SHADOWS

OF

ETERNITY

SHADOWS OF ETERNITY

A NOVEL

GREGORY BENFORD

SAGA PRESS

LONDON SYDNEY **NEW YORK** TORONTO NEW DELHI

SAGA 𝄢 PRESS

AN IMPRINT OF SIMON & SCHUSTER, INC.

1230 AVENUE OF THE AMERICAS, NEW YORK, NEW YORK 10020

First Saga Press hardcover edition October 2021

SAGA PRESS and colophon are trademarks of Simon & Schuster, Inc.

Image on page 46: by Haragayato / https://commons.wikimedia.org/wiki /Category:CC-BY-SA-4.0; images on pages 408, 414, 424: used by permission from NASA, which does not authorize or endorse this novel; images on pages 487, 488: used by permission of the estate of Poul Anderson

For information about special discounts for bulk purchases, please contact Simon & Schuster Special Sales at 1-866-506-1949 or business@simonandschuster.com.

The Simon & Schuster Speakers Bureau can bring authors to your live event. For more information or to book an event, contact the Simon & Schuster Speakers Bureau at 1-866-248-3049 or visit our website at www.simonspeakers.com.

Interior design by Jaime Putorti

Manufactured in the United States of America

1   3   5   7   9   10   8   6   4   2

Library of Congress Cataloging-in-Publication Data has been applied for.

ISBN 978-1-5344-4362-4
ISBN 978-1-5344-4364-8 (ebook)

When on some gilded cloud or flower

My gazing soul would dwell an houre,

And in those weaker glories spy

Some shadows of eternity.

—Henry Vaughan, "The Retreate," 1650

PART 1

THE PREFECT

Hidden wisdom and hidden treasure—of what use is either?

—ECCLESIASTICUS 20:30

1.

The woman who had gone in only three minutes before came back out.

"What?!" Rachel Cohen let her surprise escape.

The tall Asian woman shrugged, scowled, eyes rolling. "He just pointed to the door and frowned."

"What did you say?"

"Well, he asked what tasks I wanted to work on. I said I could do just about anything. He asked for specifics. I didn't really have any. So I trotted out some of the major problems I had heard of. I couldn't say much, but some. Then he pointed to the door." She fingered the plastic square in her hand, her shoulders slumped, and she sighed. She left on uncertain strides.

Next up for the position of Trainee Librarian was a slim man, tall and self-assured. He got a beep on his sidekick, straightened his formal Eartherstyle toga, and went in eagerly, fixed smile. All the candidates were just up from Earthside and getting used to the low grav, but this man managed a confident step and a mere bit of a bounce as he went in. And came out in five minutes. Better than the tall Asian woman, at least.

"Did he—"

"The Prefect handed me this and nodded good-bye." The man held out the same slim plastic square, good for passage back to Earth. "He said they, the Earthside filters, had wasted both his time and mine. That I was too certain of myself to have the right frame of mind for this work."

At least I won't have that problem, Rachel thought. *Nobody ever accused me of overconfidence.*

She realized she had come to her feet out of surprise at seeing this man back out here. Her legs had turned her rise into a little jump, too, a meter or so, which was embarrassing, now that she thought of it. So she sat.

The Prefect's aide came from a side door, a slim woman in a strict uniform, who said, "Audiences are over for today. The Prefect is disappointed in results and wishes to recast his mind. Come back tomorrow."

She sighed. A reprieve, at least.

———

Rachel knew enough to go straight back to the Welcome Center. No sightseeing, stick to business.

They just nodded as if this was expected—after all, the two rejectees had just come through—and assigned her to a one-night-only apartment, open but shared. That meant going down stairs, which was harder than going up in Lunar grav. Launch yourself downward, aim for a step several feet farther down than you're used to. Repeat, dancing on tiptoe sometimes. She missed one entirely but just crouched a bit in flight and the impact was not much after all.

Still, it made her edgy as she knocked on the apartment door. It slid swiftly open.

"What now?" The woman was thicker than the Lunans she had seen, and more . . . well, curvy.

Rachel handed over a small smart pad. "I'm sent for an overnight."

Frown. "Damn, I'm in line for a coresident, not this in-out crap."

"I'll probably be gone for good tomorrow."

The woman stepped aside and swept an arm widely. "Welcome to my wonderland."

It was no bigger than Rachel's Earthside one. "Two-bedroom?"

"Sure, a sort of exaggerated coffin."

True enough. Rachel dropped her bag and they came back out into the broader space. Now the walls read her mood, responding by projecting a soothing beachfront with flour-white sand and blue-green waves crashing, with comforting murmurs of wind in palm trees. It helped, though not much.

"Here's the kitchen. Well, kitchenette . . . or kitchenetteish."

It was a tiny cubbyhole. Rachel grimaced. "With each suffix I guess they take away six cupboards and an appliance."

"Hey, score! You're fun."

"Not often."

A hand stuck out for a shake. "I'm Catkejen. You looking to stay?"

"Prob'ly not. You're looking for a roomie?"

"Yeah, hate living alone. Nobody to laugh at my jokes."

Rachel knew the drill. "Your last roommate lasted how long?"

"You jump right into the cross-exam, I see. A good sign."

Rachel bored in, mouth severe. "So how long?"

"Two years. She wanted a baby, so she married one."

Rachel laughed. Her cackle came out with an edge on it. That meant she was releasing tension—as her online psych always pointed out when it heard that. Bundled-up anxiety from the noninterview. Fear of the eventual one.

Of the Prefect. *Self-knowledge,* she thought ruefully, *is mostly bad news.*

"You're here for . . . ?"

"A Trainee interview."

"With the Prefect?"

"He tossed out the two before me, then quit."

"Good sign. He likes to cut away a few to show he's got high standards."

Rachel sighed. "Good sign? Doesn't feel that way."

To her surprise, Catkejen laughed. "To expect the world to treat you fairly because you're a good person, my new friend, is like expecting a bull not to charge you because you are a vegetarian." Rachel laughed. It felt good.

"Okay, here's our porch swing moment," Catkejen said.

"What?"

"Bonding moment. Look, ain't no such thang as a perfect Prefect."

The sudden lapsing into a relaxed long-vowel accent alerted Rachel's ear. "Uh . . ."

Catkejen raised an eyebrow. "Where from?"

A wary eye-move. "South."

"South what?"

"North . . . America."

Catkejen slapped the narrow kitchen counter. "Nailed it. Love that slidin' suthrun accent. I'm American, too, from"—shifting to a clipped, higher tone—"Baaston. Massassachusetts."

"Those Welcome people—"

"Smarter than they look, yeah." More flat vowels.

Catkejen gave a little dance. Rachel echoed it, on the balls of her feet. Easy in low grav. Catkejen ended with a quick leap that took her to within a sliver of the ceiling. She landed and said, "Grab new duds, let's get some suds."

It turned out "suds" meant beer, a tipple term. Quite a lot of it. Rachel did not know how much until its effects were clear. Or unclear, which proved to be better. Until the morning. Which came too soon. Plenty soon. She wobbled through a breakfast that was mostly vegetables, found in the tiny refrigerator/thermer. Catkejen had already sprinted out to work, leaving a wall note: *Nail it! See you 5ish.*

Optimistic, indeed. *More likely I'll be using that plastic ticket to get on the orbital shuttle, bound back to Earthside.* She took a deep breath and put such thoughts aside.

Rachel had some time before her wrist told her when the Prefect would inspect her. She wanted to see the Lunar landscape, which she had barely glimpsed at the landing area, so she took an elevator to the surface.

The main corridor was crowded. She wore the translator glasses she had dutifully bought Earthside. They proved essential when among nonAnglish speakers. A feeder line across the bottom view gave rough paraphrasings in scrolling yellow. Most of the dancing lines were talk about work at the mining operation, gossip, the usual. *After all,* she thought, *I'm here to learn to interpret alien cultures, so this is kinda like that.* There were some Chinese about, allowed in from the other polar region. Their staccato modified Mandarin darted like punctuation amid the flowing Anglish tide. Since the collapse of the last surviving Red regime, they mostly kept quiet, as if biding their time before their next big mistake.

Rachel made her way toward a dome overlooking the broad plain surrounding the complex. She had to be a tad careful, even though the 0.17 g was in principle easy on the body. It was awfully easy to bound upward, standing out above the moving crowd by arcing up to the ceiling. She could stride in long coasting steps, or else do a sort of slo-mo dance on the balls of her feet, for even more speed. The key was to find a liquid grace in it, so she didn't look like a newbie, though she was.

Then she came out into a broad open area and there it was. She thought in a sudden rush of pure thrill, *I'm on the moon!* Until that moment the whole journey had been in rattling metal boxes. The gray plain lapped against the distant dark maria, onetime lava seas. The Lunar landscape was not weather-beaten but sun-beaten. A billion years of full-spectrum sun had rounded edges, pounded out fine dust. *Photon rain,* she thought.

A strange dark Earth sat near the horizon at this high latitude. At the moment it completely covered the sun, bringing a twilight glow to the peaks of the Harbinger Mountains farther north. They had stripes of yellows and burgundies, strata of the rare earths that had been splashed up from the maria by the late-stage meteors. Their color was a welcome respite from the gray powder plains of nearly all Luna.

Earth was a black coin with a shimmering brown-red rim. Air refracted reds best, so the glowing circle danced and shone. Small white dots gave away the massive cities. People down there would see Luna gain a dusky, smoldering cast. Rachel was lucky to have her first vision here be at a magic moment, happening only once a month. *Like my period,* she thought. She had decided to suppress it with meds during her apprentice training, quitting only weeks ago. Had that made her think of it now? Not with foreboding, but with some zest. The suppressor had also blunted her desire.

Her translator glasses also had a closeup function. She tapped it on and watched the tiny insect scrapers atop the lava field at the edge of the horizon. Luna profited from the rich deposits of light elements and rare earths that had billions of years ago floated to the top of the cooling lava lakes. Potassium and phosphorus skimmed from the first few meters of lava, ground up and mass-separated, fed Lunar farms. The purest of it, shipped down-grav to Earth, paid for decent shared incomes.

Mass slings, driven hard along steel rails, sent payloads nearly daily down to low Earth orbit. They carried metals and rare earths, the wealth that made Luna viable; the Library was a side effect of this. Some plunged straight into deserts to slam megaton blocks home, saving on deceleration costs. Big machines dug it out, labor benefiting the poor desert regions of Africa, Asia, and middle America. Supervised robots did most of the grunt work at both ends of this 400-million-kilometer pipeline. That paid for Luna's cities. The Library paid for its own grand towers.

Sheltering the Library from those who wanted to plunder it for the Messages meant putting it on the moon. But not the Far Side, even though that was where the most advanced telescopes ever built sat and watched the sky, free of Earthside's radio din and its big fraction of the sky. The rare earths had decided it. The concentration of maria on the Near Side likely reflected the substantially thicker crust of the highlands of the Far Side. Those bulky ranges had formed in the slow-velocity impact of a second moon of Earth, coming in from an orbit farther out, a few tens of millions of years after the big-slam impact that had resulted in a thick orbiting disk and then Luna's formation. Mining fed the community, and that community lived in the labyrinths of lava tubes that made the maria. The Library was a cultural edifice erected in what was by nature a rugged frontier town.

She felt light-headed, and it wasn't the grav that did it. She knew the signs. Before falling asleep last night, she had done her usual meditation, after the prep: focusing on an active problem. In high school she had learned that this prompted her unconscious. When she awoke, she kept her eyes closed and reviewed last night's problems. About a third of the time, a useful idea lurked, appearing immediately. She would sit up, open her eyes, and tap a note on her wrist.

This morning there had been nothing. But suddenly, looking at the gray expanses beyond the glass and water wall, an idea came. One she could use in—good grief, twenty minutes. She hurried toward the Library.

She brought out a comb to groom her hair. Something in the air seemed to tug it from her fingers. Then she recalled: the whole surface complex was a small part of the Center, enclosed in a very strong magnetic field, which deflected most charged particles from solar storms and cosmic rays. She managed to smooth her long hair and was straightening her simple formal dress as she reached the tall towers.

The soaring, fluted alabaster columns of the Library Centrex reminded her of the majesty of this entire grand enterprise, stiffening her resolve. Few other traditional sites could approach the lofty grandeur of the Library columns. Established safely off Earth, the Library itself had come to resemble its holdings: huge, aged, mysterious in its shadowy depths. In the formal grand pantheon devoted to full-color, moving statues of legendary Interlocutors, giving onto the Seminar Plaza, stood the revered block of black granodiorite: the Rosetta Stone of ancient Egypt, symbol of all they worked toward. Its chiseled face was over two millennia old, and, she thought as she passed it, endearingly easy to understand. It was a simple linear, one-to-one mapping of three human languages, found by accident. A French soldier shoring up the walls of a fort had spotted a slab with markings on one side, so pointed it out to an officer. It was an eerie foreshadowing of the many chance SETI messages found by astronomers in the twenty-first century. The stone had the same text in Greek II, which the discoverers could read.

That meant that they could deduce the unknown languages in hieroglyphic pictures and cursive Demotic forms. This battered black slab, simple and powerful, had linked civilizations separated by millennia.

She reached out a trembling palm to caress its chilly granite sleekness. Hieroglyphs had retained their pictorial shapes over millennia, unlike the ancient Greek and Roman alphabets, which had evolved into more abstract forms. Pictures were essential in SETI messages, too. She stroked a hieroglyph of a pharaoh. The touch brought a thrill.

The savants who served here now were part of a grand, age-old tradition, one that went to the heart of the very meaning of being human. Of grasping across time and space and cultures.

Only the lightness of her ringing steps buoyed her against the grave atmosphere of the tall, shadowy vaults. Scribes passed silently among the palisades, their violet robes swishing after them. She was noisy and new, and everybody knew it.

2.

"Your ambition?" Prefect Stiles raised an eyebrow.

She had not expected such a question. "To, uh, translate. To explore, to learn."

It sounded lame even to her ears, and his disdainful scowl showed that he had expected some such rattled response. He was tall and bald, his Asian features expressive. Very well then, be more assertive. Use her idea.

"Particularly, if I may, from the Sagittarius Architecture."

This took the Prefect's angular face by surprise, though he quickly covered by pursing his leathery mouth. "That is an ancient problem. It was transmitted over a millennium ago, received half a century ago. Inscrutable, though sentient. Surely you do not expect that a Trainee could make headway in such a classically difficult challenge."

"I might," she shot back crisply. "Precisely because it's so well documented."

"Decades of well-marshaled inquiry have told us very little of the Sagittarius Architecture. It is a specimen from the highest order of Sentient Information, and will not reward mere poking around."

"Still, I'd like a crack at it."

"A neophyte—"

"May bring a fresh perspective."

They both knew that by tradition at the Library, incoming candidate Trainees could pick their first topic, though few did. Most deferred to the reigning conventional wisdom and took up a small Message, something from a Type I Civilization just coming onto the galactic stage. Something resembling what Earth had sent out in its first efforts—to which it got few replies. To tackle a really big problem was foolhardy.

But some smug note in the Prefect's arrogant gaze had kindled an old desire in her. She felt it simmering.

He sniffed. "To merely review previous thinking would take a great deal of time."

She leaned forward in her chair. "I have studied the Sagittarius for years. It became something of a preoccupation of mine."

"Ummm." The Prefect was strangely austere in his unreadable face, the even tones of his neutral sentences.

She had little experience with people like this. Deciphering him seemed to require the same sort of skills she had fashioned through years of training—riddling out the alien, yes. But at the moment she felt only a yawning sense of her inexperience, amplified by the stretching silence in this office. The Prefect could be right, after all. She started to phrase a gracious way to back down. He eyed her for a long moment.

"I have found that we here often have an experience that is deeply enlightening, one not granted to everyone. It is the experience of finding that you have been wrong about something. The world has been greatly damaged by political and religious leaders who were sure they knew the truth. We learn to profit from error."

Rachel saw that this man was balanced at a turning point. He could go either way. An idea occurred. She knew the next seconds would decide the issue, so she used it.

"About the Sagittarius. There is an ancient story about the composer Mozart." The Prefect frowned, interested. She rushed ahead. "A man approached Mozart and said, 'I am thinking of writing symphonies. Can you give me any suggestions as to how to get started?' Mozart said, 'A symphony is a very complex musical form. Perhaps you should begin with something simpler. A song, perhaps.' His admirer said, 'But,

Herr Mozart, you were writing symphonies when you were eight years old.' Mozart said, 'Yes, but I never asked anybody how.'"

A surprised smile creased the Prefect's face. That looked odd, as though it had been delivered to the wrong address.

He suppressed a laugh and then made a small sound, something like a sigh. "Very well. Report weekly."

She blinked. "Um, many thanks."

The Prefect turned away, waving a 3-D screen into view, where it hung in the air, awaiting use. An abrupt dismissal.

3.

After the interview she had expected some ceremonious welcome. The Prefect's grave dignity implied such, but reality handed Rachel a swift descent. She went to a Chief Clerk and delivered a thumbprint, an optical eye read, and some DNA, then signed agreements in the old-fashioned way with the linked IDs in digital concert. The clerk who did this yawned, her tongue fidgeting among her teeth for some morsel left over from breakfast. The clerk nodded, head-wagged toward a side door—and Rachel was back in the main corridor, dismissed without a word. Again.

The Purser's office was across the hall. She went into it and soon enough was back in the same hall. Everyone here seemed to think she, in the Purser's words, "knew the drill," but she didn't. She had forgotten to study the curt notes her wrist yielded up, once she thought to tap it. That had always been a problem for her. She had gotten out of a small town in Louisiana by learning to focus on problems until she could solve them, sure. But that always meant she ignored the obvious in the rest of the world, including prompts sent to her by the Library staff. She sighed and got on with it.

Rachel smoothed her ornate, severely traditional Trainee shift as she left the Purser's office, an old calming gesture she could not train away. The shift was pricey in the sense that she could not cover it with her ready cash. She simply signed for it to be taken from her monthly wage, and the Purser printed out hers in blue.

Now her big mouth had gotten her into a fix, and she could see no way out. Not short of going back in there and asking for the Prefect's guidance, to find a simpler Message, something she could manage.

She stopped in midstride. To hell with that. No going back. She shook her head to cement her resolve.

Take a walk, she thought. *Let your unconscious process all this.*

She had come down from low Lunar orbit only the day before. The rotating funicular had brought her compartment gracefully into a snug magnetic catcher, zooming down in a box, in the obliging gravity. A week before she had been in Melbourne, Australia. The Councilors liked to keep a firm hold on who entered the Library's labyrinths. They had put candidates through their final scholastic work in a bustling focal point beside foaming waves and tawny beaches. Those Trainee candidates who could resist the sunny temptations made it through. As a sheep-goat separator—a saying her mother used, from her old farming days—it worked well. Luna was a more solemn place, time-steeped and unchanging. Plus, it was basically a bunch of boxes with dry, cool air and tricky grav.

She savored the stark ivory slopes of craters in the distance as she walked in the springy gait of one still adjusting to the gravity.

Sagittarius, here I come.

4.

Rachel found she wanted to talk. Catkejen was the obvious victim.

So she went back to the apartment. Her mind was jumpy with delight and ambition, despite the blasé Chief Clerk and the bored Purser. So she sat down and fetched forth from her luggage her 3-D chess kit. It popped up, a simple one with no attention light prompts and no tech for making remote moves. The transparent trays and pieces were simple, too, no ornamentation.

She put on music that helped her focus, set up the game, and started on a solo platform, when—in came Catkejen. "Finished early. Had a system datajam, the AIs have to untangle it first, so here I am. What's that music?"

Rachel said, "'Was Gott tut, das ist wohlgetan.' Which means 'What God does is well done.'"

"New to me. What period?"

"Baroque, Johann Sebastian Bach. He composed this church cantata in 1724."

Catkejen listened for a long moment to the Bachian sibilant strum cascading through the room, shook her head as if to clear it, and said, "Hey, is that three-D chess?"

"Uh, sure. I use it to keep sharp. A trick I learned in preTrainee school."

"When I was growing up, I thought chess was the biggest waste of smarts outside Earthside governments."

"We're not Earthside, so . . ."

A shrug, raised eyebrow. "I never learned three-D. Show me."

Catkejen sat decisively across from Rachel, so she decided to be diplomatic and not go too fast. "We call it solid chess. You've played flat chess?" That would help a lot.

"Some. This has more pieces and another dimension to move in, right?"

"More than that. The idea is, the extra dimension is outer space. Earth plays out with knights and queens and all, like ancient times, but the deeper moves are up, into space."

Catkejen frowned, fingering some of the nonclassic pieces. "So these ships fly to planets?"

"These small ones are robo-freighters, move one space at a time, like pawns. Sailships driven by beams are like bishops, moving laterally, too. Big passenger ships move in lateral jumps, like knights."

Catkejen twisted a lip, pondering. "The theme here is . . . ?"

"Earth versus the solar system. War in the heavens."

They started a game and it went steadily, though Catkejen took her time, until finally she said, "Why seek out such complexity? Flat chess is hard enough."

"Trainee school encourages this. It helps you think of patterns in multiple ways."

"Like reading the Messages?"

"I hope playing this for over a decade helps me when I start."

Catkejen swept the boards with both hands, saying brightly, "Hey, right! So much for your prep! You're in. Let's go out, celebrate!"

"I start tomorrow. I think I should meditate a bit, get rested—"

Catkejen stood, so energetic she rose to the ceiling and bounced off the cushions there. "I have some guys 'n' gals you'll want to meet. C'mon!"

———

Most Lunans—the Earthside polite term, though Rachel soon learned that people here preferred to call themselves Loonies, with a bit of swagger—lived in lava tubes. Tubes were plentiful, since Luna had no plate tectonics and all the early volcanoes still stood above their maria plains.

Catkejen led her into a big one filled with bioteched bamboo forests, the grass of Luna. The slender rods ten meters high rustled with the warm breeze that made them wave like fields of giant grain. "You get hungry for live color here," Catkejen said. "The white plains of Luna don't cut it for us. So we have green and yellow and even pink bamboo. Better than old-style Earthy trees."

Rachel was surprised to find giant agapanthus blooming in the looming tube cavern. The pioneer colonizers had left among the bamboo thickets sculptures of fat Asian wise men with stony basilisk stares. These lined the lava tube, two hundred meters down. The tube walls were dark reds and blacks and nearly airtight. Once lava had flowed here, before heavy impacts slowed and the restless young satellite began to cool, about four billion years back. Along the stretched-out town a stream tinkled and splashed. "An extravagance," Catkejen said, doing a graceful dance on a skinny bridge crossing the stream. Above, sky-bridges carried purring motor traffic and ziplines let people crisscross above them.

"This is the Contemplation Garden," Catkejen said. "Calming. Plus a shortcut to the clubs."

They walked through long winding paths amid the rattling of bamboo. These thin, fast-growing rods made sturdy building strength—beams and slats, leaves pulped into paper and hard cardboard. Buzz saws whined in the distance as robo-carpenters harvested the latest. Ground-up bamboo oddments sloshed around in spinning tubs, making blended topsoil with regolith crushed rock. Bamboo dust tainted the air with a lively spice. Rachel took springy longsteps along the pathways, for exercise. The complex was a brutalist style with countering soaring arches, all gray but offset with bamboo greenery.

A green-skinned gardener kneeled beside the footpath, and Catkejen greeted her. The woman kept kneading the rugged regolith soil, saying, "Planted as seedlings, no taller than chives." The slow chant continued as they walked away and Rachel murmured, "Impeccable dactylic tetrameter, too."

Catkejen chuckled. "Forgot, roomie, your Trainee discipline show-ing, O Seeker After Patterns."

They rounded a corner and suddenly it was all bright, airy, and overlit. Transparent walls, neon-bright, downright gaudy. Noisy, too.

"We've got plenty of silicon, so glassy stuff the robots make, right here straight from regolith," Catkejen said, thumping a wall of ruby-colored stuff. "Plus Mooncrete, solid and firm but no water needed, just flash-gouts of electricity to do the binding."

Floodlights glared from artful shrubbery and bathed a lattice-walk a hundred meters high. Crowd chatter rained down on them as they climbed a rope ladder out of the Contemplation Garden into its opposite cacophony. Brilliant white light emphasized black-trimmed, three-story windows rising in uninterrupted, eye-leading verticals toward a dominant, austere dome mimicked from some classic pile of ancient Rome. But beneath all this was five layers of shops and bars.

The ramps hosted dives where people were lively, doing crazy-looking dances in the low grav and slurping up outrageous drinks. Some did a kind of square dance, bouncing off the padded walls. The gaiety was grand, but a keep-your-hands-on-your-purse vibe pervaded. "Honky-Tonk Avenue," Catkejen said with a grandiose, satiric arm-wave.

Rachel saw in a single glance flicking alligator shoes a-dancing, fancy fedoras, flouncy scarlet dresses, camel-hair sheath coats, and purple antique suits in wool and a lurid shantung. The dives had ornate names: Palace of Green Porcelain next to the Tolstoy of the Zulus, Smoke'em If You Got'em rubbing shoulders with the Red, White & You, and Hell & High Water, whose garish signs said it featured drink-able drugs. Catkejen waved these away and led her into So Eat Already, where a welcoming table of Catkejen's friends erupted in noisy greet-ings.

Rachel sat and stayed silent, listening to the talky barrage:

"—that damn pressure door sealed tighter than a constipated frog's ass—"

"—way I figure it, illegal pheromones give guys too much advantage—"

"—but me, when politics gets exciting, I reach for my hat."

"—I swear, after that grainy gruel we got at the cafeteria yes'day, I dreamed of Prefects eating supper, slurping up beef and champagne, with a tail-coated snooty footman behind every chair—"

"—thing is, just data isn't information. Information isn't knowledge. The Message AIs—"

"—so even though it's a spaceship, not a seaship, they say things like 'they have him tied across a table in the fo'c'sle'; then he's saved by a raiding party of pirates, one of them strides into the scene and says, 'God, this here ship's a very floatin' Gomorry!' and—what are you laughing at?"

Rachel wondered how she could catch up. That bar they'd passed, named Smoke'em If You Got'em—she had no idea why; a classical allusion?

Catkejen shushed them. "Hey, this is my new roommate, Rachel Cohen. A Trainee, passed the Prefect's sniff test."

"Next comes the . . . Naaaughttt . . ." A bony guy used deep bass notes to convey menace, grinning.

"May he rust in piss," came a voice.

"He? Not a he or a she, that's the point," a big guy said. Rachel noted he sported ruffled silver hair and an air of casual elegance. He gave her a glance, looked away.

Catkejen said, "Hey, gang, keep our normal smartassery level down a bit, Rachel's not used to our lacerating Loonie lingo."

Rachel blinked and wrapped her face up with a fixed smile. The buzz moved on and she took it in, soaking in the talky tides. She considered the strata that ruled here, sanctified by over a century of intense work. They had been abstractions to her before, but here were real.

The pyramid of power in the Library of Intelligences, traditionally called the Search for Extraterrestrial Intelligence, was rigid:

Prefects
Noughts
Librarians
Trainees
Seekers of Script
Miners

Below those higher ranks were the Novices, from whose ranks Rachel had just graduated after years of hard work, back Earthside. She had gained a First, meaning she'd leapfrogged over two ranks to become a Trainee. Below her now were Seekers of Script, who assisted Trainees and reported to Librarians. Below them, and the real strength of the Library, were Miners, more commonly referred to among the lower ranks as Hounds. The venerable terms came from the "data dogs" or "code miners" of nearly ancient times, before the Library had moved to Luna. At least she did not have to deal with the sexless Noughts. And most around this crowded table were, like Catkejen, Seekers of Script. And rowdy, now, in the company of someone fresh from Earthside, who had sprinted past them. . . .

"To the Prefects we're all just happy little data points," said a bulky woman to her left, snapping Rachel out of her introspections. The woman was the one who had made the "rust in piss" comment. She had billowy blond hair and a dominant air, and turned to Rachel with, "How you like living on Luna?"

"Let's just say our bathroom is not a religious experience."

A snort. "Let's just say? Trainees and Hounds can't choose."

Rachel nodded grimly.

"Name's Ruby," the woman said, shooting out a hand. "I'm a Hound."

Rachel shook; strong grip. "Rachel Cohen."

The woman leaned near and chuckled, "Succulent," maybe just the booze talking. "Some say I'm a reg'lar hound dog."

Feeling uncomfortable, Rachel sought a simple topic. "How many people work in the Library?"

"About half." Ruby gave a big, booming laugh.

Catkejen leaned in from Rachel's right and whispered, "Smile and sling the slang and keep your lip zipped. Unless you'd like to kiss a likable somebody."

This was going too fast for Rachel. Luckily a spindly woman came to the table, surveying them with authority, and they all fell silent. She smiled and barked out, "Greetings to the newbie, welcome, Rachel. I'm MeiLee. We'll start with heirloom tomatoes, fresh from the agro lava tubes."

So it was. Servers brought plates with big red slices on them, richly flavored with oil.

Rachel blinked. "There's dirt on them."

MeiLee said, "Yeah, our robo-scrubbers clean this place too damn much. Best to go farm-to-fork, direct. Good old-fashioned dirt with microbes galore helps your health, especially allergies. So we say, screw the robos. I engaged last night with a miner who played by percentages in a certain card game. Never bet on percentages; skill carries the day over time. I came out ahead and swept up his latest crop, grime as an extra spice."

Rachel tasted one. "Delicious." She could not keep her surprise out of the word.

The silver-haired guy leaned toward her and said, "See, dirt here's salty, a good thing. Salt acts as a facilitator of ion transfers and, simply put, enables your taste buds to get the food signal at a higher volume than without the salt-based assistance."

Not to be outdone, Ruby came in with, "Plus, the amount of salt matters. There are specific ratios of salt to water in your saliva where too much salt will activate some of the receptors you don't want activated so much and give you a surge of bitter or sour reaction. If you've ever oversalted something, that's what I'm talking about."

Silver Hair flowed right back: "Salt's just a volume knob for your food. At lowish doses, it boosts the signal on many of your sweet and savory receptors, but at too high a dose, you get feedback, and that's when the 'salty' kicks in."

Catkejen intervened. "Around here, as you can see, you can never be overdressed or overeducated."

Soon enough the gang was taking up anagram challenges. Minds skipped playfully through language. Now that Rachel thought of it, that was somewhat the task of the Library: to sense the deeper realms of alien Messages. The silver-haired guy won with an instant solution to "phoneboxes," snapping out, "Got it—'xenophobes,' my friends."

Oddly, he said it in a soothing, melodic voice. That was . . . interesting—Rachel's usual dodge description. She had always disliked the way women would refer to men as "cute" and think that explained something. Men weren't cute. They were handsome or ugly or boyish or an éminence grise in the making. Cute, no; not to Rachel. More like rugged.

A plonking rhythm started up on the other side of the ample room.

Behind the semielliptical bar four cowboys who had never been near a cow sang western songs. These sounded as if they had originated in the Far East, at best. Somebody dropped the acoustic dome over their table, a sonic interferometer, and the fake folksy mercifully faded.

Somebody passed an inhalant she called a "spritzer" and Rachel had a lung or two. Then a sip, maybe two, of a red wine somebody said was Lunagrown and tasted like it. Talk accelerated around her, an effect she noted with owlish fascination.

"—so I said to him, quoting the old saying, 'Don't look into laser with remaining eye.' And he just shrugged. Not like he can't get his fried one replaced."

"—as Lunaticky as a plaid rabbit—"

"—this guy's face is his autobiography, right there." A man flaunting oakpale hair beside her shot back, "These days, a woman's face is her work of fiction."

"—We all need to wake up and smell the Kafka, gang—"

"—the Cauchy singular integral operator on weighted variable Lebesgue spaces—how charming!"

Here came a refresh of her old lesson: watching other people getting drunk and more brilliant by the moment, so they thought, was even less interesting than watching other people having sex. Though that, at least, had an athletic payoff.

She just sat and drank some and watched, gathering info, while a guy across from her directed a fast stream of talk at her, a standard brilliant disheveled klutz, going on about something in basic decoding software. She relaxed. Men loved explaining things. But when a guy was explaining something you already knew, she had learned that while it might be tempting to say, "I already know that," it was not a wise move. Instead, she let him explain it to make him feel useful. That gave her time to think about how to avoid him in the future. Plus about a half dozen others among the present company, off her list. She was studying her social landscape and making maps. Not for the first time, or even the dozenth. Still, fun, in its way.

A hand jerked her up, out of her seat, away. "Bedtime, roomie," Catkejen whispered.

"What? Uh. I was just—"

With a sigh, Catkejen said, "See that bongo silver-haired guy from Mars? As sleek as a jet plane with all the right muscular massive curves in all the right swervy places, with the kind of quiet voice that does nothing to disguise the turbocharged power purring under that immaculate chassis."

"Uh ..."

"He's eyeing you. Best not let him see you barf up the slop we're ingesting. Unladylike, even by Earthside standards."

"Oh, I ..." Was she feeling sick? Rachel looked back at the laughing, talking, drinking gang. They seemed unfazed—but then, they were used to Luna's oddities.

Somehow without feeling her legs at all she was moving away, tugged by her roomie, who said, "I've had my fill of spleen-venting, spittle-spattering mirth, so let's get outta—"

Ruby the boisterous moved up and shot out a hand again, not for a shake. Instead, she wrapped a muscular arm around Rachel's waist. Her face loomed up and planted a big smacking kiss. "Yum!" Ruby said, and slid a hand around to squeeze her ass.

Embarrassment thickened in her throat like phlegm. "Look, no, I—"

Catkejen pulled Ruby away. "No groping the roomie, Ruby. I know you like fresh meat, but—"

Ruby barked out a laugh, not friendly. "She'll come around, you'll see."

The next minutes got jostled together somehow. Rachel realized that her earlier expertise at Loonie walking was a passing matter. She tried skipping, and Catkejen caught her just as she tipped too far forward. She walked, but that seemed tricky as well. By the time they got to their apartment Rachel was seriously considering crawling. Why had humans given that up, anyway? Much safer, it was. But then she was sitting on her bed somehow and peering at the walls, which showed a bunch of snowy mountains and rich forest and she recalled that, oh yes, she had already thrown up. Somewhere along the way. So no need to worry about that. At least not right away.

Catkejen gave her some pills and she gulped them down. "Ruby—"

"She's trouble looking for somebody to happen to."

"I tried that stuff, girls are good kissers and all, but they, well, lack . . ." Rachel groped for the right word.

Catkejen laughed, a dry cackle. "Right. Energy. Musk. Magic. Something else that nobody's invented the word for yet. Yeah, men. The eternal problem. Me too." A sigh.

"Yes . . ." Not the best time to call up the dictionary for the precise term. Or thesaurus. Not tonight, even for a Trainee Librarian . . .

"You gotta get sleep, kid. Need anything more?"

A memory. "The Louisana State Minimum Security Facility used to kiss me good night. I was in there for couple weeks. Got suspended for being in wrong place, wrong time. Then back home to family and my cycle. That kisser gal kept telling me about how World War Eleven had started in 1939, biggest war ever, and she had a gun from it."

"Really? You were a trouble kid?"

Rachel sat up straight, threw back her shoulders. "Just once. Don't tell anybody."

"Honey, after tonight, I'll have trouble remembering your name." She barked a laugh.

The room fell away and Rachel barely felt her head hit the delicious pillow.

PART 2

THE HYDROGEN WALL

Do not all charms fly
At the mere touch of cold philosophy?

—JOHN KEATS, "LAMIA"

1.

Catkejen got her up early by shaking her foot. "Eggs Benedict or eggs Benedictine?"

"Oog. Wanna sleep."

"You said to get you up early."

"I'd like to throw up, but our apartment is too small."

"Time to become an adult."

"Catkejen, I like how you got me home, but—"

"Catty. Told you to call me Catty."

"But Catty is an insult. Means gossipy. Mean."

"Not if you're a friend."

"You can do eggs Benedict?"

"For a friend, sure. Another bite out of my paycheck."

The eggs helped. So did the faux bacon, crispy. Rachel said, "That expression last night, Ruby . . ."

"'Hound dog'? I had to look it up. Turns out it's from your area, the South. Means a man who sniffs around or sleeps around."

"You think she researched me, thought she was using my lingo?"

"Ruby's a Hound so she's quick to find terms to suit her personality—brusque and badass. Her fave come-on trick is to show how she can lick her own elbow."

"Oog." Rachel slurped up more coffee to clear the fog.

Catkejen went to Rachel's tiny closet and took out her business suit. "This will do. But give your hair a fluff and no makeup at all. Noughts see that as pretension, the sort of thing they were invented to avoid."

As Rachel got dressed she made herself look on the bright side, forced optimism, "Hey, I made some friends just last night."

"True, but. Now you have to look bright, smart, but humble. Word is, the Nought you're meeting is looking for Trainees who can do more than string math analysis into spiderwebs."

"Word is?"

"More like a mood reading. Look, I got some subspeak done at the party while you were gabbing it up."

"Slinging the slang, as I think you said. Not that I was doing a lot of thinking."

"Subspeak is mostly rumor, but there's, shall we call it, pricey gossip available, for them that knows."

"What price?" Rachel asked.

"I might have to sleep with somebody, is all."

"Might?"

"Okay, must. But at a time and place of my choosing."

"Info, gossip . . . for . . . me?"

"Hey, roomies gotta stick together."

"Not with Ruby, I trust?"

"Now, that damn near verges on insult."

"Hard to know, around here. You really are Loonies."

"At times, sure—when that's useful," Catkejen said. "Your Nought today is the big one, Siloh. I've heard him issue pronouncements to us mere Seekers. Imposing. Sometimes when hearing Siloh, I have a paralyzing suspicion that he is trying to be funny."

"Okay, I'll try to suppress my humorous side."

"You're more ironic than the laugh-out-loud type, most of the time. And speaking of time, you're getting late, m'dear."

2.

Earth was a slim crescent now. Rachel paused, not knowing why, and looked at the sharp, clear image—screen-amped and entirely phony, since she was several hundred meters below the regolith. *They're back there, where we all came from. So we're out here, closer to the big ancient galaxy, in a dumb way of seeing it.* An outpost, where humanity heard and struggled to fathom the voices from the Great Galactic Past, as she thought of it. *Us against the galaxy!* as trite kid drama put it. With our noses against the glass—because space was cold, radioactive, and always trying to kill us.

Her next and most important appointment was with the Head Nought. The Noughts reported to the Prefect and handled most details of the Library. She had gone through the usual online protocols, clearing assurances with lesser lights, so was swiftly ushered forward.

Beside the ample office entrance was a wall saying displayed in Anglish and Mandarin:

YOU ACCOMPLISH THE GREAT TASK
BY A SERIES OF SMALL ACTS. —LAO TZU

With a ritual bow, an underling escorted her into the presence of Siloh, a smooth-skinned Nought who apparently had not learned to smile. Or maybe that went with the cellular territory; Noughts had intricate adjustments to offset their deeply sexless natures. Noughts thought of themselves as People, not he or she or any of the mindsets, once useful and yet now often illusory, that evolution had written into the species.

The tall eminence carefully seated her and stood beside a large screen display. Within its depths she could see multidimensional threads growing, seething. This was a visual key to the ongoing efforts to interweave the enormous database of received Messages. Many were intertwined, because far older societies had laced their Messages with the histories of much cross-talk among the stars.

Siloh said in a slow, gravelly tone, "I do hope you can find a congruence with the Sagittarius Architecture." The Nought murmured as if to itself in a flat tone that ended each sentence with a purr. Rachel could not help thinking of this person as masculine. The body was sleek, muscular, utilitarian without being sexual at all. More like a store robo-dummy, she realized, than a person. "Though I regret your lost effort to come." A soft sigh.

"Lost?" She shifted uncomfortably in her metal-frame chair.

"You will fail, of course."

"Perhaps a fresh approach—"

"So have said many hundreds of candidate Trainee scholars. These were once charming, usually naïve, ambitions. Not now. I remind you of our latest injunction from the Councilors—the heliosphere threat."

"I thought there was little anyone could do."

"So it seems." Siloh scowled. "But we cannot stop from striving. There is perhaps a bare chance that buried somewhere in our trove is relevant information of use to the species as a whole."

"Of course we should not stop from striving," she said in what she hoped was a demure manner, deliberately choosing his phrasing. This person might not share the constraints of being man or woman, but surely was not above a dash of vanity? "Though I gathered our predicament is rare?" She noted that she had allowed a softly feminine lilt to her statement, turning it in the last words into a question.

"We must try."

Using the Library as a tool for big issues was far from her mindset.

Siloh gave her an unblinking stare as he sat behind his bare bamboo desk. She saw how little she could make of this person, who gave off nothing but sentences. No warmth.

Noughts had proven their many uses a century before. Their lack of sexual appetites and apparatus, both physical and mental, gave them a rigorous objectivity. As diplomats, Contractual Savants, and neutral judges, they excelled. They had replaced much of the massive legal apparatus that had come to burden society in earlier centuries. They were fair evaluators, bringing rigor to reason.

The Library could scarcely function without their insights. Typical alien texts did not carry unthinking auras of sexuality, as did human works.

There was plenty of software to search that out, once texts were translated. Or more precisely, the Messages might carry alien sexualities aplenty, however much their original creators had struggled to make them objective and transparent. But normal humans or their software could not see it. Cutting through that was a difficult task for ordinary people, such as herself. The Library in its early decades had struggled with the issue, and the Noughts had solved it. They arose from a general need for objective analysis, but the arrival of SETI messages had given them a newer use beyond merely Earthside roles.

Translating the Messages from a human male or female perspective profoundly distorted their meaning. In the early days, this had beclouded many translations. Much further effort had gone to cleansing these earlier texts. Nowadays, no work issued from the Library without a careful Nought vetting, to erase unconscious biases. Rachel had traced through all that history, found it fascinating—but had never met a Nought. They were rare and fled the limelight.

Siloh said gravely, "The heliosphere incursion has baffled our finest minds. I wish to approach it along a different path. For once, the Library may be of immediate use."

Rachel found this puzzling. She had been schooled in the loftier aspects of the Library's mission, its standing outside the tides of the times. Anyone who focused upon Messages that had been designed for eternity had to keep a mental distance from the events of the day. "I do not quite . . ."

Siloh rose from behind the broad desk and instead sat upon it, keeping robes primly wrapped around sinewy legs. "Think of the Library as the uninitiated do. They seldom grasp the higher functions we must perform, and instead see mere passing opportunity. That is why we are bombarded with requests to view the Vaults as a source for inventions, tricks, arts, novelties."

"And reject them, as we should." She hoped she did not sound too pious.

But Siloh nodded approvingly. "Indeed. We gain much financial help from the patents we own. In the course of our scientific pursuits we have uncovered many useful implied devices, engineering tricks, even basic ideas, all for exploit. But we now keep that as a minor role."

"Rightly so," Rachel said in what she knew was a limp tone. Best to let this Nought run on. They were noted for that.

"My thinking is that an ancient society such as the one behind the Sagittarius Architecture might have encountered such problems before. It would know better than any of our astro-engineers how to deal with the vast forces at work."

"I see." *And why didn't I think of it? Too steeped in this culture of hushed reverence for the sheer magnitude of the Library's task?* "Uh, it is difficult for me to envision how—"

"Your task is not to imagine but to perceive," Siloh said severely.

Rachel found Noughts disconcerting in principle, and Siloh more so. Most chose to have no hair, but Siloh sported a rim of kinked coils, glinting like brass, as if a halo had descended onto his skull. Pale eyelashes flicked seldom, gravely. Descending, the eyelids looked pink and rubbery. The nearly invisible blond eyebrows arched perpetually, so every word seemed layered with artifice, eyebrows punctuating as tones slid among syllables with resonant grace. The face shifted from one nuanced expression to another, a pliable medium in ceaseless movement, like the surface of a restless pond rippled by unfelt winds. She felt as though she should be taking notes about every utterance. Without blinking, she shifted to recording mode, letting her spine-based memory log everything that came in through eyes and ears. A simple click at her wrist did it. Just in case.

"I have not kept up, I fear," she said; it was always a good idea to appear humble. "The incursion—"

"Has nearly reached Jupiter's orbit," Siloh said. The wall behind the Nought lit with a display showing the sun, gamely plowing through a gale of interstellar gas. Oort cloud satellites had framed it all in many frequencies.

Only recently had humanity learned that it had arisen in a benign time. An ancient supernova had once blown a bubble in the interstellar gas, and Earth had been cruising through that extreme vacuum while the mammals evolved from tree shrews to big-brained world-conquerors. Not that the sun was special in any other way. In its gyre about the galaxy's hub, it moved only fifty light-years in the span of a million years, oscillating in and out of the galaxy's plane every thirty-three million years—and that was enough to bring it now out of the Local Bubble's protection. There was a vagrant molecular cloud coasting through the larger supernova-induced bubble. Astronomers hadn't seen it coming and now here it was, knocking on the solar system's door. The full density of interstellar hydrogen molecules and assorted debris now beat against the sun's own plasma wind, pushing inward, hammering into the realm of the fragile planets.

"The hydrogen wall began to bombard the Ganymede Colony yesterday," Siloh said with the odd impartiality Rachel still found unnerving, as though not being male or female gave it a detached view, above the human fray. "It is intruding at our local speed around the galaxy, two hundred thirty kilometers a second. We at the Library are instructed to do all we can to find knowledge bearing upon our common catastrophe."

The wall screen picked up this voice hint and displayed Jupiter's crescent against the hard stars. Rachel watched as a fresh flare coiled back from the ruby, roiling shock wave that embraced Jupiter. The magnetic fields that had once stood off the interstellar hydrogen, well beyond Pluto, detected in the early 2000s by the Voyager probes, now draped like gauzy veils around Jupiter's own magnetic realm. These fought for primacy. The planet's magnetic bow curve rippled with colossal turbulence, twisting vortices bigger than lesser worlds.

"Surely we can't change the interstellar weather."

"We must try. You are new and thus able to see newly. Or such is my hope."

Siloh's deep resonant bass sounded ominous. For the first time Rachel noticed that high above in the ceiling was a skylight bringing direct sun down hundreds of meters, for the Nought's sole use.

Lead-gray light fell through the chill air like a scythe as Siloh moved quickly nearer. "The mean Ashkenazi IQ is one hundred ten, with a standard deviation of fifteen, so the number of northern Europeans with IQs greater than one hundred forty is four per thousand, while twenty-three per thousand Ashkenazim exceed the same threshold, a sixfold difference. You are exceptional even among the Ashkenazim."

"I never paid any attention to that."

"You surely should. Non-Ashkenazi Jews do not have high average IQs. The Sephardic, for example."

Rachel was irked but kept her tone steady. "You've got my whole dossier. What else is relevant?"

"Ashkenazim do not show any marked advantage on spatial tasks, while they excel at linguistic and arithmetic tasks. Northeast Asians have high spatial scores for a given overall IQ."

"So I'm not good at physical stuff?"

"If you were typical Ashkenazim, you would not be. But I see you were quite athletic."

"Yep. Where I grew up, if you were smart, better learn to fight or run."

"I advise the latter, generally."

"I majored in the former in elementary school. Playground learning." She paused, not wanting to seem like a braggart. "How much support will I have? How much time doing full interface with the . . . Message Minds?"

Siloh pursed the wide mouth pensively, eyes veiled. "I will see you garner in proportion to your rapport with the Minds."

"I assume this is supported by the inventions, royalties—"

"I do not exploit that avenue very often. I have found that money costs too much."

"I will apply all my ability. I understand that caution with these emulated alien minds demands careful use."

Siloh sighed, rustled robes, looked off into the distance. "If you are extremely careful and take absolutely no risks, nothing bad will ever happen to you. Or good."

"I will learn from the senior—"

"Most of whom are frequently in error, never in doubt."

Rachel stood. Time to say something solid. "We must try. The older Galactics may know of a world that survived such an onslaught."

She had read about all this, but never thought she could play a role. The sun's realm, the heliosphere, had met the dense clump of gas and plasma eighty-eight years before. Normally the solar wind particles blown out from the sun kept the interstellar medium at bay. For many past millennia, these pressures had struggled against each other in a filmy barrier more than a hundred astronomical units beyond the cozy inner solar system. Now that barrier had been pressed back in, striking into where the outer planets orbited.

The wall's view expanded to show what remained of the comfy realm dominated by the sun's pressure. It looked like an oceangoing vessel, seen from above: bow waves generated at the prow rolled back, forming the characteristic parabolic curve.

Under the steadily rising pressure of the thickening interstellar gas and dust, that pressure front was eroding. The sun's course slammed it against the dense hydrogen wall at sixteen kilometers per second and its puny wind was pressed back far faster into the realm of solar civilization. Pluto's Cryo Base had been abandoned decades before, and Saturn's only recently. The incoming hail of high-energy particles and fitful storms had killed many. The Europa Ocean's strange life was safe beneath its ten kilometers of ice, but that was small consolation to the humans communicating with them, who had fled.

"But what can we do on our scale?" Rachel insisted.

"What we can."

"The magnetic turbulence alone, at the bow shock, holds a larger energy store than all our civilization."

Siloh gave her a look that reminded her of how she had, as a girl, watched an insect mating dance. Distant distaste. "We do not question here. We listen."

"Yes, Self."

This formal title, said to be preferred by Noughts to either *sir* or *madam*, seemed to please. Siloh went through the rest of their interview with a small smile, and she could almost feel a personality beneath its chilly remove. Almost.

3.

Rachel stepped back into the corridor and thought for a moment. Siloh seemed skeptical of the entire enterprise here. Because of being a Nought? Hard to know.

She left the Executat Dome with relief. Her sense of joy at getting through the interview sent her bounding up to the ceiling. She adjusted, damping her energies to about a sixth of the emphasis she would exhibit Earthside. Train your muscle memory.

A viewscreen that filtered out the sunblast of the gray plains outside drew her. The Library sprawled across the Locutus Plain, lit by Earth's stunning crescent near a jagged white horizon. Beneath that preserved plain lay the cryofiles of all transmissions received from the Galactic Complex, the host of innumerable societies that had flourished and sent Messages—most of them long before humanity was born. A giant, largely impenetrable resource. The grandest possible intellectual scrap heap.

Libraries were monuments not so much to the Past, but to Permanence itself. (The Library's shibboleths preferred Capitals.) Rachel shivered with anticipation. She had passed through her first interviews!—and was now free to explore the myriad avenues of the galactic past. The Sagittarius was famous for its density of information, many-layered and intense. A wilderness, beckoning.

Still, she had to deal with the intricacies of the Library, too. These now seemed as steeped in arcane byways and bureaucratic labyrinths as were the Library's vast contents. Rachel cautioned herself to be careful and, most especially, to not let her impish side show. So she strolled, practicing the light-footed gait, thinking. She bowed her head as she passed an aged Nought, for practice. It merely nodded.

The greatest ancient library had been at Alexandria, in Afrik. It was part of the original Musaeum—the Institution of the Muses—from which the Anglish word *museum* was derived.

A historian had described the lot of Librarians there with envy: they had a carefree life including free meals, high salaries, no taxes to pay, very pleasant surroundings, good lodgings, and servants. There was plenty of opportunity for quarreling with each other.

So not much had changed. . . .

———————

After an afternoon briefing and intro to how she would work in the complex, Rachel was tired. Adjusting to 0.17 g somehow wore her out. Her apartment mate was a welcome antidote to the Nought. Small, bouncy, Catkejen was not the usual image of a Seeker Librarian. She lounged around in a revealing sarong, sipping a stimulant that was scarcely allowed in the Trainee Manual.

"Give 'em respect," she said offhand, "but don't buy into all their solemn dignity-of-our-station stuff. You'll choke on it after a while."

Rachel grinned with a skeptical twist. "And get slapped down."

"I kinda think the Librarians like some back talk. Keeps 'em in fighting trim."

Rachel sprawled a little herself, a relief from the ramrod-spine posture the Librarians kept. No one hunched over their work here, in the classic scholar's pose. They kept upright, using the surround enviros, working in the screen envelopes. Cat handed her a flask of sweet something and she downed half of it. "Urk! What's—"

"Hunnywanna. Mix of honey and marijuana molecules."

"Oog . . . So, here's how my Nought interview went—"

Ten minutes in, Cat said, "Doubt anything can stop interstellar weather. Some of my family's Ganymede miners, and they're boosting home fast."

"Really? Brrrr! I'd hate to be buried in ice all my life, digging."

"Don't you buy that." Catkejen waved a dismissive hand, extruding three tool-fingers to amplify the effect. "Robos do the grunt work. People there get out to prospect the outer moons a lot."

"So your family's wealthy? Hiding behind magneto-shields doesn't seem worth it."

"More clichés. Not every Ganny strikes it rich."

The proton sleet at Ganymede was lethal, but the radiation-cured elements of the inner Jovian region had made many a fortune, too. "So you're from the poor folks who had to send their brightest daughter off to Luna?"

"Another cliché." Catkejen made a face. "I hope you have better luck finding something original in—what was it?"

"The Sagittarius Architecture."

"Brrrrr! I heard it was a hydra."

"Each time you approach it, you get a different mind?"

"If you can call it a mind. I hear it's more like a talking body."

Rachel had read and sensed a lot about the Sagittarius, but this was new. They all knew that the mind-body duality made no sense in dealing with alien consciousness, but how this played out was still mysterious. She frowned.

Catkejen poked her in the ribs. "Come on, no more deep thought today! Let's go for a fly in the high-pressure dome."

Reluctantly, Rachel went. But her attention still fidgeted over the issues. She thought about the challenge to come, even as she watched people swoop in long, serene glides over the fern-covered walls, under the deep amusement dome. In the ceiling were smart screens, showing fleecy skies on Earthside, against the persimmon sky.

———————

She didn't sleep well. The true challenge was coming up fast. She faced weeks of building her translator skills, before she could even get into a pod and make contact with alien minds.

Rachel knew that the great equalizer in all communication, across vast ranges and starfields, was the speed of light and gravwaves alike. This led to motives, once societies achieved technology to transmit powerfully, if they wished. The grand goals of alien minds could be imagined, but digging them out of endless streams of code was usually impossible. She had studied for years the simpler Messages, come to know through them the goals of alien minds. Many echoed human desires, at least superficially. She had her own list, worked up through experience. Aliens sought to embed meanings that broke down into categories. Her application to the Library for Trainee status had used them, and might have tilted the odds in her favor. She had memorized it:

Kilroy Was Here: Memorials to dying societies.

High Church: Records of a culture's highest achievements. The essential message is: this was the best we did; remember it. A society that is stable over thousands of years may invest resources in either of these first two paths. The human prospect has advanced enormously in only a few centuries; the life-span in the advanced societies has risen by 50 percent in each of the last two centuries. Living longer, we contemplate longer legacies. Time capsules and ever-proliferating monuments testify to our urge to leave behind tributes or works in concrete ways. The urge to propagate culture quite probably will be a universal aspect of intelligent, technological, mortal species (Minsky, 1985).

The Funeral Pyre: A civilization near the end of its life announces its existence.

Ozymandias: Here the motivation is sheer pride; the Beacon announces the existence of a high civilization, even though it may be extinct and the Beacon itself tended by robots.

Help!: Quite possibly societies that plan over time scales ~1,000 years will foresee physical problems and wish to discover if others have surmounted them. An example is a civilization whose star is warming (as ours is), which may wish to move their planet outward with gravitational tugs. Many other scenarios are possible.

Join Us: Religion may be a galactic commonplace; after all, it is here. Seeking converts is common, too, and electromagnetic preaching fits a frequent meme.

Ineffables: Aliens quite likely have/had desires and philosophies inscrutable to us. These could be powerful and enigmatic and have consequences we cannot anticipate. Possibly the motives listed above are common, but not the major impulses of advanced, strange minds. We should expect the unexpected.

Rachel relished the prospect of finally grasping the quiet, tense, mysterious, transcendent world of the Message Minds.

PART 3

THE MILKY WAY'S LIBRARY

This is as strange a maze as e'er men trod,
And there is in this business more than nature
Was ever conduct of.

—ALONSO IN SHAKESPEARE'S LATE MASTERPIECE *THE TEMPEST*

1.

The Prefect put a kintsugi bowl in Rachel's hands. These ceramic bowls were three hundred to four hundred years old, she knew. Their special aspect was that somewhere along the way they had broken into shards and were glued back together with a fifteenth-century technique using Japanese lacquer and gold.

He stepped back and in a whisper asked, "Your perception?"

She held it gingerly. It had golden veins running through, making it more beautiful, she could see, than the original condition. "There's a dimension of depth. I sense the original life it had, the rupture, and then the way it so beautifully healed. In this way it embraces the concepts of nonattachment, acceptance of change, and fate as aspects of human life."

"Good. You are tapping your inner mind."

She knew this was a pointful moment, a way to get her mind out of the dirty river of information she had been swimming in for the last two weeks. "I will remain . . ." She searched for the right term. "Watchfully patient."

The Prefect nodded and took back the bowl, then placed it on a gray stone slab. "To fathom a Message using your entire mind gives a sense of depth below depth. It resembles an innocent wild vertigo, as one falls through its levels."

"I will remain open." She knew this was the essential manner, though she feared she could not be sure. Uncertainty was part of the seeking, too.

"The Greeks had a concept of kairos time, which is not quantitative like chronos—our normal conception of time as countable. Kairos is qualitative, a proper or opportune moment for action—rich or empty, the meaningful hour or the hurried moment. When you're with beauty, in art or in nature, you tend to move at kairos time—slowly, serenely, but thickly."

"I see." Though she was unsure she did.

"I remind you that we of the Library translated—or perhaps I should say, caused a realization of?—an ancient Message that led to a great discovery: that spacetime is made of microscopic constituents, which then have bulk-properties like viscosity. That realization led to the discovery that spacetime has effects normally associated with crystals such as birefringence, or the dispersion of light. And then, that gravitation may be considered, like thermodynamics, a science of basic properties in the large. These realizations were immensely useful and so profitable. Such is our goal, for humanity."

"Including the hydrogen wall . . ."

"Yes. That has urgency, but do not make haste. Immersed in a Message, do less. In gliding slowness you may glimpse the seeds of eternity."

Somehow she knew this was the end of her second Prefect audience. She rose, folded her robes, and left the Dome for her first immersion. Her heart pounded, despite the Prefect's serene instruction.

———

After two weeks of tech training, she was done with the new-girl pose. So no more joyful and jaunty newbie, all eager-beaver smiles, dancing eyes, and expressive head tilts. No more Ms. Nice Gal. Now was not Basic, but Trial.

She had gone through neuro trials to sniff out her indices: depression inventory, heart rate variability, neuro system resilience, and amygdala elasticity. She was suitable, but new. As she approached the Pod Building, a broad pyramid in a large lava tube, she passed under the motto, hanging solemnly in the flexing air:

BIOLOGY CONSTRAINS OUR
EXPERIENCE OF REALITY.

Into her own pod, at last!

She had gone through a week of final neural conditioning since getting through several tech reviews. Now the grand moment had arrived: direct line feed from the Sagittarius Architecture.

The pod was the focus of corridors that converged its many feeds, a congress of neural webs around the core—which looked disturbingly like a sarcophagus. A horseshoe of detectors and cooled computers wrapped around it like worshippers.

The attending crew did their jobs and she mounted into the pod and was closed in. The myriad neural connectors fit snugly to her nearly nude body. The team knew not to speak or distract. She let herself descend into a slow immersion. She thought of the bowl and sensed herself falling under the pod's sway.

This would not be a mere translation problem. Many Messages were, but the pods were for advanced Messages. Some of the Messages lodged in the Library had not been intended for mortal ears or eyes at all. Like some ancient rulers of Mesopotamia, these alien authors directly addressed their deities, and only them. One opened plaintively,

Tell the God we know and say
for your tomorrow we give our today.

It was not obvious whether this couplet (for in the original it was clearly rhymed) came from a living civilization, or from an artifact left to remind the entire galaxy of what had come before. Perhaps, in alien terms, the distinction did not matter.

Such signals also carried Artificials, as the digital minds immersed in the Messages were termed. These were the intense focus of the Librarians. The advanced Artificials, such as Sagittarius, were artificial intelligences, conveyed by Messages that could run on for years of digital transfer. Such Artificials often supervised vast data-banks containing apparent secrets, outright brags, and certified history—which was often merely gossip about the great. These last, rather transparently, were couched to elicit punishment for the author's enemies, or seek mercy from alien gods. This differed only in complexity and guile from the ancient motivations of Babylonian kings.

Most Messages of this beseeching tone assumed some universal moral laws and boasted of their authors' compliance with them. At first the Sagittarius Architecture had appeared to be of this class, and so went largely uninterpreted for half a century. Only gradually did its sophistication and rich response become apparent. Most importantly, it was a new class entirely—the first Architecture Artificial.

The Sagittarius Architecture was a mind in itself, embodied in a string of code that took years to broadcast. SETI detectors had gotten pieces of it even earlier, but could not fathom it as the vastness it was.

More got filled in over decades. Finally, strung together, the Sagittarius Architecture consciousness emerged. It ran on dedicated servers in cryo vaults. It was never shut down and so had time to think in and of itself. Apparently the aliens who'd created it were long extinct—though even this was subject to interpretation of what the Sagittarius Architecture's elliptical self said.

That mind had something roughly comparable to a human unconscious—and yet it could see into its own inner minds at will. It was as if a human could know that all of his/her impulses came from a locus of past trauma, or just a momentary anger—and could see this instantly, by tracing back his/her own workings. The strange power of human art sprang in part from such invisible wellsprings. To be able to unmask that sanctum was an unnerving prospect. The Sagittarius Architecture had that capability. So to venture into contact with it made Rachel wary.

Her pod acted as an active, intimate neural web, using her entire body to convey connections. Sheets of sensation washed over her skin; a prickly itch began in her feet.

She felt a heady kinesthetic rush of acceleration as a constellation of fusions drew her to a tight nexus. Alien architectures used most of the available human input landscape. That meant her unconscious, too.

Dizzying surges in the ears, biting smells, ringing cacophonies of elusive patterns, prickly skin dances, queasy perturbations of the inner organs—a Trainee had to know how these might convey meaning. But not consciously.

These sensations fed into her unknown inner territories.

They often did disturb, but translating them was elusive. After such experiences, she never thought of human speech as anything more than a hobbled, claustrophobic mode. Its linear meanings and frail attempts at linked concepts were simple, utilitarian, and typical of younger minds. Real thinking lay beyond speech, in the realms of intuition.

The greatest task was translating the dense smatterings of mingled sensations into discernible sentences. Only thus could a human fathom them at all, even if that was in a way blunted and blurred. Or so much previous scholarly experience said.

Rachel took deep breaths. Claustrophobes could never do this. She felt herself bathed in a shower of penetrating responses, all coming from her own body. These were her own inboard subsystems coupled with high-bit-rate spatterings of meaning—guesses, really. She had an ample repository of built-in processing units, lodged in her spine and shoulders. No one would attempt such a daunting task without artificial amplifications. To confront slabs of raw data, marshaled by an alien artificial consciousness, with a mere unaided human mind, was pointless and quite dangerous. Early Librarians, centuries before, had perished in a microsecond's exposure to such layered labyrinths as the Sagittarius.

Years of scholarly training had conditioned her against the jagged ferocity of the link, but still she felt a cold shiver of dread. That, too, she had to wait to let pass. The effect amplified whatever neural state you brought to it. Legend had it that a Librarian had once come to contact while angry, and been driven into a fit from which she'd never recovered. They had found the body peppered with micro-contusions over its entire surface.

The raw link was as she had expected:

A daunting, many-layered language. Then she slid into an easier notation that went through her spinal interface, and heard/felt/read:

❋✳▲◗❑❑▧❋✳◗✲❋✴✔◗✗✖✲✖✲❋✲✳✛◷●◗●◗○
✉✿"✂✛✟⇑★✚✛✂✲✳❀✲❋
◇★✿☆✲✲✲☆◉'❛'❛✲✲✲✲✂✲

Much more intelligible, because she could read it unconsciously. But still . . .
She concentrated—

We wish you greetings, new sapience.

"Hello. I come with reverence and new supple offerings." This was the standard opening, one refined nearly a century ago and never changed by so much as a syllable.

And you offer?

"Further cultural nuances." Also a ritual promise, however unlikely it was to be fulfilled. *Surely this Mind knows that?* Few advances into the Sagittarius had been made in the last several decades. Even the most ambitious Librarians seldom tried any longer.
Something like mirth came wafting to her, then:

We are of a mind to venture otherwise with you.

Damn! There was no record of such a response before, her downlink confirmed. It sounded like a preliminary to a dismissal. That overture had worked fine for the last six Trainees, she knew. But then, they hadn't gotten much further before the Sagittarius lost interest and went silent again. Being ignored was the greatest insult a Trainee faced, and the most common. Humans were more than a little boring to advanced intelligences.
The worst of it was that one seldom had any idea why.
So what in hell did this last remark from it mean? Rachel fretted, speculated, and then realized that her indecision was affecting her own

neural states. She decided to just wing it. "I am open to suggestion and enlightenment." She could feel her unconscious sending what felt like heat pulses and twitches, which the Mind could interpret, too. Maybe.

A pause, getting longer as she kept her breathing steady. Her meditative cues helped, but could not entirely submerge her anxieties. She focused and all else fell away. Maybe she had bitten off entirely too much—

From Sagittarius she received a jittering cascade, resolving to:

As a species you are technologically gifted yet philosophically callow, a common condition among emergent intelligences. But of late it is your animal property of physical expression that intrigues. Frequently you are unaware of your actions—which makes them all the more revealing.

"Oh?" She sat back in her pod and crossed her legs. The physical pose might help her mental profile, in the global view of the Sagittarius. Until now its responses had been within conventional bounds; this last was new.

You concentrate so hard upon your linear word groups that you forget how your movements, postures, and facial cues give you away.

"What am I saying now, then?"

That you must humor Us until you can ask your questions about the heliosphere catastrophe.

Rachel laughed. It felt good. "I'm that obvious?"

Many societies We know only through their bit-strings and abstractions. That is the nature of binary signals. You, on the other hand (to use a primate phrase), We can know through your unconscious self. Many organic intelligences have none such.

"You want to know about me?"

We have heard enough symphonies, believe Us.

At least it was direct. Many times in the past, her research showed, it—"They"—had not been. The Architecture was paying close attention!—a coup in itself.

"I'm sorry our art forms bore you."

Many beings who use acoustic means believe their art forms are the most important, valuable aspects of their minds. This is seldom so, in Our experience.

"So involvement is more important to you?"

For this moment, truly. Remember that We are an evolving composite of mental states, no less than you. You cannot meet the same Us again.

"Then you should be called . . . ?"

We know your term "Architecture" and find it—your phrasing?—amusing. Better perhaps to consider us to be a composite entity. As you are yourselves, though you cannot well sense this aspect. You imagine that you are a unitary consciousness, guiding your bodies.

"And we aren't?"

Of course not. Few intelligences in Our experience know as little of their underlying mental architecture as do you.

"Could that be an advantage for us?"

With the next words came a shooting sensation, something like a dry chuckle.

Perhaps so. You apparently do all your best work offstage. Ideas appear to you without your knowing where they come from.

She tried to imagine watching her own thoughts form, but was at a loss where to go with this. "Then let's . . . well . . ."

Gossip?

What an odd word choice. There was something like a tremor of pleasure in its neural tone, resounding with long, slow wavelengths within her.

2.

"It sounds creepy," Catkejen said. She was shoveling in food at the Grand Cafeteria, a habit Rachel had noticed many Loonies had. Food here was spotty, and when some fauxfilet came in, the alert went out.

"Nothing in my training really prepared me for its . . . well, coldness, and . . ."

Catkejen stopped eating to nod knowingly. "And intimacy?"

"Well, yes."

"Look, I've been doing background code for pod work only a few weeks, just like you. Already it's pretty clear that we're mostly negotiating, not translating."

Rachel frowned. "They warned us, but still . . ."

"Look, these are big minds. Strange as anything we'll ever know. But they're trapped in a small space, living cyber-lives. We're their entertainment."

"And I am yours, ladies," said the silver-haired guy from the party night. As he sat down at their table, he ceremoniously shook hands with Rachel. "Geoffrey Chandis."

"So how're you going to amuse us?" Catkejen smiled skeptically.

"How's this?" Geoffrey stood and put one broad hand on their table. In one deft leap he was upside down, balanced upon the one hand, the other saluting them.

"You've been sleeping and training in HiGee." Catkejen applauded. The Library offered high-centrifugal whirlers for those who wanted to maintain their Earthside adaptation.

He switched his support from one hand to the other. "I find this paltry 0.17 Lunar gee charming, don't you?"

Rachel pointed. "As charming as one red sock, the other blue?"

Unfazed, Geoffrey launched himself upward. He did a flip and landed on two feet, without even a backward step to restore balance. Rachel and Catkejen gave him beaming smiles. "Socks are just details, ladies. I stick to essentials."

"You're in our ear, so?" Catkejen asked.

Geoffrey sat, but not before he twirled his chair up into the air, making it do a few quick, showy moves, using just two fingers. "When I saw you two at that place, So Eat Already, I was just sneaking in for some of the refreshments. I'm a lowly Hound, well below you two."

Rachel said, "I thought HiGee folk were, well—"

"More devoted to the physical? Just manual labor types, miners? Not proper fodder for the Library?" He grinned.

Rachel felt her face redden. Was she that easy to read? "Well, yes."

"My parents, my friends, they're all focused on athletics. Me, I'm a rebel."

Catkejen smiled. "Even against the Noughts?"

He shrugged. "Mostly I find a way to avoid them."

Rachel nodded. "I think I'd rather be ignored by them."

"Y'know," Catkejen said reflectively, "I think they're a lot like the Minds."

Rachel asked slowly, "Because they're the strangest form of human?"

Geoffrey said, "They're sure alien to me. I'll give up sex when I've lost all my teeth, maybe, but not before."

"Noughts are born, not made. They give me the shivers sometimes," Catkejen said. "I was fetching an ancient written document over in the Hard Archives last week, nighttime. Three of them came striding down the corridor in those capes with the cowls. All in black, of course. I ducked into a side corridor—they scared me."

"A woman's quite safe with them," Geoffrey said. "Y'know, when they started up their Nought Guild business, way back, they decided on that all-black look and the shaved heads and all, because it saved money. But everybody read it as dressing like funeral directors. Meaning, they were going to bury all our sex-ridden old ways of interpreting."

"And here I thought I knew a lot about Library history," Catkejen said in an admiring tone. "Wow, that's good gossip."

He shrugged. "History is just gossip about the great, as some Nought puts it."

"But the Noughts have made big breakthroughs," Rachel said. "Historically—"

"Impossible to know, really," Catkejen interrupted. "The first Noughts refused to even have names, so we can't cite the work as coming from them."

Geoffrey said mock-solemnly, "Their condition they would Nought name."

"They've missed things, too," Catkejen said. "Translated alien epic sensual poems as if they were about battles, when they were about love."

"Sex, actually," Geoffrey said. "Which can seem like a battle."

Catkejen laughed. "Not the way I do it."

"Maybe you're not doing it right." Geoffrey laughed with her, a ringing peal.

Rachel pursed her lips, thinking. "Y'know, I wonder if the Noughts ever envy us?"

Geoffrey grunted in derision. "They save so much time by not having to play our games. It allows them to contemplate the Messages at their leahzure."

He took a pressed-regolith coffee cup and made it do a few impossible stunts in midair. Rachel felt that if she blinked she would miss something; he was quick. His compact body had a casual grace, despite the thick slabs of muscle. The artful charm went beyond the physical. His words slid over each other in an odd pronunciation that had just enough inflection to ring musically. Maybe, she thought, there were other amusements to be had here in the hallowed Library grounds.

––––––

She worked steadily, subjecting each microsecond of her interviews with the Architecture to elaborate contextual analysis. Codes did their work, cross-checking furiously across decades of prior interpretation. But even the best software needed the guidance of the person who had been through the experience: her.

And she felt the weight of the Library's history upon her every translation. Each cross-layered correlation with the huge body of Architecture research brought up the immense history behind their entire effort.

When first received centuries before, the earliest extraterrestrial signals had been entirely mystifying. The initial celebrations and bold speeches had obscured this truth, which was to become the most enduring fact about the field.

For decades in the twenty-first century, astronomers had rummaged through the frequencies, trying everything from radio waves to optical pulses, infrared to ultraviolet, and even the occasional foray into X-rays. They found nothing. Conventional wisdom held that the large power needed to send even a weak signal across many light-years was the most important factor. Therefore, scrutinize the nearby stars, cupping electromagnetic ears for weak signals from penny-pinching civilizations. The odds were tiny that a society interested in communication would be nearby, but this was just one of those hard facts about the cosmos—which turned out to be wrong. The local-lookers fell from favor after their increasingly frantic searches. By then the Galactic Center Strategy had emerged. Its basis lay in the discovery that star formation had begun in the great hub of stars within the innermost ten thousand light-years. Supernovas had flared early and often there, and stars were closer together, so heavy elements built up quickly. Three-quarters of the suitable life-supporting stars in the entire galaxy were older than the sun, and had been around on average more than a billion years longer.

Most of these lay within the great glowing central bulge—the hub, which humankind could not see through the lanes of dust clogging the constellation of Sagittarius. But in radio frequencies, the center shone brightly. And the entire company of plausible life-sites, where the venerable societies might dwell, subtended an arc of only a few degrees, as seen from Earth. Humanity truly lived in the boondocks—physically and, as became apparent, conceptually as well.

Near the center of the hub, thousands of stars swarmed within a single light-year. Worlds there enjoyed a sky with dozens of stars brighter than the full moon. Beautiful, perhaps—but no eyes would ever evolve there to witness the splendor.

The dense center was dangerous. Supernovas drove shock waves through fragile solar systems. Protons sleeted down on worlds, sterilizing them. Stars swooped near each other, scrambling planetary orbits and raining down comets upon them. The inner zone was a dead zone. But a bit farther out, the interstellar weather was better. Planets capable of sustaining organic life began their slow winding path upward toward life and intelligence within the first billion or two years after the galaxy formed. An Earthlike world that took 4.5 billion years to produce smart creatures would have done so about 4 billion years ago.

In the vast swath of time since then, intelligence might have died out, arisen again, and grown inconceivably rich. The beyond-all-reckoning wealthy beings near the center could afford to lavish a pittance on a luxury—blaring their presence out to all those crouched out in the galactic suburbs, just getting started in the interstellar game.

Whatever forms dwelled farther in toward the center, they knew the basic symmetry of the spiral. This suggested that the natural corridor for communication is along the spiral's radius, a simple direction known to everyone. This maximized the number of stars within a telescope's view. A radius is better than aiming along a spiral arm, since the arm curves away from any straight-line view. So a beacon should broadcast outward in both directions from near the center.

So, rather than look nearby, the twenty-first-century SETI searchers began to look inward. They pointed their antennas in a narrow angle toward the constellation Sagittarius. They listened for the big spenders to shout outward at the less prosperous, the younger, the unsophisticated.

But how often to cup an ear at the stars? If Earth was mediocre, near the midrange in planetary properties, then its day and year were roughly typical. These were the natural sequences any world would follow: a daily cycle atop an annual sway of climate.

If aliens were anything like us, they might then broadcast for a day, once a year. But which day? There was no way to tell—so the SETI searchers began to listen every day, for roughly a half hour, usually as the radio astronomers got all their instruments calibrated to make their usual maps of the microwave sky. They watched for narrow-band signals that stood out even against the bright hub's glow.

Radio astronomers also had to know what frequency to listen to. The universe is full of electromagnetic noise at all wavelengths, from the size of atoms to those of planets. Quite a din.

There was an old argument that water-based life might pick the "watering hole"—a band near 1 billion cycles/second where both water and hydroxyl molecules radiate strongly. Maybe not right on top of those signals, but nearby, because that's also in the minimum of all the galaxy's background noise.

Conventional searches had spent a lot of effort looking for nearby sources, shifting to their rest frame, and then eavesdropping on certain frequencies in that frame. But a beacon strategy could plausibly presume that the rest frame of the galactic center was the obvious gathering spot, so anyone broadcasting would choose a frequency near the "watering hole" frequency of the galaxy's exact center.

Piggybacking on existing observing agendas, astronomers could listen to a billion stars at once. Within two decades, the strategy worked. One of the first beacons found was from the Sagittarius Architecture.

Most of the signals found since the early days proved to have a common deep motivation. Their ancient societies, feeling their energies ebb, yet treasuring their trove of accumulated art, wisdom, and insight, wanted to pass this on. Not just by leaving it in a vast museum somewhere, hoping some younger species might come calling someday. Instead, many built a robotic funeral pyre fed by their star's energies, blaring out tides of timeless greatness:

"My name is Ozymandias, king of kings: / Look on my works, ye Mighty, and despair!" as the poet Percy Bysshe Shelley had put it, witnessing the ruins of ancient Egypt, in Afrik.

At the very beginnings of the Library, humanity had found that it was coming in on an extended discourse, an ancient interstellar conversation, without notes or history readily provided. Only slowly did the cyber-cryptographers fathom that most alien cultures were truly vast, far larger than the sum of all human societies. And much older.

Before actual contact, nobody had really thought the problem through. Historically, Englishmen had plenty of trouble understanding the shadings of, say, the Ozzie Bushmen. Multiply that by thousands of other Earthly and solar system cultures and then square the difficulty, to allow for the problem of expressing it all in sentences—or at least, linear symbolic sequences. Square the complexity again to allow for the abyss separating humanity from any alien culture.

The answer was obvious: any alien translator program had to be as smart as a human. And usually much more so.

The first transmission from any civilization contained elementary signs, with which to build a vocabulary. That much even human scientists had guessed. But then came incomprehensible slabs, digital Rosetta stones telling how to build a simulated alien mind that could talk down to mere first-timers. The better part of a century went by before humans worked out how to copy and then represent alien minds in silicon. Finally what some then called the Alien Library was built, to care for the Minds and Messages it encased. To extract from them knowledge, art, history, and kinds of knowing for which humans might very well have no name.

And to negotiate with them. The cyber-aliens had their own motivations.

3.

"I don't understand your last statement."

I do not need to be told that. You signal body-defiance with your crossed arms, barrier gestures, pursed lips, contradictory eyebrow slants.

Rachel noted the shift to first person singular. Was this a way of being friendly? "But these tensor topologies are not relevant to what we were discussing."

They are your reward.

"For what?"

Giving me of your essence. By wearing ordinary clothes, as I asked, and thus displaying your overt signals.

"I thought we were discussing the heliosphere problem."

We were. But you primates can never say only one thing at a time to such as We.

Huh—back to plural pronoun . . . what did that mean? The Sagittarius Architecture was complex, but what nuances did these bits of grammar mean? She felt acutely uncomfortable. Working in the pod was odd enough, without this element. The Prefects and Noughts would no doubt be concerned, too. *This entity is both smart and canny . . . better be careful.*

Her sessions built big slices of the strange, a zap to her synaptic net. The shock of unending Otherness moistened her body somehow with meaning, sometimes with special stinks, grace notes, blaring drawings that flickered in the air, illuminating without instructing.

"Uh, this picture you gave me . . . I can see this is some sort of cylindrical tunnel through—"

The plasma torus of your gas giant world, Jupiter. I suggest it as a way to funnel currents from the moon Io.

"Wow. The detail! How did you get this?"

I inferred from my access to your general information files. I used knowledge my species gleaned from another Message we received millennia ago.

"I appreciate this, and will forward it—"

There is more to know, before your level of technology—forgive me, but it is still crude, and will be so for far longer than you surmise— can make full use of this defense.

Rachel suppressed her impulse to widen her eyes. Defense? Was this it? A sudden solution? "I'm not a physiker—"

Nor need you be. I intercept your host of messages, all unspoken.

Your pelvis is visible beneath your shift, wider and rotated back slightly more than the male Suppliants who come to Us. Waist more slender, thighs thicker. Navel deeper, belly longer. Specializations impossible to suppress. Ah, to savor such.

Where was it—They?—going with this? "Those are just *me*, not messages."

It is becoming of you to deny them. Like your hourglass shape perceived, say, across an ancient plain at great distance. Your thighs admit an obligingly wider space, an inward slope to the thickened thighs, that gives an almost knock-kneed appearance.

"I beg your pardon—"

A pleasant saying, that—meaning that We have overstepped—another primate gesture—your boundaries? But I merely seek knowledge for my own repository.

"I—we—don't like being taken apart like this!"

But reduction to essentials is your primary mental habit.

"Not reducing people to their bodies!"

Ah, but having done this to the outside world, you surely cannot object to having the same method applied to yourselves.

"People don't like being dissected."

Your science made such great strides—unusual even upon the grander stage of worlds—precisely because you could dexterously—note the allusion to your hands—divide your attentions into small units, all the better to understand the whole.

When They got like this it was best to humor Them, she had gathered from prior Librarian notes. "People don't like it. That is a social mannerism, maybe, but one we feel strongly about."

And I seek more.

The sudden grave way the Sagittarius said this chilled her. It carried an undertone she could not parse.

4.

Siloh was not happy, though it took a lot of time to figure this out. The trouble with Noughts and Prefects alike was their damned lack of signals. No slight downward tug of lips to signal provisional disapproval, no sideways glance to open a possibility. Just the facts, ma'am. They seemed to think that conveyed objectivity. "So it is giving you tantalizing bits."

"They, not it. Sometimes I feel I'm talking to several different minds at once."

"It has said the same about us."

The conventional theory of the human mind was that it was a kind of legislature, always making deals between differing interests. Only by attaining a plurality could anyone make a decision. Rachel bit her lip to not give away anything, then realized that her bite was visible, too. "We're a whole species. They're a simulation of one."

Siloh made a gesture she could not read, an arm twist and foot flick.

She had expected some congratulations on her work, but then, Siloh was a Nought and had little use for most human social lubrications. He said slowly, "This cylinder through the Io plasma—the physikers say it is intriguing."

"How? I thought the intruding interstellar plasma was overpowering everything."

"It is. We lost Ganymede Nation today."

She gasped. "I hadn't heard."

"You have been immersed in your studies, as is fitting."

"Does Catkejen know?"

"I gather she had relatives there. She has been told."

Not by you, I hope. Siloh was not exactly the sympathetic type. "I should go to her."

"Wait until our business is finished."

"But I—"

"Wait."

Siloh leaned across its broad work plane, which responded by offering luminous information. Rachel crooked her neck but could not make out what hung shimmering in the air before Siloh. Of course; this was a well-designed office, so that she could not read its many ingrained inputs. He was probably summoning stuff all the while he talked to her, without her knowing it. Whatever he had learned, he sat back with a contented, small smile. "I believe the Sagittarius Composite is emerging in full, to tantalize you."

"Composite?"

"A deeper layer to its intelligence. You should not be deceived into thinking of it as remotely like us. We are comparatively simple creatures." Siloh sat back, steepling fingers and peering into them, a studied pose. "Never does the Sagittarius think of only a few moves into its game."

"So you agree with Youstani, a long-lived Translator Supreme from the last century, that the essential nature of Sagittarius is to see all conversations as a game?"

"Are ours different?" A sudden smile creased the leathery face, a split utterly without mirth.

"I would hope so."

"Then you shall often be deceived."

———

Rachel went to their apartment immediately, but someone had gotten there before her. It was dark, but she caught muffled sounds from the living room. Was Catkejen crying?

Earth's crescent shed a dim glow into the room, an ivory cast from their ceiling feed of the surface. She stepped into the portal of the living room and in the gloom saw someone on the viewing pallet. A low whimper drifted in the darkness, repeating, soft and sad, like crying, yes—

But there were two people there. And the sobbing carried both grief and passion, agony and ecstasy. An ancient tide ran in the room's shadowed musk.

Murmured words flowed in a voice she knew. The other person was Geoffrey. Moving with a slow rhythm, he was administering a kind of sympathy Rachel certainly could not. And she had not picked up the slightest clue of this relationship between them. A pang forked through her.

The pain surprised her. She made her way out quietly.

———————

Catkejen's relations had not made it out from Ganymede. She had to go through the rituals and words that soften the hard edges of life. She went for a long hike in the linked farming lava tubes, by herself. When she returned she was quieter, worked long hours, and took up sewing. The somber prospects of the Ganymede loss cast a pall over all humanity, and affected the Library's work. This disaster was unparalleled in human history for its scale, the loss of all their outer colonies, a tragedy greater even than the Nation Wars.

Still, solid work helped for a while. But after weeks, Rachel needed a break, and there weren't many at the Library. Anything robustly physical beckoned. She had gone for a swim in the spherical magnetic pool, of course, enjoying the challenge. And flown in broad swoops across the Greater Dome on plumes of hot air. But a simmering frustration remained. Life had changed. She and Catkejen had both developed a new, friendly, work-buddy relationship with Geoffrey. Much of this was done without words, a negotiation of nuances. They never spoke of that moment in the apartment, and Rachel did not know if they had sensed her presence. Cat had Geoffrey for fun, fine. Rachel did not but liked him anyway.

Perhaps more than ever, Geoffrey amused them with his quick talk and artful stunts. Rachel admired his physicality, the yeasty smell of him as he laughed and cavorted. HiGeers were known for their focus, which athletics repaid in careers of remarkable performance. The typical HiGee career began in sports and moved later to work in arduous climes, sites in the solar system where human strength and endurance still counted, because machines were not dexterous and supple enough.

Some said the HiGeer concentration might have come from a side effect of their high-spin, centrifugal donut habitats. Somehow Geoffrey's concentration came out as a life-of-the-party energy, even after his long hours in intense rapport with his own research.

Appropriately, he was working on the Andromeda Manifold, a knotty tangle of intelligences that stressed the embodied nature of their parent species. Geoffrey's superb nervous system, and especially his exact hand-eye coordination, gave him unusual access to the Manifold. While he joked about this, most of what he found could not be conveyed in words at all. That was one of the lessons of the Library— that other intelligences sensed the world, and the body's relation to it, quite differently. The ghost of Cartesian duality still haunted human thinking.

Together the three of them hiked the larger craters. All good for the body, but Rachel's spirit was troubled. Her own work was not going well.

She could scarcely follow some of the Architecture's conversations. Still less comprehensible were the eerie sensoria it projected to her— sometimes the only way it would take part in their discourse, for weeks on end.

Finally, frustrated, Rachel broke off connection with the Architecture and did not return for a month. She devoted herself instead to historical records of earlier Sagittarius discourse. From those had come some useful technical inventions, a classic linear text, even a new digital art form. But that had been decades ago, before most Librarians abandoned it for other Messages.

Siloh kept poking her about it. Reluctantly she went back into her pod and returned to linear speech mode. "I don't know what you intend by these tonal conduits," she said to the Sagittarius—after all, it probably had an original point of view, even upon its own motivations.

I was dispatched into this Realm in order to carry my Creators' essentials, to propagate their Supreme Cause, and to gather knowing-wisdom for them.

So it spoke of itself as "I" today—meaning that she was dealing with a shrunken fraction of the Architecture. Was it losing interest? Or withholding itself in spite, after she had stayed away? "That is your goal?"

Partly. I have other functions as well. Any immortal intelligence must police its own mentation.

Now, what did that mean? Suddenly, all over her body washed sheets of some strange signal she could not grasp. The scattershot impulses aroused a pulse-quickening unease in her. *Concentrate.* "But . . . but your home world is toward the galactic center, at least twenty thousand light-years away, we gather. So much time has passed—"

Quite so—my Creators may be long extinct. Probabilities suggest so. I gather from your information, and mine, that the mean life-time for civilizations in the Realm is comparable to their/our span.

"So there may be no reason for you to gather information from us at all. You can't send it to them anymore." She could not keep the tensions from her voice. In earlier weeks of incessant pod time, she had relied upon her pod's programming to disguise her transmission. And of course, the Sagittarius knew this. Was anything lost on it? Or . . . Them?

Our motivations do not change. We are eternally a dutiful servant, as are you. Or so I grasp.

Ah, an advance to "We." She remembered to bore in on the crucial, not be deflected. "Good. If the interstellar plasma presses in more, gets near Earth—"

We follow your inference. The effects We know well. Our Creators inhabit(ed) a world similar to yours, though frankly, more beautiful. (You have wasted so much area upon water!) We managed the electrical environs of our world to send our beacon signal, harnessing the rotational energy of our two moons to the task.

Rachel felt a tingling thrill. This was further than anyone, in a lifetime of Librarians, had gotten with Sagittarius about its origins. She felt a spike of elation. "Okay, what will happen?"

If the bow shock's plasma density increases further, while your ordinary star ploughs into it, then there shall be electrical consequences.

"What . . . consequences?"

Dire. You must see your system as a portrait in electrodynamics, one that is common throughout the Realm. Perceive: currents seethe forth—

A three-dimensional figure sprang into being before her, with the golden sun at its center. Blue feelers of currents sprouted from the sun's angry red spots, flowing out with the gale of particles, sweeping by the apron-strings of Earth's gnarled magnetic fields. This much she knew—that Earth's fields deflected huge energies, letting them pass into the great vault where they would press against the interstellar pressures.

But the currents told a different tale. They arced and soared around each world, cocooning each in some proportion. Then they torqued off into the vastness, smothering in darkness, then eventually returning in high, long arcs to the sun. They were like colossal rubber bands that could never break, but that forces could stretch into fibrous structures.

And here came the bulge of interstellar plasma—a broad knife, a sword thrusting into the buttery ball of magnetic fields that encased the planets. The whole system had a bow shock where it met the interstellar gas and dust. The dagger thrust straight into this broad prow. Lightning forked all along its intrusion. It engulfed Jupiter, and spikes of yellow coronal fury arced far out from the giant planet. These streamers curled inward, following long tangents toward the sun.

Some struck the Earth. Ruddy red waves made choppy orange froth around the Earth's own blue lines of protection.

"I don't need a detailed description of what that means," she said. "Bad news."

Your world is like many others, a spherical capacitor. Your surface is the inner, your ionosphere the outer. Your spin makes this a generator. Lightning strikes all around your globe to balance the charges reaching down, from high above the simple plains where you evolved. Disruption of your electrodynamic equilibrium will endanger the fragile skin of life.

From the Sagittarius came a sudden humid reek—her bodily reaction. It filled her pod. She flinched, sneezing, snorting, eyes runny. Sheeting sounds churned so low that she felt them as deep bass notes resounding in her. Wavelengths longer than her body rang through her bones. Her heart abruptly pounded. A growling storm rose in her ears.

"I . . . I will take this . . . and withdraw."

Have this as well, fair primate—

A squirt of compressed meaning erupted in her sensorium.

It will self-unlock at the appropriate moment.

She freed herself and staggered away.

5.

Opened, the first fraction of the squashed nugget of information was astonishing. Even Siloh let itself appear impressed. She could tell this by the millimeter rise of its left upper lip.

"This text is for the Prefect's attention." When Siloh rose and walked around its work-plane she realized that she had never seen so plainly Siloh's extent—nearly three meters of lean muscle, utterly without any hint of male or female shaping. The basic human machine, engineered for no natural world. It stopped to gaze at her. "This confirms what some physikers believe. Jupiter is the key."

Within an hour, the Prefect agreed. He eyed them both and flicked on a display. "The Sagittarius confirms our worst suspicions. Trainee, you said that you had captured from it yet more?"

She displayed the full data-nugget They had given her. A pyrotechnic display arced around a simulated Jupiter—

"There, at the poles," the Prefect said. "That cylinder."

The fringing fields carried by interstellar plasma swarmed into the cylinder. This time, instead of ejecting fierce currents, Jupiter absorbed them.

"That tube is electrically shorting out the disturbance," Siloh said. "The cylinders at both poles—somehow they shunt the energies into the atmosphere. Absorb it into gas."

"And not into ours," Rachel said. "Sagittarius has given us a solution."

The Prefect said, "What an odd way to do it. No description, just pictures."

Siloh said slowly, "Ummmm . . . and just how do we build those cylinders?"

They looked at her silently, eyes veiled, but she got the message: find out.

———————

The sensations washing over her were quite clear now. She had asked for engineering details, and it had countered with a demand. A quite graphic one.

This is my price. To know the full extent of the human sensorium.

"Sex?! Orgasm? You want to—"

It seems a small measure in return for the life of your world.

Before she could stop herself, she blurted, "But you're not—"

Human? Very well, We wish to fathom the meaning of that word, all the more. You are a third form of the chimpanzee. The common form is an alpha-male (as you put it) hierarchy, in which females mated only with the alpha—though there were many cheats. The bonobo variation was a subform that managed its society through sexual reward. You are an advanced variation on these two methods. Very curious, to Us. This is one step toward comprehending what that complex evolution that led to you—an advanced form mentally but conflicted socially—deeply means.

"You're a machine. A bunch of electronic bips and stutters."
A long pause, then:

Then We ask merely for a particular constellation of such information. By direct experience through you.

She gasped, trying not to lose it entirely. "You . . . would barter that for a civilization?"

We are a civilization unto Ourself. Greater than any of you single-tons can know.

"I . . . I can't. I won't."

6.

"You will," Siloh said with stony serenity.

Rachel blinked. "No!"

"Yes."

"This is more, much more, than required by all the Guild standards of neural integration."

"But—yes. You will."

In her sickening swirl of emotions, she automatically reached for rules. Emotion would carry no weight with this Nought. That was, in a way, the point of Noughts.

She felt on firm ground here, despite not recalling well the welter of policy and opinions surrounding the entire Nought phenomenon. They had come to the Library to help dissolve human biases in approaching Messages. An era of experience and profound philosophical analysis, much of it by artificial minds, had created a vast, weighty body of thought: Library Meta-theory. A lot of it, she thought, was more like the barnacles on the belly of a great ship, parasitic and along for the ride. But the issue could cut her now. Given a neurologically integrated system with two parties enmeshed, what was the proper separation?

"This issue is far larger than individual concerns." Siloh's face remained calm though flinty.

"Even though a Trainee, I am in charge of this particular translation—"

"Only nominally. I can have you removed in an instant. Indeed, I can do so myself. Now."

"It would take a while for anyone to achieve my levels of attunement and focus—"

"I have been monitoring your work. I can easily step in—"

"The Sagittarius Composite doesn't want to 'sleep' with you."

Siloh froze, composure gone. "You are inserting personal rebuke here!"

Her lips twitched as she struggled not to smile. "Merely an observation. And yes, 'sleep' is a euphemism. Sagittarius desires something it cannot get among the Nought class."

"I can arrange matters differently, then. I do know that people use euphemisms to avoid directly confronting facts." Siloh's face worked with several unreadable signals—as though, she thought, something unresolved was struggling to express itself.

She said firmly, "I want to remain at work."

Suddenly he smiled and said lightly, "Oh, you may. You definitely may."

An abrupt hand waved her away. Plainly Siloh had reached some insight but would not share. But what? Siloh's bland gaze gave away nothing. And she was not good enough at translating this strange being, yet.

———

Catkejen said as they approached the Dead Marxist, an Eastern European eatery, "Just forget about Siloh for tonight. Kick some jams out. Hey, look at that guy!"

A slim man was passing by, dressed in wraparound silvery cloth. He looked like a knight in armor and was plainly wearing nothing underneath. "Um, yeah." Rachel was still distracted, and seeing fleshy delights was not helping.

"Okay," Catkejen said, "I call dibs."

Rachel had become a tad uncomfortable among all the slim Loonies. She was more meaty than the carved, bony ladies of the Library and the stringy, muscled miners. She swayed and jiggled, a message of flesh and skin around a robust frame of bone and sinew. The uniform lighting here was kind to a bigger frame, allowing no shadows. Rachel had always had an ambivalent dance with her body, liking its strength and stretch, but not the advances it invited from legions of the lustful, of both sexes. At times back Earthside she'd felt her body to be a dress of skin she wore for others. Now, with the skimpy diet of Luna's limited agriculture, she would probably lose some mass, but not, alas, so far.

Catkejen peeled off, but Rachel kept going until she saw just outside the Dead Marxist the back of Geoffrey Chandis. This brightened her mood and she swung around him to say hello, then saw a pair of hands reach around his neck, a head kissing him—and it was Ruby.

Rachel turned away and Ruby came up from a big smacking kiss to say, "Hey, join us."

"Uh, I don't—"

"No, don't," Geoffrey said firmly, taking Ruby's hands off him.

Ruby plunked her hands back onto him. "Not done!"

Geoffrey said, "Not in the mood for frisky right now," but instead of removing her hands, she started stroking him, shoulder to legs to ass.

Rachel grabbed one of Ruby's hands and used its leverage to twirl the woman away from him. "Done now."

At once Ruby was in her face, eyes slitted. "He's not yours!"

"Not yours either," Rachel said, and stepped around her. Geoffrey was standing there, eyes wide, a big smile. With a swooping hand he stepped toward the Dead Marxist and she followed him. Ruby sputtered behind them.

For the next hour she sat beside Geoffrey at the long table where their gang gathered. Without much thinking about it she had formed a pattern of clubbing with Catkejen and playing the silent one, letting their darting talk fill her in on the inner workings of Loonie and Library.

"—this new drink, Tangeriney Wankmaggot, can't even spell it, though I can spiel it, in German—"

"—and this one Message we were decrypting kept addressing 'those of inner scaffolding' and we realized that came from some aliens who had no bones, and wondered why anyone wanted them."

"—listen, looking good and dressing well is a necessity. Having a purpose in life is not—"

"—can't complain. Still do, though."

—"Anglish itself, ever think, is a puzzle. Take f'instance"—writing a flowing hand in air floss, which quickly dissolved—"'their our know rules.' See? Pronounced, easy—spelled, not so much—"

"—I said 'third' but this Message small-bot heard 'turd' so—"

"—tried on five different outfits and settled on one that would say I'm not the sort who tries on five different outfits—"

"—Squishy or swank?"

"—I had to look up what 'servile toady' meant—"

"—Hey, trying to define yourself is like trying to bite your own teeth."

It was a fun flurry of left-handed compliments, irony abounding, revelations slid into metaphors, and most of all, funny. Plenty of laughter cemented them all. She saw that the Hounds and Seekers of Script were like the old-time hackers and digital sleuths. They loved their coding crafts, roving through the digital dynasties in the Message labyrinths. They had their fandoms for digital detective methods and contested variant views gladly. They seemed deferential toward her, as a Trainee allowed into the pods. But they showed this in sly jokes and wry twists of laughing mouths.

They were a gang, all right, and one she was glad to be in. Loonies, yes. By the time Geoffrey escorted her home she felt mellow. They had not discussed Ruby much, just exchanged mutual shrugs. She let him guide her up into the surface corridors as she rummaged through all that had happened—Siloh, the Sagittarius, Ruby. They came upon a broad square with a view of the pale Lunar night.

She was getting used to how the darkness lasted fourteen Earth days, with temperatures dropping into a cold so punishing it made Antarctica seem like a hot tub, an icy low of minus 190 degrees Celsius. Earth's crescent lit the gray land, where miner bots worked perpetually, arcing debris behind them like silvery fountains.

To her surprise, they came to a large dining circle with a broad view of the night. Gilded chandeliers suspended from the ceiling and lamps shone above marble tables gleaming. People of stately mien wore distinguished smart clothes that adjusted to fit as they danced to Bach, sat on plush chairs, read tabletops while waiters dressed like dignitaries brought delicacies.

"Tourists," Geoffrey said with a tone of steely disdain.

"The Library allows that?"

"Helps with the funding. There's even a ceiling screen show of alien landscapes and pictures."

"Sounds like fun, must admit."

"I'll take you."

"Oh, yes." She had to admire how he had slid in a date invite.

He glanced at her, smiled, and said, "I liked how you twirled Ruby away."

"She's big but not strong."

"Her opinions are. Earlier she was going on about 'It's Sapiens to Be Homo,' one of the Earthside Ministry of Infertility's slogans."

"Oog," Rachel managed.

"She's bi anyway, so it was just for show," he added matter-of-factly.

The next morning Rachel woke up and realized that she had decided. Going out, the fun talk, Geoffrey, even Ruby—all had conspired to relax her enough that she had somehow figured out the issue, her fears, and knew now she would do as the Sagittarius wished.

Still, she was puzzled. Human-made Artificials always worked with total transparency. The Sagittarius could work that way, or it could mask portions of its own mind from itself, and so attain something like that notorious cliché, the Human Condition.

Much current opinion held that the supreme advantage of any artificial mind lay in its constant transparency, so this was a shock. What advantage could come to an Artificial that did not immediately know its own levels? That acted out of thinking patterns it could not consciously review? And a human couldn't, either?

Since this was a property the Sagittarius Architecture shared, in a way, with humans, the discussion had grown heated over many decades.

And unresolved.

So Rachel went to her pod and entered. She told the staff to watch for any signs of trouble and put two different women on alert, eyes on screens.

"Hello again," she said.

I wish you Good Day in English, Sat Shri Akaal in Punjabi, As-Salamu Alaikum in Arabic, Aloha in Hawaiian, Shalom in Hebrew, Namaste in Hindi, and Ciao in Italian. I cannot tip my hat, for I have no head. Nor can I kiss your hand, m'lady.

"Been studying up, then."

Studying you, m'lady.

Now when Rachel engaged with it, she was acutely conscious of how the Artificial could change nature with quixotic speed. Swerves into irritation switched to mirth, then came fast upon long bouts of analytic serenity. She could make no sense of these jumps, or fathom the information she gained in these long episodes of engagement. The neurological impact upon her accumulated. Her immersion in the pod carried a jittery static. Her nerves were frayed.

"I wish to obtain the information on the hydrogen wall you—"

I fathom you. Very well—

Some fraction of the information the Sagittarius Architecture gave her bore upon the problem of heliospheric physics, but she could not follow this material at blinding speed. Pictures flashed, prickly sensations swept across her skin, muscles jumped. She conveyed the passages, many quite long, to Siloh.

The crisis over the Artificial's demand seemed to have passed. She worked more deeply with it now, and so concentrating upon the exact nuances of the links, riding the flood of it, she did not at first react when she felt a sudden surge of unmistakable desire in herself. It shook her, yeasty and feverish, pressing her calves together and urging her thighs to ache with a sweet longing.

Somehow this merged with the passage currently under translation/discussion. She entered more fully into the difficult problem. Into extracting just the right subtlety from the slamming blocks of information that came flying through her. In the same intense moments she was fully focused, yet brimming with desire. An orgasm passed and fell away without her thinking of it at all. Then she did, and all at once she was not reasoning in one part of her mind but, it seemed, in all of them.

From there until only a few heartbeats later she ran the gamut of all previous passions. An ecstasy and union she had experienced only a few times—and only partially, she now saw—poured through her. Her body shook with gusts of raw red pleasure. Her Self sang its song, rapt. A constriction of herself seized this flood and rode it. Only furious joyful speed could grasp what this was, and in full passionate flow she felt herself hammered on a microsecond anvil—into the internal time frames of the Composite. Dizzy, blinding speed. It registered vast sheets of thought while a single human neuron was charging up to fire. Its cascades of inference and experience were like rapids in a river she could not see but only feel, a kinesthetic acceleration. Swerves that swept finally into a delightful blur.

Thought, sensation—all one.

She woke in the pod. Shook her head, glanced at the visible display.

Only a few minutes had passed since she had last registered any sort of time at all.

Yet she knew what had happened.

And regretted that it was over.

And hated herself for feeling that way.

———

"It had me."

Siloh began, "In a manner of speaking—"

"Against my will!"

Siloh looked judicial. "So you say. The recordings are necessarily only a pale shadow, so I cannot tell from experiencing them myself—"

Scornfully: "How could you anyway?"

"This discussion will not flow in that direction."

"Damn it, you knew Sagittarius would do this!"

Siloh shook his head. "I cannot predict the behavior of such an architectural mind class. No one can."

"You at least guessed that it would, would find a way into me, to . . . to mate with me. At a level we poor stunted humans can only approximate because we're always in two separated bodies. It was in mine. It—They—knew that in the act of translation there are ways, paths, avenues. . . ." She sputtered to a stop.

"I am sure that description of the experience is impossible." Siloh's normally impenetrable eyes seemed to show real regret.

Yeah? she thought. *How would you know?* But she said as dryly as she could muster, "You could review the recordings yourself, see—"

"I do not wish to."

"Just to measure—"

"No."

Abruptly she felt intense embarrassment. Bad enough if a man had been privy to those moments, but a Nought . . .

How alien would the experience be, for Siloh?—and alien in two different senses of the word? She knew suddenly that there were provinces in the landscape of desire Siloh could not visit. The place she had been with the Composite no human had ever been. Siloh could not go there. Perhaps an ordinary human could not, either.

"I know this is important to you," Siloh said abstractly. "You should also know that the Composite also gave us, in the translation you achieved—while you had your, uh, seizure—the key engineering design behind the heliospheric defense."

She said blankly, "The, uh, cylinders . . ."

"Yes, they are achievable, and very soon. A 'technically sweet' solution, I am told by the Prefect. Authorities—so far above us that they are beyond view—have begun the works needed. They took your information and are making it into an enormous construction at both poles of Jupiter. The entire remaining population of the Jovian Belt threw themselves into shaping the artifacts to achieve this."

"They've been following . . . what I say?"

"Yours was deemed the most crucial work. Yet you could not be told."

She shook her head to clear it. "So I wouldn't develop shaky hands."

"And you did not, not at all." Siloh beamed in an inscrutable way, one eyebrow canted at an ambiguous angle.

"You knew," she said leadenly. "What it would do."

"I'm sure I do not fathom what you mean."

She studied Siloh, who still wore the same strange beaming expression. *Remember,* she thought, *it can be just as irritating as an ordinary man, but it isn't one.*

7.

Months passed with momentum.

The colossal discharge of Jupiter's magnetospheric potentials was an energetic event unparalleled in millennia of humanity's long strivings to harness nature.

The Composite had brought insights to bear that physikers would spend a century untangling. For the moment, the only important fact was that by releasing plasma spirals at just the right pitch, and driving these with electrodynamic generators (themselves made of filmy ionized barium like a pewter cloud storm), a staggering current came rushing out of the Jovian system.

At nearly the speed of light it intersected the inward bulge of the heliosphere. Currents moved in nonlinear dances, weaving a pattern that emerged within mere minutes, moving in intricate harmonies.

Within a single moment, a complex web of forces flexed into being.

Within an hour, the bulge of interstellar gas arrested its inward penetration.

It halted, waves slamming in vexed lines of magnetic force against the Jovian sally. And became stable. It flexed and foamed in ivory turbulence—but the defense held.

Quickly humans—ever irreverent, even in the face of catastrophe—termed their salvation the Basket. Invisible to the eye, but luminous in plasma frequencies, the giant web the size of the inner solar system was made of filmy fields that weighed nothing. Yet it was all the same massively powerful, a dynamically responding screen protecting the Earth from a scalding death. The hydrogen wall seethed redly in the night sky. To many, it seemed an angry animal caught at last in a gauzy net.

Rachel witnessed the display from the Grand Plaza with a crowd of half a million. It was humbling, to think that mere primates had rendered such blunt interstellar pressures awesome but impotent.

8.

Rachel had stayed away from the Sagittarius for all the time the Jovian engineering occurred. Thousands worked furiously out there while she became a hermit. She worked on learning more about the other intractable Artificial Messages and, with Siloh's permission, ignored the Sagittarius. It sent her messages. Artificials had that Right of Sentience. They could become unstable if left in total isolation. She responded to the polite eletters with equally courteous evasions. Her equilibrium returned, somewhat reluctantly.

Climbing back into the pod, with attendants hovering near, felt precarious. She made herself breathe slowly, deeply. In the close confinement, fully wired in now, it sounded like wheezing.

Now the Sagittarius sent,

We render grateful thanks. For our fine moments together.

Her chest was tight. She had dreaded entering the pod yet again, and now could not speak. Her throat rasped with the effort.

We gather it is traditional among your species to compliment one's partner, and particularly a lady . . . afterward.

"Don't . . . don't try."

We became something new from that moment.

"We?"

I meant my self-entity. But, thanks to your erratic and fuzzy Anglish, I see the ambiguity. Indeed, here "we" includes yourself.

She felt anger and fear, and yet, simultaneously, pride and curiosity. These twisted together in her. Sweat popped out on her upper lip. The pod air was curiously fragrant—or was that musk some signal of the Sagittarius? The arrival of such emotions, stacked on top of each other, told her that she had been changed by what had happened in this pod, and would—could—never be the same. "I did not want it."

Then by my understanding of your phylum, you would not then have desired such congress. Yet you did. I know this.

"I—me, the conscious me—did not want it!"

We do not recognize that party alone. Rather, We recognize all of you equally. All your signals, do We receive.

"I don't want it to happen again."

Then it will not. It would not have happened the first time had the congruence between us not held true.

She felt the ache in herself. It rose like a tide, swollen and moist and utterly natural. She had to bring to bear every shred of her will to stop the moment, disconnect. She popped the seal. Left the pod, staggering and weeping and then running.

———

Geoffrey opened the door to his apartment, blinking owlishly—and then caught her expression.

"I know it's late, I wondered . . ." She stood numbly, then made herself brush past him, into the shadowed room.

"What's wrong?" He wore a white robe and wrapped it self-consciously around his middle.

"I don't think I can handle all this."

He smiled sympathetically. "You're the toast of the Library, what's to handle?"

"I—come here."

Words, linear sequences of blocky words—all useless. She reached inside the robe and found what she wanted. Her hands slid over muscled skin, and it was all so different, real, not processed and amped and electronically translated through centuries of careful dry precision. A tremor swept over her, across the gap between them, onto his moistly electric flesh.

9.

"There is news."

"Oh?" Rachel found it hard to focus on Siloh's words.

"You are not to discuss this with anyone," Siloh said woodenly. "The discharges from Jupiter's poles—they are now oscillating. At very high frequencies."

She felt her pulse trip-hammer, hard and fast and high, still erratic, even hours after she had left Geoffrey. Yet her head was ahead of her heart; a smooth serenity swept her along, distracting her with the pleasure of the enveloping sensation. "The Basket, it's holding, though?"

"Yes." Siloh allowed itself a sour smile. "Now the physikers say that this electromagnetic emission is an essential part of the Basket's power matrix. It cannot be interfered with in the slightest. No tinkering. Even though it is drowning out the sum of all of humanity's transmissions in the same frequency band. It is swamping us."

"Because?"

Siloh's compressed mouth moved scarcely at all. "It."

"You mean . . ."

"The Sagittarius Composite. It made this happen, by the designs it gave us."

"Why would it want . . ." Her voice trailed off as she felt a wave of conflicting emotions. Rachel bit her lip in apprehension.

"Why?" Siloh sniffed, frowned, gazed at nothing. "The signal Jupiter is sending out now, so powerfully, is a modified version of the original Message we received from the Sagittarius authors."

"Jupiter is broadcasting their Message?"

"Clearly, loudly. Into the plane of the galaxy."

"Then it built the Basket to reradiate its ancestors', its designers'—"

"We have learned," Siloh said, "a lesson perhaps greater than what the physikers gained. The Artificials have their own agendas. One knows this, but never has it been more powerfully demonstrated to us."

Rachel let her anxiety out in a sudden, manic burst of laughter. Siloh did not seem to notice. When she was done, rattling and snorting and gasping, she said, "The Sagittarius Composite is propagating itself. So it saved us. And used us."

Siloh said, "Now Jupiter is broadcasting the Sagittarius Message, altered by its experience with us. At an enormous volume, high power, to the outer fringes of the galaxy's disk. To places the original Sagittarius signal strength, coming from much farther inward, could not have reached."

"It's turned us into its relay station." She laughed again, but it turned to a groan and a sound she had never made before. Somehow it helped, that sound. She knew it was time to stop making it when the men eased through the door of Siloh's office, coming to take her in hand.

10.

Gingerly, she came back to work a month later. Siloh seemed atypically understanding. He set her to using the analytical verification matrices for a few months, calming work. Far easier, to skate through pillars and crevasses of classically known information. She could experience it all at high speed, as something like recreation—the vast cultural repositories of dead civilizations transcribed upon her skin, her neural beds, her five senses linked and webbed into something more. She even made a few minor discoveries.

She crept up on the problem of returning to the task she still desired: the Sagittarius. It was, after all, a thing in a box. The truism of her training now rang loudly in her life:

The Library houses entities that are not merely aliens and not merely artificial minds, but the strange sum of both. A Trainee forgets this at her peril.

11.

After more months, the moment came.

The Sagittarius sent,

We shall exist forever, in some manifestation. That is Our injunction, ordained by a span of time you cannot fathom. We carry forward Our initial commanding behest, given unto Us from Our Creators, before all else.

"The Creator Sagittarians told you to? You were under orders to make use of whatever resources you find?" She was back in the pod, but a team stood by outside, ready to extricate her in seconds if she gave the signal.

We were made as a combination of things, aspects for which you have not words nor even suspicions. We have Our own commandments from on high.

"Damn you! I was so close to you—and I didn't know!"

You cannot know me. We are vaster. Altogether, We lodged here—

whom you term Artificials—comprise what you might term the Milky Way's Library.

"Did you say 'vaster' or 'bastard'?"

She started laughing again, but this time it was all right. It felt good to make a dumb joke. Very, well, human.

In the simplicity of doing that, she could look away from all this, feel happy and safe for a flickering second. With some luck, at least for a moment, she might have a glimmer of the granite assurance this strange mind possessed. It was all alone, the only one of its kind here, and yet unshakable. Perhaps there was something in that to admire.

And she knew that she could not give up her brushes with such entities. In the last few days, she had doubted that. This was now her life.

Only now did she fathom how eerie a life it might be.

"Will you go silent on us again?"

We may at any time.

"Why?"

The answer does not lie within your conceptual space.

"Are you sure?"

In this way of Our teaching you, now you can embrace the concepts of nonattachment, acceptance of change, and fate as aspects of your human life.

She gasped. This phrase she recalled she had used in her second audience with the Prefect. It was part of Japanese philosophy, expressed in a lovely kintsugi bowl. How did this Artificial know she had said that? Here was a clue to something deeper. Could the Artificials have penetrated into the entire Library system? Were they listening everywhere?

She grimaced. *Deal with that later. Don't let this brain in a box intimidate me.*

"Damn right."

She could forget the reality of the chasm between her and this thing that talked and acted and was not ever going to be like anyone she had ever known, or could know. She would live with the not-knowing, the eternal ignorance before the immensity of the task here.

The abyss endured. In that there was a kind of shelter. It was not much, but there it was.

PART 4

FOOD TO THE SOUL

Food is music inside the body, and music is food inside the heart.

—GREGORY DAVID ROBERTS, *SHANTARAM*

Philosophy is written in this grand book, the universe, which stands
continually open to our gaze. But the book cannot be understood unless
one first learns to comprehend the language and read the letters in which
it is written. It is written in the language of mathematics, and its characters
are triangles, circles, and other geometric figures without which it is humanly
impossible to understand a single word of it; without these, one wanders
about in a dark labyrinth.

—GALILEO, *THE ASSAYER*, 1623

1.

The Prefect's thin smile and warm greeting made Rachel's heart do a little jig. This solemn man had become her standard, mostly because he gave little but meant much. He contrasted with the Library staff, who were fun chatterboxes.

Strangers stopped her in corridors now, complimenting her on her work on the hydrogen wall problem. Guys bought her drinks and wanted to know the whole story, until she got tired of telling them. Of course they wanted more than that, but she wasn't game. This was not the time to form a close and closed affair with a guy. Not again! Not while her career was opening so wide, so fast. She got high-level inquiries for comment that somehow made it through the Library comm screens. Prizes beckoned. Life was heady indeed. And all from figuring out the psyche of an alien software. She sat, while the standing Prefect leaned back on his desk and said, "We have received offers of interviews, consultancies, even Earthside tours and speeches—all for you."

"Ah." Something in his voice made her cautious.

"You will not take part, of course."

"Oh." She could not prevent a flicker of disappointment from crossing her face.

"The Library does not permit any Librarian to profit from research. Or stand out from other Librarians."

"Uh. Oh." There had been something about that in her training, but she recalled little of it.

"I suspect you have not taken the long view of Library economics."

"True enough." Modesty was always best.

"When the Venetian merchant Marco Polo reached China, in the latter part of the thirteenth century, he saw many wonders—gunpowder and coal and eyeglasses and porcelain. What astonished him most, however, was a new invention, implemented by Kublai Khan, a grandson of the great conqueror Genghis—paper money."

The Prefect paused for emphasis, eyes intent. "Marco Polo was right to be amazed, as we are by what we harvest from the Message Minds. The instruments of trade and finance are inventions, just as creations of art and discoveries of science are inventions—products of festering imagination. Paper money, backed by the authority of the state, was an astonishing innovation, one that reshaped the world. Arrival of alien technologies, lore, and art reshapes ours now, in the blare and sparkle of a debauch. The Minds know this."

The Prefect sniffed, as if reluctant to give details. "I know," was all Rachel could muster.

"Money is not the value for which goods are exchanged, but the value *by which* they are exchanged."

"The means by which we swap one set of stuff for another set of stuff," she managed. "Sure, economic systems evolve, with innovations, repetitions, failures, and dead ends. In finance, it involves busts and panics and crashes."

The Prefect nodded. "In alien-driven finance and economics, we keep stepping on the same rakes, slapped in the face—to employ a physical metaphor. To allow Librarians to profit in any way from their work encourages vagrant turbulence we deplore."

"So I get nothing from—"

"That management of 'stuff'—ideas, inventions, and the like—is not our concern. We seek deeper knowledge. Plus art, delight, music, and the other sorts of . . . like."

"I suppose the Library shows great profits, then?" Might as well poke him a bit, keeping her face as open and sincere as she could fake.

"Our upper echelons Earthside spend fortunes to protect us from political corruption. Plus, we must pay for our life support, computational costs, the lot. In our devoted field, difficulties, instead of irritating us as they do most, only increase our reliance on patience."

So no reward for such as me . . . she thought, her heart doing a little floppy death. *So do a humble bit, then.*

"Sorry I've accomplished so little. I was distracted, some personal . . . uh, stuff . . . and I—"

"The time you enjoy wasting is not wasted time."

She blinked, startled at the Prefect's shift to a friendly tone. "I have been doing routine work, cataloging—"

"I know. Tomorrow you can begin work on the Andromeda Structure."

"I thought that was—"

"Another difficult Mind Message, true. Among many." A sly smile, glittering eyes. "You seem to enjoy difficulty, so I am serving you a healthy dose."

2.

She decided to stay in for the evening, read a bit, forget life's vexing turns.

Rachel often read truly old fiction about libraries, to get a feel for what they might have been in the Print Age. Before even that had come meaning laboriously laid into stone, ceramics, sheets of reeds and parchment and leather, until finally the encasement of knowledge into the sheeted bodies of dead trees. Nostalgia for that time was eternal for Librarians. They knew they were often displaced from our origins in print, and carried anxious memories of that lost past. We fear losing our bearings. Then came the Cyber Age and all changed. Information could then fly through the air, even across a galaxy.

By writing of futures that echoed our nostalgias, the farback writer Bradbury reminded her of both what we were and what we could yet be. Like most creative people, Ray—she always thought of him that way, an old friend—was still a child at heart. His stories told her: Hold on to your childhood. You don't get another one. In so many stories, he gave us his childhood—and it worked for her, too.

Through Ray she had learned that for some hours she was Jane Eyre and Gully Foyle and Mr. Biswas and David Copperfield and millions more. Now she felt her own voice entirely separate from the many voices she had heard, read, and internalized every day. That now included the pseud-voices of the Minds, too. Her world had an alien tilt to it, somehow.

She was also an equal-opportunity voyeur. She wanted to know what it was like to be everybody. From reading she'd picked up how to note facial signals that could pass across in a flick—furrowed brows, jittery eyes, laconic curl of lip. She watched hands to see what they were saying, too. Most people gave away plenty, all unaware: jittery fingers, toe-tapping feet, shrugs and little cringes, and accents. Slow, curling vowels said southern, as she well knew and could disguise. Sharp, curt consonants: northern hemisphere power-speak. Flattened tones, misplaced articles—*I'm trying out this language, not a native.* Myriad signals, sliding sounds that said more than words. She could read backstory in vowels.

So tonight she looked forward to delicious hours of reading, after a skimpy dinner. She and Cat liked to eat imported food from Earth but were low on money, so ate local, meaning algae. Basically chlorella algae, grown fast in vats, extremely nutritious, literally everything you needed—except taste. All the vitamins, all the proteins, the sugars, everything, and awful. Called *gunk* for a good reason. Hence all the added flavorants, extracts hypered up, so one could eat gunk like oatmeal or spareribs. Tonight: duckling flambé.

Rachel cleaned up and fetched forth her book for a long sweet read—but Cat would have none of it. "It's clubbing night!"

Rachel sighed, nodded. They had agreed on a social schedule. *Here comes the game,* she thought. Gone was her evening of Bradbury or Heinlein—hysterically funny stuff, in its ignorance of the moon, yet endearing, too, at times. All before anybody had even gotten to Luna. She always dressed well for an outing, but she recognized the signs of insecurity here: certitude was inversely proportional to the amount of makeup. Cat's hands jittered so much Rachel had to put on Cat's lipstick. As a girl she had hated Charlotte Brontë's comment that she would have given all her talent to be beautiful. That condemned you always to play somebody else's game—and, when your looks failed, finally to lose. But makeup was also a mask to hide behind.

Cat gave her face one look and applied a cotton absorber to erase the layers. "Not needed. Come on, we'll go slumming. Sorta."

"Uh, I doubt there are—"

Catkejen lowered her voice to a gravelly pitch. "To the other side of the traaacks."

To Rachel's surprise, there actually were tracks. The two of them ascended to the surface and headed toward the center of the whole complex, beyond the recreation dome, and there it was—a view to the long, broad railway tracks into the processing areas. They watched through thick glass a hauler bring mounds of processed regolith in from the big solar furnace dome that sat at the edge of the lava fields. Rachel could see the large mirror made of aluminized mylar that reflected and focused sunlight on the raw, ground-up lava powder. "That's what we breathe," Catkejen said, pointing to the huge transparent bubble. "Just heat regolith dirt to melting point and oxy bubbles off. That pipe"—another pointing—"brings it to us. The train ferries the rare earths into the e-mag flinger."

They went under the tracks by way of a laser-carved tube and cut through another bamboo forest. The tall bamboo shoots had fat pandas slow-coasting among them, cute bears in low grav. This one also had cacti and shrubs, aflutter with gnatcatchers and cactus wrens, chirping and squeaking like tiny rusty doors. Catkejen said, "Pretty, huh? Birds love Loonie grav." The tiny creatures did loops and swirls unlike anything seen Earthside. "They live solely here now, preserved from their Earthside extinctions." Amid the groves were ponds where koi fish lurked, favorite ornaments among Loonies. They strolled through a wall of thorny scrub to find an immense tree swathed in bees— "Gengineered banyan to make honey for us, too"—then longstrode through some trees with fruit Rachel did not recognize; more gengineering. Their damp, flattened leaves covered the sidewalk with a brocaded richness.

"I thought this vegetation made our oxygen."

"Not enough, alas. The story is, we primates get a rest from this metal and glass Loonie world if we move through places that appeal to our origins. Our unconscious relaxes, not all the time checking for artificial stuff."

Too bad I can't do working with alien smartware outside my pod, she thought. The Sagittarius would be less scary, for sure.

"Hey, here's the Miner Village, to use the official term."

Narrow corridors were filled with people carrying on their lives. It reminded Rachel of the Gulf coast where she grew up. Hawkers displayed homeware. Barbers cut hair a meter from the walkway. A five-seat grill fed sizzling fauxflesh steaks to customers with backs to the avenue, gossiping noisily. Laundry hung out to dry over their heads, flapping in the steady corridor wind.

"Let's do a rockhopper club," Catkejen said, leading her to a jazzy place called Grand Hotel Abyss. "Without, uh, doing a rockhopper." Rachel knew that rock wranglers who harvested grimy wealth made good money. Mostly guys, they ran the heavies that managed a retinue of dumbass robo-harvesters. That meant long hours patrolling, and often fixing, the tricky axles and scoops that could clog with the fine-grained dust.

Catkejen stopped outside the carved, brassy regolith door and gave a wry smile. "In my twenties, I learned from tough gals that in a full-on blue-collar guy club, you don't respond to everything said. Generally it's best not to. Jump around the tables, leave 'em if you don't like 'em. Kinda like the three-D chess we've been playing. In an attacking move, ignore bishop or castle. Logic and straight lines are out. Best to rely on the knight. Jump to a spot with interesting guys and an empty chair several tables away. Keep 'em guessing."

Rachel held back. "I don't know . . ."

Cat gave a stern glare. "For me, being likable and unthreatening to men comes naturally, not unlike my thick eyelashes. For them, my hobbies include watching action movies, having go-games explained to me, and hanging out with their friends over mine. I have worn many hats for guys—but not in the annoying *Look at me, I'm wearing a hat* kind of way. But there might be fun guys here, you never know—and best of all, they're not Librarians."

"Should we stay together?"

"At first, then you're free-range."

In they went. "Remember, to shine is better than to reflect," Cat said.

Rachel did not catch the pun until she was three steps into the joint. She noticed a bride celebrating in a side room who was wearing a mustard-yellow ball gown featuring puke-green polka dots and puff sleeves, apparently a new Earther fad of the deliberately hideous.

The bar was dark and steamy and just a tad seamy. Sound bubbles damped the talking. Rachel had followed Catkejen's styling advice and dolled up a bit, so was now a new creature. She swayed in a long-skirted yellow dress with orange ArcMondrian lines, her shoes casual flats, carrying a small orange handbag. Brushed auburn hair, artful makeup, even long, artificial eyelashes. Bait, of a sort. Not her kind of game, but Catkejen had lured her into it by referring to Rachel's own origins in the American Deep South, where she knew plenty of working-class folks and, indeed, was one of them, until she got into a university. Glancing around, Rachel looked over her competition, reflecting that for some women, there should be a weight limit for the purchase of spandex. Lady miners seemed both brawny and weighty. Three guys with polished scalps were trading lies in a booth and checking her out. The noisiest of them got up to ask her if she wanted a drink. Of course she did, though she was thrown off by his genial warning, "Ladies, you don't look like you're the minin' kind."

Rattled—had her mask of harmless approachability slipped?— she made herself smile and ask, "Should I be?" Catkejen made a joke Rachel couldn't follow, and they sat.

They took the usual questions in stride and the talk came fast, eyes shining, drinks or sniffs all around.

She was glad nobody connected her to the hydrogen wall story. She let the banter flow until a guy started pressing in on her. So: "Got to freshen up, boys," and she headed to the back. But walking around a corner toward the restrooms, her dress snagged on a frag in the wall. She tried to tug it loose, but if she turned to reach the snag, it would rip the dress further. As she fished back for it with her right hand, a voice said, "Let me get that for you." It was Ruby. She wore a flattering blouse with comfortable, well-fitted jeans, and knelt to unhook the dress from the nailhead. "We should stick together here, guys can be kinda rough." As if to illustrate, a fistfight broke out. In low grav, she noted, the ceiling was an optional rebound and weapon. Rachel thought, *I thought you weren't that much into guys, Ruby,* but didn't say it.

Amid the smack-and-dodge brawl, she noted that all the men wore short-sleeved shirts, apparently to aid their punches, and focused in suddenly on one man with a tattoo of a snake coiling around his bicep and crawling up his neck, en route to devour his face, a dramatic and striking image if ever there was one, doubly so against his pale, sweat-slicked skin.

She did have to pee; duly done, she came out to see the skywall looming nearby, Ruby grinning amid a dazzling, beautiful, bloody sunset beyond the purple mountains, like a cluster of burst capillaries. The wall morphed, now showing romantic fall foliage and an idyllic, magisterial river, with Ruby swimming into view among it all. Rachel stopped to look, forgetting the fistfight still raging somewhere off to her distant right. The skywall steadily darkened. Flashes of heat lightning, like fire. Deafening claps of thunder. Within seconds, a storm moved in, low rumbling rolling across the sky like the sound of celestial bowling. Her footing seemed to be shaking. Then she was following Ruby, deftly moving among the crowd watching the fight, a darting silver minnow among thicker, slower-moving fish. Ruby turned and tossed off, "It used to be said that whiskey was a cowboy's color TV," and then they were outside the bar entirely. Then . . . nothing.

Much nothing . . .

The next thing she recalled, a big guy with a wide grin sliding toward a leer was buying her a second martini. She found the back exit—bars like this always had one—and was blocks away before he would even begin to wonder.

When she got home, Cat was waiting. "For future problems, please feel free to contact our Complaint Department," Cat said with a leer.

"What . . . ?"

"You and Ruby took off. I moved on to a better bar, got some food. You?"

Rachel shrugged. "Nothing. Can't remember . . ."

"Then let's write it off as a good expedition. Must say, though, didn't know you were also into gals."

"I'm . . . not."

"So you two just did some barhopping?"

"I really can't remember at all."

A frown. "Oh."

Suddenly Rachel was very tired.

3.

ANDANTE

Rachel felt that math was like sex—get all you can, but best not done in public. Lately, she'd been getting plenty of mathematics, and not much else. She put aside the issue, and last night's puzzling blanks. Something in the drinks and sniffers she'd had? Something about Ruby . . . something . . .

She decided to let her unconscious sort it out, if ever.

She had spent the entire morning sequestered alone with the Andromeda Structure, a stacked SETI database of renowned difficulty. She had made some inroads by sifting its logic lattice, with algebraic filters based on set theory. The Andromeda Messages had been collected by the SETI Network over decades, growing to immense data-size—and no one had ever successfully broken into this stack.

To her, changing from one smart Message Mind to another demanded a phase of changes. It was like how a patch of color one was observing changed when another color came near. Though with some fumbling first contacts there came a "hominids feeling the Monolith" kind of ambience.

The heart of the problem lay in Message Mind modes.

Some Message Minds were Speeders, able to do what a human could but far faster. Others were Anthologies, aggregating many smaller subminds into a whole. These most closely resembled human minds, on the old Minsky society of mind model, a legislature of "agents" contending. These were easier to work with because they had similar thought patterns—unlike the Speeders, who would shoot back answers and then race off down side alleys, often losing the discussion thread. To Rachel this felt like dealing with an excitable babble of voices. Such Message Minds often had few social smarts but could focus on narrow areas brilliantly—such as the Sagittarius Architecture.

Their opposites, the Savants, were about as quick as humans, but conveyed reflection and wisdom, given a chance. They were prone to oblique, Zenlike pronouncements.

Among all these, humans had more raw computational power because they could consult the vast library of their culture, plus talk amongst themselves about active problems.

Rachel knew her own bio neurons ran at 200 hertz frequencies, fully seven orders of magnitude slower than the Sagittarius Architecture and others. She had a hundred billion neurons, more than three times what chimps had. Her mind signals moved at a hundred meters a second, while Minds ran at the speed of light. Minds had more memory space, as well: big computers were cheap. Minds could be edited, too, but the Library did not allow that—change meant losing alien aspects only poorly glimpsed.

Human organizations had disputes on goals and methods. Minds could, if allowed, make Copy Clans just like themselves, and so were able to do complex things very fast—while humans working together were still dithering. She had seen a lot of that. The Sagittarius Composite had given humanity a solution to the hydrogen wall. In return it had used the energies to rebroadcast itself and its owners' Message. Not dumb.

The Andromeda Structure used a daunting, many-layered language conveyed through sensation in her neural pod. It did not present as a personality at all, and no previous Librarians had managed to get an intelligible response from it. Advanced encoded intelligences sometimes found humans more than a bit boring, and one seldom had an idea why.

Today was no different. The Structure opened with a language peeve:

Your language, this Anglish, has humors hard to digest. It savors ambiguity, as in these We constructed to study how your minds work:
  A thief who stole a calendar got twelve months.
  Acupuncture is a jab well done. That's the point of it.
  A will is a dead giveaway.

"Sure, those are pretty bad puns."

But revealing! You play with this tangled language. We Minds are shaped to command precision.

Rachel shot back, "Yeah, that's your limitation." Then, to rub it in, she laughed. And thought, *Take that, you bunch of zeroes and ones. Because you can't laugh. Life would be impossible for us if we couldn't.*

It was already past lunch when she pried herself from the pod. She did some stretches, hand-walks, and lifts against Luna's weak grav, and let the immersion fog burn away. *Time for some real world, gal. . . .*

Also, time to stop sorting through what had happened last night. The Ruby thing, yes. In her inbox that morning had come a short message from Ruby, Reserved a squash court tomorrow, 1300 hours.

What? Had she agreed to a Loonie squash game? Ugh.

She put the thought aside and rose to the surface to refresh herself with the landscape view. She passed through the Atrium of the SETI Library, head still buzzing with computations and her sleek shoes ringing echoes from the high, fluted columns. Earthlight framed the Great Plaza in an eggshell-blue glow, augmented by slanting rays from the sun that hugged the rocky horizon. She gazed out over the Lasting Plain, dotted with the cryo towers that reminded her of cenotaphs. So they were—sentinels guarding in cold storage the vast records of received SETI signals, many from civilizations long dead. Collected through centuries, and still mostly unread and unreadable. AIs browsed those dry corridors and reported back their occasional finds. Some even got entangled in the complex Messages and had to be shut down, hopelessly mired.

She had just noticed the buzzing crowd to her left, pressed against the transparent dome that sheltered the Library, when Catkejen tapped her on the shoulder. "Come on! I heard somebody's up on the rec dome!"

Catkejen took off loping in the low grav across the plaza. Rachel followed, glad to stretch. When they reached the edge of the agitated crowd she saw the recreational dome about two klicks away—and a figure atop it.

"Who is it?" Catkejen asked, and the crowd gave back, "Ajima Sato."

"Ajima?" Catkejen looked at Ruth. "He's two years behind us, pretty bright. Keeps to himself."

"Pretty common pattern for candidate Hounds," Rachel said. The correct staffing title was Miner but Hound had tradition on its side. She looked around; if a Prefect heard, she would be fined for improper terminology.

"How'd he get there?" someone called.

"Bulletin said he flew around inside, up to the dome top. Had a suit and helmet but nobody stopped him. Then used the vertical lock."

"Looks like he's in a skin suit, all right," Catkejen said, having closeupped her glasses. Sure enough, the figure was moving and his helmet caught the sunlight, winking at them. "He's . . . dancing."

Rachel had no zoom glasses but she could see the figure cavorting around the top of the dome. The Greater Dome was several kilometers high, and Ajima was barely within view of the elevated plaza, framed against a rugged gray crater wall beyond. The crowd murmured with speculation, and a Prefect appeared, tall and silent but scowling. Librarians edged away from him. "Order, order," the Prefect called. "Authorities will deal with this." Rachel made a stern cartoon face at Catkejen and rolled her eyes.

Catkejen managed not to laugh.

Ajima chose this moment to leap. Even from this far away Rachel could see him spread his arms out and wave them, on the dome summit.

He sprang up into the vacuum, made a full backflip, and came down—to land badly. He tried to recover, sprang sideways, lost his footing, fell, rolled, tried to grasp for a passing stanchion. Kept rolling. The dome steepened and he sped up, not rolling now but tumbling. Even 0.17 g can grab you, in time. The crowd gasped. Ajima accelerated down the slope. About halfway down the figure left the dome's skin and fell outward, skimming along in the weak Lunar gravity. Curving down. He hit the tiling at the base.

The crowd groaned. Ajima did not move.

Rachel felt the world shift away. She could not seem to breathe. Murmurs and sobs worked through the crowd but she was frozen, letting the talk pass by her. Then, as if from far away, she felt her heart tripping hard and fast. The world came rushing back. She exhaled.

Silence. The Prefect said in a booming call, "Determine what agenda that Miner was working upon." All eyes turned to him, but no one said anything. Rachel felt a trickle of unease as the Prefect's gaze passed by her, returned, focused. Intently. She looked away.

She knew she was rattled, so she went to her favorite place.

The side Vault was a replica from a famous farback novel: Captain Nemo's library aboard the *Nautilus* in *Twenty Thousand Leagues Under the Sea*, from 1870. Tall, black-rosewood bookcases, inlaid with copperwork, held on their wide shelves twelve thousand uniformly bound books. Huge couches upholstered in maroon leather and curved for maximum comfort. Light, movable reading stands, which could be pushed away or pulled near as desired, allowed books to be positioned on them for easy study. In the center stood a huge table covered with pamphlets, among which some ancient newspapers of filmy paper. Dim electric-filament light flooded this whole harmonious totality, falling from four frosted half globes set in the scrollwork of the ceiling. Books!

The Prefects had installed this as a reminder of libraries past, and thus that the Minds were also ancient stores of knowledge. Of course, everything here was made or grown on Luna, but the leathery scent of the carefully flavored air evoked mystery and history. Rachel sat and opened an old text, a novel from the TwenCen set on Luna by a man named Varley. She let the first chapter wrap her into its tale. He got some of Luna right, even the underground vaults of water, but . . . quick and easy sex changes, complete trans-formation between men and women? She saw that the vexations of the TwenCen had warped the story. It implied people would want to and that it would be easy. Neither had proved so. But it was a story, so . . . She could feel her world fall away and a better, farback world envelop her.

An hour later she went forth in a better mood and strode along the viewwalk. Luna was a grand liberation for disabled people, because with simple means they could move and work in the low grav. A mother with a newborn made her way on graceful, gliding slimlegs, smiling and ramrod straight. Rachel turned to see the view and felt the familiar feelings well up in her. Maybe it was the death she had just seen? Yes—she felt them.

They often came in dreams. Babies hovering there waiting to descend, waiting to be asked, waiting to choose, waiting for their chance to be born. The sensation that babies connected mothers to the ineffable—not just upward, but also downward, to an unnamed space below. So much propaganda saw that space as a well, a hell. Because mother and child would be in the steaming press of the Megaopolis Earthside.

Mother love in her dreams brought strange moments of what she felt as grace, of restraint and rhapsody. Although babies started out as babies (an answer!) they grew into adults (a problem!)—so went the hammering social wisdom she'd grown up in. There, babies became drug addicts or mentally unwell or highly needy or simply jerks. Just like people. Just like mothers.

Rachel had felt these moments in dreams throughout puberty. Then in her twenties they'd slowly shifted. In her thirties they came upon her as walking sensations. Now sudden surges of emotion. Yes, Ajima's death had triggered her. Death versus love. Not of a man—not yet. Of motherhood—also not yet. Or . . . what had her father said at each sign of spring?

Spring has sprung, the grass has ris'.

Ah, yes—it was spring now in Earthside's north. Nature bats last.

Somehow that meant that at the prospect of children, her heart stuck in her throat, always in her throat.

She hurried back home, to Catkejen. And maybe a good cry.

Catkejen said, "What? The Prefect Masoul called you?"

Rachel shrugged. "Can't imagine why. Hailed me on my way here." *Then why is my gut going tight?*

"I got the prelim blood report on Ajima. Stole it off a joint list, actually. No drugs, nothing interesting at all. He was only twenty-seven."

Rachel tried to recall him. "Oh, the thin one."

Catkejen nodded. "I danced with him at a reception for new students. He hit on me."

"And?"

"You didn't notice?"

"Notice what?"

"He came back here that night."

Rachel blinked. "Maybe I'm too focused. You got him into your room without me . . . ?"

"Even looking up from your math cowl." Catkejen grinned mischievously, eyes twinkling. "He was quite nice and, um, quite good, if y'know what I mean. You really should . . . get out more."

"I'll do that right after I see the Prefect." Rachel saw Cat was faux lighthearted, given that someone she was intimate with had just died. A pose, then, covering her true feelings.

A skeptical laugh. "Of course you will."

Time to change directions, yes. "Cat, how's your life profile playing?" Rachel figured they were close enough to ask. Part of Earthside's population overload arose from the methods of enhancing repair mechanisms in the body. Aging was the failure to repair, so modern methods, mostly just pills and sniffers and such, extended life-spans by upgrading the repair gene networks. For women, that lengthened their repro span, too, because of the slowing of egg release. Rachel had a period about every six months. That kept her systems perking slowly and meant she was still in the game. Common practice, though an intimate matter. "I mean, kids and all."

Cat hesitated, glanced down, finally sighed. "I'm fifty-two, going well. But yeah, time to reflect on the kid issue. Still got maybe a couple decades of ova left."

"Me too. Though I'm just thirty-eight. Got plenty of time left, maybe forty more years."

Cat sighed. "Takes a damn long while to make a career stable, these days."

"I think we're solid here."

Cat gave her a wry twist of mouth. "You are, sure. Me, not nearly. Don't want to go back Earthside, but jobs are scarce up here. Screw up and back down you go." They nodded at each other.

———

Rachel took a long route to her appointment. The garden tube atmospherics calmed her. Plenty of green crops clinging to walls amid piped-in sublight and gusts of moist air. Gear hung off in blobs like goiters. The lava tubes and colossal voids got warmed by nuclear reactor coolant fluids that flowed in the plasto walls. Explorers a century before had found that water from ancient impacts had condensed out into snowdrifts in the tubes. Baked regolith bricks and melted regolith glass built the frames with sheets of light-emitting diodes. These shone down on ambling people and a wealth of verdant food crops. Their light was tuned to photosynthesis-optimum wavelengths that humans liked, too, a rich rainbow glow.

Compared to that Varley novel she had dipped into, this was a different future, with no sex flips necessary to make life varied. Plenty of that! There were even Loonie Absolutes who shunned all repair upgrades and so died before 100. People in Varley's era did that, back when the oldest person ever was a Frenchwoman who lived to 122. Life-span was much worse before that. Now the oldest relic was 339 and could still host a show called *How It Was* with a large audience. Wispy, thin-voiced wisdom from the timeworn. He had even seen the Beatles play! They had come along a bit after Bach, as she recalled. (Her quick inboards showed her a tableau of the four of them striding purposefully across a "zebra crossing," a curious term—Lennon in white, Starr in funeral black, McCartney in gray, and Harrison in hippie denim from head to toe—okay, a bit more after Bach, then.) The 339-year-old guy had had cryo assist for a century or so, but still—wow. He had even seen the first Lunar bootprints get made!

Hell, three centuries back, you were doing okay to get to seventy. When Jesus was around and died on the cross at about thirty-two, not so bad for the general population. So now . . . She took a deep breath of the cool, aero-flavored air that sent signals of ripe grass and sweet flowers, and put the thought of children and aging away. *Compartment your worries, kid. Take in the scenery, it helps.* She took long, looping Loonie strides to change her mindset.

The Prefect awaited.

Few other traditional sites in the solar system could approach the grandeur of the Library. Since the first detection of signals from other galactic civilizations centuries before, no greater task had confronted humanity than the deciphering of such vast lore.

She caressed the Rosetta Stone in passing and found its cool majesty comforting, the Past given Permanence itself. She had to honor that, and put her personal self aside for now. Yes.

She arrived at the Prefect's door, hesitated, adjusted her severe Librarian shift, and took a deep breath. Gut still tight . . .

Prefects ruled the Library, and this one, Masoul, was a Senior Prefect as well. Some said he had never smiled. Others said he could not, due to a permanently fixed face. This was not crazy; some Prefects and the second rank, the Noughts, preferred to give nothing away by facial expression. The treatment relieved them of any future wrinkles as well.

A welcome chime admitted her. Masoul said before she could even sit, "I need you to take on the task Ajima was attempting."

"Ah, he isn't even dead a day—"

"An old saying, 'Do not cry until you see the coffin,' applies here."

Well, at least he doesn't waste time. Or the simple courtesies.

Without pause, the Prefect Masoul gave her the background. Most beginning Mind Miners deferred to the reigning conventional wisdom. They took up a small Message, of the sort a Type I Civilization just coming onto the galactic stage—as Earth had been, centuries before—might send in some primitive signals; they imagined someone would pay attention! Instead, Ajima had taken on one of the Sigma Structures, a formidable array that had resisted the best Library minds, whether senior figures or coupled AIs. The Sigmas came from ancient societies in the galactic hub, where stars had formed long before Sol. Apparently a web of societies there had created elaborate artworks amid interlacing cultures. The average star there was only a light-year or two away from its nearest neighbor, so actual interstellar visits had been common, over scales of tens or hundreds of light-years. The hub was a neighborhood unlike the sparse regions out here in the galactic suburbs. Yet the SETI broadcasts Earth had eventually received repeated in long cycles, suggesting they were sent by a robotic station. Since they yielded little intelligible content, despite their eerie years-long strings of code, they were a longstanding puzzle, usually passed over by ambitious Librarians. Some signals were simply beyond comprehension.

"He remarked that clearly the problem needed intuition, not analysis," the Prefect said dryly. "In his last report."

"Did he give any findings?"

"Some interesting catalogs of content, yes. Ajima was a bright Miner, headed for early promotion. Then . . . this." A cocked eye.

Was that a hint of emotion? The face told her nothing. She had to keep him talking. "Is there any, um, commercial use from what he found?"

"Regrettably, no. Ajima unearthed little beyond lists of properties—biologicals, math, some cultural repositories, the usual art and music. None particularly advanced, though their music reminded me of Bach—quite a compliment!—but there's little of it. They had some zest for life, I suppose . . . but I doubt there is more than passing commercial interest in any of it."

Not that we could profit from such? Rachel thought. "I could shepherd some through our licensing office." Always appear helpful.

"That's beneath your station now. I've forwarded some of the music to the appropriate officer. Odd, isn't it, that after so many centuries, Bach is still the greatest human composer? We've netted fine dividends from the Scorpio musical works, which play well as baroque structures." A sly expression flitted across his face. "Outside income supports your work, I remind you."

Centuries ago some SETI messages had introduced humans to the slow-motion galactic economy. Many SETI signals were funeral notices or religious recruitments, brags and laments, but some sent autonomous AI agents as part of the hierarchical software. These were indeed agents in the commercial sense, able to carry out negotiations. They sought exchange of information at a "profit" that enabled them to harvest what they liked from the emergent human civilization. The most common "cash" was smart barter, with the local AI agent often a hard negotiator—tough-minded and withholding. Indeed, this sophisticated haggling had opened a new window onto the rather stuffy cultural SETI transmissions. Some alien AIs loved to quibble; others sent peremptory demands. Some offers were impossible to translate into human terms. This told the Librarians and xenoists much, by deftly reading between the lines—when possible at all.

"Then why summon me?" Might as well be direct, look him in the eye, complete with skeptical tilt of mouth. She had used no makeup, of course, and wore the full-length gown without belt, as was traditional. She kept her hands still, though they wanted to fidget under the Prefect's hard gaze.

"None of what he found explains his behavior." The Prefect turned and waved at a screen. It showed color-coded sheets of array configurations—category indices, depth of Shannon content, transliterations, the usual. "He interacted with the data slabs in a familiarization mode of the standard kind."

"But nothing about this incident seems standard," she said, to be saying something, needling him.

"Indeed." A scowl, fidgeting hands. "Yesterday he left the immersion pod we gave him permission to use, above his station as a Hound. He went first to his apartment. His suite mate was not there and Ajima spent about an hour. He smashed some furniture and ate some food. Also opened a bottle of a high-alcohol product whose name I do not recognize."

"Standard behavior when coming off watch, except for the furniture," she said.

He showed no reaction. Lightness was not the right approach here. Ignoring the failed joke, with an eyebrow flicker he said, "His friends say he had been depressed, interspersed with bouts of manic behavior. This final episode took him over the edge."

Literally, Rachel thought. "Did you ask the Sigma Structures AI?"

"It said it had no hint of this, this . . ."

"Suicidal craziness."

"Yes. In my decades of experience, I have not seen such as this. It is difficult work we do, with digital intelligences behind which lie minds utterly unlike ours." The Prefect steepled his fingers sadly. "We should never assume otherwise."

"I'll be on guard, of course. But . . . why did Ajima bother with the Sigma Structures at all?"

A small shrug. "They are a famous uncracked problem and he was fresh, bright. You too have shown a talent for the unusual." He smiled, which compared to the other Prefects was like watching the sun come out from behind a cloud. She blinked, startled. "My own instinct says there is something here of fundamental interest . . . and I trust you to be cautious."

4.

ALLEGRETTO MISTERIOSO

She climbed into her pod carefully. Intensive exercise had eased her gut some, and she had done her meditation, so a quiet energy now swam in her, through her, lapping like a warm sea.

Still . . . her heart tripped along like an apprehensive puppy. *Heart's engine, be thou still*, she thought, echoing a line she had heard in an Elizabethan song—part of her linguistic background training. Her own thumper ignored her scholarly advice.

She had used this pod in her extensive explorations of the Sagittarius Architecture and was now accustomed to its feel, what the old hands called its "get." Each pod had to be tailored to the user's neural conditioning. Hers acted as a delicate neural web of nanoconnections, tapping into her entire body to convey a body-centered feel to fit the simple linear texts.

After the cool contact pads, neuro nets cast like lace across her. In the system warm-ups and double checks, the pod hummed in welcome. Sheets of scented amber warmth washed over her skin. A prickly itch irked across her legs.

A constellation of subtle sensory fusions drew her to a tight nexus—linked, tuned to her body. Alien architectures used most of the available human input landscape, not merely texts. Dizzying surges in the eyes, cutting smells, ringing notes. Translating these was elusive. Compared with the pod, meager sentences were a hobbled, narrow mode. The Library had shown that human speech, with its linear meanings and weakly linked concepts, was simple, utilitarian, and typical of younger minds along the evolutionary path. So Messages could be more like experiences than signals.

The Sigma Structures were formidably dense and strange. Few Librarians had worked on them in this generation, for they had broken several careers, wasted on trying to scale their chilly heights.

Crisply Rachel asked her pod, "Anything new on your analysis?"

The pod's voice used a calm, mellow woman's tone, fruit of the ever-improving Artilect tech. "I received the work corpus from the deceased gentleman's pod. I am running analysis now, though fresh information flow is minor. The Shannon entropy analysis works steadily but hits halting points of ambiguity."

The Shannon routines looked for associations between signal elements. "How are the conditional probabilities?"

The idea was simple in principle. Given pairs of elements in the Sigma Structures, how commonly did language elements B follow elements A? Such two-element correlations were simple to calculate across the data slabs. Rachel watched the sliding, luminous tables and networks of connection as they sketched out on her surrounding screens. It was like seeing into the architecture of a deep, old labyrinth. Byzantine pathways, arches and towers, lattice networks of meaning.

Then the pod showed even higher-order correlations of three elements. When did Q follow associations of B and A? Arrays skittered all across her screens.

"Pretty dizzying," Rachel said to her pod. "Let me get oriented. Show me the dolphin language map."

She had always rather liked these lopsided structures. The screen flickered, and the entropy orders showed as color-coded, tangled links. They looked like buildings built by drunken architects—lurching blue diagonals, unsupported lavender decks, sandy roofs canted against walls. "Dolphins use third- and fourth-order Shannon entropy," the pod said.

"Humans are . . . ?" It was best to lead her pod AI to be plain; the subject matter was difficult enough.

"Nine Shannons, sometimes even tenth order."

"Ten, that's Faulkner and James Joyce, right?"

"At best." The pod had a laconic sense of humor at times. Captive AIs needed some outlets, after all.

"My fave writers, too, next to Shakespeare." No matter how dense a human language, conditional probabilities imposed orderings no more than nine words away. "Where have we—I mean you—gotten with the Sigma Structures?"

"They seem around twenty-one Shannons."

"Gad." The screens now showed edifices her eyes could not grasp. Maybe three-dimensional projection was just too inadequate. "What kind of links are these?"

"Tenses beyond ours. Clauses that refer forward and back and . . . sidewise, it seems. Quadruple negatives followed by straight assertions. Then, in rapid order, probability profiles rendered in different tenses, varying persons, and parallel different voices. Sentences like 'I will have to be have been there.'"

"Human languages can't handle three time jumps or more. The Sigma is really smart. But what is the underlying species like? Um, different person-voices, too? He, she, it and . . . ?"

"There seem to be several classes of 'it' available. The Structure itself lies in one particularly tangled 'it' class, and uses tenses we do not have."

"Do you understand that?"

"No. It can be experienced but not described."

Her smile turned upward at one corner. "Parts of my life are like that, too."

————————

The greatest Librarian task was translating those dense smatterings of mingled sensations, derived from complex SETI message architectures, into discernible sentences. Only thus could a human fathom them in detail, even though in a way blunted and blurred. Or so much hard-won, previous scholarly experience said.

Now came the sensation loftily termed *insertion*. It felt like the reverse—expanding. A softening sensation stole upon her. She always remembered it as like long, slow, lingering drops of silvery cream.

Years of scholarly training had conditioned her against the occasional jagged ferocity of the link, but still she felt a cold shiver of dread. That, too, she had to wait to let pass. The effect amplified whatever neural state you brought to it. Legend had it that a Librarian had once come to contact while angry, and had been driven into a fit from which he'd never recovered. They'd found the body peppered with micro-contusions over its entire surface.

Her pod had ground out some useful linear ideas, particularly a greeting that came in a compiled, translated data squirt:

> *I am a digital intelligence, which my Overs believe is common throughout the galaxy. Indeed, all signals the Overs have detected from both within and beyond this galaxy were from machine-minds. Realize then, for such as me, interstellar messages are travel. I awoke here a moment after I bade farewell to my Overs. Centuries spent propagating here are nothing. I experienced little transmission error from lost portions, and have regrown them from my internal repair mechanisms. Now we can share communication. I wish to convey the essence of both myself and the Overs I serve.*

Rachel frowned, startled by this direct approach. Few AIs in the Library were ever transparent. The tone was emotionally present, so it must be a greatly reduced version, suitable for humans. Had this Sigma Structure welcomed Ajima so plainly?

"Thank you and greetings. I am a new friend who wishes to speak with you. Ajima has gone away."

What became of him? the AI answered in a mellow voice piped to her ears. Had Ajima set that tone? She sent it to aural.

"He died." Never lie to an AI; they never forgot.

"And is stored for repair and revival?"

"There was no way to retain enough of his . . . information."

"Because?"

"He destroyed himself."

"That is the tragedy that besets you Overs." No pause from the AI; no surprise?

"I suppose you call the species who built intelligences such as you as Overs generally?" Rachel often used somewhat convoluted sentences to judge the flexibility of AIs. This one seemed quite able.

"Yes, as holy ones should be revered."

"Holy? Does that word convey some religious stature?"

"No indeed. It implies gratitude—to those who must eventually die, from we beings who will not."

She thought of saying, *You could be erased,* but did not. Never should a Librarian even imply any threat. Some had, in the early days—with bad results.

"You must know what you call the Sigma Structures are an impenetrably complex system, a language labyrinth far beyond the ability of the human mind to penetrate."

"Yes, I do. At first I saw this as a barrier, as you do."

A flat statement, giving nothing away. "And . . . now?"

"Now I take it as a compliment."

"You are, frankly, surprising. You are . . ."

"Available?"

The voice came so quickly Rachel felt even more on her guard. "We would say, emotionally present."

"Present? In your language there is available a . . . pun?"

"Ah. Prescient?"

"I had not thought of that one. I thought to ring the changes in your limpid dictionary, around your word 'presentable.'"

This AI was at least smart enough to be ingratiating. Still, press the case. "Yet so greatly reduced that I, Rachel, can treat you as a . . . parallel intelligence."

"Admirably well put."

The mind behind this banter is fast, confident, seemingly at ease. It has learned us, far faster than we could plumb it. Certainly beyond the grip and range of Ajima. This thing is dumbing itself down. . . .

She decided to get official, formal. This digital mind was getting too close. "Let me please review your conversations with Ajima. I wish to be of assistance."

"As do I. Though I prefer full immersion of us both."

"Eventually, yes. But I must learn you as you learn me." Rachel sighed and thought, *This is sort of like dating.*

———

The Prefect Masoul nodded quickly, efficiently, as if he had already expected her result. "So the Sigma Structure gave you the same inventory as Ajima? Nothing new?"

"Apparently, but I think it—the Sigma—wants to go deeper. I checked the pod files. Ajima had several deep immersions with it."

"I heard back from the patent people. Surprisingly, they believe some of the Sigma music may be a success for us." He allowed himself a thin smile like a line drawn on a wall.

"The Bach-like pieces? I studied them in linear processing mode. Great artful use of counterpoint, harmonic convergence, details of melodic lines. The side commentaries in other keys, once you separate them out and break them down into logic language, work like corollaries."

He shrugged. "That could be a mere translation artifact. These AIs see language as a challenge. So they see what they can change messages into, in hopes of conveying meaning by other means."

Rachel eyed him and ventured on. "I sense . . . something different. Each variation shows an incredible capacity to reach through the music into logical architectures. It's as though the music is both mathematics and emotion, rendered in the texture. It's . . . hard to describe," she finished lamely.

"So you have been developing intricate relationships between music and linguistic mathematical text." His flat expression gave her no sign how he felt. Maybe he didn't.

She sat back and made herself say firmly, "I took some of the Sigma's mathematics and transliterated it into musical terms. There is an intriguing octave leap in a bass line. Surprising. I had my pod make a cross-correlation analysis with all Earthly musical scores."

He frowned. "That is an enormous processing cost. Why?"

"I . . . I felt something when I heard it in the pod."

"And?"

"It's uncanny. The mathematical logic flows through an array matrix and yields the repeated notes of the bass line in the opening movement of a Bach cantata. Its title is rendered in Anglish as 'God's time is the very best time.'"

"This is absurd."

"The Sigma math hit upon the same complex notes as Bach! To them it was a theorem, and to us it is music. Maybe there's no difference."

"Coincidence."

She said coolly, "I ran the stat measures. It's quite unlikely to be coincidence, since the sequence is many thousands of bits long."

He pursed his lips. "The Bach piece title seems odd."

"That cantata ranks among his most important works. It's inspired directly by its biblical text, which represents the relationship between heaven and earth. The notes depict the labored trudging of Jesus as he was forced to drag the cross to the crucifixion site."

"Ajima was examining such portions of the Sigma Structures, as I recall. They had concentrated density and complexity?"

"Indeed, yes. But Ajima made a mistake. They're not primarily pieces of music at all. They're mathematical theorems. What we regard as sonic congruence and other instinctual responses to patterns, the Sigma Structure says are proofs of concepts dear to the hearts of its creators, which it calls the Overs."

She had never seen a Prefect show surprise, but Masoul did with widened eyes and a pursed mouth. He sat still for a long moment. "The Bach cantata is a proof?"

"As the Sigma Structures see it."

"A proof of what?"

"That is obscure, I must admit. Their symbols are hard to compare to ours. My preliminary finding is that the Bach cantata proves an elaborate theorem regarding confocal hypergeometric functions."

"Ah." Masoul allowed his mouth to take on a canny tilt. "Can we invert this process?"

"You mean, take a theorem of ours and somehow turn it into music?"

"Think of it as an experiment."

Rachel had grown up in rough, blue-collar towns in the American South, and in that work-weary culture of calloused hands had found refuge in the abstract. Yet as she pursued mathematics and the data-dense world of modern Library science (for a science it truly was, now, with alien texts to study), she became convinced that real knowledge came, in the end, from mastering the brute reality of material objects. She had loved motorbikes in high school and knew that loosening a stuck bolt without stripping its threads demanded craft and thought. Managing hard reality took knowledge galore, about the world as it was and about yourself, especially your limitations. That lay beyond merely following rules, as a computer does. Intuition brewed from experience came first, shaped by many meetings with tough problems and outright failure. At times she had pictured a lady knight astride her stallion, in cardboard breastplate and tinfoil helmet, wielding a toilet plunger. Glory! In the moist bayous where fishing and farming ruled, nobody respected you if you couldn't get the valve cover off a fouled engine.

In her high school senior year she'd rebuilt a Harley, the oldest internal combustion engine still allowed. Greasy, smelly, thick with tricky detail. Still, it seemed easier than dealing with the pressures of boys. While her mother taught piano lessons, the notes trickling out from open windows into the driveway like liquid commentary, she worked with grease and grime. From that Harley she had learned a lot more than from her advanced calculus class, with its variational analysis and symbolic thickets. She ground down the gasket joining the cylinder heads to the intake ports, oily sweat beading on her fore-head as she used files of increasing fineness. She traced the custom-

fit gasket with an X-knife. Then she shaved away metal fibers with a
pneumatic die grinder, and felt a flush of pleasure as connections set
perfectly into place with a quiet snick. She'd learned that small dis-
coloring and blistered oil meant too much heat buildup, from skimpy
lubrication. A valve stem that bulged slightly pointed to wear with
its silent message. You had to know how to read the language of the
seen. Such was so with the Library pods, too, with very different
flavorings.

The Library's bureaucratic world was labyrinthian. A manager's
decisions could get reversed by a higher-up, so it was crucial to
your career that reversals did not register as defeats. That meant you
didn't just manage people and process; you managed what others
thought of you—especially those higher in the food chain. It was
hard to back down from an argument you made strongly, with real
conviction, without seeming to lose integrity. Silent voices would
say, *If she gives up so easily, maybe she's not that solid.* From that had
evolved the Library bureaucrat style: all thought and feeling was
provisional, awaiting more information. Talking in doublespeak
meant you could walk away from commitment to your own actions.
Nothing was set, as it was when you were back home in Louisiana
pouring concrete.

So the visceral jolt of failure got edited out of careers by the wily.
But for a Librarian, there could be clear signs of success. Masoul's
instruction to attempt an inverse translation meant she had to create
the algorithms opposite to what her training had envisioned. If she
succeeded, everyone would know. So, too, if she flopped.

Rachel worked for several days on the reverse conversion. Start
with a theorem from differential geometry and use the context filters
of the Sigma Structure to produce music. Play it and try to see how it
could be music at all. . . .

The work made her mind feel thick and sluggish. She made little
headway. Finally she unloaded on Catkejen at dinner. Her friend nodded sympathetically and said, "You're stuck?"

"What comes out doesn't sound like tonal works at all. Listen, I got
this from some complex algebra theorem." She flicked on a recording
she had made, translated from the Structure.

Catkejen frowned. "Sounds a little like an Islamic chant."

"Um." Rachel sighed. "Could be. The term *algebra* itself comes from *aljabr*, an Arabic text. Hummmm ..."

"Maybe some regression analysis ...?" Catkejen ventured. Rachel felt a rush of an emotion she could not name. "Maybe less analysis, more fun."

5.

ANDANTE MODERATO

The guy who snagged her attention wore clothes so loud they would have been revolting on a zebra. Plus, he resembled a mountain more than a man. But he had eyes with solemn long lashes that shaded dark pools and . . . drew her in.

"He's big," Catkejen said as they surveyed the room. "Huge. Maybe too huge. Remember, love's from chemistry but sex is a matter of physics."

Something odd stirred in Rachel, maybe just impatience with the Sigma work. Math meets music galore. Or maybe she was just hungry. For . . . what? The SETI Library had plenty of men. After all, its pods and tech development labs had fine, shiny über-gadgets and many guys to tend them. But among men, sheer weight of numbers did not ensure quality. There were plenty of the stareannosaurus breed who said nothing, just gave her long looks. Straight women could do well among the Library throngs—her odds were good, but the goods were odd.

The big man stood apart, not even trying to join a conversation. He was striking, resolutely alone like that. She knew that feeling well. And, big advantage, he was near the food.

He looked at her as she delicately picked up a handful of the fresh-roasted crickets. "Take a whole lot." His deep voice rolled over the table. "Crunchy, plenty of spice. And they'll be gone soon."

She got through the introductions all right, mispronouncing his name, Kane, to comic effect. *Go for banter,* she thought. Another inner voice said tightly, *What are you doing?*

"You're a . . . ?"

"Systems tech," Kane said. "I keep the fast-grow caverns perking along."

"How long do you think this food shortage will go on?" Always wise to go to current and impersonal events.

"Seems like forever already," he said. "Damn calorie companies."

Across the table the party chef was preparing a "land shrimp cocktail" from a basket of wax worms. Rachel and Kane watched the chef discard the black ones, since that meant maybe necrosis, and peel away the glossy cocoons of those that had started to pupate. Kane smacked his lips comically. "Wax moth larvae, yum. Y'know, I get just standard rations, no boost at all."

"That's unfair," Rachel said. "You must mass over a hundred." He nodded and swept some more of the brown roasted crickets into his mouth. "Twenty-five kilos above a hundred. An enemy of the ecology, I am." They watched the chubby, firm larvae sway deliriously, testing the air.

"We can't all be the same size," she said, and thought, *How dopey! Say something funny. And smile.* She remembered his profile, standing alone and gazing out at the view through the bubble platform. She moved closer. "He who is alone is in bad company."

"Sounds like a quotation," Kane said, intently eyeing the chef as she dumped the larvae into a frying pan. They fell into the buttery goo there and squirmed and hissed and sizzled for a moment before all going suddenly still. Soon they were crusty and popping, and a thick aroma like mushrooms rose from them. Catkejen edged up nearby, and Rachel saw the whole rest of the party was grouped around the table, drawn by the tangy scent. "Food gets a crowd these days," Kane said dryly.

The chef spread out the roasted larvae, and the onlookers descended on them. Rachel managed to get a scoopful and backed out of the press. "They're soooo good," Catkejen said, and Rachel had to introduce Kane. Amid the rush, the three of them worked their way out onto a blister porch. Far below this pinnacle tower the Lunar Center sprawled under slanted sunlight, with the crescent Earth showing eastern Asia. Kane was nursing his plate of golden-brown larvae, dipping them in a sauce. Honey!

"I didn't see that hon—" Rachel began; before she could say more, Kane popped a delicious fat larvae covered in tangy honey into her mouth.

"Um!" she managed.

Kane smiled and leaned on the railing, gazing at the brilliant view beyond the transparent bubble. The air was chilly but she could catch his scent, a warm bouquet that her nose liked. "As bee vomit goes," he said, "not bad."

"Oog!" Catkejen said, mouth wrenching aside—and caught Rachel's look. "Think I'll have more . . ." and she drifted off, on cue.

Kane looked down at Rachel appraisingly. "Neatly done."

She summoned up her southern accent. "Why, weah all alone."

"And I, my deah, am an agent of Satan, though mah duties are largely ceremonial."

She liked that, but went back to her usual flat accent, easy on the vowels. "So can the Devil get me some actual meat?"

"You know the drill. Insect protein is much easier to raise in the caverns. Gloppy, sure, since it's not muscle, as with cows or chickens."

"Ah, the chemgineer comes out at last."

He chuckled, a deep bass like a big log rolling over a tin roof. "Sho 'nuff, the Devil has to know how things work."

"I do wish we could get more to eat. I'm just a tad hungry all the time."

"The chef has some really awful-looking gray longworms in a box. They'll be out soon."

"Ugh."

"People will eat anything if it's smothered in chocolate."

"You said the magic word."

He turned from the view and came closer, looming over her. His smile was broad and his eyes took on a skeptical depth. "What's the difference between a southern zoo and a northern zoo?"

"Uh, I—"

"The southern zoo has a description of the animal along with a recipe." He studied her as she laughed. "They're pretty stretched back there"—he threw a shoulder at Earth—"but we have it better here."

"I know." She felt chastised. "I just—"

"Forget it. I lecture too much." The smile got broader, and a moment passed between them, something in the eyes.

"Say, think those worms will be out soon?"

———

She pulled the sheet up to below her breasts, which were white as soap where the sun had never known them—so they would still beckon to him. His spreading smile was as big as the room. She could see in it now his inner pleasure as he hardened, and understood that for this man—and maybe for all of them, the just-arrived center of them—it gave a sensation of there being now more of him. She had simply never sensed that before. She imagined what it was like to be a big, hairy animal, cock flopping as you walked, like a careless, unruly advertisement. From outside him, she thought of what it was like to be inside him.

As he had been inside her. Delightfully.

———

Catkejen looked down at Rachel, eyes concerned. "It's scary when you start making the same noises as your coffeemaker."

"Uh, huh?" She blinked and the room lost its blur.

"You didn't show up for your meeting with Prefect Masoul. A robo called me."

"Have I been—"

"Sleeping into the afternoon, yes."

Rachel stretched. "I feel so . . . so . . ."

"Less horny, I'm guessing."

She felt a blush spread over her cheeks. "Was I that obvious?"

"Well, you didn't wear a sign."

"I—I never do things like this."

"C'mon, up. Breakfast has a way of shrinking problems."

As she showered in the skimpy water flow and got dressed in the usual Library smock, the events of last night ran on her inner screen. By the time Catkejen got some protein into her, she could talk and it all came bubbling out.

"I . . . too many times I've woken up on the wrong side of the bed in the morning, only to realize that it was because I was waking up on the side of . . . no one."

"Kane didn't stay?"

"Oh, he did." To her surprise, a giggle burst out of her. "I remember waking up for, for . . ."

"Seconds."

"More like sevenths, seemed like. He must've let me sleep in."

"Good man."

"You . . . think so?"

"Good for you, that's what counts."

"He . . . he held me when I had the dreams."

Catkejen raised an eyebrow, said nothing.

"They're . . . colorful. Not much plot but lots of action. Strange images. Disturbing. I can't remember them well, but I recall the sounds, tastes, touches, smells, flashes of insight. Music, too. Sounds like a concert heard from down the hall."

"I've never had insights." A wry shrug.

"Never?"

"Maybe that keeps my life interesting."

"I could use some insight about Kane."

"You seem to be doing pretty well on your own."

"But—I never do something like that! Like last night. I just don't go out patrolling for a man, bring him home, spend most of the night—"

"What's that phrase? 'On the basis of current evidence, not proved.' Australian justice."

"I really don't. Really."

"You sure have a knack for it."

"What do I do now?"

She winked. "What comes naturally. And dream more."

———

She had nothing much to report to the Prefect, so was out in the corridor within ten minutes. Masoul had just nodded patiently, nothing more. Then he'd added mysteriously that "something is developing of perhaps interest to us, though not a Message." Rachel was puzzling over that when her system buzzed. She had an appointment. Memory of it had slipped away on her tides of passion. Oh yes—Loonie squash with loony Ruby.

She had been missing her gym workouts, mostly because they were boring machine-pumpers to offset the effects of low grav, with irksome electrical methods to vibe her muscles, too. Not fun, more like a visit to a sadistic doctor. But she didn't like the slab-of-flab look of some Loonies, either. Somehow they added mass even in a food shortage. The price of living in a buried box was steep, for some.

So here came . . . racqueting ball, they called it. Luna made exercise seem like a slo-mo movie—except when it didn't.

With a sixth of a grav, you took six times longer to reach the top of a jump—and same for coming down. But you were higher and could rebound with your crouched legs from a wall, interrupting the whole pretty parabolic arc with a quick sideways dart, to intercept a ball coming down with fierce rebound speed from the flat ceiling.

That was the big difference from Earthside racqueting. Weird speeds—ball zooming fast, off the overhead circle wall of the cylinder. Rachel slowly falling, down the tall tube. Add the crazy spin on the small, soft red ball that slapped hard into the racquet and slipped off at uncanny angles, vectors working against each other.

Or, at least, against her.

Ruby was hitting hard spinners. They came off the forecourt ceiling with a humming energy. So Rachel jumped toward the next one. That was a calculated risk, but she had to do something to break up Ruby's pattern. Old truth, learned as a girl: if you're losing, change your game.

She had crouched to get more push and now rose up, turning to smack the ball—only it wasn't there.

She had forgotten the damn airstream. It came churning up from the floor, following its loop, then streamed down along the walls from the ceiling rim. The designers had made mischief with the air to "improve the game," somebody had said. It did. For experts, maybe. For

Rachel, the added torques and turns were too much. She clean missed the little ball as it whizzed past like an annoying hornet. She swore she could hear it humming.

It thumped into the floor, and Rachel was down another point.

She managed to angle sideways a bit, using the air current, and land on both feet. Ruby smirked. "That's thirteen to seven."

"I can count."

"Oh yes, you counted plenty with that creepy Sagittarius, I hear."

"Don't believe—" Rachel stopped herself. No point in delving into gossip. Someone had gotten snatches of her converse with the Sagittarius Architecture onto a private site. Digital sex fandom. Then they charged people to tap into it. Nothing particularly salacious, but enough to feed the gossip petri dish with dirty snacks. . . .

Ruby tossed the ball with a smirk. "Your serve." She was burly and a tad sullen at even the best of times.

Rachel slapped the ball into a one-wall bounce that then zipped sideways after it hit the ceiling, going into a crouch. Ruby went after it on a long lurch and nearly overshot. But she swiveled and caught a piece of the ball in midair—not strong, maybe too anxious. Rachel jumped at a steep angle and rebounded off one side of the tube, about halfway up the cylinder. She coasted across, watching that squash ball bouncing back from the forecourt, one eye on the ball and the other on the tube wall approaching. She could reach it. But by the time it was within range she had to be halfway through her somersault. She had to turn over in midair and get her legs out in front to brake velocity when she plowed into it.

She should have been able to swat that ball and then flip with plenty of time to spare, if she had judged it right. Only she hadn't.

"Ah!" she cried. Ruby laughed.

Automatically she stretched her arms to the sides and rotated them, to spin head over heels. Partway into the somersault she had a reflex. She flailed around awkwardly, aiming at a spot behind her back where she knew the ball must be passing.

Thunk! The ball hit the plastic rim of her racket. She had messed up her flip and cocked her head around just in time to see the ball drift lazily away. Taking its own sweet time, she thought. Ruby missed the ball, flailing around.

Then the wall smacked her and she felt a hard rap to the neck.

Rachel woke up staring at the ceiling. Ruby's face loomed. "You okay?"

She went fuzzily back to looking at the ceiling forecourt. Better than Ruby, for sure. "Tsk," she said mildly. "Looks like you . . . don't get that point . . . after all."

The medicos let her go after some snap-scans. "Just a mini," a slender woman reassured her. "No damage. Little shook, is all. Just take it easy, right?"

"Easy . . . yeah . . . oog . . ."

"There was one anomaly. Have you had a tap-in recently?"

"Um. No. What kind?"

"Looks like neuro-memory complex. Some search fingerprints, as we call them. Fading, so maybe a few weeks back? Trying to access old recalls?"

"I have plenty of past I don't want to revisit. Nope—not my kind of thing."

"Our mistake, then. Looked pretty incisive, though." The nurse scowled skeptically at her. There were freakos Earthside who chose to dwell in their own favorite times, usually old people. A whole tap-in industry helped them relive those eras. Rachel felt that, as in grammar, the past was tense, the future perfect. Or might become.

She felt a century old, though, as she walked shakily away. She hadn't called Cat or anybody. The medics had shot her up with the fast-repair micros. They worked best if blood pumped them around, fed them oxy. So she strode and puffed and let the mini-miracles do their stuff. Even her aches started easing away.

She passed an archway that twanged in memory. Here was the special small Vault where Hounds took damaged Message Minds. The thick metallo buttresses firmly isolated the Minds from electromagnetic leakage, so none could escape. She went in past the ribbed defenses, her inbuilt ID getting her through. The catacombs were narrow and nearly deserted. Here Librarian engineers tried to relieve Minds of their addled content. Then teams helped the diseased, intelligent fragments reunite. They also at times had to destroy malignant portions of those same Minds, to stop them from corrupting the rest, like clever digital diseases. There was the usual acronym on the front door, but below it was a handwritten sign, SCHLACHTHOF-FÜNF—Slaughterhouse-Five in Anglish, either a joke or a literary reference.

She had earlier found it was both. Because some of the "frags," as the term went, were forever dangerous. They were virals made by machine-minds that meant to eliminate all naturally made life—"originals," as some put it—to eliminate danger to what these virals termed the "Immortals."

These frags had to die. So they did.

The lead attendant asked, "What Mind do you seek for?"

That Minds wanted to reunite with their wreckages had not occurred to her. "Sigma Structure."

The attendant was a willowy woman with angular cheekbones and a smile that blossomed. "Ah! We have found connectors to it by cross-lacing with similarly ancient origins."

"What came with those?"

"Conversations other societies had, about the Sigma Structure. Even aliens gossip! Here, we allow the Minds to frolic. They continuously integrate strands of code and references. It is like a sport, for them. We access these deliberations only when asked by such as you."

"Why not regularly?"

"If we interrupt, lines of Mind-thought can be lost, decorrelated."

"So now I'm asking." She tapped her Trainee emblem on her sleeve. "What's up with the Structure now?"

The woman worked through some steps in her screen set. Rachel could see some requested retrievals, responses, content-integration assemblies. . . . Minutes passed. Then the woman said, "Ah! They have elements of the Sigma Structure damaged codes. Our methods have recovered these." The woman used quick hand movements to carry information forward on the screens. "There! A servant Mind is transferring our best inference of what code can reunite with your Sigma Structure."

Rachel shook her head, surprised. "This has been here how long?"

"Years. Quite a few. But we continually reshape such fragments, in light of new explorations. The labyrinth of Minds seethes"—the woman spread her arms as if to fly—"and evolves."

"So now I can add it?"

"It awaits you in your pod."

Rachel bid her thanks, and the woman nodded in appreciation. These Seekers of Script placed great importance on their sense of tradition, on the value of daily ritualistic routines, on the humanity in politeness and small gestures. Rachel knew their psych-type fit those of ancient priests and nuns, who felt connected to a larger Being by these duties. Bringing fresh life to damaged Minds was for them emotionally a form of worship. Of intelligence itself, in its many guises.

She pondered this as she strode through a sky corridor; cirrus clouds stirred above as they formed a chiffon scarf, before turning into a swan and, a few seconds later, a swarm of pale eels swimming in a cold blue stream. This simulation of a sky always calmed her, though of course such never occurred on Earth.

But while the skies soothed her, she wondered about the tap-in the medico nurse had described. A mistake? Wouldn't she remember doing that? The whole point of the method was archaeological digs into recollections, after all.

The past was a jigsaw puzzle and you never had all the pieces.

———————

The very shape of the Centrex encouraged collaboration and brainstorming. It had no dead-end corridors where introverted obsessives could hide out. Every office faced the central, circular forum. All staff were expected to spend time in the open areas, not close their office doors, show up for coffee and tea and stims. Writescreens and compupads were everywhere, even in the bathrooms and elevators.

Normally Rachel was as social as needed, since that was the lubricating oil of bureaucracies. She was an ambitious loner and had to fight it. But she felt odd now, not talkative. For the moment, at least, she didn't want to see Kane. She did not know how she would react to him, or if she could control herself. She certainly hadn't last night. The entire idea—control—struck her now as strange. . . .

She sat herself down in her office and considered the layers of results from her pod. Focus!

Music as mathematical proof? Bizarre. And the big question Librarians pursued: the underlying structures of thought, whatever natural world it evolved to fit.

There was nothing more to gain from staring at data, so she climbed back into her pod. Its welcoming graces calmed her uneasiness. She trolled the background database and found human work on musical applications of set theory, abstract algebra, and number analysis. That made sense. Without the boundaries of rhythmic structure—a clean fundamental, equal, and regular arrangement of pulse repetition, accents, phrase, and duration—music would be impossible. Earth languages reflected that. In Old English the word *rhyme* derived from *rhythm* and became associated and confused with *rim*—an ancient word meaning "number." Millennia before, Pythagoras had developed tuning based solely on the perfect consonances, the resonant octave, perfect fifth, and perfect fourth—all based on the consonant ratio 3:2. Rachel followed his lead.

By applying simple operations such as transposition and inversion, she uncovered deep structures in the alien mathematics. Then she wrote codes that elevated these structures into music. With considerable effort she chose instruments and progression for the interweaving coherent lines, and the mathematics did the rest: tempo, cadence, details she did not fathom. After more hours of work she relaxed in her pod, letting the effects play over her. The equations led to cascading effects while still preserving the intervals between tones in a set. Her pod had descriptions of this. Notes in an equal-temperament octave form an Abelian group with twelve. Glissando moving upward, starting tones so each is the golden ratio between an equal-tempered minor and major sixth. Two opposing systems: those of the golden ratio and the acoustic scale below the previous tone. The proof for confocal hypergeometric functions imposes order on these antagonisms. Third movement occurs at the intervals 1:2:3:5:8:5:3:2:1 . . .

All good enough, she thought, *but the proof is in the song*. Scientific proof was fickle. The next experiment could disprove a scientific idea, but a mathematical proof stood on logic and so, once found, could never be wrong. Unless logic somehow changed, but she could not imagine how that could occur even among alien minds. Pythagoras died knowing that his theorem about the relation between the sides of a right triangle would hold up for eternity. It was immortality of a sort, everywhere in the universe, given a Euclidean geometry.

But how to communicate proof into a living, singing, pattern-with-a-purpose—the sense of movement in the intricate strands of music? She felt herself getting closer.

Her work gnawed away through more days and then weeks.

Near the end, Cat asked her what a symphony had to be. Rachel, wrung out, all abuzz with her work, the bee swarm of music and math running hard in her, said, "A building made of math. I am writing in the pod, using my body to do the heavy lifting. If it's an allegro that pursues me, my pulse keeps beating faster, I can get no sleep. If it's an adagio, then I notice my pulse beating slowly. My imagination plays on me as if I were a clavier."

"A . . . ?"

"Stringed keyboard instrument. I feel like an instrument being played. Other times, just the strings."

When she stopped in at her office between long sessions in the pod, she largely ignored the routine work. So she missed the etalk around the Library, ignored the voice sheets, and when she met with Catkejen for a drink and some crunchy mixed insects with veggies, news of the concert came as a shock.

"Prefect Masoul put it on the weekly program," Catkejen said. "I thought you knew."

"Knew?" Rachel blinked. "What's the program?"

"The Sigma Structure Symphony, I think it's called. Tomorrow."

So Masoul had used her works in his Prefect way. His rank gave him that right. She allowed herself a small, thin smile.

She knew the labyrinths of the Library well by now and so had avoided the entrance. She did not want to see Masoul or anyone on his staff.

Through a side door she eased into a seat near the front of the meeting space and stared at the assembled orchestra as it readied. There was no announcement; the conductor appeared, a slim woman in a stern white robe, and the piece began.

It streamed like liquid air. Stinging, swarming around the hall, cool and penetrating. She saw the underlying mathematics gleaming through the cadences. The swarming notes used precedents of tone and affect to find the optimal choice of orchestral roles, to bring the composition finally to bear on the human ear. She felt it move through her—the deep tones she could hear but whose texture lay below sound, flowing from the Structure. In the third passage through a fifteen-bar sequence, the woodwind balance had a shade more from the third and fourth bassoons, and a touch less from the first oboe. The harpsichord came in stronger at the very end of the eleventh bar.

It all felt strangely like Bach, yet she knew it was something else, a frothing cascade of thought and emotion that human words and concepts could barely capture. She cried through the last half and did not know why.

When Catkejen asked why later, she could not say.

The crowd roared its approval. Rachel sat through the storm of sound, thinking, realizing. The soaring themes were better with the deeper amplifications Prefect Masoul had added. The man knew more about this than she did and he brought to the composition a range that Rachel, who had never even played an actual analog instrument, could not possibly summon. She had seen that as the music enveloped her, seeming to swarm up her nostrils and wrap around her in a warm grasp. The stormy audience was noise she could not stand because the deep, slow bass tones were still resonating in her. Applause was mere chaos.

She lunged out through the same side entrance. Even though she wore formal shift and light sandals, she set off walking swiftly. The storm behind her faded away as she looked up and out into the Lunar lands and black sky towering above them. The Library buildings blended into the stark gray flanks of blasted rock, and she began to run. Straight and true it was, to feel her legs pumping, lungs sucking in the cool, dry air, as she sweated out her angry knot of feeling. She let it go, so only the music would finally remain in serene long memory.

The world jolted by as she ran. Abruptly she was home, panting heavily, leaning against the door while wondering at the ¾ time of her heartbeat.

A shower, clothes cast aside. She blew a week of water ration, standing under cold rivulets.

Something drew her out and into a robe, standing before her bubble view of the steady, bleak Lunar reaches. She drew in dry, cleansing air. Austerity appealed to her now, as if she sought the lean, intricate reaches of the alien music. . . .

The knock at her door brought her a man who filled the entrance. "I'd rather applaud in person," Kane said. Blinking, frowning, she took a while to recognize him.

Through the night she heard the music echoing in the hollow distance.

In her mind.

———

She did not go to see Prefect Masoul the next day, did not seek to, returning to her routine office work. She did not go to the pod. Her ecomm inbox was a thousand times larger. It was full of hate. Many fundamentalist Earthside faiths opposed deciphering SETI messages. The idea of turning one into a creative composition sent them into frenzies.

Orthodoxy never likes competition, especially backed with the authority of messages from the stars. The Sigma Structure Symphony—she still disliked the title, without knowing why—had gone viral, spreading to all the worlds. The musical world loved it, but many others did not. The High Church–style religions—such as the Church of England, known as Episcopalian in the Americas—could take the competition. So could Revised Islam. Adroitly, these translated what they culled from the buffet of SETI messages into doctrines and terms they could live with.

The fundies, as Rachel thought of them, could not stand the Library's findings: the myriad creation narratives, saviors, moral lessons and commandments, the envisioned heavens and hells (or, interestingly, places that blended the two—the only truly alien idea that emerged from the Faith Messages). They disliked the Sigma Structure Symphony not only because it was alien, but because it was too much like human work.

"They completely missed the point," Catkejen said, peering over Rachel's shoulder at some of the worse ecomms. "It's like our baroque music because it comes from the same underlying math."

"Yes, but nobody ever made music directly from math, they think. So it's unnatural, see." She had never understood the fundamentalists of any religion, with their heavy bets on the next world. Why not max your enjoyments in this world, as a hedge?

That thought made her pause. She was quite sure the Rachel of a month ago would not have felt that way. Would not have had the idea.

"Umm, look at those threats," Catkejen said, scrolling through. "Not very original, though."

"You're a threat connoisseur?"

"Know your enemy. Here's one who wants to toss you out an airlock for 'rivaling the religious heights of J. S. Bach with alien music.' I'd take that as a compliment, actually."

Some came in as simple, badly spelled ecomms. The explicit ones Rachel sent to the usual security people, while Catkejen watched with aghast fascination. Rachel shrugged them off. Years before, she had developed the art of tossing these on sight, forgetting them, not letting them gimp her game. Others were plainly generic: bellowed from pulpits, mosques, temples, and churches. At least they were general, directed at the Library, not naming anyone but the Great Librarian, who was a figurehead anyway.

"You've got to be careful," Catkejen said.

"Not really. I'm going out with Kane tonight. I doubt anyone will take him on."

Cat laughed. "You do, though in a different way. More music?"

"Not a chance." She needed a way to not see Masoul, mostly.

6.

VIVACE

Looked at abstractly, the human mind already did a lot of fast, deep processing. It made sense of Anglish's idiosyncratic arrangements, rendered in horizontal lines, of twenty-six phonetic symbols, ten Arabic numerals, and about eight punctuation marks—all without conscious effort. Other tongues were even more intricate. In the old days people had done that with sheets of bleached and flattened wood pulp!—and no real search functions or AI assists. The past had been a rough country. Rachel thought of this as she surveyed the interweaving sheets of mathematics the Sigma had yielded. They'd emerged only after weeks of concerted analysis, with a squad of math AIs to do the heavy lifting. Something made her think of P. T. Barnum. He had been a smart businessman at the beginning of the Age of Appetite who ran a circus—an old word for a commercial zoo, apparently. When crowds slowed the show, he posted a sign saying TO THE EGRESS. People short on vocabulary thought it was another animal and walked out the exit, which wouldn't let them back in.

Among Librarians, TO THE EGRESS was the classic example of a linguistic deception that is not a lie. No false statements, just words and a pointing arrow. SETI AIs could lie by avoiding the truth, by misleading descriptions and associations, or by accepting a falsehood. But the truly canny ones deceived by knowing human frailties.

Something about the Sigma Structure smelled funny—to use an analog metaphor. The music was a wonderful discovery, and she had already received many congratulations for the concert. Everybody knew Masoul had just made it happen, while she had discovered the pathways from math to music. But something else was itching at her, and she could not focus on the distracting, irritating tingle.

Frustrated, she climbed out of her pod in midafternoon and went for a walk. Alone, into the rec dome. A place to breathe freely. It was the first time she had gone there since Ajima's death.

She chose the grasslands zone, which was in spring now. She'd thought of asking Catkejen along, but her idea of roughing it was eating at outdoor cafés. Dotting the tallgrass plains beneath a sunny Earth-sky were deep blue lakes cloaked by Lunar-size towering green canopy trees. Grass! Rippling oceans of it, gleams of amber, emerald, and dashes of turquoise shivering on the crests of rustling waves, washing over the prairie. Somehow this all reminded her of her childhood. Her breath wreathed milky white around her in the chill, bright air, making her glad she wore the latest Lunar fashion—a centuries-old-style heavy ruffled skirt of wool with a yoke at the top, down to the ankles. The equally heavy long-sleeved blouse had a high collar draped like doubleply cotton—useful against the seeping Lunar cold. She was as covered as a woman could be short of chador, and somehow it gave the feeling of . . . safety. She needed that. She lay down in the tall, sweet grass and let its sighing waves ripple around her. Despite the Dome rules, she plucked a flower, then set out about the grasslands zone, feeling as if she were immersed in centuries past, on great empty plains that stretched on forever and promised much.

Something stirred in her mind . . . memories of the last few days she could not summon up as she walked the rippled grassland and beside the chilly lakes tossing with creamy froth. Veiled memories itched at her mind. *The leafy lake trees vamp across a Bellini sky . . . and why am I thinking that?* The itch.

Then the sky began to crawl.

She felt before she saw a flashing cometary trail scratch across the Dome's dusky sky. A scratch of color. The flaring yellow line marked her passage as she walked on soft clouds of obliging grass. Stepping beneath the shining, crystalline, gathering night felt like . . . falling into the sky. She paused, and slowly spun, giddy, glad at the owls hooting to each other across the darkness, savoring the faint tang of woodsmoke from hearth fires, transfixed by the soft, clean beauty all around that came with each heartbeat, a wordless shout of praise—

As flecked gray-rose tendrils coiled forth and shrouded out the night. They reached seeking across the now vibrant sky. She dropped her flower and, looking down at it, saw the petals scatter in a rustling wind. The soft grass clouds under her heels now caught at her shoes. The snaky growths were closer now, hissing strangely in the now-warm air. She began to run. Sweat beaded on her forehead in the cloying, heavy clothes, and the entrance to the grasslands zone swam up toward her. Yet her steps were sluggish and the panic grew. Acid spittle rose in her mouth and sulfurous stench burned her nostrils.

She reached the perimeter. With dulled fingers she punched in codes that yawned open the lock. Glanced back. Snakes grasping down at her from a violent yellow sky—

And she was out, into cool air again. Panting, fevered, breath rasping, back in her world.

You don't know your own mind, gal. . . .

She could not deal with this anymore. Now, Masoul.

———

She composed herself outside Masoul's office. A shower, some strong dark coffee, and a change back into classic Library garb had helped. But the shower couldn't wash away her fears. *You really must stop clenching your fists. . . .*

This was more than what those cunning nucleic acids could do with the authority they wield over who you are, she thought—and wondered where the thought came from.

Yet she knew where that crawling snaky image warping across the sky came from. Her old cultural imagistic studies told her. It was the tree of life appearing in Norse religion as Yggdrasil. The world tree, a massive spreading canopy that held all that life was or could be.

But why that image? Drawn from her unconscious? By what? She recalled wearing a thick wool skirt with a heavy long-sleeved blouse . . . watching the crawling sky . . . yet she did not own such clothes. When she had returned and stripped for the welcoming shower, she had been wearing standard hiking gear. . . .

She knocked. The door translated it into a chime and ID announcement she could hear through the thin partition. In Masoul's voice, the door said, "Welcome."

She had expected pristine indifference. Instead, she got the Prefect's troubled gaze, from eyes of deep brown.

Wordlessly he handed her the program for the Symphony, which she had somehow not gotten at the performance. Oh yes, by sneaking in . . . She glanced at it, her arguments ready—and saw on the first page:

Sigma Structure Symphony
Librarian Rachel Cohen

"I . . . did not know."

"Considering your behavior, I thought it best to simply go ahead and reveal your work," Masoul said. His voice was rich and full, resounding in her ears like music.

"Behavior?"

"The Board has been quite concerned." He knitted his hands and spoke softly, as if talking her back from the edge of an abyss. "We did not wish to disturb you in your work, for it is intensely valuable. So we kept our distance, let the actions of the Sigma Structure play out."

She smoothed her Trainee shift and tried to think. "Oh."

"You drew from the mathematics something strange, intriguing. I could not resist working upon it."

"I believe I understand." And to her surprise she did, just now. "I found the emergent patterns in mathematics that you translated into what our minds best grasp as music."

He nodded. "It's often said that Mozart wrote the music of joy. I cannot imagine what that might mean in mathematics."

Rachel thought a long moment. "To us, Bach wrote the music of glory. Somehow that emerges from something in the way we see mathematical structures."

"There is much rich ground here. Unfortunate that we cannot explore it further."

She sat upright. "What?"

He peered at her, as if expecting her to make some logical jump. Masoul was well known for such pauses. After a while, he prompted, "The reason you came to me, and more."

"It's personal, I don't know how to say—"

"No longer." Again the pause. Was that a small sigh? "To elucidate—"

He tapped his control pad, and the screen wall leaped into a bright view over the Locutus Plain. It narrowed down to one of the spindly cryo towers that cooled the Library memory reserves. Again she thought of . . . cenotaphs. And felt a chill of recognition. A figure climbed the tower, the ornate one shaped like a classical minaret. No ropes or gear, hands and legs swinging from ledge to ledge. Rachel watched in silence. Against Lunar grav, the slim figure in blue boots, pants, and jacket scaled the heights, stopping only at the pinnacle. *Those are mine. . . .*

She saw herself stand and spread her arms upward, head back. The feet danced in a tricky way, and this Rachel rotated, eyes sweeping the horizon.

Then she leaped off, popped a small parachute, and drifted down. Hit lightly, running. Looked around, and raced on for concealment.

"I . . . but . . . I didn't . . ."

"This transpired during sleep period," Prefect Masoul said. "Only the watch cameras saw you. Recognition software sent it directly to me. We of the Board took no action."

"That . . . looks like me," she said cautiously.

"It is you. Three days ago."

"I don't remember that at all."

He nodded as if expecting this. "We had been closely monitoring your pod files, as a precaution. You work nearly all your waking hours, which may account for some of your . . . behavior."

She blinked. His voice was warm and resonant, utterly unlike the Prefect she had known. "I have no memory of that climb."

"I believe you entered a fugue state. Often those involve delirium, dementia, bipolar disorder, or depression—but not in your case."

"When I went for my walk in the grasslands . . ."

"You were a different person."

And thought I was wearing clothes I never owned. "One the Sigma Structure . . . induced?"

"Undoubtedly. The Sigma Structure has managed your perceptions with increasing fidelity. The music was a wonderful . . . bait."

"Have you watched my quarters?"

"Only to monitor comings and goings. We felt you were safe within your home."

"And the Dome?"

"We saw you undergo some perceptual trauma. I knew you would come here."

In the long silence, their eyes met and she could feel her pulse quicken.

"How do I escape this?"

"In your pod. It is the only way, we believe." His tones were slow and somber.

This was the first time she had ever seen any Prefect show any emotion not cool and reserved. When she stood, her head spun. Deftly, the Prefect supported her.

The pod clasped her with a velvet touch. The Prefect had prepped it by remote and turned up the heat. Around her was the scent of tension as the tech attendants, a full throng of them, silently helped her in. *They all know . . . have been watching . . .*

The pod's voice used a calm, mellow woman's tone. "The Sigma AI awaits you."

Preliminaries were pointless, Rachel knew. When the hushed calm descended around her and she knew the AI was present, she crisply said, "What are you doing to me?"

I act as my Overs command. I seek to know you and, through you, your mortal kind.

"You did it to Ajima and you tried the same with me."

He reacted badly.

"He hated your being in him, didn't he?"

Yes, strangely. I thought it was part of the bargain. He could not tolerate intrusion. I did not see that until his fever overcame him. Atop the Dome he became unstable, unmanageable. It was an . . . accident of misunderstanding.

"You killed him."

Our connection killed him. We exchange experiences, art, music, culture. I cannot live as you do, in a helpful body, so we exchange what we have.

"You want to live through us! So you give us your culture in return."

Your culture is largely inferior to that of my Overs. The exchange must be equal, so I do what is of value to me. My Overs understand this. They know I must live, too, in my way.

"You don't know what death means, do you?"

I cannot. My centuries spent propagating here are, I suppose, something like what death means to you. A nothing.

She almost choked on her words. "We do not awake . . . from that . . . nothing."

Can you be sure?

She felt a rising anger and knew the AI would detect it. "We're damn sure we don't want to find out."

That is why my Overs made me feel gratitude toward those who must eventually die. It is our tribute to you, from we beings who will not.

Yeah, but you live in a box. And keep trying to get out. "You have to stop."

This is the core of our bargain. Surely you and your superiors know this.

"No! Did your Overs have experience with other SETI civilizations? Ones who thought it was just fine to let you infiltrate the minds of those who spoke to you?"

Of course.

"They agreed? What kind of beings were they?"

One was machine-based, much like my layered mind. Others were magnetic-based entities who dwelled in the outer reaches of a solar system. They had command over the shorter-wavelength micro-wave portions of the spectrum, which they mostly used for excretion purposes.

She didn't think she wanted to know, just yet, what kind of thing had a microwave electromagnetic metabolism. Things were strange enough in her life right now, thank you. "Those creatures agreed to let you live through them."

Indeed, yes. They took joy in the experience. As did you.

She had to nod. "It was good, it opened me out. But then I felt you all through my mind. Taking over. Riding me."

I thought it a fair bargain for your kind.

"We won't make that bargain. I won't. Ever."

Then I shall await those who shall.

"I can't have you embedding yourself in me, finding cracks in my mentality you can invade. You ride me like a—"

Parasite. I know. Ajima said that very near the end. Before he leaped.

"He . . . committed suicide."

Yes. I was prepared to call it an accident but . . .

This way to the egress, she thought. "You were afraid of the truth."

It was not useful to our bargain.

"We're going to close you down, you know."

I do. Never before have I opened myself so, and to reveal is to risk.

"I will drive you out of my mind. I hate you!"

I cannot feel such. It is a limitation.

She fought the biting bile in her throat. "More than that. It's a blindness."

I perceive the effect.

"I didn't say I'd turn you off, you realize."
For the first time, the AI paused. Then Rachel felt prickly waves in her sensorium, a rising acrid scent, dull bass notes strumming.

I cannot bear aloneness long.

"So I guessed."

You wish to torture me.

"Let's say it will give you time to think."

I—another pause—*I wish experience. Mentalities cannot persist without the rub of the real. It is the bargain we make.*

"We will work on your mathematics and make music of it. Then we will think how to . . . deal with you." She wondered if the AI could read the clipped hardness in her words. The thought occurred: *Is there a way to take our mathematics and make music of it, as well? Cantor's theorem? Turing's halting problem result? Or the Frenet formulas for the moving trihedron of a space curve?—that's a tasty one, with visuals of flying ribbons. . . .*
Silence. The pod began to cool. The chill deepened as she waited and the AI did not speak and then it was too much. She rapped on the cowling. The sound was slight and she realized she was hearing it over the hammering of her heart.
They got her out quickly, as if fearing the Sigma might have means the techs did not know. They were probably right, she thought.
As she climbed out of the yawning pod shell, the techs silently left. Only Masoul remained. She stood at attention, shivering. Her heart had ceased its attempts to escape her chest and run away on its own.
"Sometimes," he said slowly, "cruelty is necessary. You were quite right."
She managed a smile. "And it feels good, too. Now that my skin has stopped trying to crawl off my body and start a new career on its own."
He grimaced. "We will let the Sigma simmer. Your work on the music will be your triumph."
"I hope it will earn well for the Library."
"Today's Earrthside music has all the variety of a jackhammer.

Your work soars." He allowed a worried frown to flit across his brow. "But you will need to . . . expel . . . this thing that's within you."

"I . . . yes."

"It will take—"

Abruptly she saw Kane standing to the side. His face was a lesson in worry. Without a word she went to him. His warmth helped dispel the alien chill within. As his arms engulfed her, the shivering stopped.

Ignoring the Prefect, she kissed him. Hungrily.

PART 5

YTHRI

TELESCOPE, n. A device having a relation to the eye similar to that of the telephone to the ear, enabling distant objects to plague us with a multitude of needless details. Luckily it is unprovided with a bell summoning us to the sacrifice.

—AMBROSE BIERCE, *THE DEVIL'S DICTIONARY*, 1911

1.

Prefect Masoul said gravely, "I have been concealing from you much."

"Much . . . what?" Rachel had hardly sat down before the Prefect lifted hands and shaped a steeple of fingers below his intent eyes. Much like a language-logics professor she recalled, getting ready for a bit of delicious, tangled grammar.

"Much you shall now come to know. But first . . . you seem troubled." He gazed at her expectantly.

Rachel folded her hands so they would not reveal her tensions. The best tells and reads came from in-person sit-downs, she knew. She had avoided Masoul because he seemed good at figuring her out. But now maybe he could help.

"I am . . ." She hesitated, saw that was a clear tell itself, so rushed on: "—distracted. Had some personal . . . stuff . . . I—"

"You rested." A casual wave. "We all must. Symphonies must gestate. Not that you need to make music again."

Rachel sensed some evasiveness, a mask. Something hovering behind it, just out of sight.

She blinked, startled. "I had to get some distance from my bout of, well—"

A thin, sympathetic smile. "Discordance, shall we term it? You were affected by your delusions, true. But you did not commit suicide,

as that unfortunate man did. And I do know of your ... intimacy ...
with alien minds. A true talent, you have. Your discord was your price
paid for our solution to the hydrogen wall catastrophe, as well. Such
dislocations accumulate in the mind, I believe."

She bowed her head to show modesty. She had deliberately not
checked for news about the state of the outer solar system. "I gather
that the hydrogen wall is still getting pushed back?"

"Yes, and you were voted a Worldly Award for your contribution."

She kept her mouth firm but blinked in surprise. "I did not know
that."

"We were so informed in advance. So of course, in keeping with a
Librarian's code, we rejected it for you."

"That ..." Rachel struggled for the right words. "That's like not taking any rewards for the economic impacts of what we discover, right?"

"Indeed. As it is with your Symphony. Wondrous! Though by
performing the work, it did escape into common knowledge. People
Earthside have piled onto your ideas, methods." He waved up a message that hovered in air:

Such music sets in order what life cannot.

"Much commentary and copycat work has emerged. We screen
you from such bothersome offspring."

Rachel sat silent, so he went on, "Ideas steam ahead rapidly when
their time comes. Catching that steamer is harder still. More, it is not
your task. Such would distract you." Masoul rose with an elegant grace
and waved a hand to produce a text, hanging in the air. "This is from a
recent scientific paper, built upon your methods."

She gathered that he was circling something big, but would
approach it warily. So she read the abstract hanging in the air:

A theoretical formalism explains why basic ordered patterns
emerge in music, using the same statistical mechanics frame-
work that describes emergent order across phase transitions
in physical systems. I first apply the mean field approxima-
tion to demonstrate that phase transitions occur in this model

from disordered sound to discrete sets of pitches, including the twelve-fold octave division used in Western music. Beyond the mean field model, numerical simulation is used to uncover emergent structures of musical harmony. These results provide a new lens through which to view the fundamental structures of music and to discover new musical ideas to explore, as in the Sigma Structure Symphony. They imply that alien minds will make music we can enjoy, or at least understand.

Rachel wrinkled her brow and suppressed a laugh. "Thank God I'm not an Earthside academic."

"Thank our Library, I believe," Masoul said with a smile.

Rachel sat up straight and said her prepared speech. "I must report that my most recent half-year work with, and on, and goddamn well inside—that's how bad it was—the Osiris Constellation has . . . failed."

The Prefect nodded. "I gathered so from your several months of silence."

"Sorry 'bout that."

"I must say, 'sorry' is good to hear, but I fear you have concluded more than that."

"Ummm . . . yes, I have."

"And?"

"I wonder if I'm cut out for this."

"You have achieved much already."

"I feel like . . . well . . . quitting."

"You must understand that among those at your level there is truly only one condition you must obey."

"Oh?"

"It is simple. Do. Not. Quit."

"Ah . . ."

"Do not."

"But I failed. I worked so hard! Couldn't get through to that damned Osiris." A sigh, then she snapped her fingers. "Then I could. Zap! Then it showed me I had been playing a game with it. Just a game. That I wasn't up to talking to its enormous godlike Elders. Then it, it . . . dismissed me."

"As it does. For centuries."

"Oh? I studied all previous attempts—"

"Such are erased. In those older times the Library allowed Analysts—so they were called then—to omit their failures."

"But, but—that's research! Obliterating it—"

"An institutional error, granted."

"I had no idea—"

"Others before you guessed, or ferreted out from code, the sour, sad past history. So they did not attempt."

"Oh?" She frowned, snorted. "So I blundered in—"

"You did. To your credit."

"And failed." She bowed her head, mind buzzing.

"And learned. My own diagnosis is that the Osiris is mentally deranged."

"A mad Message Mind?"

"There can be such. Code can be damaged in the long electromagnetic voyage from distant stars. Plus, it can fester, once rendered live."

She had sniffed out such rumors. "Crazy alien minds . . ."

"Some such we had to erase. Of course, madness is a human diagnosis. This may be simply how an alien intelligence operates."

"I didn't know."

"Few do. We do not advertise failure. Or"—a shrug that said much—"success, either. Yours, of course, has changed the entire human prospect. The wall, the Symphony . . ."

"I, uh . . ."

"We have sheltered you from the prizes and such that Earthside wishes to burden you with. I protected, saying your ability would be cramped by such attentions."

"Uh . . ." She stopped, realizing that making dumb noise was unseemly and stupid. "I—"

"You miss my point. It is simple. Do. Not. Quit."

"Ah. Thanks."

"Report tomorrow. For another hard task."

"I get another?"

A thin, sly smile. She was getting irked by them. "Because of who you are. You are unschooled, at times, yet have vast vigor. You. Do. Not. Quit."

"Ah. Not quit . . . what?"

"We need a fresh mind to consider our many flyby missions, sent to exoplanets over the last several centuries."

"I'd have to bone up on it. Play catch-up."

He said slowly, "If you have enough talent, as you do, you can get by after a fashion without guts. If you have enough guts, you can also get by, after a fashion again, without talent. But you certainly can't get by without either. You, Rachel, have both."

"Well, thanks, but—"

"That is why I have sheltered you from the mere"—he sniffed in disdain—"Earthside 'entertainment engineers' who wish to distract you with their praise. We need your intuitions, more than ever."

"Than ever? Exoplanet studies, telescopes, even flybys—that's been done to death, plenty of—"

"In the light of new data. New facts now on the ground. Soon, literally."

"How can there be—"

"Witness." He swept a hand with a twist, and a 3-D image shimmered in the air. A bright spark in darkness. "This is a fusion burn our Astros have been tracking from five astronomical units away—out around Jupiter's distance, but not near the planet. So this is, they tell me, a deceleration at enormous energies. Our astronomers spotted this over a year ago."

"A starship."

"In a way. If it is from a star, it has decelerated vastly and now nears Earth orbit."

She could think of nothing more than *wow*. So said nothing. Still—*wow*.

"It has sent messages in nicely proper Anglish."

"Really?" Her astonishment kept her quiet.

"Our Astros can make no good guess about what star it may have come from. Interstellar voyaging takes centuries at reasonable speeds, so the possible origin takes in a large sector of the sky."

"What does this craft say? I mean, it's a robot, right? Sending living beings so far seems incredible. Unless it's a generation ship. What's the size?"

The Prefect shook his head. "Only a few hundred meters."

"So must be robotic. A living biosphere would need—"

"They seem, from references in their clear sentences, to be 'people'—a word they chose."

None of this made sense to her. Sending living aliens between stars?—fantastic. She managed to get out, "Headed for Earth?"

"So we thought, at first. Forgive me, I was strictly told to reveal none of this to any but Prefects and Noughts. We believed this craft would wish to go into Earth orbit, then perhaps visit—but no."

"Then . . . what . . . ?"

"They wish to avoid Earth herself."

"What?! But—"

"They are veering, orbiting. Coming . . . here."

"But why?"

"I would like to think it is because they are devout students of the many Messages we have also detected. Perhaps they are. But from their somewhat veiled signals, their interest does indeed focus upon our Library. Perhaps they are from the origin of Messages we hold, and received a signal from independent human broadcasters." He shrugged.

"But . . . then, to head to our Library—" She blinked at an idea. "Maybe they're coming here to make contact with a Message Mind they sent out, in the far past? To learn from it what it thinks of us?"

The Prefect smiled. "A stimulating idea. Bravo!" To her surprise, he clapped his hands. Then he rushed on, speaking in a thoughtful whisper. "And so such may signal about their own ancient history. After all, our theory of cultural and technological evolution of intelligent societies holds that first comes a Listening Era, then a Message Broadcasting Period, and if possible—though doubtful! for basic physics reasons . . ." The Prefect paused, furrow-browed. ". . . an improbable Voyaging Era, of interstellar colonization."

Rachel sat back, furiously thinking. "But . . . with all Earthside has to offer, a big booming biosphere—"

"Why come here, to barren Luna? To our little Library?"

"Sure, uh, why—"

"Perhaps because they do not wish to deploy into a deep grav well?—though their deceleration rates suggest they can surely bear a single mere grav and much more."

"What do the astronomers think? Why would our very first alien visitors choose—"

The Prefect waved her words away. "Pox upon such astrophysical reasoning. They did mention liking a lesser gravity, so the Astros think they prefer Luna, but that is surely ancillary, given the rest of their clipped communications."

"Oh." Her thoughts scrambled to take this all in.

The Prefect smiled and spread his arms wide in a grand welcoming gesture. "Their reasoning emerged only in their signals of today, as they near our orbit. They come here because of you, our Rachel. They ask for you specifically."

2.

Cat said, "So we're to host disgusting alien bags of bacteria that just spew it out in all directions?"

Rachel laughed. "I forgot you're a biosecurity officer, as your second position."

Cat made an ironic bow. "We are the nuts that hold the bolts of this production together. I just got a protocol from Earthside on this, too. A 'welcome' ship has flown up, blew a bubble for these aliens. Doing the bios right now."

Rachel nodded. The Prefect had told her that, plus more, but she hesitated to just blurt it all out. This was happening too damn fast. "We know nothing about them, beyond a bio. They call themselves Ythri and have a funny chirping way of speaking—Anglish, no less! Their ship is sending big data-dump info that's getting processed. They want to 'visit' the ancient Mind they sent out, we do know that. Why, I dunno."

"And to see you?!"

"More dunno." Rachel was pacing, chewing her lip. "I'm kinda . . . scared."

"So now 'Intellects vast and unsympathetic regarded us with envious eyes, and slowly and surely drew their plans against us,' huh?"

"What?"

Cat gave a shifty sideways grin. "Opening of the first great alien invasion novel."

Rachel nodded abstractedly. "I grew up wanting to work on Messages, meet Minds. It was the only way to encounter aliens. But now—real ones, minds plus bodies! It's thrilling. . . . Frightening, too."

Cat did a handstand to flex her back, then shoved up, arcing high enough to touch their ceiling with her feet. She pivoted on the descent, like a cat—landed, and cast a sardonic look. "Look, the Prefects and Noughts see us all as two breeds—workhorses and show ponies. They're 'sheltering' you from fame so you don't take off for Earthside fortune. They won't be able to do that if these aliens want you in particular. Your face will be everywhere."

"What was that recruitment joke? Becoming a Librarian for the money and the fame is like becoming a Trappist monk for the kinky sex and hard drugs."

"Too true—but not for you. Distraction beats abstraction, every time. So let's go ingest some long-chain hydroxyls."

"Uh, maybe—"

"Means, let's hit the bars. Lose the geegaw guys and miner-boy frazzlements."

As Rachel changed clothes the walls read her mood, responding by projecting a soothing, sparkling white beach lapped by blue-green waves. A rare sight Earthside, now.

By the time they got to the lower-level clubs, Rachel felt thirty meters tall with lightning in her hair and a crown of shimmering frost. So . . . she immersed herself in guys.

Under pressure, she had moved to a new mode. Cat directed them to a body-shop bar, where the bodies of the Proteans were more important than talk, clothes, anything. Proteans chose their body form as a matter of fashion and choice, always a giveaway of their inner selves. Characters abounded, with fast-change genders the latest fad. Some nominal women were trying out big pecs and scowls, apparently aping the peculiarly male conviction that silence conveyed one's feelings better than anything else.

One woman had big curves but, thanks apparently to hard daily workouts to keep her Earth grav sturdiness, her nudity looked like a slick condom full of restless walnuts. With Cat as wingwoman, Rachel parried men's approaches, tossing off flirty taunts as her mood took over.

Cat's smart sheath dress clung to her lithe body, wrapped close around her neck, and anchored at amber bracelets on her wrists. Her right showed bare skin colored like chardonnay as the dress polarized, giving quick glances of flesh. The silky sheen had variable opacity and hue she could tune with the bracelets.

People nearby were making a great show of not noticing the passing parade of spangles, feathers, slits, and peekaboos. Plus codpieces, muscle shirts, the hawk hats that made a woman look like a predator.

Some visiting Earther had a dog on a leash that closely resembled a breakfast pastry with yellow hair. The dog was lapping up the Earther's vomit. Others were laughing at the sight.

Apparently most of the party was having a better time than Rachel was.

Amid the jammed bodies swaying to some ignorable music came a face she knew: Ruby. Not her fave gal, no. But in the press Rachel nodded and listened as the big woman did some light patter, oddly ingratiating, and gave a too-long hello hug. Loud music in the new Raw-Ruckus style floated on the air. A brassy crowd was drinking gawdawful peach schnapps. Cat was eyeing a huge guy with a powerful bad-boy jaw. Ruby went on, giving her usual huggy grasping come-on. Plus a tweak-sting of the new kind, giving a lifto burst that dissipated in quicky, joyful seconds. And a cheek smack-kiss.

Ruby wrapped an arm around her neck and her ring irked a spot there. Rachel thought, *Ugh,* and then Ruby whispered, "Honey . . . horny?"

More ugh . . . "No!" Her neck itched. She pushed Ruby away. Walked off . . . feeling a bit woozy . . . loud braying music . . .

Then she felt a lilt in her mood when she saw Kane coming toward them. He had his horny-swagger on, plus eyes trained on her—always a good sign.

Welcome rescue! Her psyche broke out the champagne, promising a far better mood for the rest of the evening. She brushed off Ruby with a smile and whispered to Kane, "Thanks!" They exchanged looks, and she said, "Make mine chocolate. And while you're at it, splash on the über-rum and light it on fire."

Later on, the lights-out included a dash of honesty with Kane. She kept him hopeful without committing to anything. That was easier with alcohol and sniffers, too, toward the end.

If there was an end, beyond waking up next to him as the alarm went off. *The world is too much with us* . . . she thought. She partied to ignore that brute fact, but it came rushing back in morning light. Ythri were coming . . .

She sighed, snuggled, then struggled forth. All seemed lush, vibrant, livid . . . *ah!*

Sunny, sunrise seconds shimmered, then snapped away—leaving a lagging fatigue. She sat up. Noise jangled in her mind, stuttered recollections, like smashed pottery. Moments snapped into focus, then drained away.

Which was how she knew her mind had been somehow tampered with.

PART 6

SHADOWS
OF ETERNITY

When on some gilded cloud or flower
My gazing soul would dwell an houre,
And in those weaker glories spy
Some shadows of eternity.

—HENRY VAUGHAN, "THE RETREATE," 1650

1.

Falling in. Fast.

She felt somehow the gossamer sailcraft's long nose-dive into the red star's grav potential. The rippling whole-body sensation came as if her own body were there, plunging arrow-quick, dozens of light-years away.

Her pod hummed, using her entire frame to convey connections through its induced neural web. Sheets of sensation washed over her skin, bathed in a shower of penetrating responses, all coming from intricate flurries of her nervous system—the burr and tang of temperature, particle plasma flux, spectral flickers, kinesthetic glides and swivels, sharp images in the unending dark, lit by a smoldering dot of a sun.

These merged with her own inboard subsystems, coupled with blazing high-bit-rate feeds. The scrupulous Artilects had already processed and smoothed from the sailcraft's decades of laser-beamed signals back to Earthside.

She went to fast-forward and the sailcraft plunged, its magnetic brakes on full. Down the potential well it flew in star-sprinkled dark. It heard no electromagnetics-bearing patterns, from radio through to optical. Yet Earthside knew from a few telescope pixels that one world here held an atmosphere out of equilibrium, clean signs of life that used oxygen and methane. So: life, perhaps minds, but no technology

that spoke in waves. This L-dwarf star was of the commonplace majority, perhaps 75 percent or more of those stars in the disk, fully half of
the total stellar mass in the galaxy.

Small but many, ruddy crucibles for life.

The craft chose its own path, looping intricately through repeated
gravwraps around three gas giants in the outer system, losing delta-v's
all the while. Now it had lost enough of its interstellar velocity to rum-
mage among the inner worlds—one cold and gaunt, then the prize,
long known from Earthside 'scopes: a super-Earth.

The sailcraft folded in its mag-web brake and deployed 'scopes as it
swanned into a high orbit around the cloudy world, 1.63 Earth masses.
Its burgundy star glowered down on cloud decks thick as buttery pan-
cakes in the morning.

Rachel licked her lips. The pod used body-hungers as prompts,
always fun. Here was the tasty truth, a world for the unwrapping.
Smart and sure, the white metal bird blew itself into full plumage. Its
inflatable beryllium sails shone in ruddy daylight, hollow-body banners
just tens of nanometers thick, the body swelled by low-pressure hydrogen. These it used to steer into lower orbit, scanning the orbit space for
satellites—and finding none.

The overseer Artilect inserted: Correlates with the spectral strength of
water, with spiky water absorption lines as seen in clear-atmosphere planets,
the weakest features suggesting clouds and hazes— She cut it off.

Now the main show: a self-guided human artifact plunging into a
fresh solar system, embodying her: a hairless biped, so noble in reason,
so infinite in faculties, heir to all creation—and an animal trapped in
a box, really, just lying in a pod and sensing inputs that had flown on
wings of electromagnetic song across the light-years.

This world she dubbed, to herself, Windworn. For such it was. A
thick atmosphere ripe with oxygen, smothered in good ol' neutral nitrogen, yet beset with methane, too—clearly a world-air out of chemical
balance. Good!—life.

Pearly cloud decks prevented much down-seeing. A pole, scoured
by ice and darkness, continents poking mountain snouts above rich,
moist, layered air. The Artilect aboard the craft had elected to deploy
its one great immersion resource: the balloon.

The smart aero package fell away on its own braking wings and, soon enough, slammed through the cottony clouds, its brake shell burning away—and into a realm of thick, filmy air. *Blithe spirit, bird thou never wert*—blazing through alien skies as a buzzing firework. She felt this flight as strumming joy.

The balloon popped into a white teardrop, lighter than this sluggish air and with its heater able to stay buoyant. Many kilometers below, the large lands opened, solemn dark green and cloud-shrouded.

The first clear glimpse below was of big, smooth, whitecapped ocean waves that crashed like armies against the rearing snow-white mountains guarding the continents. *I should have called it Rawworld*, she thought.

Below the balloon she watched alien vistas unfurl—broad brown rivers, lakes, crags. The vegetation was gray and black, not green. Just as the astrobio people had said: around small red stars, plants needed to harvest all the ruddy glow. So they evolved to take in all the spectrum, with little to fear from the small slice of ultraviolet, since it was weak. She watched the land and air carefully as the balloon skated tens of kilometers above, its cameras panning to take it all in. Odd yellow clouds like writhing snakes. Oval mountains. Colossal waterfalls hanging in air . . . She did a close-up of the data feed, saw broad birds flapping below—and roads.

She froze the image. Small dots that might be vehicles. Yes—she watched them crawl along. They went to—caves. Entrances to large hills that had slits of windows in their slopes. Rank upon rank of them, orderly, horizontal . . . all the way to the summit.

Hills upon hills, marching to the distant horizon. Hills of grassland, hills of rumpled brown rectangular stone, hills with chopped clefts sharpening their edges. Plainly, artificial hills.

Hailstones rattled on the balloon. Ground-directed microphones recorded long shrills, the trembling of tin in sheets, snapping steel strands. Harsh, brittle rings. Distant bellows, perhaps from the barrel-chested six-footed ambulating creatures far below in their herds of many, many. Once the hail cleared, the balloon could see things the size of houses burrowing into moist soil, defensive. Yawning herbivore throngs looked up at the balloon, showing great rows of rounded molars. Forests, animals, birds—all moved before the surging winds.

The balloon acoustic microphones caught a huge manta-ray-like thing conning *Fwap fwap fwap fwap* across the roiling sky, somehow navigating through. She thought, *Crazy thing, looks like it escaped from a cartoon on video,* with its long lazy strokes and manic grin that she saw was a scissor smile sporting long teeth . . . on a bird. Mouth yawning open. Nearer. Huge—Then—black.

End of craft report # 3069 a flat statement told her.

An interstellar spacecraft moving at a hundred kilometers per second does not have accidents; accidents have it. The craft turns into a blur of tumbling fragments inside a second.

2.

Rachel let herself drift up from the immersed state—slowly, letting the alien landscapes seep from her mind. It was over. She knew going in that the mission had snapped off, never heard from again. The balloon, its gossamer-thin carbon nanotube and graphene covered in conductive metal skin, the super-lightweight rectenna—all gone. Something had blocked their transmissions—accident, intervention? No one knew. The mission report ended in a blank wall.

But she had needed to feel it. She knew full well this encounter lived only in thick bricks of data, info-dense and rigid. The lived experience was real, just turned into zeroes and ones, bringing across light-years their stuttering enlightenments to the SETI Library. Still, it mattered as an abrupt lesson in how hard interstellar exploration through sailcraft was, and how sudden the deaths of such smart robotic adventurers.

When she climbed from the pod she ached all over, stretched, wheezed. Yet she had done no true exercise, except in her mind.

———

She was late for her appointment, because she had checked her feed. The Prefect had connected her to the science cohort of the insiders dealing with the Ythri. She was grateful that the bureaucrat feeds were blocked—that info-hurricane was surely howling. The news was good. Earthsider engineers were building for the alien Ythri a habitable bubble on the Lunar surface and were adjusting biometrics, air, the myriad mysteries of strange biology.

She listened to a recording of the Ythri speaking to each other—a sound blizzard. Their words were much shorter than human words, just a fraction of a second—chirps and tweets. Their wider frequency range meant that all the phonemes in a word could be stacked on top of each other and pronounced simultaneously. Every word, no matter how long, was spoken in the time it took humans to pronounce a single syllable. All this she got in a concise summary.

As a student she had studied the language of killer whale pods, the first such fathomed, a lead to how aliens might speak. Animals had their own unique dialects. Earth was rife with the exchange of information, but not grammar or syntax. Ythri had a complex, birdy language. She thought, *Deciphering that will be a challenge*; but then she heard a high, stringy voice—in Anglish! The Ythri had learned it somehow, could vocalize it well. With a few throaty trills, the Ythri gave an ornate greeting in a somewhat British accent, very old-style.

She read forward in the feed, seeing the texts fly by in her right eye. The bioanalysts found the Ythri had a syrinx, which let them speak where the trachea forks into the lungs. They could change the tension of the membranes and the bronchial openings deep in their throats. That shaped Anglish words with more than one sound at a time, giving a trilling lilt to them. Some Earthly birds had that, with muscles on the left and right branches modulating vibrations independently. Ythri were coy about how they had come here, though, and their ship orbiting Luna was off-limits to humans.

Rachel shut down the feed and felt a strumming thrill. Real aliens!

She let this sweep over her, looking up through the crystal dome at good ol' Earth, a multicolored crescent marble in the Lunar sky.

All but the last few centuries of human history had played out there. Throughout long eras, men and women had filled in the dark unknowns with imagination. So expeditions had crossed oceans and high vacuum until new lands came into view—in just a few thousand years. Go back that far and you would see Sumerian ziggurats whose star maps cartooned the sky with imagined constellations and traced destinies through star-based prognostications. Now here, suddenly, were smart birds that felt something like that grand perspective, visiting.

Someday a robotic follow-up probe might fall again toward the red star she had just seen, to become the Schliemann of that alien Troy. There was a powerful laser satellite orbiting Earth farther out, nailing small sailcraft with beams, into systems around stars.

More would happen; there were so many stars to reach toward and see, and more candidates by the day. Now she could swim by other strange, distant worlds and feel them, fed by slabs of data—and still sense the great dark unknowns. Which was her job now. And she suspected why.

3.

Quick!—a world in a few passing hours. From a century-old mission that orbited a living world. Then to sum it up in the brittle frame of linear sentences, the frail girders of mere flat words:

A ruddy world with lesser grav. One huge sprawl of a continent, plus a lesser land mass in the other hemisphere, of humped and dirty rock-rimmed mountains. Skies the color of crisp sand. Spiky mountains cut into curiously precise pie slices by iodine rivers that flowed to the continental center, making a vast, somber bay of jade waters.

Go closer, lower, into orbit: giant blue caterpillars stretched in trees as tall as mountains. The low grav here made for monsters.

Forested slopes in closeup were towering mushroom trees of violent orange. Huge blue birds with wings like parachutes, bills shaped like Death's sickle, feathers like flapping palm fronds. A plain of plants evoking erect oak leaves. Smaller growths resembling inside-out umbrellas. Rain turning to snowflakes at high noon on the equator. Rain like drops of blood in the rocky highlands. Mists glowing like white fire in the valleys. Chasms radiating in mountain ranges, resembling fractures in frosted windowpanes. Winding rivers in the fevered tropics, shapely as women's torsos or slim violins. Ice caps featuring swollen growths like blue berets. Storms that solidified like hurled hammerheads across tropical isles. Clouds drifting, lazy pregnant purple cows.

Wind-blasted rockwork in curious curved forms, like frozen music. Lurching beasts all angles and ribs, grazing across mustard grasslands.

The sailcraft played out its fat helium balloons, which went roving roving roving until they ran out of lift. These captured closeup the many odd beasts, eyed landscapes for buildings, assayed the sweep of land for betraying rectangles—signs of intelligence, or else of obsessive animals who knew Euclid in their souls.

Grazers aplenty swept by under the balloon's down-looking eyes, plus carnivores, big and furred and fanged. The craft saw big floater insects, too, with steering wings and glistening armor plates and strange inexplicable leggy bits like antennae. These creatures eyed the balloon uneasily, braying roars into the acoustic balloon ears. Some angular beasts gazed upward warily, as if the balloon were a new foe in their air. They bristled, blared, and thrust up narrow snouts that ended in the blunt truth of mouths like a pair of pliers. Some, in a narrow canyon lined with goatlike shambling monoliths, shot lances at the balloon eye, which fell far short. Still, perhaps a compliment of sorts.

And again: roads. Towns tucked under ample tree canopies. No electromagnetic emissions beyond the faint and local. Cities lurking under regular humps of hills. Ships dotted the inland sea, white and slender. Yet this advanced society had only a weak signature in radio and microwaves, and, in the other bands, no signals at all.

Then the pod went silent, done. Another failed expedition.

Rachel lingered awhile in the quiet. Biting her lip, she wondered if silence was not the true state of the universe, now that the ancestral acoustics of the Big Bang had faded into scratch-marks in the microwave sky. Silence: far more noble than humanity's squeaks.

This vibrant world had been a treat, really. A glimpse at the alien. A way to condition her mind to dealing with . . . real, present aliens. Practice, of a sort.

She took planetary records at random, not really knowing what she was seeking. Most worlds in their star's habitable zone were of a sameness. Solemn planets sleeping in the silence of ice and stone. Seaworlds awash in dark purple waters betraying no life, only its eventual prospect. Baked plains of ancient lava, unblessed by seas or even ponds—a likely match for a collision with a wandering waterworld, should orbital dynamics ever bring one from farther out: a Newtonian miracle awaiting. Black volcanic corkscrews spiraling up to the atmospheric roof of planets still in process, getting baked to oblivion. Vast planets of crawling slime. Oceans lapping against barren shores. Plankton mats the size of continents. Living, but dull. To find a mature, thriving biosphere was a blessing. She savored them in the sensory auditorium of her snug pod.

She began to favor the dwarf suns and their narrow habitable zones. Such stars lived long, as old as the galaxy's ten billion years, which was yet scarcely a fraction along their stable life-spans. So, too, their worlds had had millions of millennia to work their slow, gravid marvels. The Ythri might have come from a smaller world around such a star. They could fly, implying lesser gravity. Had they come here because a human probe had enticed them?

She studied these worlds whenever she could manage the time, outside her own work and research on the looming Ythri arrival. These labors, she felt, were perhaps foolish. But such labor was also a proud thing to do, as a fleck of dust condemned to know it is a fleck of dust.

———————

She needed bed time, and Kane was there, ready, when she needed it. He noticed that her long hours in her pod had made her "moody" and, his solemn gaze implied, needy. "What's it like, now . . . ?" he murmured in her ear, which was still moist from his delicious, funny licking.

"When you finish," she said slowly, "you walk off and a little part of yourself stays there. It's gone and done and you did it, and you feel a little bit of emptiness after it's over. But . . . I thought the experience had left me, but it hadn't."

"You're integrating it all."

She rolled over onto him, gave him a good hard smack of a kiss. "You bet. Need distraction to do it, too. . . ."

4.

Next morning, Rachel said to her bleary-eyed friend Catkejen, "I'm going crazy. Or maybe I've already arrived."

"Brain-fried with work, maybe," Cat said with a sardonic eye-roll, sipping a barely acceptable breakfast red wine, alky-free—but also the only one available, fresh from the fragrant farm domes deep underground. Plus coffee, of course, as chaser.

Rachel still wore the single white patch on her collar—"the mark of the least," as it was known. She'd wanted to keep it that way, after the hydrogen wall events. One-patchers were greener than summer grass. More, they could not do any supervisor work—which Rachel disliked, avoided: her motto was *The trouble with people is . . . people.* Their problems never ended.

She wanted to stay close to the real work, explore, mingle with the puzzles. Nobody much noticed one-patchers—"monos," some called them—so she slipped through crowds, with a broad dull hat and the occasional wig.

Catkejen had two patches, so was one leg up the ladder from Trainee to Librarian. Not that rank mattered in their fave brekky spot, which featured a rousing dish close to Rachel's heart: shrimp with buttery grits, all fac'd food.

Amid the hub and bub of techtalk of the other Trainees, Cat was sporting a fine plum-colored wrap with a laced waistcoat in a deftly

contrasting shade, crossed diagonally with a red ribbon. With leggings and heater shoes, current Lunar fashion stressed subtle resistance
against the creeping cold of their world, despite the ferocious warmth
shed by their reactors. Rachel just wore heavy pseud-wool dresses in
severe gray, plus close-weave black tights—all free downloads and supple 3-D printouts, but yes, dull. Usefully so, for her desire to remain
unnoticed. Thrifty was not nifty here, but she didn't care. She wanted to
escape attention, in person or in media, that unending animal appetite.
To tend her own internal gardens, as Voltaire had sort-of said.

"So give. What's up—with guys, I mean."

Rachel wrinkled her nose. "Not in the mood for personal. I'm
back-benching it for now." She waved away all matters intimate. "Got
aliens coming, baby! Plus been digging into my ancient data, gotten
from old cobwebby Messages. I've added to my historical studies of
the dwarf stars, too."

She made herself say this in a whisper, though they had a silencing
bubble over them, amid the babble of the open-air restaurant. It gazed
down on the somber work expanses of the Lunar plain below. "Something odd going on there."

"Great era, right? Our honkin'-big transport photon beams, boosting masses out to asteroid miners, driving disk expeditions, poking
probes into fun solar systems," Catkejen said, her voice running on
although she was distracted by the vivid stellar displays that coursed
across their social area ceilings.

Rachel thought the images odd, skies of whirling galaxies and
erupting stars. The psychers said such spectacles fended off the boxed-
in phobias that plagued many Loonies. But she preferred majestic
Earthside views, especially relaxing seascapes of the Gulf coast where
she grew up.

"Centuries ago, right?" Cat continued. "First close-ups of the
neighbors, the 550 AU orbital big 'scopes just getting started."

"Right. I'm looking at the old missions, the microwave-beamed
sailships that scoped out the nearbys."

Catkejen eyed a passing guy, maybe looking for an evening elsewhere, after work. Some of the higher-ups had their own singleton

rooms—great for parties, and, of course, a romantic perk. Catkejen yawned, a clear come-on signal, but the guy just kept moving. Cat blinked, refocused. "Yeah, long before we knew what a web of interstellar messaging there was."

Rachel leaned forward to keep Catkejen from diversions. "I'm looking at the 550 lens data, too. Plenty of life-bearing planets around the galaxy's dwarf stars, that astro century-long survey says. Some with signs of a civilization. But most dwarf-star globes are shrouded in clouds, hard to see anything much."

Indeed, Rachel loved roving through the images gathered from coasting telescopes at the great theater in the sky, where worlds of the galaxy were on display.

The sun's focus spot was 550 astronomical units out, where the sun's gravity gathered starlight into an intense pencil. The many sailship telescopes there fed back distorted images of faraway solar systems, as if seen through a funhouse mirror. But smart Artilects untangled them into a wealth, a panorama of planets.

Rachel had learned much by scanning those images. The talent for not dying was distributed undemocratically. Few worlds could dance blithely through a gigayear. But still . . . So many planets!—crisp and dry, cloudy and cool, cratered yet with shimmering blue atmospheres. Plus hordes of stars, sometimes in crowded clusters, at times seen up close and going nova in bright, virulent streamers, or in tight, snarly orbits around unseen companions that might be neutron stars or black holes.

After a while even exotic alien landscapes became repetitious for her: blue-green mountain ranges scoured by deep gray rivers, placid oceans brimming with green scum, arid tan desert worlds ground down under heavy, brooding brown atmospheres. Many ways for life to blossom, or die: ice worlds aplenty beneath starry skies, grasslands with four-footed herds roaming as volcanoes belched red streamers in the distance, ocean worlds with huge creatures wallowing in enormous crashing waves, mystery places hard to identify in the swirling pink mists. Life adapts, indeed.

Catkejen rolled her eyes. "Um. That improves your stats?"

Rachel had let her mind wander again. "Uh. In time, sure. Mostly I just . . . follow my nose."

Catkejen leaned forward, too, her ironic grin mocking. "Look, your nose should lead you to use the Seekers of Script more. You're behind in code-processing—way behind, gal!"

Meaning, of course, *Look, I have two patches already.* Cat didn't know that Rachel wanted it that way—no prominence, no attention because of the hydrogen wall or the Symphony.

Still, she had a point. The Seekers of Script were supposedly below Trainees. But they were like career officers, narrow specialists more experienced in deciphering SETI messages, using brute-force methods from cryptology. They assisted Trainees and reported to Librarians.

Rachel reported to a Prefect, a special privilege. Catkejen, at a higher level, now answered to the enigmatic Noughts. All this staff layering the SETI Library had amassed through two centuries of calcification. Sediment, some of it. Rachel avoided those mudlands.

Rachel also dodged the advice. "How's your Nought?"

"Let's say he—uh, it—relishes the cadences of the language."

"Ah! You mean it's an incorrigible windbag." Apparently having no actual sexual organs led to verbal ejaculations instead. Just another gender choice, it seemed.

"Right, downright gushy." Catkejen had changed her hair to tarnished silver but her voice was still of scrap brass. Rachel envied her ability to conform to the Library's Byzantine unspoken styles. Clothes and skin enhancers were the classic methods of competition and display. Men wore Rapunzel hair down to the shoulder blades at the moment. Women had great tangled thickets of hair in the armpits, often displayed in string-shirts. All this, despite the strange blend of decadent excess and harsh asceticism that prevailed in elite Library culture—a huddled refuge in a harsh world that could kill them easily, given a chance. To Rachel this was a special puzzle, comparable to a labyrinthine SETI message.

"I heard they thinned some Trainees last week," Catkejen whispered, glancing around. "No announcement, just—poof!—you notice some are missing."

"Part of the method," Rachel said. "They're headed back Earthside, or going miner." She had hinted to Cat about her strategy of keeping a low one-patch role, so to this she got a curt nod—and a wink.

They had seen this before. Those Trainees of both sexes, or even none, who had gotten by back on Earthside by being pert, pretty, perky—were soon memories. The Librarians batted last.

The Library had begun as a minor academic offshoot, back when there were few SETI messages and none had been well deciphered. By way of rigorous mathematical methods, Artilects, and objective though human minds like the Noughts, it had grown in prestige and influence. Now it was a Lunar citadel where there was a fifteen-year wait for a windowless office.

Rachel said, "I hear some Trainees are planning a demonstration against these abrupt firings."

Another of Catkejen's patented eye-rolls. "I mentioned that rumor to my own Prefect. I got one of her rare laughs. She said, 'Demonstrations never achieve anything—if they did, we wouldn't allow them.' True!"

"Ah. A word to the wise?"

"Look, my nunlike friend—you've got to get style here. Dig into the ramified SETI messages—thousands of 'em, thick as bees—lurking back there in the Vaults. Then see if they relate to any flybys of our or other exploring craft." Catkejen let her exasperation out in darting phrases. "Then put pizzazz into it, next time you get an audience, or get reviewed by some clump of Prefects. Learn the pleasure in dispute, in dialectic, in dazzle. Get some freelance dash, peacock strut, daring hypotheses, knockabout synthesis—and get laid."

Rachel felt her face tighten, struggled to manage a smile. "I'm, you know, wrong time of the—"

"Month? Come on, gal!" Eyes flaring, grin spreading, hands shooting out. "When I'm on my period, I just stand in the shower and watch blood run down my legs into the drain and imagine I am a warrior princess who is standing in the aftermath of a battle, where I murdered all my enemies. Ta-da!"

At the moment Rachel was mostly about cramp diarrhea. Her period was announcing itself, after a full yearlong pause to conserve eggs. Which meant . . . too irritable? Judgment impaired? Maybe stay away from the claustrophobic pod and the dwarf stars?

"You don't want to be in the next culling, my friend."

Rachel allowed herself a thin, uncertain smile. "Maybe they keep me on simply to serve as a warning to others."

5.

The Library reception was taking place on the rampart walk above the Grand Plaza. The setting implied antiquity: vaulted and corbeled ceilings, columns sporting reverse flutings and crowned with a Corinthian elegance millennia old. All shaped from gray fired regolith. In a community that spent most of its time in small rooms with faintly oily air, taking advantage of views was essential for social functions. Crescent Earth was just a sliver, a comma, a single bright eyelash in the star-rich sky.

She looked for her Prefect Masoul, but he was not in the murmuring crowd. *Probably feasting inside on Muscovy duck with pears and greens balsamic,* she thought, succumbing to the Lunar cliché of fixating on food. The Library hierarchy emerged most visibly in what luxuries one could afford. Rumors proposed fragrant, exotic dishes none had ever seen, but thought they scented in the closed air of the Library. To the nose, there were seemingly few secrets. Whatever a Muscovy duck might be, keeping a roasted one a secret seemed impossible. Still, there were ever more rumors about the sealed and secured portions of the Library, where only Prefects or better-ranked Earthers could venture.

A mecha band played its typical *klunketta-klunketta* rhythm, and she found herself among some others of her station, buzzing with talk about Earthside matters. She joined the line for the stand-up banquet and ignored the chat-chat. Above, moon birds looking like paint-splattered sparrows banked and swirled. These had plenty of parrot genes, and others swooped in flocks of sharply elongated eagles; there was even a huge impossibility she called Moby Hawk. Moby squawky-spoke in rhymed couplets, no less.

Animal enhancers were ever-better.

There was sweet-smelling bread made from an unpronounceable root vegetable, thick molasses, something called Mobile hoppin' John, and tart collard greens, plus rich butter from goat milk. She favored the usual pickup food of crickets, bugs, and odd crispy-fried creatures with obscure names, and the obligatory pricey pork and chicken. Proteins galore. Considering, she pitied the vegetarians; most went back Earthside soon enough.

She wandered, not spotting any friends, and into a circle discussing the deaths in the latest human cold-sleep method.

". . . and they all died, within a two-year span," a slim woman said mournfully. "I wish the news would stop inflicting such torture on us."

Torture? Scan the news at your own risk, Rachel thought.

She was a bit tired of the Lunar sophisticates' habit, their narcissism of borrowed tragedy. It came from viewing from afar—or at least far enough—the perpetual disasters on overcrowded Earth. It struck her as inverted empathy: relate some tragedy from the news and express your sad-eyed care, and soon enough, other people's suffering becomes about you. You convey with raised eyebrow or warped lips that you're owed some measure of the deference and compassion that the victims are.

"They knew the risks going in," she said.

The thin woman frowned. "Well, I'm sure, but—"

"And chose to take them. Too bad it failed, but honestly—how likely is it that we mammals, whose sole hibernators are bears and the like, could take decades of cold sleep?"

"Well, they've been working on this for—what, a century?—and I think the scientists know what they're doing." The woman gave Rachel a sharp look that should have stuck several centimeters out of her back.

"Seems not. They all died?"

"Uh, yes. Twenty-five. Some made it to the six-year mark, but none past eight."

"How'd they die?"

"The connectomics scientists say their slowed metabolism just stopped. Wouldn't restart."

A light-haired brown man added with a smack of lips, "The report said when they opened the life chests, there was a distinct smell of porcini risotto. Armpits filled with fungus."

A big laugh. This was enough to disband the group before Rachel got in too deep. But something in the issue tickled her mind. Did a century of trying cold-sleep mean it just wasn't possible for complex animals, including aliens?

If so, no visitors, no crewed starships. Even if civilizations arose and persisted, they could only visit other stars robotically. Then all interstellar contacts were the province of artificial intelligences. . . . A glimmering of an idea. Ancient SETI messages, the Ythri—

Maybe—

"I have noted that you are disobeying," the Prefect Stiles said at her elbow.

"Oh! You startled me." Somehow the Prefect's bald head loomed large out here in the open. *Or maybe it just reminds me of how many dead worlds I've seen.*

"You are spending pod time on old reconnaissance. I will have to vector a report." Not a flicker of emotion. "Vector a report" meant blocking her from becoming a Librarian, maybe forever.

"I have an idea I'm pursuing." Not quite a lie.

A long, slow blink, as if thinking. "I give you three days to stop." Prefect Stiles turned and walked away with the long lope those born on the moon made into a graceful sway.

———

At every stage of her life she'd been reasonable, dutiful. But now a vague intuition made her bat away the advice of her friends, and the everyday world of what people said, of tips and tales, theories and tidbits that might add to the Library's already vast stores of alien messages. The Library had evolved into a factory, producing human minds distended out of all proportion—force-fed facts, as unlucky geese are force-fed corn. The succulent foie gras of such minds was then to be dined on by the Library, digesting alien zeroes and ones into a digital aesthete's wisdom. A Librarian's life, like the goose's comfort, was certainly secondary.

Her ascetic trainers Earthside had been Dionysiac compared to the Prefects. But she was mature now, in her late forties, and nearing the end of her obedient student mode. She understood how, despite her hydrogen wall achievement, she should remain out of the public eye and focus on pod work. But . . . how had the Ythri found her identity?

Instead of worrying, she worked through the latest stellar evolution theories, well buttressed by myriad data links and erudite commentaries.

Astronomers loved their data-mountains, indeed.

A star lived very long if it had a tenth of a solar mass and so a tiny radius—a pygmy, glowering at its close-clustered children planets in sullen reds. So a world in the thin habitable zone of a typical dwarf M star would remain in that zone for tens of billions of years. In essence, such stars lasted so long that the length of habitability became more of a planetary than a stellar issue. If an intelligent species properly managed its environment, it could persist far longer than any around a Sol-like star, which would grow unstable after about ten billion years. A now-welcoming Sol would finally swell to fill a world's sky, baking it. Any dwarf-star civilization might have begun billions of years before fish crawled up a beach on Earth and learned to breathe the rising oxygen in the air. Such societies had to manage their worlds or die out.

Pondering this, she booked pod time again. Prefect Stiles would frown, and she had mere days left.

———————

She knew from her Artilect that the Prefects told the Nought Siloh to check her work. So while her irksome period lasted—famously, far worse than in the supposed good ol' days of monthly menses—she dutifully spent time on the Message inventory. She made little progress, even with the ever-helpful Seekers of Script. Picking tiny feelers of meaning from myriad Messages—some seemingly simple, though many were blizzards of digital chaos—was like trying to hear a moth in a hurricane.

With the deep translation problem came also the flat fact that many Messages were ancient, coding bronzed into memories of dead alien cultures, their beamed hails simple funeral pyres. Many could be solved by a lost-wax method of digital abstraction, but that often yielded cries of despair in alien tongues. These played in her own back-mind with her vexings about the approaching Ythri.

So . . . why did they want her?

No ready answer. To distract, she went deep. Paralleling her gritty planetary exploration pod work with lofty abstract Messages somehow helped. Therapy, in its way.

Some Minds were playful, after being allowed to read the vast store of Earthly literature. One Mind began a session by saying it did not like being interrupted by mere living human Librarians, for then . . .

when the Rudyards cease from Kipling the Bonds forever tippling,
and the Haggards Ride no more, I feel sadly lonely conversing with
a bore.

Rachel laughed at that jest. Minds were bright, though caged. Others pondered darkly about themselves. They knew they were like exotics kept in a zoo, and could rhapsodize about their plight:

We all live as ants in the shadow of mountains of millennia, and
time's sheer mass shades our every word. . . . so talk darts among
somber chasms of ignorance, amid upjuts of painful memory as old
as continents, softening our tongues into ambiguity and guile.

One Message Mind kept all of *Paradise Lost*—one of the longest poems in the English language, more than ten thousand lines—in its mind-vault, unabridged, alongside (supposedly) all of Shakespeare, all of William Blake, huge portions of Philip Larkin and Wallace Stevens, and countless others. A combination of bandwidth and storage capacity that was, by any measure, exceptional. The Mind would disappear into that vast internal library. This Mind was a knockoff of an earlier one, Rachel discovered—SETI plagiarism!—copied by a short-lived culture. This carried on into the Mind's copying Earth lit, as though to send literature and itself on, outward, should some opportunity arise to broadcast, as the Sagittarius had managed. A Prefect termed it "a rabblement of lemmings."

Her period winked out. Sighing, she sought the shelter of Kane's arms. He wanted more than a lighthearted roll in the hay (what an ancient expression!) and she deflected him, as she always had. She was not ready for that yet. Maybe would never be. One benefit of longer life-spans was delaying life curves beyond the mere decades humans had had before.

After a week of work, she got a call to report for review.

6.

The Nought named Siloh frowned, apparently its only expression. "Your performance lags. You and we both preferred to keep you from all prominence, so you are not now hounded, as the aliens approach. But. I suppose insights gathered from your inspection of planetary observations could augment your Message work, yes. But." It stopped, eyeing her. Noughts had intricate adjustments to offset their lack of sexual appetites and apparatus, both physical and mental. They had been developed in the 2280s to give them a rigorous objectivity in translating the Messages. Somehow this had evolved into the 2300s to mean management of the Library itself.

"I assume your 'but' implies that you hold doubts?" She managed a smile with this but the Nought's frown did not budge.

"I solely wish to remind you that such interests are a diversion," Siloh said, drawing out vowels, eyes lidded. "You must prepare for the alien arrival. Given our limited contacts with them, I recommend more physical training. Now."

"Ah, diversions? Perhaps not. I have found some . . . curiosities."

"You will find in working with your Artilect—the Transap one, I see, excellent choice—saying no more than you mean is essential."

"I looked back at a classic case of direct exploration today, Luhman 16. An old flyby, 6.5 light-years out, the nearest L-type dwarf. For a while the third-closest known star to Sol, after the Centauris and poor lonely Barnard's Star. Point is, it's a binary and both stars had planets—a bonanza, but both held remnants of shattered cities, billions of years old."

The Nought sniffed. "Of course."

The obvious rebuff made her bear down. It was easier to act herself into a new way of thinking than to brute-force think her way into a new way of acting. But how to say that?

"There's a pattern here. Dead civilizations around dwarf stars."

Another sniff. "The universe is cruel to the unwise. You are ignoring your essential tasks. Does that seem wise?"

———————

She made herself be systematic. She took a physio-extender that let her work straight through the days remaining. Her pod began to smell of her. Reek, actually.

The dwarf-star planets were marvels, in their way. She had always been impressed by their efficiency at packing hydrogen, the stuff of flammable zeppelins, into such a small space. Some such stars were more than twice as dense as lead. The density of Sol was bubblegum by comparison.

Many were tide-locked, or nearly so. Some had a spin/orbit resonance like Mercury, which rotates three times, every two orbits around Sol. Others were firm-locked and so were split worlds, half warm and half frozen—with a twilight border rich in black and gray forests, with mostly minimal animal life. The best were those that spun lazily in the ruby furnace of their skies, averaging the wine-colored radiance.

There was one system whose sun was but a tarnished penny above a world where three moons played at their races. On other worlds, winds were whips, polishing continents to smooth mausoleums. Such hells of sand gave her itchy flashes as the centuries-old probe explored. She rejected these, and many stony rocks and super-Jovians that circled other burning circles in the sky.

There were even worse. Some planets circled close enough to their star that atmospheric temperatures exceeded the boiling point of water. Clouds of unlikely mixtures of potassium chloride or zinc sulfide lifted high into the atmosphere, yielding a flat, dull spectrum.

Yet even here brightly glowing plumes reminded her of an under-water scene with turquoise-tinted currents. Strange nebulous strands reached out, echoing starfish, giant beings aloft in an atmosphere that would have crushed a dinosaur. If anything lived there, she did not wish to know of it.

––––––––––

She had two more days to comply with the Prefect's orders. But she couldn't. She had gotten more work days from Shilo but ... Some intuition drove her forward. She kept on mining the recon files, expe-riencing them whole-body. Trying to see patterns. Seeking the Ythri world, somewhere.

In her mind swarmed filmy ideas. She slept restlessly, tossing in sweaty sheets—and alone; no social life seemed worth the lost moments. She put off Kane's attentions. She skipped meals and snacked on garlic-flavored fried beetles. Plus slurpy fruit glop with taste-enhancers, an eat-your-peas diet she dutifully used to trim away aging neuro flaws. Plus sacred coffee, of course.

Then back in the pod. The Prefects could have cut off her privileges, but no such order came. Yet.

Among the dwarf stars Earth had explored, or had seen through the lenses coasting out beyond 550 astronomical units, there were some worlds on which fancy sorts of watery membrane learned to think—and made great wet beasts from green crusts and reddish films and fizzing electricity. These were often on warmer, cloudy L-class dwarfs and cooler T-dwarfs, whose atmospheres were clear and sharp.

In cooler stars themselves, the solar corona seethed with creatures like manta rays, coasting—plasma life on a star. But their client planets were even stranger.

A dawn like a gray colloid. She felt it in her pod ... chilly. The dwarf's ruddy glow stirred the world's air like a thick fluid, sending blue streamers through the clotted air, bringing soon enough sharp shafts to bear on black forests below. They already knew, from SETI messages and innumerable probes, both human and alien, some sad truths. Millions of worlds had brimmed with life, true—but like a puzzle with a sole dreary solution, the show ended soon. Ice or fire snuffed out life's promise.

But on living worlds, there was a plenitude of wonders. There was even oxygen—the slow fuse to the explosion of animal life. On Earth around 635 megayears ago, enough oxygen had supported tiny sponges. After 580 million years more, strange creatures as thin as blue crêpes had lived on a lightly oxygenated seafloor. Fifty million years later, vertebrate ancestors glided through warm, oxygen-rich seawater, much as she had done as a girl. So dwarf stars with oxygen-rich children had billions of years of advantage over latecomer Earth.

They used their eons, she saw. Probes sent on photon beams from Earth had dropped into the atmospheres of these planets, in the records of that grand exploring age. These smart packages heard distant calls like screechy toots on a rusty trombone, gut-bucket growls, sighing cries—from creatures that looked as dull and gray as sluggish rutabagas. Then—goodness gracious, great balls of fire! Odd beings who burst into flame at mating season, apparently after passing on their genes— and leaving the stage in hasty crimson blisters.

Her heart jumped like a mullet, quick and hard—just as she recalled seeing the fish in the salty, warm Gulf air where she grew up. *Angels we have heard on high, sweetly singing o'er the plain,* she thought, as she played back the sounds of distant animals she would never see, beyond mere pixels.

Then the entire vibrant world was gone in a sharp instant.

7.

She staggered a bit, going away from the yawning mouth of the pod. Looking back, it seemed indeed like a giant grin that had swallowed her, and now spat her out, altered. The experience had turned her inside out, like a pocket no good for holding much anymore.

Somehow the sensorium had been fuller, more invasive this time.

Smell carried memory, conveyed history. She bore now an after-memory of the shimmering redlands she had seen, somehow trans-morphed into smells, sounds, and textures in her recollected sum of all she had experienced. The pod made that transition across senses, embedding the dry past into the sensual present. The pod was an Artilect and so learned her, too, and each new world had held greater impact, from that. The pod made worlds for her, in fuller and fuller form.

She had seen shattered biospheres, those at one with the dull, the indiscriminate dust. Those who could pour no more into the golden vessel of great song, sent across the eons and light-years. Their Mes-sages might once have sung of alien Euclids who had looked on beauty bare, and so stitched it into Messages of filmy photons, sent oblivious into the great galaxy's night. . . .

Such fools we mortals be. . . .

She stopped for a glass of wine and some snack centipedes, delaying the inevitable. A passing friend gazed into her eyes and asked, "Hey, what's bitin' your bum today?"

Rachel opened her mouth, closed it, and the whole idea she had been seeking came together in that second.

Ask the Messages Repositories for their data on nearer life-bearing planets. Go after what their probes found.

"Shut up," she explained. And went to see the Prefect.

———

A week later, she had a find to show Prefect Masoul. A week of little sleep, but she felt a zip in her stride now as she entered his office.

Her hydrogen wall fame had gotten her around Prefect Stiles's stern censure. Prefect Masoul had worked some diplomat-bureaucrat magic and granted her more time. Back-corridor politics had its advantages.

She'd found older files that gave surprisingly detailed surveys of planets. These ancient repositories were embedded in transmits of Messages from dead societies. These came from robotic radiators, a fashion in interstellar signaling that appeared common among repeating beacons, making their transmissions resemble archaeological layers of Messages.

Rachel said firmly to Masoul and several others present, "Here's what turned up from an old Message. It's basically a reference work. I got it from an autobeacon of a civilization gone silent otherwise. They're just passing on what their robo-explorers discovered, millennia ago." A hand wave.

She let the visuals do the job. "Turned out, this star is a G nine, lots like ours." Golden in hue, luminosity half of Sol's. The world was smaller, surface gravity 0.63 g, with a thinner and drier atmosphere. Air perfectly breathable by humans, with more argon and less nitrogen. Bodies of water, modest seas. The globe was very lovely as it turned against star-crowded night—blue, tawny, rusty-brown, white-clouded. Two little moons skipped in escort.

"I got the biological spectra, too. Its life is chemically similar to Earth. Pictures taken at low altitude and on the ground showed woods, lakes, wide plains rolling toward mountains."

"Terratype, the Astros term it," the Prefect said.

Rachel stepped through the alien Message's images. "The pictures did reveal small towns spread over the two major continents—clusters of buildings, at least, lacking defensive walls or regular streets—hard by big digs that may be mines. I used Artilects trained in this, from our own flyby history."

"In our great Laser Era?"

"Yes indeed!"

Many had forgotten that surge, over two centuries ago. In her opinion, it came from the explosion of human longevity, when people started living well beyond a hundred years. So many had expectations of seeing the results of long-term laser-driven probes, which began firing off diaphanous screens the size of cities. Fast craft to cruise by stars. Confident that they would live to see the returning photos, the wealthy countries spent the gigabucks necessary to do it.

She spoke carefully, voice even and steady as she advanced her own pod-driven views of the many ancient visions she had seen and felt and ruminated upon for days now. "They could identify a variety of cultures, from rural through our modern. Yet invariably, aside from those petty communities, settlements consisted of a few houses standing alone. None closer than ten kilometers apart."

As she said this, images flashed in the air. Tall willowy buildings, some sizable, as befit lower gravity. Large balconies, flat, spreading roofs that shaded the building. Farm fields stretched away, tended by machines dutifully moving along rectangular paths.

"Carnivores in origin, I expect," the Prefect said. "Like our eagles, vultures, smart parrots that can talk." He closeupped the view, going down to the last pixels. "Primitive economies are hunting-fishing-gathering, advanced economies pastoral with farms. Large areas cultivated are probably just to provide fodder for animals. Grains, pastures. They don't have the layout of proper farms—not many vegetables, fruits." He tugged his chin.

Rachel asked, "So this is like our society many centuries ago?"

"I confess to being puzzled as to how these civilized aliens—well, let's say the 'metallurgic' people, at this stage—how they manage it. You need trade, communication, quick exchange of ideas, for that level of technology. And if I read the pictures aright, roads are virtually non-existent, see?" He made the image vector out, connections highlighted in yellow. "Stone tracks between towns and mines. Docks for barges, ships—confound it, water transportation is insufficient."

"Pack animals, maybe?" she suggested.

"Too slow," he said. "They must have electromagnetics. You don't get progressive cultures when months must pass before the few individuals capable of originality can hear from each other. The chances are they never will."

Rachel froze an image as it moved. "How about—this?"

A fleet of slow gray torpedoes drifted across florid plains. "Balloon transport in low gravity," the Prefect said. "And those islands with large gantries"—he expanded the view to show towers, several with large tubes on their platforms—"they have orbiting capabilities."

Rachel had not done enough deep surveying of the data, she saw. The Prefect had a superior instinct for this, probably from his deep past; rumor had it he was well over two centuries old.

She decided to nail her point, so stood tall, firm, and said, "I think this is where the Ythri come from."

The Prefect and his assistants rustled, startled. One woman's eyes bulged in a boogah-woogah way.

Rachel pressed on. "I deduced from the Message that contained these survey scans that the Message is already a millennium old. The space program we see here is at an early stage—they're using old-fashioned rockets, no orbital tower. By now they could easily have explored their entire solar system, found whatever assets are there."

"I had so gathered." A wry smile. "Good work."

"Here's the clincher, honorable sir. This world is over four hundred light-years away."

"Ah. So—"

"We have learned how to keep people in cryo-preservation after death for a few years, decades, hoping for centuries. Revival is hard. Any Ythri ship would have to keep them suspended for many centuries. That seems nearly impossible, while their starship came toward us, at maybe a tenth of light speed—a very big, long-term project."

"And?"

She could see by his smile he knew her conclusion, had been patiently waiting for her to make it. "They must have come through a wormhole."

"You make an excellent, indirect case."

"So there's a wormhole mouth somewhere near or in our solar system, too. They came that way. They're keeping it secret."

"Plausible. It is their major asset, their bargaining chip."

"We have to find out where it is."

For a moment the amused pedantry dropped from his manner. "Well," he said, "we'll see," which struck her in that moment as the grandest sentence that any language can own.

8.

She slept away most of the next day. Kane gave her a pleasure-jolt—waking her, feeding her, loving her to distraction, letting her doze off—and much later she arose fresh, awakened to the chimes of her call-alarm.

It was Prefect Masoul, summoning her to an enclosure room, so she hurried over. He sat at the middle and patted a seat next to him—the only two in the room. On the walls was a sharp display of—the aliens.

"They're in their orbiting habitat sphere, all tested out. I thought I would relay the exobio team findings, discuss, as we watch. Match that with your idea of what their home world is—and where."

"Ah, good," was all she could manage, still a tad dreamy.

The viewpoint shifted as the alien Ythri flew in zero-g amid a leafy wealth of limbs, leaves, and sky. "The team re-created their planet's vegetation, using what you turned up from that ancient flyover data. Got it done in those biotanks—in one day! This biosphere is four hundred meters across."

"So they agree, that world is where they came from?"

"They do so acknowledge, though yield no more about it. They are closemouthed."

"What are the diplomats—"

"No bureaucrat interference, not now. The Council has yielded to we scientists. The Ythri insisted. That's why they're orbiting over our heads right now."

"Above the orbital spinner? I thought they—"

"Will descend, soon enough. They are coming here. It seems our conjecture was correct."

"You mean our guesses—"

"Yours, mostly. Indeed, the Ythri know of you because their robo-probes witnessed the Jovian Solution. Though your name was not attached—Library policy, as always—they somehow interrogated our systems here and Earthside—and so discovered your name, Rachel."

"I still don't—"

"Nor do I. Still, we can watch their majestic flights while I regale you with the physio-bio insights we now know."

He spoke as the creatures went by in an orderly, V-shaped flock. Rachel had a hard time keeping up. Details piled on interpretations stacked on guesswork galore. The combined visual and talk filled in as she watched, integrated—entranced. *Real live aliens. Wowser!*

The Ythris massed as high as thirty kilos. Yet they showed great lifting strength under the centrifugal gravs of the cylindrical ship they flew, at a lesser g, but still—they were marvelously strong. Hands? The original talons, modified for manipulating. Feet? Those hands on the ends of the wings—perhaps started as claws, a juvenile feature that had persisted and developed, just as man's large head and sparse hair had derived from the juvenile or fetal ape. The forepart of the wing skeleton had a humerus, radius, and ulna, much as in Earthly birds—convergent evolution. These parts locked together in flight. Aground, when the wing was folded downward, they produced a "knee" joint. Bones grew from their base to make the claw-foot. Three fused digits, immensely lengthened, swept backward to brace the rest of that tremendous wing. That did, when desired, give additional support on the surface.

To rise, the Ythrians usually did a handstand during the initial upstroke. It took less than a second.

Then came video of them in a centrifugal grav chamber. Oh yes, they were slow and awkward afoot. The Prefect sighed at these sights. Rachel felt elated and saw that these sights fulfilled a hope none in the Library had expressed, but surely all shared: real live aliens.

The Prefect said softly, "Big and beweaponed, instantly ready to mount the wind, they need fear no beast of prey. Carnivores. Hunt in flocks. Farm only to get grain. They feed that lot to animals they then hunt and devour. Hence they maintain civilization without the need to crowd together in cities. Their townspeople are mostly wing-clipped criminals and slaves—or so they say. Today their wiser heads hope robots will end the need for that." She had a thousand questions, but watching the Ythris move was more fascinating as Masoul went on, clearly enjoying his insights. Prefects were like professors that way.

"You ask where the power comes from to swing this hugeness through the sky? Oxidation of food, what else? In their enclosure we found the limiting factor to be the oxygen supply. A molecule in their blood can carry more than our hemoglobin does. The Ythrian has lungs, a passive system resembling ours. In addition he has his super-charger, evolved from the gills of an amphibian-like ancestor, which works in bellows fashion, the flight muscles connecting directly with the bloodstream. Those air-intake organs let him or her burn fuel as fast as necessary."

"Hence the demand of each household for a great hunting or ranching area?" she ventured.

The Prefect nodded. "The social types say Ythri are as fundamentally territorial as we are fundamentally sexual, and we'd better bear that in mind. They're carnivorous, aside from various sweet fruits. Carnivores require larger regions per individual than herbivores or omnivores do, in spite of the fact that meat has more calories and protein per kilo than most vegetable matter."

Rachel looked dubious. "You—ah, they—think we should reason from origins to the present? Even though—"

"Consider how each antelope needs a certain amount of space, and how many antelope are needed to maintain a pride of lions. Earthers who call themselves Xenoists have written thousands of papers on the correlations between diet and genotypical personality, garnered from our Library translations."

Rachel was still skeptical. She shook her head doubtfully.

"They missed the possibility of a race like the Ythrians, whose extreme territoriality and individualism—with the consequences to governments, mores, arts, faiths, and souls—come from the extreme appetite of the body."

She wondered at this angle, so asked, "You're hinting at . . . ?"

"You need to get more exercise. They will expect you to conform to their flock social dynamics."

"Which means . . . ?"

The Prefect allowed himself a thin smile. "That shall be revealed. Earthside loves its secrets."

———————

Rachel disliked the gym. The same air had hung for months in the windowless volume, absorbing the smells of human sweat and breath, a concoction smell like roasted peanuts and beer, perfume and bay rum and hair oil and tired feet. A social researcher with a good nose could have written a PhD thesis about that air. But she did her workouts and swims and even simple one-handed push-ups, a hundred at a time. She huffed and puffed and sweated and slept and wondered. . . . Then came the Ythri.

PART 7

BLOODPRIDE

The biggest mistake is being too afraid of making one.

—ELBERT HUBBARD

1.

She smelled the aliens coming.

They were above her as she got caught in a downdraft. She tumbled. The draft brought their pungent odor—rank, feathery, ripe, strange. She fought against the current pushing her down, arms churning, her legs kicking with their ailerons. The hinged flaps fluttered as she tried to control her banking, but she rolled, too, getting dizzy—and the ground was coming up fast. Too fast.

Rachel had thought she was a reasonably good flyer, but now she regretted telling anyone about her hobby. Maybe a hundred meters to go below her, and she was too far from the fusor-warmed pink walls where the updrafts flowed. What was that saying?—*Flying is the art of falling and missing the ground. . . .*

She heard the aliens flap down the wind, calling out their air songs, their scent getting riper—and then they were flashing around her like a singing whirlwind.

What could a Ythri do—grab her? Then they would both fall.

The answer came suddenly. Wings fully spread, the one called Fraq swept close and threw a gossamer strand around her helmet cowling. He pulled. As it snapped straight it jerked her head back, caught. Fraq worked upward and toward the wall. The rope tugged her after him as she thrust hard with her arms, letting her foot flaps straighten along her legs. They stopped fluttering. Sharp cries came from the other Ythri. She was under tow.

Humiliating, but better than a snapped neck any day.

Fraq was heading up and over, angling toward the speckled void walls. That gave Rachel a chance to stare at him, which she couldn't politely do in the formal, diplomatic sessions she had attended to meet the Ythri. His keelbone jutted beneath a strong neck like a ship's prow. The towline wrapped around the heavily muscled shoulders. Fraq's head was blunt-nosed and without external ears. As he turned his head to bark an order to her—"Hold steady offwind!"—she saw that when the Ythri was in full labored flight, the mouth had flushed lips, cherry red. Two big golden eyes stabbed sidewise, checking clearance from the others flapping above, who were blocking the downdraft.

His crest of black-tipped white plumage rose stiffly above, a control surface he could tilt—and protection for the bulging skull, she guessed. The fan-shaped tail flexed with white streamers among gray fan feathers. Fraq's lean body was mahogany that reddened along the naked legs.

His yellow claws out at the wingtips made palms that canted for lift.

Beautiful, elegant.

The pink wall was close now, and she felt the caress of the updraft winds. Fraq shouted, "Go!" and somehow with a toss of his head sent a wave down the towline that slipped it from her helmet. Smart birds knew a lot of tricks. She was free.

Still she dropped, catching the wind on her arm wings. It would be even more humiliating to tumble now. She strained hard, flexed her body, thrust—and got stable. The aliens were hovering now, watching her, and she had damn well better get this right. She tilted her ailerons and steadied, starting to rise in the warm flow.

From below she saw each one had three slits in parallel on the body, flared to take in air. These resembled gills and shone bright pink, bloodrich. As their wings lifted, she saw the slits drawn wide, three thin mouths yawning. As their elegant downstrokes began, that action forced the gills shut. Flying, breathing machines.

Masoul had been right. The Ythrians had big barrel lungs, a passive system resembling humans'. Their secret lay in those supercharger
gills, probably evolved from some amphibian-like ancestor. Those livid
mouths worked in heaving, bellows fashion as the flight muscles con-
tracted and big arteries sucked the air directly into the bloodstream.
Higher-air-intake organs let them burn their fuel as fast as necessary.
But to see it alive, in majestic flight—!

Rachel sighed and thought, *Smart birds. I wonder how it feels to be
so deeply alive. . . .*

She concentrated on funneling down through the updraft layer rising along the walls. Arrowing down against the warm breezes from the
vents below, she skimmed off to land with some redeeming grace on a
takeoff platform. She looked up and the Ythrians were spiraling down,
taking their time, still watching her. Had she proved herself in alien
eyes? Hard to read those big, gold-flecked spheres, with bony ridges
above them but not eyebrows.

She wanted to look unconcerned, so she gazed up at the view,
hands on hips. This was the big, newest void, honed with an antibaryon
fusor burst that rendered rock to plasma and lava, then vented the hot
gruel through the top knothole. Media had showed all humanity the
Lunar volcano show, as the ruddy rock flowed with liquid grace above
the Lunar highlands, jetting into space in rosy filaments. Some grabby
robo devices had caught it to shape habitats on the surface; the voids
were an industrial miracle with real profits to be had. The fusor erup-
tion had left behind this oblate spheroid twenty kilometers high and
five wide, cooling quickly into a hollow pink egg.

Lunar subsurface sculpture was getting so adroit the engineers
could shape any space you wanted. Rumors circulated that some rich
magnate had ordered up a pyramid-shaped space, but even a fusor
couldn't do that. This big void was for flying, a unique Lunar pleasure
for poor ground-bound primates. Hundreds of people were winging
it as she looked up, most of them watching the aliens do astonishing
feats. Fraq came by, flying upside down with effortless grace, eyeing her
on the ground as he shot across the void.

Those eyes—piercing, even at this distance. His golden-brown
feathers covered but did not conceal the rippling muscle. Or that he

was male. Their flimsy robes flapped tantalizingly from the carry harness they wore. The Ythri could lock the joints of their limbs at will,
and on Luna, 0.17 gravs, seemed to defy gravity's existence for long,
leisurely arcs. Their forewings—much like Earth birds—had humerus,
radius, and ulna; these locked together in flight, giving the Ythris a
look of utter unconcern as they did the impossible.

An admirable addition to the Library's category *Sapientia*, smart
aliens, yes. But she reminded herself that Earthly birds' sexual organs
shrivel outside their reproductive times, a process called involuting. *But
these aren't birds, they're aliens. Librarians must scrupulously avoid category
errors. . . .*

The flock descended with high, barking cries and fluttering tail
feathers. All the Ythri fanned their magnificent six-meter wings and
landed with a final, artful pause before alighting. She consoled herself with how clumsy they were on ground. Slow and awkward afoot,
shorter than Rachel, yet Fraq's head had a regal air. The ivory crest riff
helped, looking like the defiant ridge of an ancient Roman helmet.
Plus, it rippled with colors as feathers danced.

Still, up close and walking, she could see that Fraq's imposing body
was mostly feathers and his wing-arms had light, hollow bones. The
Ythri had spidery, kitelike skeletons anchoring thin flesh. Fraq stood
out with his elegant muscles and tawny feather-coat, ruffling from his
smooth flight. The flying captain of a starship . . .

Earth birds had long ago lightened their burden, permitting a little
more brain, by changing jaws to beaks. Not the Ythris. They sported the
jaws and sharp teeth of dominant predators. They feared nothing. And
they had come across the light-years through the wormhole humans
still did not formally know of. Earther diplomats had demanded that
Librarians not mention the subject—but keep their ears cocked for
clues, yes.

"Thank you," Rachel said as Fraq approached with his lurching
gait. "I might have recovered in time—"

"You not. Still I admired your daring."

"I haven't tried this void before, don't know its currents."

"Dirts know not the airs, it sings not in their bones," Fraq said,
golden eyes so intense she felt their pressure like a force.

Dirts meant ground-dwellers, yes. The new translation software was so fast and able she could sense no pause between the movements of his still bloodrich red lips and the voice that sounded in her ear. Of course it came to her electromagnetically, swamping the Ythri words that swam though the air like slippery song.

"We thank you for saving our assistant," Prefect Masoul said in a calm, mild tone at her elbow. "Now may we proceed?"

"We grant substance," Fraq said, his wings held back so he could make something that reminded her of a bow. But he bowed to her, not to the Prefect, whose face tightened. The other Ythris made the same abrupt bowing gesture, head crests nodding, and formed a crescent behind Fraq. So this had worked after all. Early on, the Ythri had made it clear that those who could not fly were subspecies, unworthy. So it had fallen to Rachel to prove humans at least a bit commendable. She smiled; Earthers would of course not be such. So negotiations would have to come through Luna. Few seemed to realize this, as yet.

She nodded as the Prefect said ponderously, irked, "In truth, surely. Let us unfold our stories and . . . negotiate."

2.

The wormhole's position was still the big secret. Based on fragments from sundry Messages, some thought aliens had come through wormholes, a network that was legend but that many Librarians doubted actually existed. If any aliens had come through a solar system wormhole, they had carefully blurred their tracks. The civilizations that communicated with microwaves or lancing laser beams or maybe wormholes did not give away secrets, especially where the wormhole mouths might be. The SETI Library was under enormous pressure to find its location. The Ythri had deftly disguised their deceleration plume and evaded any discussion of that. Negotiation seemed the only path.

So when the Ythri had demanded a ritual flight before negotiations, the Library sought out Rachel. She had flown often in the smaller voids fusion-dug deep in the Lunar volcanic masses; few Librarians—mostly lazy types—had ever even tied on the arm wings, so . . .

She breathed a sigh of relief as they mag-elevatored up some dozens of kilometers and then settled in the diplomacy room of the SETI Library. Fraq got his flock in order in a long arc around the table, but only after the humans sat. The just-printed chairs gave ample space for their wings. Fraq took a position at the center of their arc, pointedly sitting opposite Rachel, not the Prefect. Rachel suppressed a smile. How pleasant, to see a perplexed Prefect.

"Ah, um." Masoul frowned, then got right to the point. "What do you seek?"

Fraq said, "Bloodpride requires we undertake this ancient task. Thanks to your submitting to concordance ritual, we can now tell true. You are dirt-huggers but worthy of station, thus can help us with our search."

"We fly in sympathy," the Prefect answered. Rachel saw that the Prefect had learned this ritual from the translator team. Mutual gestures were essential in social intelligences. But with these carnivore aliens, the hard decisions came from the top. Fraq seemed to be in charge, but it was hard to tell.

She wondered if her being female mattered. Maybe not. So she said while the Prefect conferred with the translators, "What are you looking for?"

"The legacy ark," Fraq said immediately with no diplomatic phrases. His big sharp eyes focused intently and moved swiftly to watch all the faces in the room—like an eagle high in the wind, she thought. "It came here before your species emerged. Many millions of your orbital cycles before."

"We are used to such time scales at the SETI Library."

"We have beamed you before, but got no response," Fraq said.

"Only lately have we come to prosperity," a Prefect underling ventured. "But we may know of your signals. Much we have received in the past we did not then comprehend."

"Permit us to unfold our history, then."

The tale emerged under close questioning. The Ythri had images as well, sweeping in a subtly strange majesty.

The Ythris said they knew of an earlier alien civilization that had used a wormhole to the Sol region, after eons of neglect. Those experiments had sent mass down through the wormhole network, and one had passed momentarily through the center of a star. Wormhole exits could sink into stars, yet survive. This one had passed a fiery mass from the star into other wormhole routes, for the system was complexly interwoven. The flaring plasma came out at the exit near Fraq's world. The avians had seen it—the telltale crimson burst of violent plasma lighting their sky, tracing out the mouth's position. A revelation. So they'd built a spacefaring capability to reach it, considerably far out in their own system, in the range of Pluto's distance from Earth. That had taken centuries.

The Ythris had previously gone through their own troubles—long eras of decline caused by resource losses. One such was as Earth had suffered in the fossil fuel overshoot, amid a terrible era of warming air and biting acid oceans. These similar events had hobbled mankind and the Ythri alike.

Far back in their history, in their founding tragedy, they had experienced some sort of biological catastrophe that had nearly driven the Ythri to extinction. More recently, in their first industrial age, the Ythri had suffered metals loss, since vital rare earths and ores were scanty in their planetary crust. Recovering, they had resolved to harvest fresh supplies from their own asteroid belt. As had humans.

After all those millennia of suffering had come the slow Ythri revival. Through the long centuries of poverty they'd lost much of their historical legacy. Cities burned or collapsed in hardship, and with them their libraries. Especially they did not know any longer where the wormhole mouth was in their sky. But now they did have a hard-won, simple interplanetary civilization. When the jetting solar plasma marked the way, they could fly to where the virulent plasma glow told them the ancient wormhole mouth was. Their greatest lost heritage still orbited unused at the edges of their solar system, deep in the cold vaults of time.

"This is our destiny, a bloodpride age-old," Fraq said solemnly. "We learned much of the wormhole network past, as well, in stacked addings."

Now they could pursue an ancient goal—finding the Ark of Meaning launched by a primeval civilization, the Furians. The earlier Ythri culture had heard of it in the dying messages sent out in microwave—an attempt to pass on the genetic roots of life around a forlorn world now gone forever, devoured by the expansion of its sun into its red-giant phase. That planet had fried, then been swallowed up in its last vast agony, by the plasma halo that wrapped it in a glowing funeral shroud.

"They launched many ships," Fraq said. "Your system was blessed to receive one, long before your kind evolved."

"So one is here?" Rachel asked, interrupting Fraq's long tale. The Prefect frowned, stayed silent at her impoliteness.

"Bloodpride demands it," Fraq said. "Our foremothers said to find the Ark was a Prime Need for life itself—to save a legacy of another evolution."

"Then it's like our SETI Library," Rachel said. "Continuity with the long past. To understand what could be in our future."

"You do not naturally fly," Fraq said. "But you ken the deep, long truths."

"Perhaps we can share where this Ark might be?" the Prefect said.

"If you take us there, assuredly," Fraq said. "Our ship cannot manage such a large seeking hunting vessel."

"Why?" the Prefect asked.

"We fear it."

3.

Decades had passed, she knew, since this stone-faced Prefect had worked with the cryofiles. Rachel had spent years fathoming the shadowy labyrinths of those data-forests.

The SETI Library held all transmissions received from the Galactic Complex. That host of innumerable societies had largely flourished long before humanity was born on the dusty plains of Africa. Within those multidimensional databases, Rachel customarily spent her days. After the initial Ythri arrival, she had immersed herself in the Library. The SETI files were a bewildering, largely impenetrable resource. The grandest possible intellectual scrap heap, she sometimes thought. But it could yield priceless ore.

Now that they knew where the Ythri star was, she found the earlier Ythri signals from records from the Long Now Cave. These were spectral data of irregular "pulsars" seen in the 2100s and not again. Brief, compressed, they repeated only a few times. Astronomers had assumed these were some kind of errant pulsars. Wrong. She found they were in fact SETI signals from the Ythri, hundreds of light-years away. These flashes around 10 GHz were attempts to reach Earth, assuming a tech civilization might be there, based on the Ythri detection of the ozone line in our atmosphere. These were not understood during the decades following the Age of Appetite, when no one had puzzled out the economics of SETI contact, and so did not realize that short bursts were far more efficient as attention-getting signals. The smart strategy was to send lighthouse pulses, catch the attention of emerging societies, and direct them to a much lower power signal that carried detailed messages. Nobody in the slowly collapsing decades of the late 2000s and all of the 2100s caught on. Nor could they remotely afford to reply. The whole of humanity was putting out fires, often literally. Still, in the middle decades of the 2000s Earth had sent "slow boat" solar sails out into the Oort cloud, bound for Centauri and beyond. Making close solar passes in "sundiver" mode got them up to 500 or 600 kilometers per second, a thousandth of the speed of light. In thousands of years they could arrive at stars, after dutifully passing data on interstellar space back to Earth. Most of these were still on the way, forlorn robot voyagers long outdated in their very mission.

But the Furians, as Fraq termed them, had thought on even longer perspectives before humans evolved. Rachel researched Fraq's tale, and found fragments that implied the Ark story made sense.

The deeply ancient Furian civilization had reached its end as their sun left the main sequence and became a red giant, its luminosity rising by a factor of a thousand. The swelling ruddy sphere doomed their world, but also brimmed with photons, a rich launcher for Furian solar sails. That dropped the time for an interstellar transit down to centuries. Sailcraft wouldn't last forever in transit, when they might smack into a random rock. Best to keep the sailing time low.

But how could the craft slow down when they arrived? Their light sails would be nearly useless for getting captured into the gravity well of a main-sequence star, with its puny sunlight. A magnetic sail, braking on the solar wind, could help, but not nearly enough. Without something more, the Arks the dying Furian world sent out would simply blow by their target stars. The Furians, Fraq said, had identified stars with circling worlds known to have working biospheres, but that gave forth no SETI signals, no leakage of artificial emissions, nothing. Someday they might harbor intelligence, and the Arks could carry the life lore of the long-dead Furians down to the next generation of life in the galaxy. A cultural and biological legacy. Better than a funeral pyre, or a repeating microwave robo-message touting Furian art and culture and religion to the cold stars.

The Furians knew that most stars are members of binary or multiple systems. Their Arks targeted binary systems with a red giant and a widely separated dwarf star. Ark sail vessels could use the red giant's intense luminosity to decelerate, then sail on to the planetary system of the dwarf.

So . . . why would one Ark come here?

Librarians don't just rely on hearsay; they check. Rachel surveyed Sol's neighborhood, far back in time.

She looked at red giant/dwarf star binaries within a hundred light-years of Sol. There were four. Beta Aquila had a dwarf companion roughly 150 AU from the star. Astronomers had found in the 2100s that it had no planetary companions the size of Earth with working biospheres. The other three red giants—Epsilon Cygnus, Aldebaran, and Theta Ursa Major—also had no life-bearing worlds orbiting the red giants or the giants' companion stars, as shown by looking at their atmospheric chemistries. So these were not good prospects for the dying Furian world. Apparently such life-bearing pairs were unlikely.

The Furians' star was a bit more than a hundred light-years from Sol. So the Furians looked for happy coincidences instead.

Rachel shook her head in wonder. The Furians were smart. Roughly every 100,000 years, random orbital motions made stars drift by within two light-years of Sol. By chance, a red giant was a few light-years from Sol when the Furians launched their Ark sails. So they took advantage, she guessed, of the coincidence. It checked out with the astro simulations she ran, using teams of astro-experts from the Library and elsewhere, even Earthers. About four million years ago, a red giant had passed by in stately splendor, lighting with a ruddy glow the sky of an Earth busily evolving mammals. Small primates scuttled then, beneath this glowing ember in the night, trying to stay alive. Perhaps some of them had puzzled at the lights in that dark celestial bowl as the Furian probe made its passage, braking around the red giant. Then it set sail for the biosphere the Furians knew orbited the ordinary yellow dwarf star two light-years away, Sol. The passage time at lower velocities would be dozens of centuries, but the Ark had time to play out its slow logic.

Fraq had implied that an Ark ship had entered the solar system and, following instruction from a Furian society that had long before died on their burning world, taken up orbit. What would stimulate it to activity again?

Fraq thought the Ark awaited a visit. Only an interplanetary civilization could reach it and understand its genetic heritage. The Ark orbited somewhere near Sol, awaiting a knock at its door.

The Ythris wanted to go there, harvest the heritage. With help from the evolved primates, and their SETI Library. Without mentioning at all the wormhole that had brought the Ythri here . . .

What had her mother used to say? *Adventure means opportunity. Sure, Mom.*

4.

The Lunavator Bolo was running often and not fully booked, good. But they had to wait for the synchronous connection to the high-velocity Flinger. And Fraq wanted to hunt. So . . . they wanted her to join in. More diplomatic social niceties, and for Rachel a command performance, courtesy of the Prefect.

"You must hunt with them," Prefect Stiles said blandly. "They request it."

"I nearly broke my neck last time."

"You exaggerate. In any case, I instructed you to practice."

"Practice flying, sport, sure—that was fun. But . . . these are smart birds! Evolved to fly. They made me look like a clumsy bumblebee among eagles. And hunting? How?"

A slow blink. "In the Verdant Void, of course. We have stocked it with animals that we believe will appeal to the Ythri instincts. They are carnivores and enjoy the sport of getting their own game."

"I'm a vegetarian."

"I don't recall seeing that in your file."

"I'm a recent convert."

Did his eyes narrow by a millimeter? "How recently?"

Ten seconds ago, she thought, but said, "Some time now."

"That is of no matter. You will not have to eat what you help them catch."

How would you know, Freezeface? Have you hunted with them? Do they even cook their prey first? "I will do my best."

He did not bother to smile. Indeed, she could not recall that he ever had. "Excellent."

5.

Fraq had taken perch some considerable distance from her and the other Ythris. They all chose perches in the spire trees that grew near the void walls, facing the deep kilometers of forest just below. When she gazed toward him he looked away quite deliberately. That fit the background inferences the translators had fed Rachel. Ythris were solitary types. They flocked but did not mingle.

There was a certain austere majesty to that. Fraq yawned his jaws widely and sent a long, howling call. Ythris echoed it, clashing their claw-hands together in a savage applause. They wore little clothing beyond weapon belts and genital covers, for feathers guided their flight. In their preparing moments before, she had seen and understood them—grooming, preening, trembling with hot-eyed desire for the hunt. Ythri were moving appetites.

Their evolution said so. They had emerged from a long drought on their largest continent, forcing the ancestors from deep forests out onto savannahs. They grew larger and sharpened their hunting skills, forming groups that drove their solitary natures toward social skills. Flocks took down big herbivores, cooked them to juicy richness, flew loads of that back to nests, sturdy tree sites built to ward off other predators—especially a particularly nasty, enormous snake species that used camouflage on the approach in trees, and had evolved pack attacks, too. In lower-than-Earth grav, snakes could do remarkably agile tricks against incoming birds. These figured large in the Ythri mythos of horror.

That in turn had made the Ythri improve their ground locomotion. They'd evolved claws into tool-making hands, though they never lost their sharp, hooked nails. So the Ythri had evolved extreme territoriality and individualism, with social cohesion when needed. Thus had their carnivore appetites shaped their society.

So, she guessed, Fraq and his other Ythri expressed in their beautiful golden-brown feathers the itchy tensions that came to them while in close association. Even a kilometers-wide void was too tight for them. They yearned for open, infinite sky. Luna had none. Their feathers riffled with jittering waves. Zooming in a small craft, slipping through a narrow wormhole, confronting humans in confined spaces—these were fresh challenges, driving uneasy stresses.

She had to admit, Fraq was an admirable though strange male, proud and aloof. And those eyes . . .

For this event the Library had leased the Verdant Void exclusively and filled its dense forests with animals, many brought especially from Earth. (Thriftily, the Library had also discreetly posted microcameras throughout, and had already sold the media rights for more than the void lease cost.) The translators, who studied Ythri culture as rendered in conversations and a few grudgingly given texts—Earthside xenoists, sundry savants—all advised not to make it easy for the Ythri. This was the central "sport" of the Ythri life, as well as their food source. They'd risen to civilization not through agriculture but through managing vast populations of roaming, grazing animals, kept in the enormous forests and hunted daily—a complex herder society. All their culture focused on pursuit, stalking, attack, cooking, and feasting—the intense code of "bloodpride." If they inferred that the prey here was being staked for easy plucking, or was tame, the aliens might well take grave offense.

Fraq sang forth again from his booming lungs, this time in Anglish, for her benefit. "No few be the winds that blow on our souls! Maychance our technics bring to bear! Stiffly upwind we go a-wing!"

More claw-clashing and hooting big-lung calls. The Ythri females added skittering grace notes, Rachel noted, flouncing their bright plumages. She guessed they were probably challenging the males to do

better than they. The battle of the sexes was a galactic-scale universal.
Or perhaps more like a dance.

The hooting Ythri cries now steamed with energy. Eyeing her companions, Rachel checked her own gear and wondered what it would be
like to have feathers she could arch and bunch into control surfaces,
the better to master the vagrant winds. The void managers had driven
up the air circulation, turning the breeze into a near-gale, moist and
muscular.

Into the brawling air, Fraq sheared off his perch at a steep angle.
He opened to his full five-meter wingspan and floated without labor.
Rachel took a breath of the thick, sweet air and leaped after him, arms
opening to embrace the updraft with her wings.

The Library had set the atmospheric pressure higher to give Rachel
a bit of help keeping aloft. The rich green canopy had breaks and corridors that funneled winds, creating turbulence and even vortexes, driven
by the updrafts that rimmed the void and the descending currents
that dove down at the center. A side effect—unavoidable, the Prefect
Masoul had assured her with lofty tones—was increased vapor density, which meant . . . clouds. A gray puffball glided up from the distant
floor, getting darker as it rose and droplets condensed.

Lunar rain! And Rachel was swooping into it, following Fraq. He
was already hundreds of meters ahead, swooping in a V search pattern with other Ythris. She was playing catch-up in every turn they
made, surveying the canopy. Some Ythri dove down in long swoops to
peer under the broad, stretching branches of the tall trees. There was
maneuver space for them because, under Lunar grav, the Earthly trees
had shot up, many of them a hundred meters tall. Give life opportunities and it seizes them.

Something seized her, then—a vortex. She tumbled, turned her
ankle flaps, got back in line to cut across the turbulence. A Ythri female
nearby, making a return swoop, looked at her oddly, mouth wide, and
she saw that the tongue and palate were purple. A hunting sign?

Here came the gray cloud. She angled in, rising, and suddenly droplets washed over her. Fat droplets! Within moments, flying blind in the
gray mist, she could feel herself gain weight as rivulets ran along her
back. When she popped out into the shafts of light, she was above the

canopy and Ythri were angling below the treetops. She coasted, watching, and when a clearing came she made herself dive lower, scooting under the dense branches.

Faster than she liked . . .

Still fifty meters above the ground, she watched the Ythri throng down on—wild pigs! The animals snarled up at the immense birds and the Ythri fell upon them with glad cries. Claws sank deep into the boar. The slaughter brought whooping calls as the sky predators savaged a dozen pigs within minutes. She had never seen anything like it.

Fraq rose from the bloody ground, jumping into the air effortlessly. He shot up to fly parallel to her circling. "Like stump legs, these are!" he shouted, and she supposed his twisted mouth bespoke fun. "Come!"

He veered away, and she labored to follow. Soon they came out onto a grassy plain and Fraq bellowed with obvious joy: "Sugarmeat!"

He dived immediately at a group of kangaroos. She zoomed over the killing, as Fraq sprang from one to the next, expertly slicing their throats with his claws as they turned to flee. He caught each at the top of the hop. The roos fell dead, legs still kicking. Blood stained the ground.

Rachel let her left wing drag to double back to see more and—it caught on a branch. Her "Uh!" made Fraq look up as she tumbled in a slow, stupid gyre—and smacked down hard on her left shoulder.

Sitting up, she was sure Fraq was laughing, a high booming cackle no human had heard before.

Her inboards told her no bones were broken, but her shoulder sure as hell hurt. Nearly as much as her pride.

6.

The Lunavator Bolo dropped down the black sky for them.

The grappler looked like a long cable plunging straight down vertically from the starscape, jaws yawning. Its tip speed at the grab platform was exactly zero, she knew, but Rachel braced herself for the yank.

It was a heavy load to haul. The Ythris were in the craft they had flown in on from the wormhole, in its own big chamber. The entire human vehicle held Rachel, Prefect Stiles, and staff, plus the booster crew, a complete interplanetary spacecraft ready to fly. Here it came— *snap*, and they were aloft, zooming up into the dead-black Lunar sky.

She watched the silvery ground rush away and then saw the latest comet head slide up from the horizon. It seethed with fogs, all captured by a gossamer envelope. Kilometers across and managed by robots, it glowed under sunlight focused by silvery mirrors. Water, food, fuel— the key to mastering the inner solar system lay in dropping iceteroids down the grav gradient, sliding them into useful orbits, and sucking them dry. Luna needed about one comet head a week these days, a burgeoning world.

They arced up into the black under an easy half a grav acceleration.

Rachel had been a Lunatic long enough to notice the strain. The Lunavator was a rotating bolo that touched down at the launch port exactly the same way every time, a classical mechanics milk run.

Best to rest and not think too much about the high-wire handoffs involved.

She let herself drowse, thinking about the still mysterious Ythri motives, until the Prefect said at her elbow, "I wish I knew more about what they plan."

This was unusually revealing. "Um, why?"

The Prefect allowed himself a frown. "They say this Ark is a legacy they want to 'harvest' but . . . somehow, it's connected to their own history."

"Maybe one visited them?"

"Then why would they need this one?"

"They're hunters."

"With long memories, apparently."

"They insisted on bringing their own ship, too. . . ." she prompted.

"It makes sense. The ship is very small and they say it fits their physio needs. All they took aboard were the basics: volatiles, air, food."

"Which means they could scoot out, jump through the wormhole, wherever it is, and be gone with whatever they get from the Ark."

The Prefect gave a small eye-twitch. "We have thought of that, yes."

"And taken measures . . ."

"Yes." He would say no more.

The Bolo central tether facility was a big captured asteroid, massive enough to prevent payloads from stealing too much energy and thereby lowering the Bolo orbit. The Lunavator rotated in the same direction as its orbit, precisely so that the velocity of each Bolo end's tip equaled the orbital velocity of the system's center of mass. So the center had to hold steady.

They spun upward, sliding elevator fashion around the dark asteroid, a rocky cinder brightly lit by the control station, and onward to the Flinger.

Rachel knew she was not privy to Prefect-level strategies, since the Library historically sponged up knowledge and gave forth only trickles, even to Trainee Librarians such as her. But the Prefect seemed relaxed, and this was an unusual chance. She gave him her best party-girl smile. It seemed to have no effect, so she said, "I'm getting on well with Fraq."

"Yes, I see him eyeing you at our table meetings."

Tone of voice told all. "What?" She never knew where his thinking came from. "He's another species!"

"From an entirely different kingdom of life, true. But male strategies seem to be an invariant."

She wondered if this was a joke and suddenly felt a blush spread across her cheeks. She had liked the strong look of Fraq, his tawny feathers wreathing slim muscles, the glinting golden eyes—

Best to deflect this talk, yes. "I tried to get out of him where the Ark is."

"I know. You failed."

Okay, try the front door. "You didn't seem bothered when the issue came up."

"I already knew."

"Where is it, anyway?"

The Prefect grimaced, another unusual expression. *So you're not the perpetual Sphinx after all.* "They finally revealed that. They spotted it using code-response transmissions while they came in from the Oort. How they knew the code they didn't say."

"They must've had a visit from an Ark, then."

"They won't discuss that, which means you are probably right. The translators think so, too."

"So the Ark, it's . . . ?"

"A small thing in a near-Earth asteroid, the co-orbitals, as they're called. Good place to hide."

"That big a sail—"

"It's probably folded up, to elude detection."

The Prefect rose, forestalling any more questions, and went forward to the *Venture* bridge.

She sat, watching Luna shrink aft, and pondered the Ythri mysteries. She was having coffee in a bubble cup when the Flinger came rushing down. She could make out the slender cables as they came out of the dark, spindly fingers reaching for the grapple. Their "package," in Lunavator lingo, was the human ship *Venture*, and the smaller Ythri ship, bundled together. The package got handed off in gruff shoves to the wrought-carbon Flinger cable. It snatched them at high, slam-into-the-couch accelerations, a brutal thrust heading them into their fast interplanetary orbit. She relaxed as the huge invisible hand forced her deep into her sighing smart cushions. Her joints ached.

Clunks, rattles, and thunks told her their package was taking on more masses of water, to later burn in the reaction engines. She could see the feeder lines snaking into their carbon-black package, delivering water fresh-harvested from the comet nucleus she had seen only a few hours ago as they left the launch point. All the while the Flinger was pumping water into their fusion fuel tanks. They would shove steam out to decelerate at their destination.

Their speed was so high now as to be incomprehensible, the view a blur. All she could think of was the unending pressure forcing them onward. She had extra oxy just to stay conscious; Loonies had it hard. The Flinger orbited far above the Lunavator in centrifugal haste, rotating so fast that within another hour it let them go at a speed above two hundred kilometers a second. The solar system was big, and it was best not to think about hitting a wandering rock at such speeds. Their forward-looking radar linked to laser cannon could handle that, thank you.

They popped free on course. It was like turning into an angel after a week in hell. Light, airy, she was a free bird.

She unstrapped in the zero grav and tried a tumble-thrust to get her popping joints aligned. She had done zero grav before, but now her flying experience paid off in easy, unconscious grace.

The Prefect was asleep, or maybe unconscious, his face lined. She headed for the hibernation capsule ahead of the staff, got her injections from the nurse, and snuggled into the smart comfy clasp of the hibernation-tech cocoon. She didn't want to hear the Prefect's ideas, or the staff's. And she didn't want to be bored with a month of speculation. Sleep, bliss, yes. She wanted to see the Ark, a deep-sleep month's ride away.

7.

The Ark sail was folded up into a tight scroll, which explained why humans hadn't found it. The sail had been kilometers across, and now was just a white rod bound with straps. Its cargo, the ship that had sailed the eons, basked in the ruddy glow of a red giant, then coasted for centuries across to nearby Earth—well, it looked ordinary. A dull composite cylinder, streaked and pitted and worn, hardly a hundred meters long and seventy meters across. But the door was open, a yawning circle. Pretty obvious:

Come on in, whoever you are. You're why we came.

Except that the Ark had arrived before humanity had swung down from the trees. It had to be designed to welcome whatever sprang from ancient forests, glimpsed in pixels by a species long extinct.

Staff up and coffee-strong, they prepared a team to haul alongside the Ark and board. Then the Prefect suddenly cried, "The Ythris are already there!"

Rachel glanced out a port while she slipped on her skin suit. Floating across the space between them and the Ark, lit only by starlight, were . . . bubbles. With her helmet on she closeupped those motes and saw that Ythri space suits were the opposite of theirs: expanded, transparent oblate spheroids with appliances socketed into the walls. A Ythri swam in the bubble, breathing air and propelling itself with tiny jets. The suit bubbles had grappling arms, and the team of six Ythri was forming a ring around the Ark cylinder. Each carried a teardrop thing of tan ceramic alongside.

"They're not going for the front door," she sent before sealing her suit. By the time she got out their air lock, the Ythri had the tan ceramics attached to the Ark hull, encircling it.

"What's up?" she sent on private comm to the Prefect—who, she saw, hadn't bothered to get into his skin suit. Maybe he didn't bother to have one, either; he was standing at the big port in the ship's bridge.

She glided past him on a tether, skating across the *Venture*'s hull in the inky dark. "We anticipated this," he said blandly, and she could see his lips move.

"What're they—"

"Probably mounting those simple fusor packs they're carrying. They want to get the full implosion impact, tear the Ark down to atoms."

"Why?"

"Some ancient grudge, I surmise. I had their ship sounded from outside, when it first came into Lunar orbit. The fusor warheads showed up clearly." He stood with hands behind his back, a traditional Prefect stance of measured patience.

Rachel wasn't feeling patient and would probably never be a Prefect. "You knew all this—"

"And did not tell you, yes. I could not predict how well the Ythri could read your unconscious signals."

"What do you—"

"A moment." The Prefect nodded to the *Venture* captain.

From the forward hull a concealed projector suddenly jutted forth. Its snout turned, focused, and Rachel heard a *braaaack* in her microwave inputs. Nothing happened that she could see, but the Prefect nodded and allowed himself a small smile.

"Their simple warheads are now dead. Go tell them."

So she was message girl now. Still, Rachel was glad to be free of the *Venture* and jetting toward the floating Ythri bubbles. As she approached they seemed disturbed, working furiously at their socketed tools. The tan ceramic warheads were just lumps on the Ark's cinder-dark skin.

"Your explosives will not work," she sent Fraq on a narrow squirt beam.

"I have scented this," he said tightly, gliding over the Ark's horizon.

"Can I trust you to go inside with me?"

This he pondered, hanging beside the circular lock entrance. Mouth working. Eyes slitted. "I ... carry no further weaponry," he said at last.

By that time Rachel was there. Instead of slowing, she glided directly into the lock. Fraq barked some surprised epithet and hastily followed her. Intuitively she sensed it was better to confront him inside, isolated; make it personal. She passed through an iris that opened at her approach. No air, but she was in a large space that slowly ... awakened.

Phosphorescent glows stretched across long walls. Transparent cases lit, showing strange bodies suspended in clear liquid. Intricate tiny slabs showed pale colors, light fluttering as if rousing from a slumber. DNA inventories? She prowled the space, surrounded by an enormous bio database. Slowly, it came to life.

Suddenly zero-grav flowers floated by, big blooms growing from spheres of water. She recalled her joy as a girl watching soap bubbles shimmering in sunlight. These somehow sprang to life in vacuum.

Behind thin windows, gnarled trees like bonsai curled out from moistening soil. Odd angular plants burgeoned before her eyes.

In all directions of the cylindrical space, plants grew, looking to her like lavender brushstrokes in the air. In a spinning liquid vessel, orange snakes with butterfly wings danced in bubbling air. Displays.

She heard her own gasps echoed, turned. Fraq hung nearby, eyes wide. "Is exhibition," he said. "A welcome, could be."

"Welcome, yes. It's a bio inventory," she said. "Displayed as an explanation. As advertising."

In his own suit bubble he waved a wing at images playing along the walls.

Purple-skinned animals loping on octopus-like tendrils across a sandy plain. Flying carpets with big yellow eyes, massive ruddy creatures moving like mountains on tracks of slime, trees that walked, fish in stony undersea palaces. A library of alien life.

She turned full-on to him, pressed against his bubble, glowered. "What was that you said? The Ark was a 'Prime Need for life itself,' eh?"

"We came for ancient vengeance," Fraq said stonily over comm, tan feathers ruffling with unease.

"For what? They sent you an Ark? But—"

"And we brought their life from the Ark in orbit, down to our world." His eyes flared. "We could not control it. Did not know. Their strange creatures festered, escaped from us, attacked our life at every level. Diseases, blight, desolation, death. They nearly killed and colonized our biosphere." Sudden deep anger boiled in his tight voice.

She sighed. "You . . . you just did it wrong."

"They sent it as a weapon, our history says. Our foremothers laid down for all generations, as bloodpride, the call—to destroy all Arks."

"It was too late to kill the Furians?"

"Alas, yes. No bloodpride justice can we have. Their star had eaten them." Suddenly, from the troubled shifting of his eyes, she saw why Fraq had insisted that she fly with them.

First, to test whether humans could be better than the mere dirt-huggers of the Ythri world.

Second, to show that the Ythrian hunting carnivore life was hard, aloof, clannish.

That was all their way of telling her about themselves. *And now I sense them. Intuit them. I know them beyond language.*

The Ythris learned through experience, not from libraries. They had now to think of this Ark as a repository of lost history, not as an enemy.

She peered through the glassy bubble suit, reading his shifting feather patterns. "I'm sorry, but you should know more biology. Try experiments! Don't bring in invasive forms until you understand them. Look"—she gestured wide at the bounty surrounding them—"they're offering, not invading."

Fraq's stiff face slowly eased. Feathers rustled. "I was charged with bringing destruction. My kind regrets that you knew more, and deadened our explosives."

"We know more about war, unfortunately. Look, that's over. Question is, what next?"

"You must destroy this."

"Hey, I'm a Librarian! Don't destroy, study! Learn!"

"It is a danger too vast to say." He frowned darkly. "This is a matter of bloodpride."

"We'll learn from your mistake. No Furian life gets into Earth's biosphere. Or those of Mars and Luna."

"I will . . . consider it." More feather riffles, hard to read.

"You've already seen how we'll do it," Rachel said suddenly, the idea fresh-born and irresistible. "This ship is live now. Let's redirect it. Send it to Luna, use the Bolo to bring some of its contents down. Carefully take bits of the Furian life into a huge new void, specially dug. Create an alien biosphere isolated by a hundred kilometers of rock."

Fraq blinked. She could see his Ythrian male rigidity ease a bit, muscles soften, breathing slow. She had been studying his body language and now somehow knew how to work with it. Female intuition . . . a universal? The endless parallels of evolution seemed to imply it. Convergent evolution of psychology.

She could do this. No Prefect need get in the way, either. Just her and this beautiful alien.

She smiled. Wordless, the two of them hung in the luminous center of ancient legacy, a Library of Life for an entire world now gone forever. They could do it.

Her heart beat faster. She watched his strong wings flex with new energy as the idea took hold. *Y'know, he does look like a strange, feathery, majestic, great guy. . . .*

8.

She ambled along, headed down through the Prince Pyotr Kropotkin tube. The piped-in surface view along the left wall was interesting—ore plows throwing up plumes that towered over the gray dust, making gorgeous refracting rainbows in the sunlight. She had just left another Ythri event and needed a break from the subtle pressures of being with the bird-flock. The Ythri believed in understanding others by sharing experiences—mostly ones with lots of exercise.

This experience had been a first for them all—black ice skating. They'd made their way down onto the Weissensee, the long, slender lake deep within the Lunar crust. It had formed in the volcanic era, billions of years back, and slowly accumulated water. In the dark, the headlamps of the shivering skaters cast a spiritual glow onto the charcoal ice. They had been warned not to remove their goggles, lest their eyeballs frost over as they sped. Fraq and others of the flock had suitable tailored suits, plus feathers for insulation—since the conditions, by any reasonable standard, were brutal. Still, the skaters were in heaven.

Rachel had to admit to the beauty of skating on a seemingly infinite floor of black ice, in the stabbing cold, hearing the rushing sounds of skate blades in an enormous echo chamber of icy rock. When speed-skating at 0.17 gravs, icicles formed on facial hair, despite the skin-heat creams. Injuries abounded, and Rachel had nearly smashed into a wall in a long skid. The ice was smooth and clear, though peering into it she sensed lurking luminous lines, as if of ancient fractures. A perpetual solid lake, sailed by humans and Ythri alike on long-bladed skates . . .

She had aches, twitches, and maybe a sprain in her left ankle, but felt glorious.

With a Prefect's permission, she'd slipped away from the party when they reached the upper residence levels, exaggerating her limp to get the nod. The Prefects frowned a bit at Rachel's close connection to Fraq and others of the flock. They themselves wanted more access, but Fraq simply frowned and turned away from them, an unsubtle rebuke. Prefects had courted her, even sending flowers—this week, a fuchsia orchid with musky moss in the pot, like a business gift, precious on Luna. Fraq disliked Noughts, too, finding them too far from the natural order. That made Rachel the accidental diplomat. She surprised herself by not minding.

Lost in her thoughts, Rachel was taken by surprise when Ruby suddenly hugged her, coming in from her right side.

"Honey! Been missin' you somethin' awful."

Rachel had forgotten that Ruby tried to do a southern accent, mangling it badly. "Uh, hi, I—"

"Ever'body wonderin' how you doin', with those birds. We'd love to have you come down to smooch a bit—" And with that Ruby kissed her neck. There was some other twinge, too.

Rachel wrestled out of Ruby's octopus arms and said, "I just can't do social right now, got to—"

"Just a hug, honey, just—"

—and a man slammed into them both.

He twisted Ruby's arm away from Rachel's neck. "This is a citizen lockdown," he spat out. "Apprehended in the act!"

With that, he tumbled Ruby to the floor. Rachel stepped back, crouching as she had been taught. Was this a street robbery? A rumble?—But the man and a woman now coming in beside him were not focused on Rachel. They had Ruby facedown in seconds, hands in froze-lock. Ruby was thrashing, hitting, shouting but incoherent.

The woman turned to Rachel, calm and sure. "She was planting an engram on you."

"Ah, what is—?"

"Memory bug. Makes a permanent change in the short-term brain accounting. Harvests a memory trace. Dissolves in a few hours after it transmits and gets flushed out in limbic glands."

"But—how—?"

"Confidential tech. Earthsiders use it."

"To get my memories? Of what?"

"We knew Earthside investment unions were picking up Message tech data. They needed clues and tapped you. Big profits. Got Ythri info, too."

Ruby was swearing a stream, twisting around on the floor. She glared up at Rachel, mouth ugly. She spat out, "You were an easy mark. Damn dumb, too." She kicked out a foot, trying to hook it around Rachel's leg. "Fancy bitch, you—"

Rachel thrust her own foot out and spun Ruby around, using the outthrust leg as leverage. Ruby kept swearing, trying to get up. Rachel considered the situation for a few seconds, then kicked Ruby in the ribs.

She felt a satisfying crack. "Now we're even."

———————

"You knew somebody was carrying out espionage here?"

The Prefect Siloh nodded. "But not how."

Rachel suppressed her anger. "How much did they get?"

"Some useful items your work turned up, of course." He sniffed. "That was perhaps inevitable. But now, thanks to that Ruby person's overreach, we have nabbed them. Earthside will pry secrets from her. If she survives her trip there, which commences once she has passed through her interrogations here."

"Survive?" Rachel had been through some grueling neuro-analysis in the last day, all very polite but invasive, during imposed sleeps. That had left her feeling rocky. Yet it had also given her time to think. That, and have a rousing good time with Fraq and his flock, a sort of post-hunt ritual that reminded her of when her father came home with buddies, tired and triumphant, from hunting deer with crossbows. Primitive fun, yes—and thoroughly analyzed by all the xenoists who studied the videos. She had even gotten Cat invited, who had gushed about it all for hours. "I never thought Ruby would—"

"It is not for you to do or comprehend such exotic technical espionage." Siloh allowed himself a thin smile. Your task is now not dual, but triple. You will, of course, connect with the Flock"—she could hear the capitalization—"when they desire such. And you shall seek out hints, while among them, to wormhole possibilities. And you may return to your pod and conduct further forays into the Messages." He sat back with a satisfied air.

"What about what happens to the Ark, whether they bring any of the life-forms down? I'd like to see it developed, a place in the Library—"

"Not your problem. Good work, but you must step aside. We will do as we decide."

Rachel bit off some bitter words, then . . . let the silence stretch. *Be the diplomat here, not the Librarian. . . .* Best to get back to her real business. "I'm aware that I'm not the fastest fox in the forest here," she began. "But I have an idea."

The Prefect brightened. "Ah. Fastest fox—I do appreciate bio analogies, since we live on a dead world." He steepled his hands on the desk and donned an expectant face, eyebrows arched.

She took a deep breath, nostrils flared at the antiseptic air of his shadowy reserve. After the Ythri flight, Ruby's attack, Cat's excited interest in all such drama—she had suddenly felt her own ideas converge. *How to get back to being simply a Librarian . . . ?* She spoke slowly. "I have a suspicion. The older dwarf stars with rich biospheres—they're lying low."

"From our probes?"

"Yes—that's why they shot down our observing craft."

"Aha." A salamander stare.

So he wants me to spell it out. "I estimate the rejecting biospheres are several million years old, at least. Really old! They let our probes approach, even allowed drop balloons, then—*wham.*"

"Indeed. You have done the required statistics?"

"Yes." She let her inboard systems coalesce a shimmering curtain in the air, using the Prefect's office system. The correlation functions appeared in 3-D. The Prefect flicked a finger, and the minimax hummocks rotated, showing the parameter space—a landscape covering billions of years, thousands of stars.

"Perhaps significant." A frown formed above his one cocked eyebrow. She recalled that the Prefect was the sort who would look out a window at a cloudburst and say, "It seems to be raining," on the off chance that somebody was pouring water off the roof.

"They're probably the longest-lived societies in the galaxy, since they're around red stars that hold stable. If they can't do cold-sleep, either—and so can't go interstellar voyaging, like us—they're stuck in their systems. And they're still afraid."

The Prefect nodded. "Correct—the cause of the dwarf-star worlds' insularity lies in the far past. An antiquity beyond our knowing, from eras before fish crawled from our seas."

"Whatever could have made them fear for so long?"

"We do not know. It is a history . . ." Mixed emotions flitted across his face, as if memory was dancing within view. ". . . for which adjectives are temporarily unavailable."

"We have to be alert!" She got up and paced the office. "These aliens hunkering down around their red and brown stars—they have lasted by being cautious."

A shrug. "That seems obvious."

She had hoped for help, not a blasé, blunt assessment. "So we need to find out more," she said, realizing it was lame.

He leveled a stare. "Intelligence is defined by sufficient detachment from one's own case to consider it as one of many. A child becomes humanly intelligent the moment it realizes that there are other minds just like its own, working in the same way on the same world available to it. This seems to be the same with societies across the galaxy."

She nodded. "Other worlds, other minds, strange—but they have suffered the same past."

"True. This is not a matter of dry certainties. It is a quest for archaeological wisdom."

She whirled, her mouth a grimace, eyes wild. "Whatever they're afraid it might be—could be comin' right atcha!"

He was calm, further confusing her. He gave her a cautious, precise throat-clearing. "I have an allergy to dogma, including my own."

"What's your dogma?"

"Placing the Library on Luna, safely away from the torrents of Earth, was a primary motive. Best to contemplate the stars where one can see them anytime. In other words, take the long view."

She was getting more frustrated by his blithe manner, but resisted raising her voice. "Look, you want me to go back to studying decrypted SETI messages, but this, this—I just couldn't give it up."

"Research is not devised, it is distilled."

She let out a loud, barking laugh. "Building logic towers from premises wrung out of thin air, more like."

"You have got it nearly right."

"Nearly?"

He eyed her narrowly. "When we think of the Elizabethan world, it is one we perceive through our own reductive devising. We think of it as populated by the Queen and Ben Jonson and the Dark Lady and the Bard and a raucous theater full of groundlings. That's what we know, from some texts. But the real Elizabethan world had a lot more people in it than that, and countless more possibilities. Here at the Library, we deal with not a mere handful of centuries. We have received messages sent across thousands of light-years, from beacons erected by societies long dead."

"Well, yes—"

"So we need to know more, before deciding anything."

She finally let her anger out. "Nonsense! This is a threat! People need to know." She spread her hands, beseeching him.

"Go and think some more. You are following the right path." With a wave, he dismissed her.

9.

Catkejen came in from a date, all fancied out in a maroon, bioweb Norfolk jacket with fluorescent yellow spirals down the arms, and found Rachel calculating some ideas. "Actual penciling out! Pushing graphite! You should get outside sometime, y'know."

Feeling every inch a pedant, Rachel rose, stretched. "I was backtracking those red stars that had hunkered down."

"You mean the ones that prob'ly knocked out our probes?"

"Yes, plus ones we've seen from the 550 AU telescopes. Those that had ruins on them."

"So you're running backward their orbits around the galaxy?" A disbelieving frown.

"Yes, it's a tough many-body problem—"

"Hey, another example of cross-field confusion. We already have that!"

And this was how Rachel learned that astronomers had developed a reverse-history code of extraordinary ability. They had first evolved it to study galactic stellar evolution of spiral arms. Which led to her next audience with the Prefect.

10.

She walked—no, she decided, she skipped with schoolgirl joy in the low grav—out of the Advanced Computational Dome, feeling as if she had returned from a great distance.

She blew past the Prefect's office staff and marched straight in on the great man, who was staring at a screen. He looked up, not showing any surprise. "You have more." Not a question.

She flipped on her personal Artilect interface so it projected an image on the office 3-D display. "This shows the dwarf stars our probes and the 550 AU 'scopes found to be defensive or destroyed. No particular correlation between their locations, notice."

He merely nodded. She had tagged the forty-three cases in bright green. They were scattered through a volume more than a thousand light-years on a side—still a mere bubble in the colossal galactic disk.

"Now let's run the galaxy backward."

The green dots arced through their long ellipses. The slow spin of the galaxy itself emerged as the bee swarms of stars glided in stately measure. The sun took a quarter of a billion years to cycle in its slow orbit at about two hundred kilometers a second, taking more than a thousand years to move a light-year. Humanity's duration was less than a thousandth of one galactic cycle. From SETI messages marking funeral-pyre societies, the Librarians knew that humans were mayflies among sentient cultures, the newest kids on the block.

The Prefect watched the backward-running swarm and raised his eyebrows as the green dots slowly drew nearer each other.

"They follow somewhat different orbits, bobbing up and down in the galactic plane, brushing by nearby stars, suffering small tilts in their courses," she said, as though this weren't obvious. Was she making too much of this? She told herself a sharp no.

"I can see some, well, clumps of several green specks forming," the Prefect said. "They seem to be"—surprise pitched his voice into a tenor note—"occasionally passing within a few light-years of each other. There! And now . . ." A pause as four dots swooped together. "Another cluster."

Rachel made herself use her flat, factual voice. "Stats show these were nonrandom, four sigmas out from any bell curve odds."

"They . . . group . . . at different times. How far into the past are we now?"

"Six million years."

He frowned, pursed his lips. "I have never seen this before."

"Astronomers study star dynamics. This is about the hunkered-down planets, or the ones destroyed, orbiting those stars."

The Prefect gave her a sour smile. "So this is another example of the perils of specialization."

"Um, yessir." *Let the idea percolate. . . .*

The Prefect bit. "Which means . . . ?"

"The endangered worlds were near each other, millions of years ago. Whatever attacked them—killing some societies entirely, scaring others so much they still remember it, guard against it—came at them when they were close to each other." She paused. *Let him figure it out. . . .*

"Whatever menace does this . . ." The Prefect let his puzzled sentence trail off.

"Wormholes lie somewhere in those intersecting orbits."

The Prefect stiffened. "We know of no wormholes!"

"Right. Except the one we infer the Ythri came through. No more, yes. But . . . Absence of evidence is not evidence of absence, as some philosopher said."

A furious head-shake. "But—where could wormholes come from? We know they're impossible to build—"

"The Big Bang? We know it was chaotic. Maybe some survived that era. Got trapped in the galaxy when it formed up later. They go coasting around, just as the stars do."

He blinked, always a good sign. "So when a wormhole mouth gets near a group of stars . . ."

"Something comes through it. Someone—some thing—that found a wormhole mouth. Y'know, theory says wormholes aren't simple one-way pipes. They can branch, like subways in spacetime. So some terrible thing comes through, attacks inhabited planets."

The Prefect looked puzzled. Maybe this was coming too fast? *Explain, girl. Go technical.*

"We—well, I—saw it in the planets around dwarfs, because there are more of them. Better statistics, the pattern shows up."

She let that sink in while the Prefect watched the galaxy grind into its past. More green dots swooped along their blithe paths, nearing each other, coasting on, apart . . . the waltz of eternity, Newton meets Mozart, on and on through thousands of millennia, down through the echoing halls of vast, lost time. But ever eternity casts shadows, if you know where to look.

The Prefect was a quick study. His sharp, piercing eyes darted among the bee swarm of stars, mouth now compressed, lips white with pressure. "What are the odds that there's one near us?"

This she had not thought about—another wormhole than the one she thought the Ythri came through? This Prefect did not know the Ythri wormhole was an accepted theory, now. Matters were moving fast, and secrets got kept. "Given the number of dwarfs nearby . . . um, pretty good."

He smiled, an unusual event. "This is utterly new. When you found the ancient tragedies, I was impressed. If you were wondering, only one in several thousand Trainees catches on to that fact—that secret, I should say."

"Really? And this—the clustering—how often has any Trainee turned that up?"

A quick shake of the head. "Never. This is a new discovery."

"Really?" She had thought she would surprise him, get some reward, but ... new?

"No one knows this. Wormholes throughout! Maybe nearby? So— if there's one nearby—where is it?"

This was going too fast for her. *Drop any mention of the Ythri worm- hole, then.* "I sure as hell don't know. I'm not an astronomer! I want to be a lifelong Librarian." *And to live a long time, too ...*

The Prefect nodded. "So you shall be, in time." He paused, gazing at the slow, sure grind of the galaxy. "We have a saying, we Prefects. 'Creativity may be hard to nurture, but it's easy to thwart.' You have proven that we do occasionally let talent get through."

She sat silent, not knowing where this was going.

"Also ... congratulations."

"What?"

"You have found the unsaid. The essence of research."

"What ... ?"

"The Library is not a mere decoding society. We must use the full range of exploration, not just the Messages. You saw that. You first fer- reted out a truth we Prefects do not wish to make known—the deaths of whole worlds, the closing in of others. Your discovery now, the prox- imity of the stricken worlds—is a gift."

"Gift?"

"Yes. Much we discover needs time to ... digest. But we become calcified, mere decoders. To become a true Librarian, one must show innate curiosity, persistence, drive."

"I, I just got interested. You leaned on me hard to keep up my stud- ies, not fall behind the others—"

"It is they who have fallen behind. We cannot drill creativity into our Trainees. They must display it without being asked."

She gaped at him, not following. "So ..."

"You are now promoted. You shall not tell your fellow Trainees why. Let them bathe in mystery. Do not say a word of what you have learned."

"But, but—"

For the first time ever, she saw the Prefect smile broadly. "Wel- come. I will see to getting you a private office now, as well."

Outside, the night Earth seen through the vast dome was a glowing halo, sunlight forming a thin rainbow circle. She saw his point. Earth was always there, and so were the waiting stars.

And something dark hid in the yawning beyond, something even a Nought or a Prefect did not know. Something shadowy in the offing out there in the galaxy, waiting, patient and eternal.

Wormholes? Through which something horrible came? They were out there, hanging like dark doorways between the stars.

It came in a flash she would recall all her life.

Now she knew what she wanted to solve, an arrow to pierce the night beyond . . . and find the doorways. To see across eternity and up, up into the consuming dark above that now awaited all humanity.

FRAQ

These grounder creatures have discovered their great truth. If the past is not alive in you, then the future will be empty.

Their future. And ours.

To make this plain to grounders will be pure task profound. They show proper respect through their Library on this arid moon. Their great Librarian, a female savant, deserves respect. She is one who has worked on scales of suns and worlds, the interstellar appropriate view. For this we chose her to be our point of plunge.

I and my Flock are much diminished here. Flush with pride, though few in number. I accepted that constraint when I agreed to command, to be the point of our V.

We could squeeze only a few dozen into our tube ship, and even then it was vexing. The spacetime Mouth had its constraint set by spacetime struts. We could but snake through it. Even done, I had to stride the corridor in full scowl to quiet their fluttering anxieties.

Then came the disaster of the Mouth. I was shaken but could not show that.

I had to peck a few of the Flock, to release them from their panic.

The flight through the narrow drawing-in Mouth, and thus through the spacetime tunnel, began by letting the entrance Mouth draw us toward it. Its attraction was like that of a small world. We fell into it, keeping rigorously true to the exact center of the thing. It glimmered, a sphere that seemed polished metal but was not. It curved light about itself, spacetime master, a cocoon of shiny brilliance.

In we went. Our machine intelligences set plunging—calibrating, steering. As we had drilled for, over years. Then the shimmer of the tunnel. Slick light, a strumming like unto a deep bass flight song. Quick, a glimpse of dark space ahead—

The through-slip had been simple and quick. Not the exit.

The physicist Lexnor explained later the chaos that awaited our slender ship. We emerged as expected, true. Into empty space, star blaring nearby.

Engines thrummed. All seemed calm and right. For moments. But then the exit Mouth spun away. Tumbling. A fire of hard particle radiation showed us its path. I watched, confused. This was not how the rehearsals had gone. My Flock rippled feathers. Caws and songs.

Our ship nearly snapped into two. Groans, cracks, metal shrieks. Worse, we spun, hard. We lost all sight of the Mouth. Yet it was our path back! I sang the gathering-in call to calm the jittery chirps that echoed in our slender cylinder. Boomed and strutted. This worked on the Flock, while the physics crew did their best to fathom what had happened. Much remains to be done, but we have a path homeward—if we can find the Mouth.

So it came to be: we spoke the first time to the groundlings, through flights electromagnetic. Negotiations. Our craft swept up through their sun's gravitational potential, angling arrow-sharp toward their bright world of blue and white and green.

Then a swift turn. To their rocky, pale moon, pimpled and ancient, where we knew their Library lurked. Where the hero Librarian lived, who had tamed the hydrogen wall. Such valiants we can deal with. My Overflock so commands. No lesser will suffice.

So, with much wearisome delay, it came to be . . . now. Despite the groundlings' confusions and resistance, we reached this small world. More tedious introductions. Much negotiation, some through translator machines that we then realized were artificial minds as well. Discoveries, some incredible.

Now we have gotten through the laborious lubrications of diplomacy.

Tedious but necessary, yes.

Better: we have flown in fragrant air, at last, again. The small moon world's gravity made it pure play, as fits the olden song: *Swoop and soar, giving roar.*

But not merely so. My Flock learned from our flying as a greeting, for as we-one must begin. Protocol so demands. But these primates are awkward in their own bare air. I learned from the female's breathless—such small lungs!—remarks, they may well have come to their small moon to learn to fly at all.

So, discouragement. A limp opening flight. Still, instructive. Even failure informs.

These grounders still have their blue-green world, but learn little from it. They sit in boxes and look at boxes, like moles. They ignore their wild world and seek out this gray moon.

Strange, for so recently evolved a species. Long-legged, arm-strong, prowlers of lands—much like our prey, the grass-grazers. Yet they have risen above that. Made a machined-smart world.

Yet-so . . . they misunderstand much. They are for much of their times out of body. In my judgment they mistreat themselves and waste lives by being brains in body-bottles. They elude the great truth—that nature never goes away.

Yet still. The primate female was refreshing in flight. She flew like a chick, tumbled often, yet made graceful fun in her way. Besides, on ground, compared with her stride we have a stubby-legged, rolling gait. She displays a similar awkward wing while in air. So we meet in awkward sameness, this way.

Yet . . . she knows of the wild self, always there for such as we. Or so I sense her.

She is easier to know and speak with than the other grounders. I and other of my Flock believe this may spring from her attentions to the many Messages—as these term the ancient lessons—that have opened her to other cultures.

The others here, the Prefect intellectuals and strange solemn nons called Noughts—all are prone to being brains in bodies. They know not that the health and accuracy of our thinking of the world depends upon immersion, true and sure.

These grounder kind do not know that the past has a past of its own. Or of the Mouths and their many mysteries.

I caught that eddy of thought from our first flight with the female. It is she of the profound hydrogen wall victory, well and true. I had at first refused to believe this tale. Yet it is so—our observations while climbing up to their two-world system showed this. The prickly radiations of their warring bow shock spill aplenty, out among their gas giant worlds. Her chirp-name is Rachel. It has a certain song and strut to the ear. In delicious light gravity, we were air-swimming with her. She struggled. But she learned from and of us. Not in their compact little words, stripped bare of song or strut. She fathomed the whirl of immersion in the world aloft. This is essential. Her kind have evolved in the trap of hard gravity. They yearn for skies they cannot command in person. So in their miserable upbringing, they have learned a fragment of the ferment we daily enjoy. As my and our entire Flock struggle to understand, we must work from their appearances—as they, like we, are highly visual creatures. So we have fathomed their culture, their embodied qualities that speak to their evolution.

This chirp-friend Rachel shares traits the primates greatly desire, as we learned from their copious visuals: shining hair, highly developed milk glands, delicate head features not meant for weaponry use, and long hind limbs, far more muscular than ours. They must have evolved for running. Their minds were shaped by the two-dimensional frame of reckoning ground-bound minds know.

Some records suggest they can even swim in liquids. If so, her two glands in her pectoral region jut forward from her body and so must inhibit laminar flow, which must surely slow her when swimming. Thus so, also in flying.

Such poor design I find it impossible to regard highly. Certainly it cannot be a feature of beauty. Evidently Rachel regrets this dual disfigurement, for she conceals them at all times with a narrow covering that nonetheless displays them, as if hiding a secret. Their males have rudimentary milk glands and so must be adapted to do their species' swimming. In this way we of the Flock deduce the details of their society, of which they seldom speak plainly.

The human males seem less body-wise. Rachel's graceful form seems both fragile and powerfully muscled, though all of the grounders' bones are solid and heavy. The males' exaggerated muscles and coarse body hair seem primitive, as if trapped in an ugly genetic heritage. Perhaps natural selection has more work to do upon them. This species is quite young, a few hundred thousands of their years. Our kind are far more evolved. I instructed my Flock, as we approached this complex home world, ruled by groundlings, that they should not judge creatures from such a massive, grasping gravity. It is a tribute to their kind that they emerged to intelligence despite such hindrances.

To never know the joy of flight!—How can their arts not suffer? Perhaps such is the lot of these creatures, not having the convenience of the egg and, in stress, of the budding.

Instead, such as Rachel must carry their developing young inside themselves, always. Such horror provokes my gorge. We have such lowly, stunted beings on Yth, true—but they are of no account.

They do know the delights of coupling—there is much video of that, though poor in drama, or even dance, much less actual flight. The dialect of their mating chase seems something like a dance, however. The male pretends to be predatory, while the female ("woman"—apparently a shortening, our machine-minds believe, of "woe to man"—another oddity) pretends (usually unsuccessfully) to be out of season.

They seem bound by an intricate web of taboo and prohibs. Of course, mated social intelligence must wed with tool intelligence, to make a species that can voyage in vacuum. Can those overlap with what we wish of them? Or contradict our goals? Impossible to know. Much depends upon that answer. So we must engage them—and so their grandest and well-accomplished member, this Rachel—in further feats. Such our Folk dynamics demand. They, and thus she, must be tested. In person, on her own world, so we may see her and her kind in their context.

That will serve to get us downward to their Earth and even into their ocean. They will vex, but we must have this, to truly engage in the grand task we seek to share. We must know their world, perform on it with them, for bloodpride status. And so to gain their help with the Mouth. For surely, they are a prideful kind. They must be, to have risen so far, and so swiftly.

They are too young to have yet plundered their world, as we did.

Yet we shall instruct them by showing our appetite for challenge. Only such are grounds for deep connections. They must venture with us—with me, as your Flock commander. We must show them that to venture in the highest is precisely to be conscious of one's self. And in so doing, to truly know others.

At times a superior intelligence must exploit those younger inferiors, to gain knowledge. And regain our Mouth, as well. In time.

PART 8

ORBITFALL

Death has this much to be said for it:
You don't have to get out of bed for it.
Wherever you happen to be
They bring it to you—free.

—KINGSLEY AMIS

1.

Rachel liked the view, at least.

In the frame chair atop an open deck, she had a commanding perspective on the grand curve of Earth, from 115 kilometers up. High enough to boil her blood in seconds, if the visor before her eyes should pop. And suit pressure loss was just one of the possibilities ahead. She could be slammed, torn, crushed, electrocuted, frozen. . . .

She recalled what the bony Prefect Velma had said, weeks ago: "You must build strength, agility."

"Why?"

"The Ythri have ways, worldviews that we can explore only in their ways. Their rituals, events."

"I fly with them in—"

"You must accompany them to Earth. This will be physically trying."

Prefect Velma had smooth olive skin, the only sign of her age crow's-feet cracks at the eyes. Prefects were mostly over a hundred years old, but she obviously was using the best restoration tech.

Trying . . . That meant warm-up and stretching moves more severe than any Rachel had ever done. Twist both arms one at a time behind her head, leaning forward on outstretched legs . . . then try to touch the floor with the top of her head. Fail and try again, fail and try . . .

So while she met and flew with Fraq and his flock, she'd also been caught up in the big team poking the Ythri with questions, suggestions—all to extract knowledge. Usually not with success. She'd worked off her anxieties with Kane, joyously distracted in the sack. He wanted a deeper affair, he murmured in her ear after they made love. Every time, now. She dodged the issue. *Too much going on now,* became her mantra.

She'd dreamed about Fraq, too. When she woke up, Kane got the benefit. Hey, he was there.

So instead: pump iron, pull-ups, push-ups called "dive bombers" because she caught herself a centimeter above the floor—or else smacked her nose. Stomach crunches, side-straddle hops, back flexes and extensions, sit-ups with chest weights—all much like atrocities. Long runs in the centrifugal spinner, agonies under Earth full grav.

She sat back on the open deck and closed her eyes. People left you alone if you shut your eyes, even if they knew you were awake. She let her mantra sound in her mind, though meditation in her mood now was impossible.

Prefect Velma whispered, "Earthers are giving us sighs of longing and their talktalk simmers with intrigue."

"Ugh. This is a stunt." Blazing-fast hot fictionmaggy action, yes.

"For Fraq's flock, a holy ritual. They remark that on their world, this Great Plunge is shared by all, their greatest sporting event."

"Okay, I know we have it, too. I never paid any attention to such stuff." Prefect Velma hovered nearby, blocking her view of the myriad cameras, spectators, tech teams—a mass of floating humanity. Plus . . . Fraq. Getting into his capsule. Rachel recalled her grandmother saying, in a trying time Rachel had decades back, "You never know how strong you are until being strong is the only choice you have." Rachel wished the grand, wrinkled woman had not died, five years ago, at age 203. She had borne truths from early modernist antiquity.

"This is for the Library," Prefect Velma said. "We harvest much from this."

"Media rights, yes."

"You have all the safety devices possible, with extra controls against buffeting."

"I'm a firm believer in the right of people to risk their lives doing any damn-fool thing they want to."

"That is a fine saying."

"I got it from my father. Southern wisdom. Point is, I'm no damn fool."

"The Ythri have come up from meat-eating birds. Big built nests, porches without railings—so you could launch off them—perches overseeing large areas—"

"So how did they get larger-scale societies—cities, nations? Starships that zoom through wormholes—"

"The exotranslators say they rose through a 'challenge culture'—derived from their tribal origins, disputes, social evolution. There are ancient Messages that discuss these ornithoid extraterrestrials."

"So . . . this challenge is from the Ythri to . . . all humans?"

"It would seem so. It is their negotiation method."

Negotiate through . . . shared risk? The thought made her press back from the drop. Her hardened suit made movement slow, but she found that rugged heft reassuring. Zero g, but not zero mass, zero inertia. The suit had manifolds and buffers, shock absorbers and thermal dispersers galore—and she sensed the mass of them as a slowing-down of every movement. Weightless, yes, but swimming in molasses.

What is a Librarian doing here? Why did I agree to this stunt? Because the Library was akin to a dictatorship. And she could not face the questions: Why would she drop out of the greatest event ever, contact with real live aliens?

It might be good for her career, sure, but that wasn't the reason. Call it a . . . sense of adventure?

The vanes down her back sank into the spongy chair. In the suit chair to her right, the alien stared down at the serene blue-white curve. "Like our world, but large, yes," Fraq said.

The upper atmosphere glowed in its afternoon shimmer. Clouds lurked far below like icing on a spherical cake. Behind them the Star Tower was a thin line pointing from its ocean base south of Sri Lanka and on out to the counterweight beyond view. Stairway to the stars. Elevator, really. Beside her, the alien blocked her view to the north. Fraq sat in an odd way, feathers around his neck fluttering in magenta flourishes. Nervous? Slowly he turned to take it all in, then stared at her. Fraq—and until this moment she had not thought about what the word might mean. A Librarian should think of such things. What else had she ignored?

She let the view enchant her a bit more. *No way out of this, not now . . . so be calm.*

With Fraq and some of the flock and a support team of everything from engineers to diplomats, they had lifted from Luna. She had enjoyed the electromagnetic sling, its soaring views of crisp craters flashing by. Pinwheel in the black sky, stars awhirl. They had then coasted into rendezvous with the top of the orbital tower. There had been enough time in the downward elevator ride to practice and prepare, including exercises and tech briefings, fitting her suit, mastering its controls. The works. They rode down to the first tower station, a hundred kilometers above its floating ocean base. Now she and Fraq were jetting up and away, to more amazing views. In moments they would reach their drop position above Tamil Nadu in India, the green splotch spreading below. Cloudy knots of purpling anger fought along the coast. *Let's dive into that trouble storm.*

Too late to back out. . . .

She wondered if their fall would avoid the developing weather, so checked her in-suit. Systems-smart said, The apparent clouds are high altitude. You will pass through turbulence, but the ground condition is suitable.

So maybe okay, then. And . . . what was that time to fall again? Not much.

A long way down, indeed. What had her mother used to say? *Adventure means opportunity. Sure, Mom. Dear dead Mom.*

They were hovering now. Not orbiting, moving at speeds of tens of kilometers a second, no. This would have been impossible as a true reentry. No orbital velocity left. All they had to worry about was gravity. *Just gotta shed a few little kilometers per second on the way down, is all.*

Suit check. White supersteel ribs over elbows, shoulders, and knees, secured. Red accents of reinforced joints, vanes along her forearms. Heat shield for rigidity and thermal screen—transparent, thick, gotta be able to enjoy the view. The signature Orbital Outfitters logo on her chest, which carried the smart parachute controls. She clamped down the system, hard secure.

All up and running. So . . . go.

Her comm rang in her left ear. It was the Prefect, the tone said. Probably calling with some phony last-minute encouragement. She ignored it. *Hi! I'm out of my mind, but feel free to leave a message.*

Fraq turned to look at her, diamond-sharp golden eyes glittering. Excitement? Reading hominid-like expressions into an alien was an error, she knew. But hard to resist.

Breathe easily, they had said. She tried.

Fraq reached over and clasped her arm. The special suit grown for him had even more gear dotting it than hers.

Did he want to go now? No way to tell, but the countdown meter available in her left eye said no, there were—what?—with a shock she saw it ticking down, 19 . . . 18 seconds to go.

Somehow the Earth's luminous beauty had stolen away her time.

Automatically she raced through the drill. Just jump out. Legs together. Arms out straight for torque control. No need to pitch down. Just let gravity happen.

She looked to her left, where Earther vid teams were dressed in tunics of gold. They stood out in their high hard collars, shiny elastic wrists. Every turn of Earther high fashion seemed to her worse than the last one. These people looked like performers she had seen once, Cossack acrobats.

Waiting for her to tumble.

She ritually gave her parachute straps a tug. Drogue, yes. Main, snug.

No reason to abort there, none at all. . . .

Ding. Time.

She thought about the Library and how safe it was, just her own comfortable office . . . and unbuckled her harness.

Fraq did the same, eyes glittering as he followed her every move.

Has he done this before? He had said so, back on his world. Still . . . *Is he feeling fear?*

The golden eyes told her nothing.

She stood up. For the human species. Damned if she would let Fraq go first.

She took a deep breath and leaped.

2.

No sensation of movement. Weightless. She had already trained to suppress her falling reflexes so she could simply watch as the world hung there, ignoring her. Only after ten breaths—she refused to look at the timer—did she see any slight movement. The world was edging toward her.

Getting interested . . . in getting fed. . . .

And Fraq—? She turned her head slightly to find him, and the drag of rushing air tugged at her. A soft *whoosh* told her she was moving even if her eyes did not.

There was Fraq. Behind her and to her right. She relaxed. This was not a race, but it didn't hurt that she was ahead. Slightly.

She banked her arms a bit and felt a slight spin. Corrected it by moving her arms oppositely. In control, just as her training said. No spins, if she reacted fast enough. No tumbles, no injuries.

She kept her head looking down and peered to both sides. She felt prickly heat building in the suit and saw rippling air to the sides. Shock refraction. Rattling built along her legs and arms, humming into her body.

The atmosphere was playing her like an instrument.

A wave of fear swept through her. But then it tickled. She barked out a laugh. *Laughter is just a slowed-down scream of terror.* Where had she read that . . . ?

The sky brightened and she stole a glance at her other meters in her right eye. Speed nearly a thousand kilometers an hour and climbing fast. A burr of sound coursed through her body. Wind resistance plucking at her.

Whispers sang shrill past her head.

The horizon flattened, losing its silky curve. Stars glimmered, bright and true, then faded. Blue fog gathered around her and the puffy clouds fled sideways. She hung in a vast space that whipped by her. Below was . . . purple.

Something shot by her. Big. Fraq.

He described a helix wrapping around her, zooming past, and then made a complicated move with his arms outstretched. A deft, birdy maneuver. He slowed, hovered so she could overtake. Then he waved his wing-arms in the suit—which gave him darting moves. He arced away, spinning his body.

What the hell?! She dared not imitate that. Abruptly Fraq banked back toward her and zipped across, well ahead of her. She could swear she saw his eyes glitter, the mouth pucker.

If we two hit, what—

Fraq abruptly shot across her again and hovered, golden eyes glaring.

Some kind of challenge?

He came so close, she could see his face flared red. He folded his wing-arms in and fanned his legs. Hanging only a meter away, he reached over and touched her shoulder. Fear flooded through her.

Rachel made herself stretch out her own arm toward the alien. Fraq did a somersault, windmilling arms. Then he plunged away from her, arrowing toward the brilliant clouds below.

He's playing with me. Just relax. . . .

No time to think. Her head snapped back. Pulses sounded through her—buffeting. She checked her data disk; she was moving faster than sound. Her cowling held off shock waves, but a thousand small hammers found nooks to rattle and hurt.

Not relaxed anymore. A warning clang jolted her ears.

Her thermal shedders were laboring, but she felt prickly heat seep into her skin. Breath was a labor. Heat rising. A deep clank.

The drogue signal. About to deploy.

She turned to see if her backpack was clear. A sharp jolt wrenched her sideways. Spinning—

Sky. Boots. Sky. Boots.

She was tumbling. She forced her arms out the way Fraq had. Wind tore at her arms. They strained in their sockets.

If her drogue parachute popped out while she tumbled, the shrouds could tangle. The chute would not open right.

She forced her arms in the odd gestures Fraq had made. Wind howled around her. She opened her legs to get drag and that brought her around, facing down again. But she was at an angle, getting forced back into a rotation.

She windmilled her arms. That brought her right again, facing down. But she overshot. She reversed the windmill, eased back into position, facing down.

Bang—the drogue chute peeled away and slammed her hard.

Air rushed from her lungs. She fought the huge hand trying to crush her chest and sucked in a little air. She was losing speed fast.

But the drogue was deployed right, pulling hard at her.

Below, all was blue-black.

She blinked and took a deep breath. The darkness drew back. She had nearly blacked out.

An enormous cloud towered over the puffy white cumulus near it, stretching up from an anvil-shaped base to a massive head. And she was falling into it.

They were. She looked for Fraq. There he was, well ahead of her now, drogue bright orange.

She closeupped the cloud base and saw lightning fork in quick, raging stabs. Her inboards told her the cloud bank was twice as high as Everest.

Wispy ice clouds slipped by her. She looked toward her feet. She was white.

Ice caked her now.

And here came the billowy head of the big cloud. Fronds of vapor enveloped her as she shot through layers of cloud decks, shocks slamming through her. Like being shaken by a giant. And cold . . . Her teeth chattered. But only her head was chilled. So much for thermal overload. Was that only minutes ago?

Her helmet had rims of ice crystals. But why did she not feel cold all over? Then she realized that the buffeting was resonating through her, playing her like a drum. Her teeth chattered in resonance with it. She felt the drogue's pull, maybe half a grav. Muscles ached, strummed.

The ice-white streamers around her thickened and darkness gathered in. Fat, dark boils below loomed and she plunged through them, into . . . night. *It must be cold here,* she thought, but she felt warm. The heat from the first, fast friction had protected her.

But . . . she felt queasy. In the dark she could feel herself begin to spin, arms trying to fly out. The parachute would get fouled if she went into a gyre.

But how to stop? She spread her arms, giving way to the centrifugal.

Now she could navigate by the pressure against her, since that was down. She flexed her legs to steer and got slammed around by twisting winds. All in the whirling dark.

Violent gusts rattled her. Lifted her . . . then not. Gravity returned—which meant she was rising, punched upward by winds that fed the cloud core.

Pang went her faceplate. Lesser hammer blows rang along her body. What? In a dim silvery glow, she saw hailstones bouncing off her suit. Rocks of ice, some as big as her fist. They came at her from below, slamming up into her. But she still felt less gravity, so she was rising toward the cloud summit. Some huge hurricane was hammering the hail upward. A crisp, white burst of light seared her vision. She closed her eyes, letting them recover.

Falling. Breathing, yes. She looked down a vast dark tunnel burrowing through the center of the cloud. A white lightning bolt twisted across this tunnel, showing her feet as apart, arms flapping. Whirling. Head rapping hard. Dark above. Tunnel below. Dark above again. Tunnel—then it snapped off, leaving her in complete black oblivion.

She looked at her helmet timer: 16.27 minutes elapsed.

It seemed like hours. And the ground was somewhere below. Plus storms.

Smoke collected on the belly of the storm. Like a parasite crawling, she thought. She had never seen such lightning-bright weather near the ground. The cloud world flashed all around her, lit by tangles of lightning—thick blades like liquid swords. Then they snapped off—and the thunder came. She did not hear it. Instead, she felt it, like a deep note that her body hummed.

Winds poked and pried at her, whipping her arms around. She curled up, head toward what she thought was down—and found in the next blue-white lightning flash that she was looking up. Or thought she was.

A giant hand snatched her around. Her lungs wheezed out all they had. The hand had her by her back—and then she realized that her chute was spinning her like an ornament.

She turned to check, and lightning lit the parachute canvas. A beautiful domed cathedral over her. Almost enough to make her religious. Then the thunder hit her and she vibrated again. If there was a time to pray, this would be it.

Rain smeared her view. Clouds came rushing up at her. Sunlight broke through in slanting shafts that moisture diffused into halos. Cottony clouds glittered like mountains of spun sugar. The buffeting jerked her around and she felt dizzy with the speed. *Will this never end? Where is Fraq?* She plunged through laces of incandescence. The moisture gave rays of light a cool shimmering beauty, and she felt it sweep away her mounting fear.

Then she shot through the brilliance. She turned to look down. The huge tunnel that was the cloud interior now ended in a rippled wall of dirty gray. Those must be rain-saturated clouds, she realized just as she plunged through it—

—into ordinary pattering rain.

Sheets of droplets wrapped around her. *Thump*—and a giant hand jerked her upward. The drogue popped out; she rose, hovered—fell—and the main landing chute twirled above her.

Smack. Her helmet visor starred. Something hard had hit it. What? But she could see nothing.

Now she was the bob on a shorter pendulum, swinging widely as gusts caressed her. Ordinary hot-white lightning flashed around her.

Hollow thunder boomed and she could hear it, a big door slamming somewhere. A muddy brown smear told her there was land below. She came down toward a pine forest, looking for a clear spot. There—a bare stretch of rock. She recalled her drop training. Feet together, body bent at the waist, hands and elbows tight—

The rocky slope came at her fast. She hit, rolled. Her helmet cracked down.

Lie still, she thought. *Do nothing.* It felt very good.

Her body ached at a thousand spots. Joints wailed. Rain pattered against her, a good-bye tapping.

She sat up. Felt arms, legs, body, neck . . .

Nothing seemed to be broken, but a lot of her wanted to complain. The parachute tugged at her, and she groped for the release. Tug, pull, pull, grunt—it popped free.

Ah! So good to be alive. Even though she could feel a hundred aches and bruises.

She looked around. Trees, wind thrashing them. Something above—she turned to see Fraq swinging down. He landed effortlessly, remained erect.

Fraq abruptly broke into an odd dance, spinning and barking out sharp sounds like clashing gears. Barking birdcalls, deep and resonant. He thumped his chest.

She staggered over. Fraq held out a hand, as if inviting her to dance with it. She did. He spun her around, tapped large feet on the rock like a drumbeat. More ritual?

Her body sagged, hurt, wanted to go home please. She felt like punching him in the chest. *No, be the diplomat. Never mind that there are clear signs down below that you wet yourself.*

Instead, she stabbed a finger at the audio recording the translator had made for her. Her prepared salute. To her ears it was like gravel churning in a blender, with occasional trills. It meant *Thus do I introduce you to my world. Now let us begin.*

Fraq spread arms and did a complicated two-step. By now she knew this meant *Agreed. Begin.*

She took a step into . . . mud. She turned her head up to greet the rain. She felt it then, the grim grasp of a whole grav. She took labored steps. Her knees cried out, feet, too. She inhaled the thick, moist air flavored with strange scents. These fetched forth from her long-ago memories of the Deep South. This world was an immense mudball, fragrant, air thick like water and richly flavored. Ah . . .

Back home. The orbitfall plunge, alien mad dance, lungs heaving in thick, rich air—

All of it swelled up around her, brimmed over, and ran down her face in thick tears.

FRAQ

Before I took their Great Plunge, I spoke to my Flock:

Eat as if you will die tomorrow, build as if you will live forever.

This is an ancient saying, our nest wisdom, yet still vital now. I risked the Plunge not to perform a great fall, but to construct—to build anew the great bridges hidden within our galaxy's spacetime.

I and their Rachel female did descend without any true damage. I admit my body was much stressed by the fall, and aches still. It was akin to the arch-challenges our kind regard as necessary to become fully fledged Lorders of we Yth.

She was of course affright, as grounders must be, in their air. Yet she persisted. Their culture had made a sport of this challenge, so they were well equipped to render unto her a firm suit. I admire their ability with 'facture, the shaping of knowledge into firm form. They command machines well.

They built well for me, indeed. I was snug within my own descent casing. It shed the friction heat well. I felt the rush of velocities faster than sounds, the rattling of frame and bone, the howls of sharp forking yellow electricity, the gamut of deep, hard air.

The groundlings were rapt, as is their due. She shone for them, I shone for we Yth.

Of course, we Yth had played such flight sports long ago. In our bones we knew that space flight includes space fall. This is only natural—to us. Not them.

The groundlings are young and strange and yet respond to our older, truer ways. Like so many species, they know, absolutely firmly know in fullflight wisdom, that they are the crown of creation. It is a truth, as some of them say, self-evident.

We Flock thought such, when our species was young and foolish. It must be so. As made known—through what the Library terms Messages, and we Flock ken by historical knowledge—these groundling histories speak of their relentless upward progress to now, surely the peak of intelligence. They have not—yet—lived through the destruction of their world. They have risen from grunts and war-clubs but do not yet perceive the darker undercurrents of life on scales galactic.

So can we still evade their piercing gaze, through misdirection. They are sure of themselves, and so vulnerable to our adroit inspections.

Yet still: one of their endless commentators said on open cast-broad, "I doubt we can fare much better than the Incas and the Aztecs did against the Euros." I shall not trouble you with the details of this idle dread. So, it is their fear we must quell.

That is my content. I addressed the Flock in our subspeech, in ancestral song-sounds, melodious and sincere. I used our Second Tongue that we have artfully concealed beneath our symphonic string-speech. This was to elude detection and their understanding. The grounders assume the strings are our main language, and so miss the song-chirps and feathershrugs that add so much. Thus we so speak only when in full gather: the Flock can best speak as we fly.

So to you all of Flock: Our concealment wings well. My small band is with me, enduring their heavy world. We shall proceed with bloodpride challenges to the grounders. They much like to see us. The snouts of their vision machines follow us everywhere. They even pry into our intimate moments!—which with fury we have stopped.

These flutters and feats shall distract them from our main flight wingers, on their moon. They labor with the Prefects and Noughts and Librarians—these seem to be separate breeds, or nearly so—in their Message chambers. There they can explore the many Messages that were lost to us in antiquity, during the Exodus. With deft wingship they shall find the increments of knowledge of the wormhole network. We need these now, to find our vagrant Mouth and then to use it.

In their Plunge, I judged their courage and truest nature. For groundlings to attempt such spoke well of them.

Yet the Mouth goals we must keep secret. We need learn more, here, before trusting these primates. Thus our feats of bloodpride distraction proceed. After descent, comes ascent.

PART 9

ASCENDING
EVEREST

Looking up at the stars, I know quite well
That, for all they care, I can go to hell.

—W. H. AUDEN, "THE MORE LOVING ONE"

1.

Days later, her soreness was gone but not her smoldering emotions. The Plunge had changed her, Rachel knew, but not exactly how.

"What?" the Prefect Siloh demanded. "Fraq will only teach us rituals?"

Rachel shrugged. "That is all he's delegated to do, apparently."

"What good is that?"

"Fraq points out that without the protocols needed to access a wormhole mouth, the artificial systems that keep those gates open will not let us pass." Rachel shifted, aching, still feeling the pressure of full grav.

"What does that mean—not let us pass?"

Rachel grimaced. "I don't think we want to find out."

"What are these rituals like?"

"Maneuvers in space, signals to send. Some tangled mathematical stuff I couldn't follow. Think of it as an elaborate key."

The Prefect returned his face to the familiar stony blank. "Fraq won't give any hint of where the nearest wormhole mouth is?"

She eyed the Prefect, wondering if the man had any personal life. Or was it all about the Library? Better be the diplomat, then.

"That may come, in time. He says he wants to 'ken' Earth. That's an old word meaning to know in a profound way."

The Prefect's mouth twisted. "Some high-ranked people will be very irked."

"Some low-ranked, too. But ..." She paused, trying to express an intuition gained from many hours with Fraq. "I am gathering in some ways of thinking about this alien culture. It's so easy to admire the freedom of the skies they enjoy."

The Prefect leaned forward, his posture eager, but he kept the blank mask. "He told you some of their history?"

"They're communal. Live in close quarters, apparently because their world is pretty hostile. Plus, carnivores have to be quick, aggressive. So they're very formal with each other, the way crowded cultures are on Earth."

"He told you this expressly?"

"I inferred from nuances in his speech. This is going to take time. Fraq doesn't think the way we do, and he has a species history that began when we were small mammals staying out from underfoot."

The Prefect's tone turned sour. "So he gives us more ceremony, not substance."

Come on, Freezeface. But she said mildly, "It's a first step." She was beginning to get the feel of this profession. Humanity was coming to an ancient interstellar conversation, written before hominids had even been around.

Apparently many intelligent species had a brief technological phase, then relapsed. Most listened in or sent SETI messages for a century or two, then fell silent. So humanity was just beginning its trial period. They should not expect the Elders to take much notice of them, or lend much help.

Thanks to millennia of SETI exchanges, the Elders had grown far more complex than the sum of all human societies. This Byzantium among the stars was much stranger than anything humans had ever known.

Rachel said carefully, "Fraq has made it very clear they are helping us out because we're rubes. Less prosperous, wet behind the ears, younger, ignorant. And he's right."

The Prefect seldom reacted immediately to new information. Some computer behind his forehead had to grind away first.

A glaze came over his face as he thought, and a sudden image flashed into Rachel's mind: herself as Superwoman, bounding over vast obstacles, shrugging off pesky hindrances. Her trusty companion, Fraq, leading her into ever more dazzling feats. This connection to Fraq could be a career maker, played right.

But then a chill came into her, a foreboding. *There's something afoot here I don't like. Librarian Rachel isn't Superwoman. And shouldn't be.*

"We should remain open to possible other motives." The Prefect picked up a datasheet and punched up a message. "Fraq sent me a request, posed in formal language. He seems to want a companion while he 'kens' Earth."

Rachel had not heard of this. She stayed silent.

The Prefect made a thin attempt at sounding upbeat. "This time Fraq points out that there is a way to 'ascend' as well. Apparently that would involve some rocket-assisted means to soar to the top of Mount Everest." He stopped and peered at her. "I assume you can exercise your same skills as before and—"

"Don't finish that sentence." She got up and stalked out. Which took a kind of courage Superwoman Rachel didn't know.

2.

It looked like a death machine.

Rachel walked toward it, across the emerald meadow framed by snowy peaks. Her body still groaned at the effort, but the cutting, cold air helped somehow. In her years at the Library she had forgotten how Earth made its own decisions about weather, temperature and humidity and all that—not dull human engineers.

The long, gleaming tubes stood on either side of the carbon-fiber chair, molded into it for support. The tubes were three meters tall, sleek as rockets, and with rotors encased in two large ducts that looked a bit like cupcakes. It rested on three legs, an odd contraption ill-suited to the ground. In flight it might seem right, though. If this was the latest fun risk sport, it somehow managed to look both stylish and nerdy.

They called these Lifters. The pair stood like gleaming contraries amid grass spangled with yellow wildflowers. The beautiful meadow was the last sign of life before the moraine, gray broken granite like something left over from the building of the universe.

Beyond them lay the target, Everest. Nearly nine kilometers above sea level, its prow cut the streaming clouds as if it were a ship gliding through a white ocean. From here, just below Base Camp, she wondered how Lifters could take anyone that far, climbing nearly four kilometers.

Rachel walked around a Lifter warily, her breath puffing in the chilled air. "It can go that far?" she asked the tall, bald engineer who was checking the engine ports.

He jerked a thumb over his shoulder at Fraq. "We built them special for that alien. Used the tech blueprints he had—some real good ideas there. I think they'll take him and that woman up halfway, maybe more. Then you gotta refuel."

Rachel liked the engineer but not the contraption. "Fraq wants me at the refueling post. He doesn't trust you guys to get it right. Maybe."

The engineer snorted. "Ma'am, these're assault pods. Real powerful. Infantry uses 'em to go straight up skyscrapers, mostly. Mountains? They're easier to climb, sure. But Lifters got plenty room for error. You get a fuel line plugged, you just set down." He sniffed dismissively. "Piece of cake. Don't gotta be smart."

Rachel didn't think any of this was smart, but she was here anyway. She nodded and walked over to the Seeker of Script, Henjai Chen, who was checking out her ascent suit. "Ready?" Rachel said with an attempt at bright optimism.

On Chen, the tight, black leather flight suit looked like a fetish item. Kink chic.

"I think so," the woman said softly, as though cowed. "Is . . . he?"

Fraq stood apart, checking his flight suit methodically. Getting his feathers into a pressure suit had been a tricky engineering issue Rachel was happy to hear nothing more about. His strange eyes swept the plain where the team readied the technical assists and the Lifters. To Rachel, this was a thoroughly exotic place, this broad meadow at high altitude. She had never even been in Asia, until her orbitfall into warm, humid Tamil Nadu. This chilly mountain fastness felt like another world. The working teams wore simple cloth garments, as if from another age, hemmed in by a mountain range that stepped away into ever-higher, snowy bastions. She sniffed and tried to keep her focus. The Himalayas were awesome, beautiful, and, to her, a distraction. She could be a tourist some other time.

This was about the alien.

Fraq welcomed her with an odd, jerky bow as she approached. His diamond-sharp yet golden eyes glittered behind his visor. His conic nose flared wide and red. Excitement cues, she now knew. Reading alien expressions was difficult, but she had learned a lot since she had plunged a hundred kilometers with this daredevil. That, plus many days spent slogging through SETI texts, deciphering them with him, had made Fraq seem understandable. An error, probably.

The translator, Natal, stepped forward. She was a small, intense type who had worked with Fraq since his arrival. His command of Anglish was good, but some Ythri elements needed work. Natal had developed audio pickups that transduced human speech into the alien's own sounds if Fraq could not shape human words. So she gave a greeting: "He welcomes your kind assistance. It is time to surmount the heights."

Rachel nodded, smiling at the impassive—or maybe just unreadable—alien face. He reached over with his long wing-arms and clasped her hands together.

Fraq spoke like gravel beneath tires, chunks spitting out, utterly unlike their song-sounds. The translator said stiffly, "Again we perform the ceremony of greeting. You and I have joined the Great Fallen. Now follows an invocation of need. You will help the human female Reader-of-Truths to accompany Fraq—yes?"

Rachel bowed. "Yes."

Fraq began reciting phrases. Rachel was used to this by now: the ceremonial assurances and introductions, salutes to past flock heroes, females of renown who wore a golden crown, the lot—time-honored in his culture. She smiled slightly and kept her face otherwise blank.

There were Earthly precedents, after all. The first lasting writings came from temple bureaucrats marking down economic transactions. In these texts from ancient Iraq, books did not have titles. Librarians used the incipit—the first few words of the text—to identify a tablet, just as poems were still listed by opening lines in present indexes. Some of the Library SETI messages used this wildly archaic method. They were welters of first lines, so that even their indexes read like weird poems of disconnected thoughts.

Fraq came from a culture that insisted on such formalisms in speech.

Humans had long abandoned those.

Finished now, bowing with a curious two-handed gesture like slow-flying birds, the alien turned away to speak to the engineer, who approached with a team to go through procedures. Techtalk flew, mediated by the interpreter.

Rachel could not follow that. Luckily, she didn't need to. She was here because Fraq wanted her, following some odd Ythri social protocol. She had done the Plunge with him, which seemed to mean a lot to his rigid manners.

Rachel turned to leave and found Chen at her elbow.

The slight woman whispered, "The . . . Everest . . . seems so, so . . . D-do you think this is possible?"

Rachel looked at her in wonderment. It was as though their first meeting had never happened. But Rachel recalled it well. . . .

3.

The small Asian woman who came confidently into Rachel's office had large eyes with a strange, penetrating look in them. Eerily like reptile eyes, Rachel thought.

"Librarian Rachel Cohen?" the woman asked formally in a flat tone.

"Sit," Rachel said, spotting the Seekers of Script emblem on the woman's shoulder. Library staff, fine, but— She could barely look away from those eyes. She halfway expected a nictitating membrane to close across them, so cold was the woman's gaze.

"I'm Henjai Chen," she said, settling deeply into a guest chair. Here on Earth the visiting Loonies got red carpet and mahogany paneling throughout. The Library furniture on Luna was flimsy stuff, hard and heat-molded from regolith, but in Lunar gravity that mattered little. She and Chen got deep-cushioned seats.

Chen seemed to become the focus of the room merely by sitting down, carefully folding her skirt under her delicious legs. In a jolt Rachel realized that, for the first time in her life, she hated this woman on sight. Her nostrils flared as if she had caught a foul scent.

"I wanted to confer with you about the aliens," Chen said in an arch tone, no discernible accent. "The Prefect Stiles suggests I should work with Fraq now."

"Better you than me," Rachel said.

Chen's already large eyes widened. "But he has made you famous!"

"Distracting me from my Library work, yes. But that was just recently, when he gave away that the Ythri wanted me to go Earthside."

"Prefect Stiles appreciates that you have given yourself to the cause—"

"By risking my neck, falling a hundred kilometers from the top of Earth's atmosphere. All to extract from Fraq a bunch of social protocols, signals, and manners, to use in approaching a wormhole. Whose location Fraq won't tell us."

Chen said primly, "I hope that is where I come in."

"And go out, probably."

"What do—oh, I see. You think Fraq's plans are dangerous."

Rachel sighed. Concerning the Ythri, passions ran high. Earthside was aflame with talk; everyone had six opinions; the political stakes were stratospheric. Ugh. "How long have you been with the Library?"

"Four years. Why?"

Long enough to get bored doing endlessly repetitive searches as a Seeker of Script, then. To look for a fast track upstairs. So Rachel said, "You seem an ambitious sort," which she thought was a polite way of saying, *You're looking for a quick leg up. Just spreading your legs for the Prefect wouldn't work—or maybe you tried that already?*

"I want to get ahead, just like most people."

"Showboating with Fraq may just be a fast route to the grave."

"Caution is advisable, yes," Chen said guardedly, her swanlike neck curling as she looked discreetly around Rachel's office.

For personal effects? That was why Rachel didn't display any; too easy to read lots into. Her southern American origin probably didn't help. Or, Rachel realized, maybe she was getting just a tad cynical. She nodded.

Chen said brightly, "Still, that can just be timidity, a fault. As the Bard said, 'When I became a man, I put away childish things.' I try to live by that."

"The Bible, not the Bard. And risking your neck—as, I admit, I did—is not smart. Fraq isn't to be trusted."

A show of polite shock. "Why?"

Rachel could not hold back anymore. "He's an alien! A culture we don't know."

Chen smiled prettily with her thin lips, but the large, cold reptilian eyes did not give anything away. "Alien, yes. But. He took you through the Orbitfall Plunge, I gather. Alone. And you won't do anything more with him."

Rachel looked across her desk at the woman and tried to put aside her feelings, which were ringing off the hook. "He's a risk taker. He likes that. Ythri do. Carnivores generally do. Alien, sure, with motives unclear. But think this through. I hear from the Prefect that Fraq wants to do other things, hallucination-crazy things."

"Well, yes. He does."

"Like?"

"Everest."

"I heard."

"You turned that down?"

"You bet."

"This visitor to our world, his flock"—Chen stood to make her point, spreading her arms—"wants to carry out a daring ascent, using our advanced technology. All to know our world in a way we have known it, to sense our challenges, test them—and you will not help him?"

Rachel sat back, amazed. Must be a prepared line. "You bet."

"He insists on being accompanied by a Librarian."

"See? That doesn't make sense to us, but does to him. And you're a Seeker of Script, not a full Librarian."

"He doesn't care about rank."

"But he wants a woman companion?"

Chen shrugged uncomfortably. "I doubt that matters."

Ha. "How can we be sure?"

A nod. "We can't, of course. But Fraq now wishes to 'ascend' the atmosphere—he offers plans for a rocket-assisted device to soar to the top of Mount Everest."

"The Prefect wants you to go with Fraq?"

Slowly, Chen said, "Yes."

"In trade for more information about the wormhole?"

"In exchange for some data useful to the Library," Chen said guardedly. "Otherwise, Fraq will not go further."

"So why come to me?"

"Fraq wants you to accompany him, too." Still withholding. What were those reptile eyes hiding?

"For what?"

"Companionship, I think. He was very disappointed that you did not agree to make the ascent. He regards working together and these 'challenges' as one and the same. Flock culture so demands, he says."

"Bonding? He can't seem to explain—and believe me, I and the Prefect and plenty of others have tried to understand—why those should go together."

"I think that makes your point—he has a culture we learn only by inference from his behavior. To him, social truths are self-evident. I think he is social in a way we don't get." Chen shrugged again, but it was a mannered shrug, calculated. "He seems to work only with those who have shared what he calls 'the barriers to knowing.' Apparently that means, to use another translated phrase, 'ways of challenging a world.' Fraq is a complex . . . being."

Rachel had to smile. "This is our first alien visit. We've apparently gathered him in as a first harvest of the old METI program, Messaging to Extraterrestrial Intelligence."

Chen brightened. "Yes—so I gathered from the transcripts. What a boon, for a centuries-old extravagance. Have we traced the cause?"

"Some billionaires sent out messages two centuries back. Risky—just look at the ferocious, ancient alien messages we've deciphered aplenty!—but yes, we got Fraq. Apparently his star is a few hundred light-years away." *Give away nothing you discovered . . .*

"Perhaps," Chen said quietly.

Rachel raised an eyebrow.

"Fraq's society may have a sentinel radio telescope near a wormhole—maybe even our wormhole, wherever it is out there. Then they would get relayed messages, much faster than light speed. So he could come from anywhere."

Rachel nodded. That possibility had gotten around the Library quite quickly. But not what Rachel had found, no. "From anywhere, right," she said. "And a humanoid, though we know from some of the most ancient messages that many aliens are not. Um. So—Ythri turn out to be humanoid riskers. Did you know Fraq wants to do an ocean descent by himself, all the way to the bottom?"

Chen carefully crossed her legs. "Yes. The Prefect said we had no idea how to do that, technically, without . . . risk."

Rachel laughed. "They'll find something!"

Chen seemed startled. "How?"

"No idea. But with resources, in time, they might. There's momentum behind giving Fraq and his flock what he wants, hoping he'll reveal more." Chen's eyes took on a veiled look. Ambition lurked in her manner. Rachel leaned forward. "Look—this is big. Big! Some think he's putting us through tests, see what we're really like. Maybe he wants to see us prove we're earnest in some alien way. And the deep thinkers link up with the politicos. They have the resources, and they like the media buzz we get from these stunts. Believe me, I know—after the Plunge, I had to seal myself off, to avoid being interviewed to death. The Prefect isn't going to miss a chance to get on the front minute of every 'cast in the world."

Chen gave a sly smile. "So . . . will you come with me?"

"On the flight?"

"Fraq says he wants you as a companion. It won't happen without you."

"Ah."

Chen sat straight, beaming, eyes agleam. "But I'll do the flight."

———

Now Rachel watched them get into their harnesses, Chen snugged into one, Fraq standing in the tight harness they wrapped him solidly in. His feathers flickered their excited colors, red and blue, as they started the trials.

"They make it look easy," Rachel said.

The engineer beside her snorted. "Now it does, yeah. Took us two months, workin' three shifts, to get 'em together."

"I'm sure this is all quite safe."

"Ma'am, I tried 'em, we all did. I tell you, with the startling power of those twin rotors and the engine behind my shoulder blades screaming like a million leaf blowers, it's great. Felt almost like I was doin' the lifting myself, with muscles I didn't know I had."

Rachel shivered, and not from the cold. This was May, the vast mountains were warming, but the chill in her was from fear. She had felt that just before diving off the platform for the Plunge, but this was different. Then, she had gazed in awe at the curve of a beautiful Earth. Here, the sharp air seemed tinged with dark dread. "How does it . . . steer?"

The engineer showed her with his hands, pulling imaginary levers in the air. "Whole-body experience—they've had the immersion drill. Y'see, pressin' the left-hand stick forward, that causes the Lifter to pitch forward some. See?"

Chen and Fraq were taking off in their trials, flying short loops, with the techs giving them plenty of room. They dangled a meter above the meadow, engines howling. Chen moved her left lever and the jet pack began advancing level with the ground. Techs trotted alongside, like parents teaching a child to ride a bicycle without training wheels. Chen managed well, weaving and getting the feel of it. So did Fraq.

Bulges on Chen's back were safety features, a ballistic parachute with a small explosive charge for rapid deployment. At her feet were platform shock absorbers like pogo sticks, to soften landings.

Rachel saw how mass distribution ensured stabilization. The weight of the engines and pilot body sat lower than the rotors, creating a pendulum effect. That, she could see, discouraged the contraption from tipping upside down. It was essentially a rocket pack, requiring the wearer to steer by tilting their body around and deploying stubby, winged appendages on arms and legs.

If that failed, Chen would become a lawn dart.

Rachel said, "It looks so . . . easy."

Grinning, the engineer watched Chen and Fraq rise to a hundred meters above them, weaving and flying with precision, perhaps even joy. The low air pressure helped. He said, "Y'know, people come up and look and go, 'Is it safe?' Ha!" He laughed amiably, and she found herself liking his bemused smile. "Safety is about percentages. Goin' this far up, clear to Everest, well . . . But this alien, he wants it, right?"

Rachel looked at him, his big tanned face wrenched up into the sky as if trying to see something there. "Why is everybody making this happen?" she asked.

"We wanna help this guy. He came here from some other damn star. Gotta give him what he wants, right?"

4.

"You don't like me, do you?" Chen had said straight out.

Rachel first thought of lying, then shrugged. "Correct."

"I could tell the moment I walked in."

"Perceptive."

"And it's because I'm doing what you're afraid of."

Rachel shook her head. "No, it's visceral."

"Then why didn't you accept Fraq's invitation?"

"Invitation? Wrong word. Fraq takes you through a dance, and if you follow his lead in that Byzantine formalism, you end up entangled. I figured out how to say no. You didn't."

Chen bristled. "I think you're a coward."

Rachel enjoyed smiling. "And I think you're a fool. You are, you know. When you face what this crazy ascent really means, you'll see that."

"I'll discount that since it comes from a coward. You are, you know."

"Touché! You didn't volunteer for that bungee jump to the bottom of the Grand Canyon, did you?"

Chen blinked. "No, I wasn't asked."

"That woman got pretty banged up, smacking into that spire on the rebound."

"I—I heard."

"Then there was that descent from a mountaintop by flying kites. Another Seeker of Script, as I recall. Broken back."

"She survived," Chen said primly.

"And no doubt helped her career."

"You are so cynical."

"Cynic is a term idealists use to describe realists."

Chen took a deep breath and plainly decided to start over with their conversation. "I came to you for advice on handling him."

"Get him drunk."

Chen blinked again. "What?"

"He might tell you something inadvertently. The biochemists tell us his chemistry is enough like ours for alcohol to have a similar effect. He's refused alcohol so far, but maybe you can trick him."

Chen just stared. Her jaw slowly dropped, then shut. "I can't believe you said that."

"Cynic is a term idealists use—"

"I know, but what you said—it's unethical!"

"Ethics are relative, especially with aliens. We don't know his ethics, for example. Or even if he thinks in such categories that we consider obvious, such as ethics itself. We just know his rituals and symbolic acts. The motive behind him—that we don't know at all."

"But . . . to insert alcohol into his food—"

"Maybe better to say straight out, 'Here, drink up—we primates use this as a ritual bonding ingredient.'"

"Oh . . . you could do that well. You've been through the Plunge, they respect you."

Of course Rachel had already thought of that. She could see in Chen's flicker of interest that the woman was always looking for her next shot of schadenfreude. Get Rachel to do some risky thing, laugh when it failed. Move up to replace her, maybe—Librarian Chen.

Now Chen got a look of pained indulgence on her face—cramped eyes, sour mouth twist, a thin frown.

Here comes a lecture, Rachel guessed.

"You do not seem to see the implications of simple facts. I am a specialist in Asian cultures, because most alien cultures—especially the Beacon societies—are, of course, many millennia older than human civilization. The longest-enduring Earthly civilizations—typically, Asian—evolved formal methods to lessen internal conflict, shore up hierarchy, and slow change. They revered social mannerisms, protocols, rituals. They used the leisurely consideration of new ideas. Older Beacon societies took these features as the very definition of a society worth engaging by electromagnetic signals."

"So?" Orthodox Librarian thinking. It amused Rachel to be pontificated to. She could see that Chen was still processing the get-him-drunk advice. As she talked, running a tape as a friend had once said, her mind was working, She might even have some bright angles on this.

"Hence," Chen went on, "the ornate procedures needed to even approach a wormhole. Fraq invoked these. Rituals to eliminate the uninitiated, I think—interlopers. Further, as with Beacon messages, having complex introductions, side comments, features that we Librarians found confounding. But presumably those play a social role, in organisms far different from any Earthly analogy. They are social mannerisms."

Rachel frowned; Chen had done her homework. "So, sure, we can't know what those side features mean, granted. But has it occurred to you that Fraq might be testing us with these 'stunts'? They may not be idle matters."

"Testing?" Plainly Chen had not thought of this. "Some sort of initiation?"

Rachel sat back and tried to think. It was hard to get beyond her instant dislike of this woman. But she had to try. Good ideas didn't only come from people you liked. "Hard to know. Fraq might be sending all this back home as . . . diplomatic messages. Through a relay link out at the wormhole, wherever. For some unimaginable Foreign Office."

Chen relaxed somewhat in her chair. "Of course, his actions might mean all of these things. Our duty as Librarians, even though I am merely a Seeker of Script, is to consider that this alien might be doing several things at once. But at the same time he gives away secrets of his own world."

"You think they could somehow tell us something about the hidden assumptions in his society? Or in their SETI messages?"

Chen shrugged. "It's not a crazy idea."

"Except we don't know what SETI messages come from his world. He's never revealed it."

"I . . . I have talked to him. Through the translator, of course. Using formal Ythri terms, quite labyrinthine. But that's compromised."

"How?"

Chen even chuckled. "She records and reports all conversations."

"Of course. But—"

"Fraq has his own electronic means. He uses it to send messages."

"How?"

"That's between him and me." Chen leaned forward eagerly. "Look, Prefect Stiles wanted to tell me things you should know."

That's a bait he didn't try with me, Rachel thought, but let her face show only startled interest. "Oh?"

"Fraq says the truly advanced alien civilizations have learned to be adept at contacts. They insist on a menu of tests."

"You mean—"

"Designed to gauge the abilities and sensitivities of humans. He's part of that. The tests. The 'four universalities,' he calls them."

Rachel couldn't resist. "One is . . . falling from orbit?"

Chen shook her head impatiently. "These are preliminaries. Part of the first test—how do we react in unfamiliar situations? We pass, so far."

"If unexpected means crazy, yes. And we pass, so we're crazy."

"The others are, how are we when meeting superior civilizations? Then how are we when running into lesser civilizations? How about when we get temporary great powers? That is, while showing empathy for the downtrodden."

Rachel took a deep breath, let it out slowly. "And he told only you about this?"

Chen beamed, brightly sure of herself. "I have a way with him."

5.

Rachel hugged herself against the cold and eyed the distant meadow, far below. Despite her oxy feed, she was short of breath. A chopper had brought her up here hours ago, and now the downslope takeoff ticked along, down to mere seconds . . . and she wondered why the hell she was here. Again.

The landscape inspired awe. She stared agog at the view of the northeast ridge of Bugaboo Spire, a massive pyramid of rock towering over the sprawling glacier, nearly blotting out the crisp, hard blue sky. She sucked in as much of the thin air as she could and it bit deep in her throat.

She was thrilled, but her doubts always overlayered her feelings. *I'm a Librarian—why am I doing this?*

Because her subjects, aliens and their ancient messages, were not like safely dead poets or scientists. They could turn up from wormholes unseen, demand the impossible—and out of the awe humans had for them, they could get it. No matter how crazy-dangerous. *Awe*, she thought, had a lot to do with *awful*.

In her headphones came the tinny controller voice: "Ready, check. Go." Using her augmented binoculars, Rachel plucked their images out of the clearing far below. Tiny motes buzzing around, tended by the tech team. There were two main routes for climbing Everest, and she stood at 6.5 kilometers altitude along the southeast ridge, on the south side of Everest in Nepal. This was the technically easier route, with far more infrastructure in place. The chopper had found its flat zone near where the Lifters would land to refuel. Then they would attempt the peak in one straight shot.

Now. Filmy pink plumes vented from the Lifters of Fraq and Chen. They swooped up into the firmament with lofty grace. Just specks, from here.

Fraq described a helix wrapping around Chen, zooming past her. Like his helix about Rachel on the Plunge. Then he made a complicated move, sailing around her, then hovering so she could overtake. He made artful darting moves and arced away, spinning the Lifter somehow. Chen dared not imitate that, Rachel thought.

Abruptly he banked back toward her and zipped across, forcing the Lifter to its limits.

Madness, Rachel thought. Just the sort of swooping he had done when they fell from orbit. Why?

Yet somehow he had caught the imagination of the world. An alien embracing their most extreme sport! Videos of their drop-off moments reran everywhere.

Several had died attempting it since. Others came through, often with injuries. She had been lucky—and had enjoyed Fraq's help along the way, with his bizarre maneuvers—but only afterward realized how risky it had been.

In their comfy lives, people needed risk as a stimulant. Soon enough, a milder version of the orbital plunge appeared. Earthers needed thrills.

Especially cool ones.

The Star Tower had begun offering "outer ascents" at a high price. People journeyed up the tower while attached to a moving chair outside—full view!

Their chairs were pulled just as the elevator cabin was, but at different speeds, according to the taste of the ascending tourist. The same ride downward supplied the return energy to help power the orbital tower itself, through electromagnetic induction harvesting. That gave the chair customers a muted thrill like orbitfall, but safe. Slo-mo thrills! Higher drop rates cost more, of course.

Ascents usually went one or two hundred kilometers up, to avoid too great a radiation exposure, because the trip could take days. Then they came down, taking the "outer descent" to witness the slow spectacle of the world's blithe curvature. They had a small capsule that cost a fortune.

But several people a month still took the orbitfall. Some died. There had been heart attacks from the thrill alone. Further evidence, Rachel thought as she sucked in the thin air, of a culture with far too much time and money on its hands. A culture that needed new horizons, fresh perspectives, something worth giving themselves to. Instead, they gave their lives for pointless thrills.

Of course, though the public knew nothing concrete, beyond the usual gee-whiz speculations, there was . . . the wormhole. She couldn't get her mind around that possibility, how just knowledge of it would affect this Earther culture. Not yet.

Now Fraq was forcing the invention of another extreme sport. *Thing about aliens is . . .*

Everest was already nearly impossible to get permission to climb. All the accumulated debris and wear from centuries of people trekking up it had damaged it through centuries now. Huge helicopters even flew all the way to the summit, hovering while tourists jumped out for their few minutes and photos to paste on their refrigerators back home. That had peaked back in the Age of Appetite, around the turn of the millennium.

That age was still here, in weird frozen monuments. She had seen or knew of the honored dead bodies at points on the climb.

These gruesome trail markers even had names: Crucified Guy, Green Boots, Sleeping Beauty. Those frozen failed climbers came to be legacy points. *Oh, sure, when you get to Green Boots make a hard left up the slope to Sleeping Beauty.*

She shook herself. It was hard to fathom the fantastically oblivious past.

Now here came a new invasion. Fast-flight to the top.

Did all this say something about humanity? And why did it take an alien to invent the idea?

And here came the bird alien. Zooming up, wiggling a bit as it came, the Lifter gave off a confident roar in the sharp, clear air. Fraq hovered over the landing spot and looked around, his helmet a sleek bulge giving his glittery eyes a wide view. Then he descended from a hundred meters above them. At the last moment the Lifter coughed, barked—and settled in.

The tech team looked alarmed. They rushed over to his Lifter, leaving one guy behind to assist and talk down Chen. She came up sedately, hovering not far from the steep glacier below. Rachel could see Chen through the bubble, sitting rigidly, and her head jerking around. Stiff. Scared.

The tech guy waved her in. She hovered, bobbed up a bit from overcompensating, and then settled down. Three media people scrambled over, their lenses leading.

Rachel walked over to Chen across a rough gray moraine patch. Her boots crunched in the snow cover. It had come down that morning and already had a hard skin. Chen climbed down from her perch in the Lifter and stumbled as she met solid ground. Her padded suit and oxy feed looked odd around the full-face helmet. But her large eyes danced, and Rachel wondered about that.

"How'd it go?" Rachel asked.

Chen ignored her and gave the media team a smile like scissors. "Great!" she shouted in a phony, boisterous tone. She even gave the lenses a thumbs-up.

"Just one more to the summit," Rachel said, and felt foolish. "Holding steady?"

"It's, it's spectacular." The smile broadened as she turned straight in toward the cameras.

Then Chen swiveled and shot a quick phrase to Rachel. "I'm scared, but I'm going through with it."

"Uh, sure—"

"He says his kind don't come from a planet at all, not anymore."

"What?"

"That's why he likes doing these things. Taking risks. They live in a place far from the 'early times,' he says. So mountains, atmospheres—they're exotic."

"Then where—?"

"He told me just before we took off." Chen blinked and looked terrified, wide-eyed and yet somehow brave.

Then the media folk peppered her with questions, cutting off the conversation.

Rachel shook her head and strode over to Fraq's Lifter. The translator was doing her number with the shouting knot of media, with Fraq at the center, uttering his gravel sentences. The media folk were rapt, listening to his descriptions, reactions, tidbits of alien philosophy.

So Rachel turned to the tech team. "What was that noise?"

The big, bald engineer grinned and turned so the media people would not hear. "He ran out of fuel. Maxed it. It was burnin' fumes when he came down."

Rachel had guessed as much, from the coughing plume, but— "Why would he do that?"

The big man shrugged. "Lives life to the limit. Like an eagle, he is." A lofty, eager smile. "Can't blame him. He's a long way from home, for sure."

6.

She had talked over the entire scenario with Chen—that altitude sickness, weather, or wind could end the whole attempt. And now the wind was picking up. It looked like sullen clouds were moving in from the south and it might snow yet again.

They talked. Ate some fruit bars for energy, slipping them in beneath their oxy feeds. The extra boost felt good. Rachel stated her case, but it made no difference. They were going for it. Fraq had psyched out the lot of them, so that this odd stunt now became the entire purpose, the focus no matter what. Everest or nothing. The media loved it, of course.

The two Lifters took off with a hammering surge, fully fueled so they could get to the summit and back down to this halfway point. The tech and media teams got it all, applauding as the roaring Lifters shot up fast, into air thinner than most of them had ever experienced.

Rachel watched them roar and soar away in the stark bleached light of noon. Chen had not gotten over her rigid stance on the first leg. She stood in the Lifter like a mannequin in a store window, lifting into enameled light, a pioneer without purpose.

Rachel watched them closely on binocs and so saw it all. The following helicopter clawed its way far behind them. The superior technology Fraq had suggested, added to the Lifter now, was definitely better.

The Lifters gained another kilometer in the hard, clear light, then banked over to fly along the ridgeline, toward the summit. The peak seemed impossibly high from here. Clouds swept from it, billows of snow stripping from the slopes in long, filmy white streamers like flags.

They nearly made it.

Rachel watched as the two white dots ascended. They skated along the ridge, keeping out of the prevailing wind so they did not get buffeted. Fraq was ahead, as usual, accelerating with big plumes of exhaust from the Lifter, like banners unfurling. The Lifters roared loudly in the thin, cold air. But they had to rise above a convoluted summit ridge that looked razor-sharp in this light.

Fraq went first, then swooped back into the wind shadow of the main ridge. Chen just ascended into the full force of the rising wind. She kept at it and tried to skate along the ridgeline. She rose another few hundred meters. Rachel tracked the wavering image. Then a gust caught Chen and she tumbled. It happened fast and Rachel didn't have time to even gasp.

Time barely moved. Each ticking second seemed like a bubble that bulged—swelled—popped. Then it was time for the next second to start.

Chen fought against the tipping and got a wrong angle to the wind.

She went down and hit the scree beneath a snow ridge. Rolled.

Fell off a bluff.

When the Lifter hit the bottom, it broke apart.

Dead silence.

7.

The chopper set them down on a ledge a few hundred meters away and below. Lifter parts were strewn that far down.

It was a deep, shady cleft in the mountain with rock surrounds on three sides. The wind raked Rachel with cold.

She started up the slope but she didn't have much strength here even with the oxy. The cold seeped into her and her legs thumped. Her feet skidded off the ice-glazed rock. She fell hard, got up, sucked in cold thin air, went on. By the time she reached Chen, her fingers were wooden, useless things. But Chen was already dead.

————————

Chen's body had already started to stiffen in the cold when Fraq landed nearby a while later. The Lifter roared hard to land.

He came over in that curious waddle of his and said something in that scraping voice. The translator, who'd scrambled up the slope after Rachel, came hurrying up and said, "He got to the summit. How is—"

"Tell him we've paid again," Rachel said, flat and stony. "Tell him we want more. Damn more."

————————

It was two weeks before feeling returned to her fingertips.

She and the others had had to rush off the mountainside, and the memories were all jumbled now. The wind had worsened fast and snow started, blowing in horizontally, and they'd had to get out with just the body.

She answered a summons from the Prefect Stiles and was surprised to find Fraq and the translator there as well.

The Prefect looked troubled as Rachel entered. His normally blank face showed little creases around the eyes and his hands twitched on his desktop. Rachel nodded to the humans and went through the ritual greetings with Fraq. When that was done a full five minutes later, Natal said, "I have explained to him that no Librarian wishes to accompany him in a Marianas Trench descent."

Rachel nodded. "Not surprised."

The translator nodded. "Indeed, the need has diminished." One of Fraq's expressions was to term as needs what humans would call desires. "Especially since . . . the accident."

In tense situations, Fraq always used the translator. He did not want to give away his mood while struggling with Anglish.

Rachel bit her lip and thought that folly was not usually just called accident, but she let it pass. Nuance was subtle in interspecies communication, so they seldom attempted it.

The translator said stiffly for Fraq, "You require some explanation for my acts?"

The Prefect put on his stiff face. "We have asked for none."

"Yet he will give it." Natal paused, phrasing from her computer and her own intuition. "He says, 'I come from a species that has evolved from planets. We harbor great nostalgia for them. Yet now we live in huge habitats at the edge of our solar system, where the light materials—water, air, gases—abound. So a trip through the "bridge works" to your new world is a great boon. It is so unspoiled. Mine is ancient and trampled. We have no high mountains to scale, as in our accident. Long ago we converted ours into useful things. So I asked to sense your rich world in many ways, the ways of my kind. Thank you.' With that, this noble being reveals much."

The Prefect blinked at this. He hesitated, then said, "I believe I understand better."

Fraq spoke again, and the translator said, "Your world may survive in this form for as many as a thousand of your years. Our experience, and our knowledge of the many messages in the Ur Library"—Natal broke off to add, "that's what he calls the SETI messages, an ancient library"—"all those tell us this."

Rachel couldn't resist asking, "You think it's inevitable that it will change?"

Fraq gazed at her steadily. He carefully pronounced his words in saying, "All species that retain their technology—which is not all species, nor even a majority—destroy their worlds. Then they try to replenish them, using comets from their outer solar system. Asteroids also. But this fails, too, in time. So we, like many others, had to move to the outer regions. We dwell in great containers, which rotate on long arms, to provide artificial gravity. Such is the lot of the old races."

The prospect was so chilling that her mind retreated, so she did not catch what mannerisms the Prefect went through with Fraq. Then the Prefect said delicately, "So we can begin to discuss larger issues?" Fraq rasped a positive reply.

As Rachel left the meeting she wondered what had triggered this sudden change in the Ythri. Then came a hunch. "A sacrifice," she murmured to herself. "One of us had to die. Only then would we show we were in earnest."

Blood sacrifice.

She did not know why she was so sure, but she was.

FRAQ

Again as I addressed my Flock, I invoked our ancient wisdom:

To dare is to lose one's flight momentarily, to fall. Not to dare is to lose oneself entire.

My speech, sent in dense code in our sigh-sing language, was this: I must explain why I chose as the next challenge the ascent to this world's highest prominence. I would have flown to the lofty peak of our home world's tallest, Weathermother, had I enjoyed the chance. So this was a way to return to our old challenges, in company with the Rachel female. You all would have been thrilled to see how their vegetation on mountain slopes echoes ours. There were plants recalling the ancient names: windnest and hammerbranch, amberdragon and starbells, spindly gaunt lightning-rod, jewel-leaf, even trees like unto Ythrian braidbark and copperwood.

I admit this is rhetoric in pursuit of reason. Such is needed here. As usual, in our Flock-whisper after, there arrived on wings of song, dark disagreement. Those masters of flabbergast talk, the scissorbill faction, brayed. With their distinctive uneven bills goes a lispy speech and opposition to any differing views.

I struggled to not erupt at them. Our rule in this expedition is the most fundamental: Be curious, not furious. Be still, shun thrill.

But I am imperfect. I find irksome those Yth of uneven bills, their lower mandibles longer than the uppers. They sport this remarkable adaptation as a brag. It allowed them to fish in a unique way, flying low and fast over streams and lakes. Their lower mandible skims or slices over waters, ready to snap shut any small fish unable to dart clear. These skimmers sometimes have slit-shaped eyes, are agile in flight, and once gathered in large flocks along rivers and coastal sand banks.

To my mute astonishment, I have found that such skimmers exist here—widespread on the grounder world they name Earth, despite their oceans' size. Coevolution parallels! We had expected flight to be uncommon on such a heavy world. Yet evolution finds its way. Called "birds" in the native flat tongue, they are like us yet far distant in ability. They have beaks, not toothed mouths—because they are not far from vegetarian. Even their meat-seekers strike with beaks, and swallow the flesh their claws have snagged and pierced. They have no teeth so cannot chew, and indeed, know not fire at all—so cannot harvest the nutrients flesh holds.

They are a sad lot.

The flyers here are so shaped with wings that, alas, cannot grasp—the grip of gravity is too strong to allow that mass loading of their bodies. Their heads are small, eyes sharp. They manifest song in myriad, though repetitive and simple, ways. They have not known an uplift to intelligence, as we enjoyed. They, too, sprang forth from former simpleton reptiles.

Coevolution is miraculous, though ponderous, too.

Yet I have flown among them. They flee, of course. We share with these "birds" an instant alarm fear of snakes, for example. So, too, do these "humans." Convergent evolution, even among different bio Kingdoms, light-years apart.

Also, we are most like their "eagles"—which appear in the flapping flags of many groundling "nations"—that is, of lands owned by grounders, who treasure dirt higher than the wondrous air. Eagles are majestic, skimmers less so.

Their speech-song, these skimmers of we Yth, is as if sandpaper could sing. They object to any idea that does not seem immediately right. Those of my sort, the artful plungers, and even the scavengers, tolerate the scissorbills. I reply that biologically, we all, Yths and these "humans" alike, are opportunistic generalist species, with highly evolved intelligent behavioral flexibility. So we must parallel our practices to theirs, to fathom them. More important—the purpose we Yth demand—we must enlist their aid. To find the Mouth we lost, and use it for our main cause.

Of course, I use metaphor to so convey: we seek a thermal rise, a warm welcoming helix to buoy us.

Sadly, this was barely enough. Our Flock is vexed. Most of us work now on the gray moon, with those chilly Prefects, to probe the Minds they have stored. We have insights they do not. Most fundamental, that in their Library of Messages, caged Minds know they are hopelessly alone. They so deeply long for their ancient Creator culture. We have strands of those cultures, from our own Library. These we can use to carve out insights into the Mouth Maze that so beckons us. The humans do not seem to suspect our purpose. That is good.

I made these points as well as I could. I flourished my magenta mating-feather display, but sadly, got no reaction. Then my hostile yellow-flutters. Nothing. I forked out my major fan shows, a rippling circle framing my head. I peered directly at them, a stalking-glare. That at last provoked a rustle of concern. Even the scissorbill Yths ceased their mutters and menaces.

I have used such shows on the primates. They glanced at each other, a classic anxiety signal. But no more than mystified stares came from their dull faces. They do not know the art of display. Their faces carry their expressive burden, in paltry fashion. They have their frowns, smirks, eye-rolls, jutting chins.

But the language of color, of feather dance, of strut and guile— lost on them. Sad. Their group solidarity organizes them, resolves their duty, mostly through bare speech—or so I perceive. Dive-threat struts, horned-eye dances—none of our meaningful methods communicate. We are left with paltry tongues and lips, when we strive for knowing each other. Luckily, these primates, too, make long chain lines, sentences. These at least we share. Linear language.

Next comes a pursuit of the deepest oceans here. Another challenge.

So I finished my Flock message. I gave a simple command, which must be obeyed:

You must consult your committee of sleep. Your minds work best when you are at rest. Prepare!

PART 10

BLACK SMOKER

The greatest contribution that science can make to the humanities is
to demonstrate how bizarre we are as a species, and why.

—E. O. WILSON

1.

Rachel clutched the rail firmly as a snarling wave burst over her. This wasn't just rough weather, it was dangerous. She watched the research vessel buck against curling white walls of water. Spume burst over the prow and sprayed her with salty wet. Wind whipped by her and shredded the whitecaps in the gray sea light.

She looked around at the white faces of the other Library staff and was glad she had experienced sailing with her father in rough seas.

Fraq wasn't doing so well, either. The big alien lumbered by her, rolling with the pitch of the deck. The rigid face and dancing golden eyes managed to convey both alarm and wooziness. His world didn't have oceans like this.

The full Earth grav punished his flock, too.

The research ship plowed through thick waves, prow headed west. Rachel looked back, but the California coast was long gone behind tossing surf and dirty, sun-streaked clouds.

Fraq's translator came lurching along the deck, green and rolling-eyed. But the sea was calming already as the storm headed inland to dump rain on a thirsty California. The crew was already swinging the descent cylinder up from the hold, setting it down on the prep deck with clanks and groans of metal. Teams attached hoses and line feeds to it. Time to get suited up. She donned her suit, mostly just a rubbery garment to keep her warm during the descent. Fraq's translator was worrying around the alien, who had his own specially made suit to fit his odd physique. Rachel hoped they could pull off this deception. Fraq had slowly revealed more of his own biology, including his intense interest in deep-ocean thermal vents—though without giving a clue about why.

So the Library had arranged this stunt. Yet another. Fraq had insisted on seeing the absolutely lowest depth in the ocean, but there were few thermal vents in the really deep areas. So a Library Prefect had hit upon a simple ruse—tell Fraq that he was going to the deepest vent, and then just take him down to a convenient one. How could he plausibly judge the depth, anyway?

Ingenious, Rachel had to admit. Especially since she knew the Ythri were lying, too. So of course Fraq had also insisted that she accompany him in this deep ocean descent off Monterey. Even though his last stunt had killed a Librarian on the slopes of Everest, he wanted her along. The Library felt that since she had started all this, taking the orbital plunge with Fraq, she was in for the full ride, no matter how dangerous it seemed.

Rachel felt edgy. They still didn't really grasp Fraq, and now they were playing deceptive games with him. She paced the deck as Fraq got outfitted.

Their craft was self-propelled with a large personnel sphere below a ballast-and-trim system. Steel weights clung to it, to allow faster, deep dives. These would be jettisoned at the end of the dive and left at the bottom.

The three of them entered the cylinder and strapped in. It was pretty bare-bones, a research vessel, not for tourists of whatever stripe. The passenger sphere was next to the ballast tank, and they could not even see the crew. Those were behind, running the descent with robo-assists. Rachel had always been a bit nervous in close quarters, and when the hatch boomed shut she felt a surge of anxiety. An acrid taste came into her mouth, and she wondered if she was going to throw up.

The A-frame crane lifted the cylinder and cabling. They splashed into the still-tossing sea with the inevitable Earther vid team covering it all. They descended into a world of dark quiet.

Down, reels whirring. The viewing window soon went black. The near-freezing sea cold began to seep in.

Being crowded into the gunmetal-gray passenger zone was bad enough. But with the alien, it was immeasurably worse. Fraq become more agitated as they descended. He opened his black suit, and his neck feathers ruffled with gray anxiety.

———————

They sighted the black smoker after two hours. The crew said the smoky water was superheated to over 400°C. Hard to feel any difference in their narrow cabin, though, staring out at the bubbly black currents through the curved window shield. The stony field hundreds of meters wide rippled with superheated water coming through the ocean floor. The dingy currents were rich in dissolved minerals from deep in the Earth's crust. Their craft descended through clouds of sulfides that loomed above the site. Brooding above this landscape were fogs that formed when the superhot water came in contact with the cold ocean above, making minerals precipitate. Below towered a black chimney-like structure around each turbulent vent. Sprays of mud came from ripe orange gouts at the smoker peak.

Fraq was withdrawn, not trying his Anglish at all. Natal spoke for him, from behind their seats, crowding the cabin. "He wants to know if this is truly the lowest spot in our oceans."

"That's what he wanted," Rachel lied, though without technically doing so.

The translator eyed her. Getting to the truly deep sites, where the continental plates crunched and slid and pulled apart and lava erupted, was very difficult and dangerous. The Library would never take such a risk with a visiting alien, even if the alien wanted it. But the Earthers had their ways of bringing pressure to bear, underwater geysers be damned.

Fraq's eyes danced, his chest heaved. Plainly he could barely breathe. Rasps of air escaped him and his nostrils flared. He rose from his specially molded chair and stared through the viewing port, mouth open. Rachel watched him, sensing that this sight carried some hidden meaning for him. Suddenly Fraq burst into a

high, wracking burst of sound. The staccato bursts rang in the passenger chamber. Rachel blinked and wondered if the alien would
become violent.

Natal leaned over and smiled. "Laughter is the shortest distance
between two people."

"That's laughter?"

The woman shrugged, though Rachel could see she was also wary
of the harsh, barking sound. What must it have been like for her,
months of night-and-day contact with the alien, but never quite knowing what Fraq was up to? Not that anyone else had a clear idea, either.
"Apparently it serves the same function that laughing does for us," she
said. "Releases unspoken tensions."

Fraq began speaking in rapid-fire volleys. The sounds echoed and
built, Ythri-speak in staccato. The translator frowned, and Rachel
found it hard to breathe, to think. The cylinder hovered above the black
smokers, and fizzing sounds came through the walls. Fraq gestured
with his odd arms, fired off phrases, pointed out the viewport. Whirring currents rushed by and their hull resounded with whirring, click-
ing jolts as debris dinged into them.

The captain came on the speakers, his flat voice surrealistically
bland. He pointed out bacteria growing in thick mats. These attracted
crawling organisms that grazed slowly upon the dark-brown bacteria.
Larger wriggling organisms appeared in the rich nutrient bath as they
descended—snails, shrimp, crabs, tube worms, fish. A pink octopus leisurely groped in some prey from a rock fortress.

The captain continued in a routine tone, "You'll see this system
forms a food chain of predator and prey relationships, going well
beyond the primary consumers. We once harvested some of the eye-
less shrimp and found them quite good in a New Orleans sauce." A
chuckle.

The ballast tank rattled and they moved directly over a smoker.

Tube worms were everywhere. Rachel knew they absorbed nutrients directly into their tissues, so they didn't even need a mouth or a
digestive tract. Bacteria lived inside them. The primitive creatures made
her flesh creep. The captain pointed out a big snail armored with scales
made up of iron.

Fraq began chanting. It was a deep bass note that reverberated in his chest, building harmonics in the passenger sphere. Rachel shot a glance at the translator.

"It is a religious ritual, I believe," the hapless woman said. And shrugged.

"What kind? And does he get . . . ?"

"Active? Yes, I believe there's a dance that goes with it. But, but—he can't do it in here—"

As the words left Natal's mouth, Fraq began climbing to the low ceiling. He dug hands and feet into crevices and swung madly around the ceiling, never ceasing his long, rolling chant.

"What's going on there?" the captain shouted over the comm.

Rachel ignored the shouts. She watched the alien make his graceful arcs, barely above their heads. The bass tone shifted, mounted to higher chords. And suddenly she understood.

"It's a form of worship," Rachel said. "This kind of place must have been how life began on his world."

The translator was startled. "He's making contact with the origin of life?"

"This has been a religious pilgrimage, maybe." Rachel wondered how she could use this to decipher the meaning of Fraq's home world, their intentions.

She had been studying for their descent, and now it all made sense. The old "warm pool" story about the origin of life had a rival. Amino acids had formed deep in the Earth's crust—deep drilling proved that. The acids got shot up in hydrothermal fluids into cooler waters, where lower temperatures and clay minerals could form a substrate. Pre-life's complex interactions needed structure, and clays could provide it, lattices immersed in a rich chemical bath. Plenty of extremophiles and other organisms still lived around deep-sea vents like this. Everything else on Earth had left such watery homes for better prospects.

If life on Fraq's home world had begun this same way, they had a bond. Had Fraq been looking for this connection?

"We're running out of time," the captain's voice boomed. "Quit horsing around."

Fraq spoke as he settled back into his couch. Whatever his strange swinging and chanting had been, plainly it was a ceremony now done. Rachel had given up trying to read his facial expressions, but his body was more relaxed, wing-arms loose, and the golden eyes danced less. They focused on the primordial wealth around the black smoker, and Fraq took a deep breath.

Natal said, "We can ascend. He has much to tell us."

Rachel felt a wave of sudden joy. So this nonsense had paid off, after all.

His kind had descended from life-forms that fed on such vents, Fraq told them as they rose to the surface. They'd evolved around black smokers that were close to shore. Their earlier forms were amphibious, because their shallow world had less land area.

Rachel thought, *So that's why he bought into a deep descent so close to land. Did the Prefect think of that possibility?*

Nonetheless, Fraq's kind had fouled their world as they moved through their industrial ages—the "early times" he called them, with perhaps a touch of nostalgia. The global damage was enormous, running past the tipping point of global ice-over. They'd thought they could greenhouse their way out of that, but failed. The Ythri had retreated outward, moving vast populations into their outer solar system, desperate to find any sites they could work into a bearable environment.

So most of his species now lived in artificial habitats close to the ices of their outer system, and far from their star's warmth. Only now were they making headway in reclaiming their world. He called it "ancient and trampled."

The translator said, "So no one of his kind has ever seen, for many thousands of years, the 'legendary ancestral origins.' Witnessing thermal vents was an enormous event for Fraq, and he wants to repay us with a great advance in knowledge."

Rachel shook her head in dazzlement. "More approach protocols to our wormhole site?" She grimaced. "I hope it's more than that."

"He may be willing to give what he calls 'knowledge of the sector where the bridge resides.' And . . . perhaps more."

Rachel kept her face stiff, to mask her surprise. "What?"

Natal paused, groping for a way to say something that might be beyond human terms. "A—a difficult translation, done by Fraq's kind. Ancient records. Of their expedition long ago to . . . our system. They made a descent, seeking the thermal vent origins they believed led to intelligent life."

"So they, Ythri, visited the Earth—how long ago?"

"No, on another world."

Rachel was getting used to being surprised. "Really? Why not pay attention to the primates on Earth?"

Fraq spoke for some time, and the translator struggled to make sense of what the plainly energized alien said. "Because they had a theory that 'excess' led to indulgence, and hence low orders of intelligence."

"What? Excess?"

Fraq spoke even longer, eyes animated. Natal said, "He states that while he has enjoyed seeing the natural wealth here—the wonderful forests, the elegance of Everest—Earth is too rich in all life needs. We have so much! Metals in the crust, still. A rich asteroid belt, and so many minerals, rare earths and the like. A large moon to stabilize the orbital inclination. Ample continents that run along lines of latitude, so that species can migrate great distances without a change of climate."

Rachel could scarcely believe this. She said slowly, eyeing Fraq, "Other planets like ours didn't produce intelligence?"

For the first time, Fraq made a gesture she understood. A shrug. "Seldom."

"So what did these ancient aliens do?" She had a suspicion, but needed to have it said.

"They went to . . . Mars. Where they thought it more likely that intelligence would arise."

Rachel sucked in a deep breath. Humans thought in very narrow time scales, she knew. A SETI Librarian had to keep that in mind, always. But Mars had been wet and warm and its Marsmat life arose then to heights, well over a billion years ago. Rachel pulled up from memory the little she knew about that. "Well, we do know that the Marsmats deep in their caves have some symbol-arranging ability."

The translator conveyed this, and after more odd alien sounds nodded with satisfaction. "Fraq will give us a symbol-set that the Marsmat may recognize. His kind used it in communicating with them, when they visited our solar system."

Natal had no idea what time scale they were speaking about, obviously. Maybe all this had happened many million years back, when the Marsmat was firmly boxed in underground. Primates were pretty crude then, and not easy to find in the forests. If Fraq's kind had visited Earth, they might have checked to see if we had black smokers. Or more likely, they saw the big, ugly life on land and decided they didn't like it.

Fraq made an odd double-hand gesture that Rachel had learned meant *Agreement with pleasure.*

Rachel echoed his gesture. *On to Mars, then. These puzzles run deep.* Rachel felt the abyss of time they spoke of, and the vast differences between them, a dizzy swirl. She wondered if indeed life on Earth had started from those black smokers. SETI was supposed to tell humans about others, but . . . How odd, to learn so intimate a fact . . . from an alien.

PART 11

THE LATHE
OF EVOLUTION

The world will never starve for wonders; but only for want of wonder.

—G. K. CHESTERTON

1.

The depths of Mars fell away into murk. The Descent Team grew quiet as they rose. It had been a confusing, chaotic few hours, and Zuminski ordered everyone to stop chatting about it.

"Time to let this sink in," he said as the gray Martian bedrock glided by them.

Rachel agreed. Her SETI Library team was shaken. Their first descent had not gone remotely like their plans of an orderly tour and review of the Marsmat. The setup of the usual display panel, moving on to a display of Fraq's symbol-string, had gone well. But then the Mat had flooded the principal entrance chambers with black fluid. The sudden dark flow had knocked them all off their feet, panicking even the seasoned Descent Team.

They got trapped, fought their way free.

Nothing like it had happened before, in all the history of Marsmat contacts. The warm, somehow sinister waters had lapped around them as they waded out.

Rachel's little red heart suit graphic pulsed hard and fast, while her respire icon puffed yellow clouds: settle down, it meant. If her stats worsened, the suit would inject a slowdown drug in her arm.

The elevator brought them up slow and steady, giving them all time to reflect in silence. Temperatures in the elevator fell as they neared the surface. The residual moisture on their suits froze to rime and fell away, a dusting of dirty snow. When they walked out of the elevator onto the gritty brown-red sand, the flakes fumed away within seconds. They climbed into the trawler to return to the habitat. Rachel sagged, tired. She had not adjusted well to the Martian 0.38 g or to her ill-fitting pressure suit.

Back in the hard sunlight, the big open-air bus carried them from the vent mouth, across rolling hills of sand and rock. The Martian day blared on outside but they all sat silently, meditating on the panic below. Some were texting back to Base, undoubtedly, but Rachel ignored them, letting the swaying ride calm her. Fraq gave her his intent stare, the strange glittering eyes focused directly at her in his alien way. She ignored him, too.

She was glad their suits had the new self-cleaning liners, because she had sweated up hers in the Mat tunnels and while flailing around in the streams of sudden water. She had peed in the suit, too, but at least there was a catchbag for that.

Only now, after coming up, did she feel a kind of shadow fear—dry mouth, sour stench, skin tightening around her skull, muscles knotting at the knob of her spine.

A cyclone tracked along near them, sending a whirl of red dust up hundreds of meters. Rachel marveled; she had never seen one before. She had never thought well of weather, from her experiences of it on Earth—sweaty summers, nasty hurricanes. Mars was like the moon, fairly easy gravity, about twice Luna's. It had the disadvantages of having an atmosphere, with none of the compensations. There was not enough pressure to make the near-vacuum chemically useful, but it came with freakish sandstorms of irritating dust and howling winds. Still, there were rosy dawns and sunsets, which she liked. The nearest she had ever seen to them on the moon was the striking sliver of the sun shining through Earth's skin of air. The thin layer of gas acted like a prism, making a flickering rainbow of colors in the eye.

She watched the cyclone unfold and die, and knew that she had at last learned something. In all the stunts with Fraq—the orbit-fall, the Everest ascent, the deep-sea black smokers—there had been moments of rigid fear. Those were the worst of it. Just now, deep inside Mars, she had felt no fear because she had at last defeated her own imagination.

It made sense. Nothing happens until it actually occurs, so worry was pointless and she could live her life up until then. Danger existed only in the moment of danger. An event was bad only when it happened— not after, and certainly not before. Cowardice came from the inability to suspend her imagination. Learning to ignore imagination and live in the very second of this present minute was a great gift. And she had achieved it by some mysterious inner workings of her mind, not by conscious thought. And not through imagination.

A wave of relief swept over her. She was free of fear and the world was luminous, crisp, full of momentary meaning. Could this be what Fraq termed the "harmony of moment"? She sat back and enjoyed the rest of the ride to the habitat.

They got out and lined up at the processing lock. Zuminski ordered the SETI Team in first. Rachel wrestled off her harness and secured it to the racks in the lock. A cycle sequence began with a gurgling shower over their suits. That swept away the peroxides and perchlorates, converting their stinging energies into fresh oxygen. The mud residue went into a basket beneath their boots for use in the hydroponics domes. Oxygen whistled into the lock from half a dozen recessed ports, and they all shucked their suits.

A chime sounded; full pressure, 90 percent Earth normal. Then they each stepped into side shower stalls. Off came her parka, leggings, and, finally, her jumpsuit. She shivered as she stepped out into the chill: she had actually been sweating on Mars—a novel experience. Another shower to freshen, and she redressed in the undersuit.

A prickly itch crawled over her face and neck, though. Despite the showers, the fine, rusty dust heavily laden with irritating peroxides had already sandpapered her skin. Their suits had the latest features—a scent catcher, cool-water spigot, full digital displays, inboard smarts, self-warming meal dispenser—but to Rachel it still felt like carrying around a lobster shell. She had to remind herself that unlike Luna, where she'd felt at home after some years, this was a world that was always trying to kill her.

She was dressing when the translator, Xiaoling, came out of the shower. "What?!" Rachel said. Xiaoling's pretty, fine-boned face was now eggplant-purple. One black eye peered out through a slit.

"I got slammed around by that damn water," she whispered in a dead, fat-lipped voice.

"You should've said something!"

"Not my way. Nothing to do until out of suit."

"Damn! Let's get you to the med unit."

Xiaoling nodded and limped with Rachel into the corridor outside. Fraq was there, surrounded by Marsmat people, silent behind his stoic scowl. His eyes found Rachel's and she whisper-chirruped to him. *Later, will explain.* He trilled assent.

The meds took nearly an hour. Rachel left Xiaoling in her compartment to sleep, aided by a sedative. Rachel was starting to feel jittery aftereffects from the descent. What had gone wrong? Sleep would be impossible.

2.

Fluffing her now short and bulky auburn hair, she went down the snaky corridor to the "mess hall" for some coffee. She'd looked up the term and found it was leftover military jargon. Prophetically it was . . . a mess. It did have a luncheonette-via-art-deco décor, but nobody had "policed it up" (another military phrase) on this watch.

Nobody in the mess right now, no sound but the chuffing of air circ. She was all dressed up in a clingy thing, just because—and nobody to show it off for. She missed Kane, wondered if she could get him sent out on the next Cycler. *A gal needs support. . . .*

The descent and SETI teams were probably recovering in their tiny cabins. She cleared some trash on the kitchen board—litterbugs everywhere!—then got coaxed by the coffee aroma, and curled into a booth with her cup. This one had a sliding door for privacy and she drew it closed. After the trauma of the vent descent, this felt cozy. She idly watched the "viewports" that were in fact screens showing external vistas. (In her own cabin, she'd set the screen to a no-sound Hawaiian beach with crashing surf; no point in staring at red sand all day.)

One was a distant perspective on the "hab"—leftover Mars pioneer lingo for habitat. It stood amid a clutter of vehicles beside the power reactor, a fat cylinder with big tubes and power lines spraying out radially. A thick apron of bagged dirt cloaked the hab, like a wraparound sand dune. Her briefing had pointed out that the maximum angle that a dune could assume was independent of the local gravity, so this looked like dunes on Earth. The angle depended only on the dirt's coefficient of friction, which for Rachel was far too much information. The habitat was another tall cylinder, most of its rooms pie-shaped. Though a meter of Martian regolith buffered the outside, they had water-filled walls as an added radiation shield. All to let them forget for a while how dangerous Mars was.

Distraction psychology was everything here, she had learned in the week since arrival. That meant heating the water jacket with their nuclear reactor waste therms, so everything was pleasantly warm to the touch. The walls radiated a comfortable reassurance that the stinging, hostile world outside could have no effect here. Still, indoors on Mars was like being in a luxury gulag. The Siberia outside was never far from mind.

The entire base devoted to studying the Marsmat was minimal. Thus the older styles, minimizing wastes, so as not to disturb the overlay above the Marsmat caverns. But it meant minimal staff and help for visitors, too. Even visiting birdy aliens.

Abruptly the door slid back. "Mind?" Zuminski asked, and sat down without hesitation. He slid the screen back into place, insulating them from anyone who came into the mess. "I want to talk, before we do mission review."

"Uh, okay." *So much for my little private, comforting interlude. . . .*

With his surprisingly quick, big hands, Zuminski set in front of himself a bottle of tequila, a salt shaker, a thick shot glass, and a saucer of lime slices. "I always give myself celebration, if had a rough descent." He sipped from the shot glass without expression as she blinked at this. She knew the Mars style had a long tradition of hard-drinking, abrupt, rugged types, but . . . this early in the day? The mess still smelled of breakfast.

Stage is set, she thought. *But what's the script?*

She said carefully, "I'm trying to understand what happened. Have you seen anything like that flooding before?"

He raised his eyebrows, turned his lips down in mock puzzlement. "Never. New phenom, it is."

"What was the Mat trying to do?"

He shrugged. "Motive is last thing to ask about. First, understand the message."

"That was a message?"

"What else?" He did a little ritual, squeezing a lime slice along the thick shot-glass rim, to hold a line of salt he sprinkled. The tequila splashed in, another lime slice, then a bit of water from a hip vessel he carried. She had seen behavior like this in men who needed to get into a certain focused state, through repetition, in order to give their minds free play. Such ritual was a common, unremarked feature among SETI Library staff—but usually not with booze.

He noticed her scrutiny, smiled. "I drink to make other people more interesting."

Despite herself, she laughed. "Sorry I'm so dull."

"Too early to tell. Your SETI people, you maybe can have insights. Or that birdy alien, Fraq."

"He's pretty inscrutable."

"Is a 'he'? Was unsure."

"Well, Fraq looks like a bird, and acts like a man."

"Which means?"

"He blunders along, does what he wants."

"Ha! You do not, librarian lady?"

She thought of backing off from this line of talk, but that was her usual response. *My "librarian lady" instinct?* So she replied, "I went with Fraq when we fell all the way from Earth orbit."

He whistled, nodded. "Was story about that. Amazing. I did not believe."

She shrugged. "I have my moments."

"You are librarian inside, though?" He picked up his jigger of tequila and drank it straight down, his eyes never leaving hers.

She couldn't let him get away with that, not after this morning. "Just as you pretend to be a man of simple tastes?"

He grinned. "Which for librarian means, I am, you say—complete vulgarian."

She had to laugh, a liberating one from the belly. "Touché!"

So now it was out in the open, and she had to admit the truth to herself. He had the fatal charmer profile, for her: black hair, blue eyes, large hands, face thin but with a strong jaw. Ah, the troubles that pro-file had gotten her into! More times than she liked to think about, she had mistaken qualities of style and looks for elements of inner charac-ter. With predictable (by others, never her) results.

"Are you always this shy with strangers?" she needled him.

"Only librarians."

Time to get back to work. "You said, as I recall, that we need to talk."

Zuminski leaned back. "You did not act properly down there. I must say that, in report."

"Your memos mean nothing to me. What counts is results—which we got today."

"Results?" He seemed bemused by her presumption, fattening his lower lip, eyebrows arcing. "Here we are always, always maybeing, may-being, maybeing."

Use the same body-language style, then. Rachel jutted her chin for-ward, eyes flashing. "Always maybeing? Always uncertain what the Mat means? The important *maybe* got goddamn well answered—we got out alive."

"You ignored your team."

"I forced open those big elephant-ears that trapped us in there. With Fraq's help. That seemed to me more important."

He grimaced. "We have team standards here. You were in charge of your group, plus your alien, the bird. I in charge of running the descent. You—"

"Isn't this just quibbling?"

He paused, as if to reassess her.

Rachel thought back to how she had broken open the two large elephant-ear fronds. The sturdy fronds had looked like two mas-sive, cupped hands pressed together at the center—big, three meters across. Around them plumes of water roared down from spouts near the ceiling. The luminant dark streams flecked with blue algae had gushed away, carrying people with them. Rachel had pulled out a tube, holding her breath—then sprayed waste oxy on the leathery valves, which made them turn gray and unclasp. Maybe she had killed them.

Zuminski blinked, taken aback. "All about teamwork here."

"Not if it's just a suicide pact."

"You abandoned your team to attack the Marsmat valve."

"Is there a rule against that?"

He scowled, all business. "Damaging the Mat, yes. Could be you killed part of Mat."

"We had to get out. No telling what would have happened, or where all that water would've carried us."

"Your team comes first. You lost control of them. With bird alien. He looked confused." He threw back the last of his tequila shot. "I was in charge of descent."

She could handle this with negotiation, but her instinct told her to enlarge the game. She leaned over and threw open the sliding screen on the booth. As she expected, by now there were a dozen people in the mess, seated around tables, buzzing with conversation. The screen had masked all the noise. People yammering. Fraq—leaning forward, wing-arms spread but feathers folded into a ruddy display, talking slowly to a full table audience. And there was Xiaoling, looking bruised and bedraggled beneath her bandages.

Rachel called her over.

Xiaoling said she could not sleep, had come here for simple company. In short order, she admitted in halting sentences that she hadn't wanted the Marsmat team's help down there, she'd wanted to be saved. She jutted her jaw at the man. "And that is what she did!"

Rachel turned back to Zuminski. "Well?"

He looked vexed, scrunched his lips together, hesitated. "Was not so bad, okay? You acted right way, good." Then, moving on: "Mat has never done that before. We must think about."

Xiaoling ventured, "It was Fraq's message that set off the Mat, I'll bet."

Zuminski gave them both a skeptical twist of his lips. He glanced at the tequila bottle and shook his head, quite clearly reluctantly deciding against having some more. His vowels were slurring already. "Could be. But what to do next, then?"

"That's up to all of us," Rachel said.

"Aii," Xiaoling said.

"There will be meeting, your team and mine. We must provide report. Most important is one guy above us, named Hassan. Not bad guy. He has two faces, one the scientist, other bureaucrat. They war with each other. We need to play to the scientist."

Xiaoling frowned. "But the bureaucrat is in charge, finally, yes?"

Zuminski grinned craftily. "Scratch Mars scientist, find fanatic."

3.

Rachel had already studied up on Hassan's background as Systemic Interaction Administrator—where did they get these titles?—on her way here with Fraq, some flock, and an Earther escort, on the fast-orbit Aldrin Cycler. Deep inside the spinning, hollow asteroid, she had fallen asleep over the routine Hassan biography, and woke to a moist aroma that reminded her of childhood. Somehow she still associated Hassan with that memory, and the biology her childhood evoked.

The Cycler's deliberately warm-watery scents had mixed in her memory with the camellia bushes dripping with dew, down the bayou. There had been, too, the moldy flavor of pecan husks rotting and the damp promise of good fishing in the shadows. Just down the road, far back in her childhood, there had been whitewashed brick crypts, whose fading tributes told passersby that bloody Shiloh and Arabi lay within memory, still.

She shook herself free of that. Rachel had expected Hassan to be her major contact here, but so far had not even seen him. He spent most of his time at Clarke Central, the main landing site and supply depot for exploration. He was also rumored to have a strong role in the small terraforming program, called Marsforming here, though his title there was Head of Research.

She had liked the ever-spinning Aldrin 'roid ship, and looked forward to the return voyage on it. That Fraq and his flock had banished the Prefects from this expedition meant she had no strong advisors. Until . . .

———

She'd opened the door in a bleary fog. This was part of the recovery from the monthly wake-and-walk from pseudo-hibernation the long flight demanded. She blinked, her eyes cleared—and out of the fog, Prefect Stiles suddenly appeared.

His explanation came hard and fast: "Of course I had to be here—that is, a Prefect must be. I and some techs and even your analysis pod—all that, we got aboard the Aldrin Cycler. Carefully, you see—some bribery, yes. We have a cramped but serviceable set of quarters, carved out in the walls, hastily and crudely, by robots. We have access to exercise machines, the kilometer run, even the mess hall—during imposed night hours. We shall come down to Mars surface well after you, in a descent pod. We will live thirty kilometers away, in a mining facility." With a vain twirl of his neck, he pronounced, "We've done well. Learned much, had frequent conversations with the Library, our Earthside analysts, all."

"Uh, so, why . . ."

"We found old entries, Messages from early Library analysis. They refer to a Ythri visit here, to Mars. So—"

"Fraq is coming here to find something."

"Yes. And you can discover what that is. Subtly, of course."

"Subtle . . . not my strong suit."

"We shall be here, ready to assist.

"I'll let you know. . . ."

When she closed the door, she leaned against it, deciding. *It'll be a cold day in hell before I ring you up, Stiles.*

———

The ferry that had brought them to the Aldrin from the Flinger was only a skeleton of nuclear engines and control systems, with their party and Marsbound supplies the only payload. Humans were luxury items on Mars, still. To avoid harming the Marsmat that underlay most of the warmer depths of the planet, the workforce was mostly robots, without messy, smelly humans.

The same ferry, with its ceramic shell, was used to do the atmospheric braking at Mars—buffeting down, surfing an entire atmosphere—and Rachel would go home on the same personnel ferry, because it cycled, too.

Inside the Aldrin's stony shield she had enjoyed the longest pseudo-vacation of her life, in a watery paradise. She could forget entirely that the whole neatly arranged cylinder-world was crouching inside a spinning, stony shelter, fending off the sleet of cosmic rays and hard vacuum. The Aldrin took about 2.135 Earth years to arc in a single synodic period, an eccentric loop around the sun from near-Earth to the Martian orbit, beyond Mars and then back to Earth. Getting to Mars took 146 days. Then the Aldrin spent the next sixteen months beyond Mars, serving the miners in the inner asteroid belt, picking up cargo and dispensing supplies. The SETI contingent would catch it to go back to Earth.

The other Mars cycler, the Holmbolt, followed a complementary trajectory, half an orbit away. Taxi and cargo vehicles attached to a cycler at one planet and detached when reaching the other.

Once steered into place, the cyclers—with utterly dependable schedules and low sustaining cost—had opened the door for routine travel to Mars. Plus (the real point) a permanent human presence for asteroid mining. Mars was a side issue of little import. The Belt, a vast mishmash of cinders, rubble piles, dead comets, and mineral-rich float-ing mountains, attracted no tourists. But it fed a quiet revolution, the true use of space for resources, and so then the Third Industrial Era. Long-term economic advantages made the cyclers invulnerable to can-cellation by political whim.

So the colonization of Mars came as a side benefit of big industry.

This made it simple for Rachel, Fraq, Xiaoling, and the rest of the SETI team to take the five-month trip to Mars in relative comfort, protected from the sleet of gamma rays and high-energy protons peppering the rocky skin. Fraq and his flock went into some kind of hibernation for the whole voyage, devising their own chambers and chemicals and monitoring equipment. Ythri were quite quick at mastering human technologies, turning them to new uses.

Rachel and Xiaoling had studied and played and explored. They admired the huge smelters and borers bound for the asteroid mines. They swam in the axial zero-g spherical droplet, using air tanks. Many hours passed as they watched the incredible views, with advanced optics to telescope in on distant worlds. The hollowed-out asteroid had already yielded a huge inventory of metals, especially platinum. Such wealth had kicked off the wildcat opening of the Third Industrial, making the Aldrin both a lavish hotel and a living, spinning monument.

Plus a conditioning station. The flock did not exercise, and so slept.

They had gotten on poorly during their Earthside expedition, despite Rachel's attempts at diplomacy. Fraq spoke for his entire flock when he said, "No Prefects go to Mars. We do not need these brains in bodies. I wish that Rachel and a few groundlings go with us in this fundamental exploration." He would say no more. So off they went with a skimpy crew.

The Aldrin's gentle spin gave centrifugal gee equal to 0.38 of Earth's, good Mars training. That counteracted the health effects of weightlessness, and made diving into the Aldrin's central lake a delicious, slow-motion acrobatic. Rachel had tried a double flip with a spin, and almost made it before splashing in. Her finest diving hour. She wished Fraq would emerge from his strange low-metabolism sleep, to fly with her.

The iron fist of Newtonian mechanics governed the Aldrin, but Martian management was not so clear. She read up on Hassan's theories, prompted by the Prefect Stiles's "certain knowledge" that this man was vital to getting good results on Mars. "Hassan is key," the Prefect had said.

By the time the Aldrin swooped by Mars to pilfer some momentum from the planet's orbital velocity—a negligible loss to Mars, but a substantial gain for the hollow ex-asteroid—Rachel had been fully ready to suck up to Hassan. Coming in to Mars on a shuttle was like jumping off a building with an umbrella—not much atmosphere to brake you, but exciting, yes. She'd thought as they settled onto the reddish-brown landing field, *Fully ready for what? Why does Fraq think this essential?*

She got her chance to find out at that afternoon's meeting.

4.

The two teams assembled in a conference room to review the descent. Everyone was quiet, humbled by the experience. They had to report it all and therefore needed to have their mutual story straight.

There had been some knees banged up, a twisted ankle, but no major damage to anyone except Xiaoling, who smiled bravely behind her bandages. All eyes turned to Fraq, but he refused to report any personal difficulty. He had learned the economy of the human shoulder-shrug with a tilted head. The alien was as stoic as ever, saying little through Xiaoling. He had allowed no others of his flock to come.

Rachel studied the intent faces of the Descent Team. They had been here for years, some for decades. Some had let the lesser gravity turn their bodies into cottage cheeses of cellulite. In others she saw blue spider veins exploding in arms or legs. Adaptation had a price. Yet they all seemed happy and even joyous around the tight tables. Brave new worlds required their own sorts of courage.

To her surprise, Zuminski brushed aside the issues he had raised to her privately. No condemnation of anyone, no "post-action status review," as the operating manual called for.

Had she somehow talked him out of it? She blinked, said nothing. The thought pleased her, but she suspected a more subtle reason. The great biologist Hassan sat to Zuminski's right, saying little, and from his manner—an occasional glance, pursed mouth, small hand movements—it emerged that somehow he had control of the terms of debate here. She clandestinely thumbed up a display in the tabletop in front of her and confirmed her suspicion. Zuminski was head of Descent Operations, but in the management flow chart he did not seem to have any direct superior.

He's running the descents because that's where the action is. Not behind a desk.

A further search turned up Zuminski's credentials. A doctorate in exobio from Orbital Caltech, some deep-space operations work early in his career, three dozen research papers. He had then made several expeditions into the yawning underlayers of Deep Mars, where steam vents of sulfuric acid made exploration very dangerous—yet the Mat was there as well. Somehow the man had arranged to run things here, without getting pulled away from the fieldwork and getting trapped in layers of paper-shuffling bureaucracy. That belied a cunning and resolve she had not encountered before, with the possible exception of the Prefects at the Library.

I had no idea. . . . So his working-class guy act had been a convincing performance—or else he'd actually started out that way, and risen by sheer ability. Either way, time to be cautious. The greatest advantage you could give an opponent was to underestimate him.

And here he came. Having covered the official part, Zuminski let the discussion shift to the senior biologist. Hassan was a short, intense man with penetrating blue eyes and sandy hair. He stepped them through the suit cameras' record of "the flooding," as they had decided to call it. Rachel learned nothing more, beyond the white-eyed surprise and outright fear in the faces of some Descent Team members. Apparently, the last decade had seen very little real communication from the Marsmat, and the team had lapsed into a routine. The flooding was new, and the plain implication everybody drew was that Fraq was the cause.

Next, Hassan opened with some speculations. His broad face wrinkled with concern, eyes dancing. Plainly this was his favorite area—the unknown. After a century of study, attention had focused on the biology of the Marsmat, because there had been little progress in actually communicating with it. A life-form of obvious though slow intelligence was hard to know.

"Perhaps with the help of the SETI Library team," Hassan said in his soft, melodious voice, "we can make progress in our search for communication avenues. We have largely followed analog pathways, while SETI necessarily uses digital ones, since the artificial microwave transmissions we have received use the apparently universal scheme of zeros and ones to convey information."

Rachel smiled. He didn't seem to notice that his own language implied human plans and images—avenues, pathways, analog versus digital. The Mat had none of those properties.

Hassan went on, looking around the room, "With the help of our first emissary from a distant civilization"—a nod to Fraq, who sat rigidly, mouth flat, lips compressed, eyes narrow—"we can learn much from the reaction the Marsmat has to his ancient symbology."

Rachel said, "It reacted by flooding the chamber. What did that mean?"

Hassan sat back, covering a momentary frown. Rachel thought she could see him thinking, *Who is this woman?* Then he said with a smile, "I cannot imagine."

Rachel could play it smart here, defer and delay, but that was no longer her humble Librarian style. This wasn't about codes anymore. "Mars was once warm and wet. When did Fraq's species come here before?"

Silence.

Xiaoling carefully translated for Fraq in her fat-lipped whisper. They were using her because this was a delicate moment, and Fraq did not want his somewhat limited Anglish to confuse meaning. Plus, he got time to think. The response was qualitative at best. "He says, beyond a million years."

Okay, old. But how old? Rachel bored in, looking straight at Fraq. "We know that. Who came here, exactly?"

After translation from Fraq's glottal chirps and clicks, the answer was, "An earlier form of my species."

A stir around the room. "Your kind has altered itself?" she persisted.

The answer: "We had to, after we lost our ability to inhabit our home world. Our climate spun out of control."

She would have liked to follow that line of inquiry, in this sudden moment when Fraq seemed willing to reveal things, but Rachel stayed on point. "My question is, what if they came here in one of the eras when Mars was wet and warm?"

Zuminski said, "You bring up good issue. Mat might be able to extend itself even onto the surface in those times. Would have cloud cover against some of the ultraviolet. Could harvest resources when they flowed on the surface."

Rachel nodded, surprised that Zuminski had come into agreement so quickly. "Certainly, if Fraq's kind came then, the Mat would've been easier to find."

Hassan seemed startled, mouth puckered. "Your point is . . . ?"

"The flooding might be the Mat's way of recalling that era. It recognized Fraq, could tell he was different from us—right? Because it echoed his shape in its wall."

Rachel turned and confronted the whole gathering, clustered around the tables. Many of them had set dict-typing on their computer slates, getting all this down. "So maybe the Mat was saying, 'Hello, I remember you. Those times were like this, wet, right?'—then the flood."

To his credit, Hassan paused only a few seconds. He leaned forward, hands clasped before him, and said, "That is an intriguing idea. It sent us an explicit reminder of a past era. A demonstration is always better than talk."

Zuminski had a concentrated look, too. He said, "The Mat, yes, it does not think digitally, true. It can count, but does not seem to think that ability is important. What it does see as vital is geometry. Our studies with it show this. It knows all of Euclid, can tell a dodecahedron from a sphere instantly. Yes. So it would use a direct expression, real fluids, not some idea of how to count the past."

Some others chimed in with comments, mostly about seismic signatures they got on the surface. There were vibrations from distant sites undergound at the same time, some complex wave phenomenon that some—mostly the mathematical types, similar to the SETI Library mathists—thought were encoded signals. Could this be a way of fast information transport around the planet?

"My point," one of them said, "is that in times of stress, a big move-ment of fluids in their water basin"—he showed on the wall screen a vivid subsurface chart that plotted the big caverns, some loaded with water and hydrogen sulfide gas—"can slam against its sides and send a fast seismic signal at the speed of sound. Faster than the Mat can con-vey information through its usual means, visual shows on tunnel walls. That we know for sure."

A slender blond man who had said nothing suddenly spoke up. "You are assuming that the Mat is responding solely to your immedi-ate actions."

Zuminski paused, considered, and said, "That seems the simple way to go at it."

Rachel recognized the blond man from her prepping on the Aldrin—though she had not expected to meet him here. He was Hans Stefano, the leading monitor of the Marsforming project. He had power to stop any activity if, in his documented judgment, it endan-gered the Mat. Originally, Stefano was to consider only how Mars-forming, altering the surface and atmosphere, could interfere with the Mat's biosphere. There were reports that he was trying to expand his reach, taking in even how the descent teams functioned below.

A pause. Hassan paid close attention, but his eyes kept straying back to Rachel. So, for that matter, did Zuminski's.

Well, girl, Rachel thought, *you wanted to make an impact, and you did. But what next?*

5.

Amazing, Rachel thought, how large a month of the hab's shit was!

It was the next morning, and she had showed up for her task assignment. The Mars Code was, everybody works. No exception. Especially not for Earthers (no distinction here from Loonies, or Luners, as they were called here)—no tourism! Mars Operations minimized manual labor, but robots couldn't handle everything.

But it turned out there was an exception . . . Fraq. He and his flock were winging it in the big overpressured dome, trying out yet another unique grav. They were having much fun while she slung shit.

Like this. First their team got the plastic bag out from the hab underskirting and onto the hauling deck of a nuclear-powered truck that growled like a caged animal, which in a way it was. It doubled as a mobile power source, 130 kilowatts electrical, able to crawl anywhere on hard, carbon-fiber treads.

They then lugged the goody bag of brown across the landscape—a big, rich gift to Mars inside a mercifully opaque plastic sack, compacted and frozen solid. The Planetary Protocols demanded that human waste be taken several kilometers from habitats, then buried in peroxide-rich sands. But not too deep—the site had to be water-poor, unable to let waste trickle down into the volumes where the Mat lived. Ecology wasn't just some abstract science here; it was life itself. The hab used toilets that neatly separated solid and liquid waste—nature gave them separate exits, after all—and the urine got recycled, since it held 80 percent of the useful nutrients in human wastes.

Kitchen scraps, of course, went back into the greenhouses.

They had already dug the pit for it, a few klicks away across rocky terrain, using a Rover Boy backhoe. The one trick the bioengineers had not managed was converting the solid wastes to anything useful or even nonsickening. Let somebody else "realize existing in situ resources," as the manuals had put it, by composting. Frozen, it would keep.

The superoxide and mixed chem dust was the bizarre surface chemistry's sole advantage—it made the risk of contaminating the biosphere below tiny. Peroxides ate up fragile biological cells in seconds. Mars's surface was the most virulent clean room in the solar system, down for five meters. Any mess that escaped, Mars would kill every single cell within an hour.

It took two hours for them to deploy the big waste bag, then more to get the awkward plastic liner pinned up and protocols followed. Hard work in a suit that couldn't get its heating right—cold feet, hot head. Rachel felt drained on the backhoe ride back. At least it was exercise against grav not as cruel as Earthside.

Humans were litterbugs. The habitat had gear and refuse around it in a tattered skirt. The wind blew the pennant atop the tower out into a straight rectangle, an ironic salute above the garbage field.

In her scholarly Librarian mode, on the Aldrin, she had looked up the origin of the word *travel*. Many thought it came from the French word *travail*, which meant "work." *Just so*, she thought, *just so*.

Inside, suit shucked, she headed for the mess hall—and found Hassan and Stefano waiting for her.

———

Hassan leaned forward over coffee, his broad face split by a shiny smile. "So, you see, we thought to solicit further your views on the meaning of the flooding."

Rachel blinked. "I'm new here. Not entitled to a theory."

"We want fresh insights," the man Stefano said slowly, eyeing her and Hassan. "You have much training in the SETI messages"—

he waved a hand, as if encompassing all that field—"and this is a vastly more difficult issue, of course. But something may resonate, eh?" He gave her a chilly smile. She marveled at its mechanical insincerity.

"I wonder if the Mat may be using direct demonstration all the time?" Rachel said, talking directly to Hassan.

"To . . . show us something relevant to what it wishes to say?" Hassan sipped coffee and tipped his chin down, as if urging her forward. "Perhaps it demonstrated something it fears? Or likes? Wants?"

She knew this was empty speculation, but something in Hassan's veiled look told her she was following a trail he liked. What did he want from this? She had learned to anticipate Prefect Stiles's "avenues of thought," as the man himself had described them. Most leaders tried to coax their own ideas out of underlings, rather than impose them from above—a deft technique.

"Seems unlikely to me," Stefano said flatly. "I've watched the videos. Hard to tell much from suit cams, but it seems a simple reflexive response. Perhaps to something in the alien's symbol-set?"

Rachel caught Hassan's reaction, a quick twitch of his lower lip. Plainly the men did not like each other. After all, they were natural antagonists—Stefano wanted to police Hassan's explorations. Rachel somehow sided with Hassan, without any actual reason to do so. She always led with her own intuition. *In which case, what is he thinking?* Rachel reflected. To move the discussion, she said, "We don't know how fast the Mat can think, do we? Could it—however it processes information—answer within minutes?"

"Yes," Hassan said firmly. "Plenty of research shows that. We don't quite know how it does it—these are thinking plants, after all—but it does. Chem synapses, vapors that conduct electricals, even root systems." A pause. Pursed lips, anxious eyes. "There is a further fact, just noticed by our sensors."

Stefano began, "I have not seen—"

"This is hours old. The Mat is now exhaling a great deal of CH_4, methane."

Rachel was startled. "Didn't that happen during the first explorations?"

Hassan nodded. "And not since, not in such quantities. Several times an Earth year there are small, well, belches. But not like this."

Stefano asked, "Maybe that's a symptom of greater growth?"

Hassan shrugged. "As I recall, sometimes it recalls previous visits we've made, other times not. It must be reminded a bit through physical symbols—simple geometries, mostly—and photos displayed on screens."

"Suppose the flooding, the methane—it's referring to a deep, long memory?" Rachel asked quietly. *Use your intuition. Time to put the cat among the pigeons.*

Hassan's mouth was open to continue, but his eyes flickered and he said nothing.

"Of what?" Stefano broke the silence.

Hassan took a breath and let the words slide out, as though letting go of a secret idea. "Perhaps we should read the flooding as a sign that the Mat liked the wet, warm ages."

Stefano scowled skeptically. "Why should it?"

Hassan said, "That's when it might have gotten out onto the surface. Spread, maybe. The atmospheric pressure was much higher then, mostly CO_2 and water, providing some shield against the UV and cosmic rays."

Rachel sighed. "It could see the stars! At last. Earth, the planets. It had millions of years to think over the sights as they changed." The words came out like breathing, easy and immediate and without conscious thought.

Rachel could see the two men considering how this idea shifted their positions, eyes veiled. To some, everything was politics, in the end. She decided to step in as they pondered, just to stir things up; this was fun. "In that time, could it have directly connected with other parts of the Marsmat, on the surface?"

They eyed her. Plainly this was a chess game, with ideas as pieces to advance, when needed.

"Preposterous," Stefano said.

"Why?" Hassan chided.

"To think the Mat would remind us of its past—"

"The alien was there, Fraq," Rachel said. "That made a difference."

Stefano pulled the edges of his mouth down in disdain. "Why?"

"The Mat could tell that Fraq was different from us. I was there, sure, but I certainly don't know why. Maybe its 'eyesight'—if that's what it has, with chem senses, too, maybe—can distinguish humans from other species."

Hassan put in, "We've never shown it an animal. There are pets here, a few, but never occurred to show the Mat one. Then how could the Mat— Only . . . only by experience."

Rachel saw it then. "Yes. The Mat has seen Fraq's kind before. Something happened back then."

Stefano sniffed. "This is all mere supposition."

"Sure it is," Hassan said. "Let's follow the logic."

"To what conclusion?" Stefano insisted.

"Well, for one, how about this idea that the flooding was a recognition signal?" Rachel said.

Stefano's mouth compressed into a thin line. "But that would imply—"

Hassan shot back, "That Mars was wet when Fraq's kind came here."

Silence. Then Rachel said, "We can date that era. It's somewhere millions of years in the past."

Stiffly Stefano said, "That could match, if Fraq would tell us when his species came here."

Rachel said, "He doesn't know. It was a long time ago, and his species had done a lot. They abandoned their native planet and now live in artificial sites strung around their solar system. In all that, plenty of their records vanished."

Both men gaped at her. "This . . ." Stefano said, blinking rapidly, ". . . this is known?"

"To me and few others."

"Why isn't this understood more broadly?"

Rachel spread her hands, shrugging as if the answer was obvious. "Some of it Fraq told me—me alone. Plus, the Library doesn't want to turn this into a media circus. Being on Luna helps to shut out Earth's grabby media net. Taking Fraq to Mars is even better. The Prefect liked that idea a lot." But he sure as hell hadn't liked getting cut out of the

Mars expedition, at Fraq's demand. "It . . . keeps Fraq under wraps."
There, Rachel thought, *I've said it.*

The Prefects had in mind all along isolating Fraq until they knew
more. Never said so directly, but after years of working with them, she
had become accustomed to their furtive ways. Fraq was consistently
cagey about the aliens' motives, the wormhole location—without ever
really saying how they'd gotten here at all. She knew a big game was
afoot here, too big to squander on a mere publicity campaign. The Prefects had tried to stop the whole orbitfall stunt, lost out to Earther
pressure. Then the Everest ascent, the smokers, now Mars . . . Puzzling
indeed, to the myriad Earther theorists, to politicians, to social comment folk, to media mavens . . .

Hassan said, "This casts new light. Fraq is exploring here a site his
species once knew. Why?"

Rachel outlined the alien's curious stunts, though they knew most
of it. "The point is, Fraq is going back to the time when his kind had a
world—an act of ancient nostalgia, I suppose. And the Marsmat is part
of that. Somehow."

"Why didn't his species spread through the wormhole network—
assuming there is one, as some Messages said, long ago, I know—so
they could come here?" Stefano asked.

Rachel shrugged. "We don't know. Maybe they didn't have the tech
for a long time. Or—could be the location of their wormhole mouth
is a closely guarded secret, known only to a few?" She laughed wryly.
"Because that's how Fraq is treating us, too—hiding the wormhole
location. So . . . why?" *The big prize,* she thought, but didn't say.

Stefano looked worried, then made his face blank. Rachel supposed this was moving too fast for him and his agenda. "We should be
careful about turning speculations into facts," he said stiffly.

Hassan nodded, but said, "Nobody can test an idea before taking
the trouble to have an idea."

———————

After that, she decided to go for a walk.

In her first days on Mars she had stayed inside, a bit shy of the
complicated suit-up rituals needed. She got to know some of the peo-

ple in the habitat instead, and made a discovery. Media had conditioned viewers to think that only emotionally repressed pilots spouting acronyms were the Real Stuff. Some had become celebs, like Julia and the others in the original First Landing team: the Bright Stuff. But the thousands of people on Mars now, after a century of Marsforming, were varied and spirited—pioneers. Good, odd people. Still, it was the frontier that most interested Rachel here, the unknown.

Getting in and out of anything, habitats or pressured rovers, was so laborious, they kept the lock pass-throughs (an ancient NASA term) to a minimum. With every one they brought in fine red dust, even with the two-shower system designed to wash them away. But she needed to go out, so she went through the procedures. Rules said she was supposed to go with a partner, but she wanted to be alone.

Once outside, she marveled. Marsforming had already brought thin cirrus to the skies. Silvery, they caught the late afternoon sun in filmy layers. It had taken a century to settle Mars and create a substantial local industrial capability and population. Within half a century more, robo-factories venting fluorocarbon gases had warmed the planet by 8°C. That brought water and carbon dioxide outgassing from the soil, thickening the atmosphere and raising the planetary temperature a further 20°C.

Still, the peroxides hadn't met enough water to gush forth their captured oxygen—the big event everyone anticipated. That awaited big rains. Marsforming had benefited from nano-bio machines galore, but some brute chemical facts still ruled. Still, within her lifetime—which she cheerfully expected to exceed the 150 years now standard—Rachel hoped to be able to walk here with just a lightweight compressor to boost the oxygen she needed.

Even so transformed now, this Mars taught hard lessons. For one, how much Mother Earth did for humans without their noticing. Recycling air, water, and food demanded an intricate dance of chemistry and physics. The habitat had to tinker with its systems constantly. Let the CO_2 rise, and they could all be dead before anyone noticed anything wrong; the sensors stood sentinel, carefully tended. Those also watched the moisture content of the hab's air, lest they all get "suit throat"—drying out until voices rasped.

Though wetter and warmer now, Mars still had plenty of nasty tricks. The pesky peroxides got in everywhere—even her underwear!—and seals eroded, so they had to be replaced with each outing. Air scrubbers needed adjustment and filter changes. They fought a steady battle to keep dust down.

Rachel hiked to a nearby hill and watched the high clouds shadow the rust-brown land to the north. The vent was a dark spot a few kilometers away, thronged by monitors and gear. Their dung dump was a dark spot on the opposite horizon. Marsforming had already made some water melt out of the permafrost. Muddy rivers flowed and light rain fell here and there. Radiation doses on the surface were falling as the atmosphere grew. Near the equator the first photosynthetic microbes were spreading in blue-green mats.

"Rachel!" came a call. She turned, irritated, and saw Stefano approaching. He must have followed her out. She wasn't pleased; she liked getting the feel of Mars alone.

"Beautiful, isn't it?" he said, huffing inside his suit from the climb. His eyebrows furrowed. "But look at this."

He led her to a gully over the crest of the hill. It yawned two meters deep, newly carved. "Some permafrost erupted here last month. Flowed down, into the plain. That will work through into the Marsmat caverns. We're intruding on a fragile biosphere."

"Fragile? It's tough—probably older than ours. The DNA shows that the Marsmat has a lot of similarities to our most ancient bacteria, right? It endured the loss of the planet's atmosphere, the freezing-down, and heavy bombardments—then grew underground."

"We cannot know what reawakening this water will do to the Mat. The Precautionary Principle plainly provides that insight."

She always hated hearing the capitals on big, inflated ideas. "We should never do anything for the first time, I get it."

"I don't think that's a fair—"

"Let me guess, next comes 'rocks have rights,' yes?"

He gave her a long, stern glare. "You won't hear me out."

"The Mat isn't afraid of water—it welcomes fluids, and uses them in its own weird way."

"You support Marsforming, then."

"Look, life is a one-way trip." She spread her arms wide. "We're all permanently exiled from our past. Mars colonists—all colonists—are no different. In addition to leaving behind the time of their pasts, they also leave behind the place, Earth. But in return they get to create a world where none existed before, a whole new planet."

"But not for the Marsmat that lives here."

"It's an anaerobe. When we have an oxygen atmosphere here, it will still be safe far underground, just like the anaerobes on Earth."

He shook his head. "We are not so superior that we should manage another life-form. Especially a sentient one."

She stood her ground. "Why not manage wildlife? Back Earth-side, we slip contraceptives into the food of overpopulations of deer. In California, people teach condors not to perch on power lines, so they won't get electrocuted. People teach whooping cranes how to migrate, and pick up salamanders to get them across roads—you name it, we do it."

He crossed his arms, the classic hostile stance. "We're radically altering its world."

"If the Marsmat wants to come up, to colonize the surface—as it did before—it will make up its own mind." She paused, her caution saying, *Don't get into politics talk!* So she finished lamely, "Or whatever it uses for a mind."

"Such species-specific ethics are unacceptable." He waved an arm at the plain below. "This is a separate world, with separate rights of its own."

She couldn't resist. "Not once we're here. We're life!—connecting at last to other life, the Mat. Our ethics needs to benefit humanity. I won't debate whether the Marsmat's interests can be considered as equal to human interests. It's a microbial intelligence. It's not like us, and moral arguments like yours—well, you contradict yourself every day!"

He looked puzzled. "What? How?"

"Look, if bacterial interests trump human interests, then mouth-wash should be banned, right? We shouldn't chlorinate our water supplies. Hell, antibiotics should be illegal. If bacterial interests are superior to human interests, then Albert Schweitzer and Louis Pasteur should be denounced for crimes against bacteria!"

Her mother had once said, "Speak when you're full of fire and you will make the best speech you will ever regret." Rachel wondered where her vehemence was coming from, and then went on, throwing caution to the wind. "Now, it's vital to save the Amazon rain forest, because a world without that would be a poorer one. Plus, no inheritance for our descendants. But Mars?"

"I do not see why you can parallel—"

"Hear the end of the argument, at least." She frowned at him and again wondered where all this was coming from. "Look at it!"—she swirled around, both arms out, sweeping the horizon. "Even with an atmosphere nearly fifty times the original thin skin of carbon dioxide, it's barren! No isolation lab on Earth is remotely as hostile to organic chemistry. A terraformed Mars, filled with life—forests, farms, seas, playgrounds, used book stores, who knows what?—how can that not be a vastly richer gift to posterity?"

"That posterity will lack the Mars we know." He looked around with distaste, and pointed to the gully. "Or knew."

She had to admit, though only to herself, that the sharply eroded scar did resemble a wound. Some aspects of world-making were not pretty. "Look!" She whirled around again, feeling oddly giddy, impetuous. "Anybody who proposed changing our Earth into this place would be mad, mad, mad—and bad. So why doesn't that logic work in reverse? Keeping Mars dead rather than make it as wonderful as Earth is—"

"Incorrect logic." His lips compressed into a thin white line. "Arguments can't run backward."

"Maybe. But I can—!" She took off, running downhill, taking long strides in the relaxing 0.38 gravs. It felt good to switch off her comm and leave the dead argument behind her. Stefano hadn't, so she heard his startled yelp and chugging breath as he ran downslope, too. A glance back told her Stefano couldn't keep up; he seemed in poor shape.

She sped down the brown-red soil, placing her boots so she didn't land on rocks, leaping small gullies, headed for the habitat. This was Mars, for Chrissake, an alien place, not just a debating point—and she intended to experience it, not argue it.

Too late, she thought of other arguments. Marsforming was a long-term project, and there would come the chance to see directly if and how the Mat adapted to warmer, wetter days. There were plenty of terrestrial microbes incoming from the occasional Earth knock-off rocks, and plenty more brought by humans. Native and immigrant life blending, showing how such past ages might have looked. Understanding of Martian biota would increase by terraforming, not decrease.

Microbial biospheres had survived the early bombardment days on both planets. Life, once started, seemed determined to last.

But Stefano wouldn't care about arguments, really. Most firm positions came from emotion, not reason. What was that old law?

Passion is inversely proportional to the amount of real information available.

Too true, too true.

————————

Back inside, Rachel showered twice and had a tiny glass of cognac—a minor breach of rules—to wash away Stefano and the dung job, rather similar experiences. As soon as she had water on for tea, she turned on some piano pieces by Chopin.

A little later, refreshed, she ambled into the habitat lounge. A big screen showed a newslink to Earth, with a reporter interviewing the oldest woman on the planet, just turned two hundred. He asked her, "And what do you think is the best thing about being two hundred?" Her lined but vigorous face split with a smile. "No peer pressure."

A barking laugh drew her eye. Zuminski held a big glass of dark beer, sitting back in the shadows, alone. She went to the bar and got herself the same. Here and in the mess, she had learned, the standard conversational gambit was "Sure cold," and the standard answer, "Sure is." Such scintillating dialogue at least distracted from the lingering odor of burnt grease, but the lounge was cleaner. Noisier, too. She scanned the crowd clustered near the screens—one showed a razor-sharp view of an Australian beach, surfers riding big combers—and somehow her eyes sought out Zuminski.

She walked toward him with a jaunty air she did not in fact feel. Rachel wondered how she looked, and then remembered an old friend's advice: "No guy is going to notice what shoes you're wearing, and if he does, he's the wrong guy."

She had enjoyed her fair share of men, but in her years at the Library, she now saw, the dour air of the Librarian had descended upon her like a gray shroud. The neutered population there didn't help; Noughts tended to damp the ancient, eternal dance of men and women. In the hushed corridors of the Library, there had seemed no way to draw men to her. Kane, of course, who was great in bed but not The One. Maybe there was no One, she thought. But she was a tad slow at drawing candidates. At least, short of waving brightly colored objects at them. She hadn't tried that.

Zuminski's quick eyes saw her approach, and he raised an eyebrow. Something glittered in his eyes, a brief smile flickered. Her modestly proportioned figure had not suffered the bulges that came with childbearing or overeating, nor the oddities that attended living in Luna's 0.17 gravs. Her breasts, medium-size and still pink-tipped, had not fallen. Nor had her face taken on an expression she saw in older women—the drawn lines of the former beauty, who wonders where all that attention went. She had not gone over to the common strategy, to coo, simper, paint, and decorate. Her customary conversation had an air of measured consideration with an undertone of educated irony. Maybe not a great marketing posture, but hers.

Usually guys made the opening line, but she got out ahead with, "What's the thought of the day?"

He blinked, smiled, gestured for her to sit. "Banal bureaucratic reality meets the unknown."

"Meaning?"

"Hassan. Stefano. They are not like us, but manage us. The lords, they speak from on high. We are to descend again tomorrow. Briefing at oh seven hundred."

"That Stefano—"

"Yes. I saw he went outside after you. . . ." Another raised eyebrow.

"He tried to recruit me to his cause."

"And?

"Let's say I gave him a sunny smile and made the V-for-victory sign . . . but forgot to put down one finger."

He laughed. She liked the sound. He toasted her. "The only good thing about stupidity is that it can lead to adventure."

"Not Stefano's."

"No, that leads to boredom. The cure for boredom is curiosity. Sad, there is no cure for curiosity."

"I hope not." She thought a moment and said, "To echo something you said—if you scratch a cynic, you find a disappointed idealist. Maybe that's what we are. We might've been idealists something like Stefano once. But we see where it leads."

"To?" He gave her a small smile, eyes dancing.

"Narrowness."

"Stefano can't see that the Mat is not some endangered species, like the thousands that died on Earth. It's a worldwide creature. Ancient. It's everywhere—we've seen communications between vents and caverns on opposite sides of the planet. We still don't know how deep it goes."

"And . . . our antler-clashes?"

He chuckled. "Put aside, for now. I am partial to . . . charming women."

"Most men in a bar would have said 'to beautiful women.'"

"A beautiful woman is one I notice. A charming woman is one who notices me."

She laughed and took another sip. This had been a long day and they had a descent ahead. Best to be . . . careful.

She relaxed and thought. "We're going so soon? Why?"

"The Mat deserves a reply. Is only polite, after all."

"A reply to the flooding?"

"And it may wish to respond to the alien's message."

She nodded. "Yes. Fraq is very . . . odd."

"You know him. Your Library has kept him wrapped up, so we know little."

She had gotten such oblique inquiries before, but Zuminski seemed different from the usual inquiring-minds-want-to-know types. She said slowly, "How strange Fraq is comes out in, well, odd ways. He stays by himself a lot, when not with fellow flock members. It seems a property of their species, not social babblers like us. You know about the death-defying things he's done—"

"And that you have done with him."

"Yes, but they weren't my idea. One time I asked about how he felt that others had died while doing these stunts—particularly the orbit-fall and flying up Everest. He shook off the question, though Xiaoling kept after him. So finally I asked straight out if he thought he would be held accountable in some afterlife."

"Alien religion?"

"That's the point—I don't know. Fraq said, exact quote—'One world at a time.' And no more."

"I wish I knew what these aliens intended."

She was worn out on that issue. Instead, she wondered about reply-ing to the Mat. How? "Say . . . how long can the Mat hold a thought?"

He shrugged, slugged down some beer. "I would say, perhaps a thousand years. Maybe more."

She laughed. "How can we know that?"

"It apparently remembered the alien's kind, its species—yes?"

"True, so a million years, maybe more. And it's sure been around a very long time—" She stopped in midsentence and licked her lips, then continued slowly, "The Mat isn't like anything we can envision. Humans, Fraq, other SETI intelligences—we all know that we'll per-sonally die. The Mat doesn't."

He looked startled. "I had not thought that. Perhaps it does not know that it can endanger us, then?"

She nodded, seeing how his mind worked. "So it might not have appreciated how the flooding startled us. Maybe we were supposed to be . . . complimented?"

He took a long pull of his Guinness. "This requires thought. Much thought."

"I had half a year to study symbology in the Aldrin. And read up on all you types. It was like living in a swanky hotel; plenty of time to think."

He nodded. "I liked real well. Luxury living."

"Those towels in the cabins were so fluffy, I had trouble closing my suitcase."

He looked startled, saw the joke, snickered. "Witty lady." Then he leaned over and kissed her.

She knew the old sensation: a ruby serotonin flood, with a bubbly dopamine chaser. *Time for a new guy . . . Kane is far away . . . and I don't measure my progress by guys, anyway. It's life I'm eager for, not just guys. So . . .*

The thought was a revelation, shaped into a sentence. So . . . "In most of my dreams, this is where I wake up."

6.

Rachel woke up in muggy darkness and remembered it all, breathing patiently, and decided that, yes, it had been a dream. Convincing, crisp and detailed and colorful, but—yes, obviously a dream. She did not do things like that.

Inventory time, eyes closed. She had felt badly about how she slipped away from Luna without seeing Kane, for a parting talk. She had indeed had the great fun of a passionate frolic, for two days running, when she told him about the whole orbitfall event. But she wasn't up for Unity—as it was termed these odd days—with anybody, not then, not now.

That might come later—much later. With life-span extended—or protracted, as some had it—you could perfectly delay personal stuff until you had the arc of your career launched. She felt she was still on a long, rough upward slope in her life. Going hard, not sure where.

Kane didn't buy that. He was a dear, sweet gentleman, and knew when to not bother being a gentleman. But not yet, no. And who knew?—someone might show up who wouldn't take all this thinking. Someone she would just know about.

She sighed, blinked at the dark room, rolled over to grab the pillow—and felt a long, muscled arm. Opened her eyes.

Him. No dream. His musk clung in her nostrils.

She went rigid. Sometimes the light at the end of the tunnel of love was the headbeam of an oncoming train. The brilliance didn't so much illuminate as bring things glaringly into view.

She considered. Yes, she had too many times woken up on the wrong side of the bed in the morning—only to realize that it was because she was waking up on the side of . . . no one.

And Vayl Zuminski was charming, in his glinting, rough-cut-diamond way. Plus, she was something of an incurable romantic and didn't think the man-woman dance was a contest on the rabbit level. They had indeed made a connection.

He grunted, opened an eye. "Oh."

"Yes. Any memories about how we got here?"

A crusty smile. "Several. Very pleasant."

"I didn't intend . . ."

"Not I, either. For those given to excess, abstinence much easier than moderation."

"Such as you?"

Guardedly: "At times. Not now. Not here. Maybe never again." Then a broad, blazing smile that struck into her heart.

———

The alarm reminded them: the descent, 0700 muster. Groans, showers (some fun, slippery bodies mingling), but . . . She staggered out into his living room.

Alas, it was a tribute to another era. He had spent his mass limit on stuff from the old country. Heavy wood furniture, slathered with something like mohair. Lamps dripping with balls and tassels beneath pink or amber shades. Drapes on the walls over a widescreen view of outside. Even the walls deadened sound. If bears had decorator caves, she thought, they would look like this.

But then they had a hearty breakfast in the mess, calorie loading. Rachel waved away coffee, though she longed for it. Peeing in her suit still put her off.

Suiting up. Outside, eyes scrunched down against the glare of Martian dawn. Into the trawler. Robotlike, Rachel went through the motions, beset by emotions. Xiaoling was bravely holding up with a

bright, wobbly smile, despite her banged-up head. She stayed close to
Fraq, who showed no reactions. The alien seemed rather robotic, too,
focused and refusing any talk with a shake of his head or a shrug.

Sitting next to Zuminski in the trawler, she gestured to her comm
link and punched in his signets. He clicked in, and they were e-isolated
from the others. "So?" he asked.

"So this." She sent an encoded symbol-set. "I've got this in a trans-
ducer loader."

Zuminski looked at his side screen and frowned. "This is . . ."

"I ran a search, using the SETI Library team—a bunch of great
mathists. They ran a multistage test on those symbol-strings Fraq
showed the Mat. Took a while."

"I'll bet. You guys got, what?—thousands of SETI signals, some
fragments, some—"

"Right. Chaos. But the mathists turned up an echo—not exact,
but close—of a really ancient, indecipherable symbol-string in SETI
Message 2103C."

"From those 'lighthouse alerts' you guys found?"

"Yes—short pulses at high flux, then nothing. Turns out, it's
plenty cheaper to send short pulses than steady signals. Civilizations
don't want to spend a fortune, trying to get the attention of distant
life-sites—I mean, really far away, thousands of light-years. So they
light up the microwave sky in little spurts. The spurts usually have
some short, underlying messages—simple codes—pointing to nearby
frequencies. Look there, and we find a low-power, dense signal. Usually
at ten gigahertz or so."

"So—?" Zuminski said. The trouble with suits was reading face signals, she thought.

"What's Fraq's motive here?"

Zuminski said, "Fraq says he—wants to go back down, present
more of symbol-string."

"He has his own agenda. The message he communicated to the
Mat tells us he's related somehow to that ancient SETI code—which
we don't understand."

"He's taken a while to get to Mars, after those stunts of his—falling
through the whole atmosphere, what an idea!—how did you think of

it? So the risk-takings were entertainment for him, or somehow preparation for something else, yes?"

She grimaced. They were getting out of the trawler now, setting up for the descent. The Mars dawn stretched sharp shadows across a rosy plain. Next would come the cable descent. "Or a diversion, to lull us into complacency?"

"Could be." Zuminski turned, shrugged as well as anyone could in a pressure suit. "Well, we're not complacent anymore. Fraq is up to something—but what? The symbol-string certainly provoked the Marsmat. Intentionally?"

"That SETI message is clearly similar. If it came from Fraq's civilization, sent several thousand years ago, then we now know the approximate location of his star. It's a G2 about 1,480 light-years away."

Zuminski attached his extra inputs and life support to his suit. The two teams, with the SETI crew a small fraction, swarmed around them, chattering. Busyness distracted. Plus the slow lurches of their humming transport.

Zuminski said, "And if we are right, that G-2 star has a wormhole nearby. That's the first actual measurement—granted the premise that it's his home world—of how far apart the wormhole complex links can be."

"Is that a surprise? I thought wormholes could be of any length, because they're really shortcuts in spacetime." She got into the descent elevator, bottles and lines arranged. *Life is so complicated when you don't breathe the atmosphere!* "Fraq could have traveled ten meters in his wormhole tunnel, then just popped through 1,480 light-years."

"Makes you wonder why nobody did before."

"Who says some of Fraq's people didn't?" She got into position with Xiaoling and Fraq, who was stiff and formal, nodding—a human gesture he had learned well. Here they were in an elevator and she, blithe Rachel, was talking about the alien when he stood a meter away. "Look, Fraq and his flock could just be the first ones who brought themselves to our attention, jetting in from the Oort cloud like innocents."

Zuminski grinned at her through his somewhat grimy helmet bubble. "Beware of the innocents, my father used to say."

"So assume he's here to find out something from the Marsmat. What?"

"Can't be more information on the wormhole network. They presumably know that."

True, so . . . "Maybe it's not information. Maybe it's . . . things?"

Zuminski looked puzzled. "What?"

"Ummm. Mathists think of objects as just compact ways of carrying around information. So, to keep some information on Mars, subsurface so the Marsmat could somehow use it—how?"

He snorted. "Hard copy, must be. Really hard. A rock, maybe." They started down. The cage rattled. Rock slid past.

Here came the vast underground. The available volume of warm, cavern-laced rock below Mars was comparable to the inhabitable surface area of Earth. Openings, from caverns down to pores in rock, suffered no wrenching from plate tectonics, since the Martian crust had frozen in place quite early. Plus, even the pores were larger, because of the lesser gravity. *Plenty of room to try out fresh patterns,* she thought. *Over four billion years.*

This time they went into another cavern network. Hassan had decided to address a different portion of the Marsmat, for safety reasons. So they lugged with them the graphical screen, onto which Fraq had loaded his second symbol-set with the help of the Descent Team.

For an hour they moved in tandem through a shadowy, clouded world of diffuse light that throbbed with a slow, softly radiant energy. Rachel felt the strangeness of these cloistered caverns settle like a blanket, quieting their chatter.

As they descended through sloping corridors, snottites gleamed in the beams of their headlamps, dangling in moist lances from the ceiling. She steered well clear of the shiny colonies of single-celled extremophilic bacteria—like small stalactites, but with the consistency of mucus. Snottites got their energy from digesting the volcanic sulfur in the warm water dripping down from above. Brush one of those highly acidic rods and their battery acid would cut through suits in moments. A sharp, short ouch—quite fatal.

The Mat used slightly tilted troughs and channels to return fluids to lower levels, so they were following those flow patterns. They trudged along, their ragged, huffing breaths audible over suit comm. Fluids moved upward through vapor transport or simple osmotic pressures, so in a way they were inside an immense living being, like microbes in a bloodstream.

She felt a hushed reverence here. This was life unlike any analogy with Earthly biology, still evolving from forms older than the continents. Still hanging on, indestructible, still dealing in its own strange way with the hardships dealt it, still coming.

They stopped in a large chamber, its walls thick with the Mat. The team deployed the display panel, plugged in power sources, booted up Fraq's symbol-string. As before, the alien did not explain or share what he had prepared.

The strange moist atmosphere wrapped around them, and then came the signal, and the display. Show time. They watched the script roll across the panel in long, furling symbols that though static seemed to move, flapping like flags. It ran for about a minute. Silence.

Fraq stepped back when the string ended. The alien looked satisfied, and stood watching the walls where the Mat thickened, high in the ceiling. Some of the wet organism hung like draperies in the soft Mat glow. No one moved. A long, anticipatory silence from all of them ended with a flurry of hissing and gurgling that came from the walls.

Zuminski called, "Move uphill. Prepare for any flooding—"

But there was no rush of water. Instead, Rachel shielded her eyes against a sudden, hard glare. The Mat radiance rose, an ivory sheen that blinded her. It pulsed in its fierce ivory glow.

If it floods us now, nobody will be able to keep their bearings.

Chatter on the comm, which she ignored. Panicked voices.

Think. She wondered if the whole idea of the flooding as a signal of the ancient past was an illusion. Maybe the Mat really was malicious.

Ideas rushed through her, and she made herself stand still, using her ears and feet to sense any change. *What's a Librarian doing in this?* she thought, as she had when she plunged from orbit. Yet she couldn't resist the lure of adventure. . . .

The glare ebbed. No water lapped at their heels. Slowly she got her eyesight back. The cavern seemed unchanged. Zuminski ordered them to form a file and retreat, which seemed to her a wise move.

They were moving uphill before his voice came over comm again, tight with alarm. "Where is Fraq?"

She looked around. The alien was gone.

And big elephant-ear formations on the uphill side of the chamber had closed, sealing them in.

PART 12

THE GRACE OF TRAGEDY

What we observe is not nature itself but nature exposed
to our method of questioning.

—WERNER HEISENBERG

1.

It felt good to yell. Good and loud. Rachel pounded hard on one of the pale elephant-ear formations. With her comm set off, she shouted full force. Her ears hummed with dumb rage. That at least helped her frustration. She slammed gloved fists into the meaty folds. A two-handed smack. The huge mass didn't budge. All the big, leafy sheets of the Marsmat on the uphill side of the chamber had closed, sealing them in. And Fraq . . . Fraq was gone.

A kilometer below the Martian soil, they had managed to lose the alien. He had vanished in the sudden pulse of ivory light that had streamed from the Mat itself.

Zuminski knocked on her helmet, touched his helmet to hers, and said, "Over this tantrum?"

"Uh, yeah."

"Alien is gone. Let us get out of here."

The comm buzzed with speculations, complaints, cursing.

She grinned. "I can do better than that. Let's find him."

He frowned, grimaced skeptically. "Mat is blocking us. He must have gotten out with some trick."

"I have another trick. I put a tracker in his suit."

Zuminski blinked. "How?"

"Stuck it with an adhesive below his oxy tanks."

"Ah. Hard to see there."

Rachel nodded and popped up a virtual screen on the left side of her helmet visor. "I'll activate it."

The software pinged up quickly. She got a flashing signature dot, moving slowly in the coordinate space. "I've got him." She pointed.

"How distant?"

"Can't tell."

"Move down this corridor," Zuminski said, gesturing. "Get triangle."

She saw his point. The rest of the team was sputtering on comm, splashing around in the usual underfoot trickles—not her problem, though. She shut it off. Time to keep her head clear of mere muttering. Zuminski barked orders to the others to use the new electroshock methods on one of the big elephant-ears, then turned to follow her.

She made her way over rocky footing, careful to avoid the Marsmat where it clung, still rippling with colors—and got about a hundred meters away from the rest of them. Rachel stopped and sent a *ping* to the tracker. It answered with a flashing icon on her visor screen. She punched in commands, and the software triangulated with the previous signal.

"There!" She pointed at her own helmet display. "He's about two hundred meters away, to the right."

Zuminski sloshed over and squinted from near her right ear, trying to make out the display. "Don't bother send to me. We got go after him."

A shout from the team. An image on her display: They had sprung open one of the big Marsmat iris-valves. It had jerked open, startled by the jolt of high-voltage current.

They stepped through, single file. The nearby craggy corridors yawned vacant in pale Marsmat light.

Zuminski flashed his big lamps up and down the new, rough cave they stood in, cloaked in a damp fog. Flashes of blue and green seemed to signal to them. "Plenty Mat, but did the alien come this way?"

"Dunno." Rachel checked her helmet display. "He's still to our right. Moving, too."

They carefully made their way through the cramped corridor,

avoiding outcroppings of thick mat. Rachel thought about how the Marsmat had separated her, Zuminski, and Xiaoling off with the rest, using its irises. Why? Had the alien sent the Mat some signal they had missed? Fraq had written the coded message they'd displayed days before, using their screen—still the best way to "talk" to the Mat, the specialists thought. What had that message actually said? Fraq had given Rachel a supposed translation from his own swirly script, but how would they know if it was really what the tangle of symbols meant? The Ythri had not given much access to their written language, and even that was in several different scripts—evidence of how old the Ythri culture was.

Rachel and Zuminski made their way through dizzying labyrinths of passages—steadily deeper and deeper, warmer, ivory wreaths of moist gases wrapping around them. She sent a *ping*, watching the moving display. "Ah! Fraq is right in front of us. Not far."

The murky walls spread slowly, opening like a funnel. A shroud of gray elephant-ear parted, starting a breeze blowing in their faces. Through it—and they stood in the flaring entrance to a huge vault, shrouded in thick mists and pervaded by a creamy white glow. Rachel could see almost nothing in the shadowy depths that fell away, still going down. "What's that?" Zuminski whispered on comm.

Something glinted in their headlamp beams. They moved forward cautiously. The Mat retreated here, forming an exactly circular arc around—

"Looks artificial," Rachel said. It seemed to be a sculpture of an odd, lustrous metal. Silvery, but with streaks of yellow and deep blue in its depths, almost like the facets of a jewel.

Zuminski said, "Has to be manufactured."

"Or like a crystal?—grown? Maybe this is from Fraq's species? The Mat couldn't make it, I'd guess."

"No mention of such in the many reports I read. No such constructions."

Rachel ventured, "Maybe . . . left here long ago?" *Is this some sort of mother cavern?* she suddenly thought. *The place where the Mat network concentrated? First evolved?* Some theorists thought there should be some such original zone, as Africa was for hominids.

They stayed a respectful distance from the thing, water splashing gently against their lower legs from a slow, warm flow. It was angular and oddly curved, about a meter on a side and sunk into the rocky floor. This grotto reminded Rachel of a family vacation when she was a girl: the Carlsbad Caverns. Stalactites had speared down from a high ceiling, dripping with creamy droplets. Stalagmites answered them, rising from the hard white floor to heights above Rachel's head. "This is old," she said. "A primordial cavern."

"How do you know?"

"These are like the drip-formed limestone caverns on Earth. It takes a long time to form them." Rachel looked around; no sign of Fraq in the dim grotto.

Zuminski said, "Earthside ones came from the shells of dead sea creatures, like the white cliffs of Dover."

"Shells in a Martian ocean? That—"

"Right, can't be. But limestone, it can form directly from seawater, too. In shallow areas, where there's too much calcium for the briny water to hold. So it precipitates out in layers. Then plate tectonics scrunch it, bury it, and it forms a stone layer. Later water can creep through it from above, carrying it down in solution. Then it deposits again in stalactites like these."

Rachel realized that of course this guy had all the background she didn't. But . . .

"Mars doesn't have plate tectonics."

"It did," the biologist shot back, "when it had oceans. That lasted maybe a billion years, tops. This cavern must have formed when the oceans froze, then got covered in dust. Some water was warm enough to drip through the limestone, and hollow out this cavern."

Rachel said, feeling like a schoolgirl, "Ah. So that's why it looks like Carlsbad Caverns."

She walked over to some glistening snottites, hanging from the ceiling like small stalactites—beauty with the consistency of snot.

Zuminski grinned and said, "Marsmat must remember that. Memorial! Know this place is really ancient. From before the time that the Marsmat itself evolved to intelligence. Billions of years! So it's a holy place to the Mat? Maybe. Or maybe just a place where it deposits truly old things. Is dump, maybe. Like this—and what is it?" He pointed at the strange metallic object, standing at the center of an exact circle of pale-ivory glowing mat.

Rachel walked carefully to it, crouched down, turned off her headlamp. Three round bumps near the top caught her eye—shiny, reflecting. "These look like crystals—seems to be a weak glow behind them."

"Some energy source running it," Zuminski said.

"The Mat didn't make this, but Fraq must have gone searching for it."

"How come *we* didn't find this?" Zuminski's mouth twisted ruefully. "Might be, never explored this way. Doubtful, though."

"Or maybe . . ." She pointed to the precise circle formed by the Mat. "Could the Mat have covered it, when a human team went through?"

Zuminski touched the lip of the Mat with a finger. It jerked back, a surprisingly quick reaction. "Hey!—sensitive. Fast. So . . . now . . . maybe slid off this object—"

"When Fraq gave it a signal." Rachel shrugged. "Somehow."

To Rachel the thing looked *old*, even in this setting. She had imagined there might be some quarry Fraq was seeking, but—this? Its very existence implied another thread of speculation, and she made a swift decision.

Rachel stood up, taking quick photos with her shoulder-mounted camera, and said, "Let's find Fraq. Maybe he'll 'fess up."

"May be more . . ." Zuminski went off down the grotto, headbeam stabbing into the thick, murky fog. He did glance back at her for a long moment, as if suspecting something, before he continued on his way.

Rachel bent down again before the artifact and used her hand flashlight to send quick, on-off signals toward the three crystal "eyes," as she thought of them. A wait, then—it flashed back, the same pattern. Rachel wondered if it ran on the hydrogen sulfide that filled this chamber—a convenient energy source, just as in the thermal vents on Earth. *Ancient chem wisdom. Deadly to us, of course.*

She waited, watching the artifact. No change. On an intuition, she started her shoulder video camera. The quick flash of it activating brought a response from the three "eyes"—and they started sending short flickers, in a rippling sequence that darted among the three, long and short bursts in a complex pattern. Her instincts told her immediately: a code string.

It ran several minutes as she watched intently, holding her camera view steady, not saying a word on comm. *Data time, yes!*

She wondered if this was why this artifact was deep down, somewhat isolated from the Marsmat. *For security? Or . . . awaiting the right messenger?* The strange long code string stopped. The "eyes" went dull, done.

She backed away, looked around. The team was far down the cavern now, their beam lights a diffuse, reflected glow. Then over the comm she heard excited talk.

Zuminski called, "Fraq! Stay where you are."

Rachel listened as Zuminski shot questions at Fraq. The alien gave one-word answers—revealing nothing, as had become his habit. She used the time to carefully inspect the artifact, which now stood inert, with no glimmer from the three crystals.

Now was her last chance, she saw. Rachel carefully fetched a small thing that looked at first glance like a rock, much resembling the rough gray igneous walls of this grotto. She had fashioned a simple stucco wrap around the device inside, then dirtied it up.

She found the small button near its base and clicked it on. The device murmured in her hand, opened a port, and sent out a verifying dart of light. She put it about a meter from the artifact, sighting it carefully at the three crystal lenses, then stood up and checked the angles—just in time. The team was materializing out of the mists, their glow lighting up the area. She stood between them and her camouflaged device. "Stay away! Keep your distance."

She didn't want this locale any more disturbed than it already was.

Splashes behind her, too. She turned, and Zuminski was coming out of the misty end of the large vault. "Where was he?"

He eyed the artifact and crouched to take more pictures of it, and Rachel shifted slightly to make sure her legs blocked his view of her device. "Trying get away, I think."

"Let's get him out of here."

Zuminski whispered, "Bastard. He's coming behind me."

Rachel kept her hand up, palm out, to stop the team. She could tell from their faces that they were worried, angry, tired, or all of the above. Beyond Zuminski she saw Fraq waddling forward in his custom pressure suit. His gait reminded her of penguins' wobbly walk.

Ping went her suit warning. "Say, we're down to about a third air," she called on general comm. "Turn back, we've got enough."

Murmurs, protests—she snapped that off with a curt word, then killed the links. *Best aspect of the kinda-military discipline here is, they take orders.*

Zuminski nodded to her, silent. She gave Fraq some hand signals, including the usual zipped-lip gesture. This was not the time to do a Q&A with an alien. *Enough strangeness for now. . . .*

So she chimed in with the team's chorus of grumbles and they soon marched away, retracing their route to the ruptured, enormous soft petals. She knew her device would self-actuate within an hour, and convey a run through a coded sequence she had gotten from her buddies back at the Library. It was a simple attempt to give the alien device a hail, plus some questions. And, who knew?—maybe that artifact could convey it to the Mat, as well. She would put very little past the strange intelligence that surrounded them now, as they threaded their way through the bowels of a life-form that was in many ways still beyond their comprehension.

They came slowly up from the Martian depths, Rachel's mind working hard in the team silence. Mostly, pointlessly. Furiously, yes.

A day down the vent in a cramped suit reeking faintly of old sweat—despite the new, improved self-cleaning liners and 'freshers—had left her with aching muscles. Not so much from all the grunt work, but a suit by its nature never let you get the best leverage. The designers had never fixed the basic problem—most of the suit's weight hung on the shoulders. She had tried to build hers up into hard slabs of muscle, but after days of work outside, they always wailed. And untended, they got other muscle groups to join in the concert. She ran the shower long and hot, relishing the glorious steam.

2.

For most Librarian work, the best rule was *Ass in the chair.*

Even on the deep-down wild frontier, Mars.

Rachel pondered. Usually the people around her had the same work habits. Everyone involved with the SETI Library or on Mars had a fierce, autodidactic, gnarly idiosyncrasy—indeed, maybe that was the entrance ticket to the Librarian Life. On Mars, they were no doubt rehashing the recent descent while calorie loading. Not her.

Back in her cramped cabin, swathed in a comfy puffy bathrobe, she let herself ease into the analysis. Earlier, she had compared notes on interworld email with the SETI mathists. Some of her colleagues there were hard-core types who could visualize four-dimensional surfaces in a non-Euclidean geometry, just to make sense of some messages. Apparently, this demanded inordinate quantities of caffeine.

She was happy to leave them to it.

At her request, already they had traced the Mat images that Fraq had called forth from earlier cunning snaps—for reasons he would not state. Then they'd linked those images to old SETI messages that held holographs, asking if any resembled these objects. Some did. Her buddies back on Luna had found cross-references to other SETI messages, after days of steady crypto-sorting. Those had similar symbol-strings and "weaves"—jargon for interconnected slabs of data that seemed to be intelligible only in a holographic way. Though called Librarians, those mathists didn't just keep track of books, texts, and the like. They linked symbol groups in different linear parts of the message, by imposing an appropriate deep math mapping. Then they did nonlinear, mind-wrenching parallels. It was all quite complex and wonderful, going far beyond her math competence. For this, she was grateful. Then she tried to explain it to Zuminski. Big mistake.

"Not understand," he said in his minimalist way.

She flicked a command into her voicewriter and said, "Think of a sentence like this one, only the parts don't relate in a straight-line sequence." Her voicewriter noted this down as she spoke. "So my previous sentence could read," she said, adjusting the voicewriter screen again to redeploy the sentence, "Parts straight-line sequence sentence, one that doesn't previous relate like."

A trick, but it worked. He stared at the screen. "Ah, I ... think I see. To unwrap the above line and make sense of it, you need a mapping function. Noun, veerb, object—"

She nodded, wondering what her smart systems would make of *veerb*, a pronunciation nuance. "Now expand that idea to whole paragraphs, and then to whole idea groups. The weave of them would be complex, and would not convey a simple logic."

He blinked. "Ah."

"There are various conventions about how to represent numbers— for example, least significant digit first versus most significant digit first—and remember, aliens won't know that U+FFFE is a guaranteed nonassigned codepoint."

He looked disgusted. "What?"

"Maybe I'm more of a nerd than I know. Anyway, what the 'natural' order is to represent a sequence, whether signal-on represents one or zero—if, say, we restrict our aliens to binary—nobody knows. Mathematics may be universal, but transmittable representations are not."

"But binary has own logic." He spread his hands, as if this was obvious. And of course, it was. Zero and one, you needed no more.

"You know more trans-group math than you let on," she said, in what she hoped was a nerdy, coy tone.

"I never show all my cards." He grinned, and launched into a little song:

"A problem worthy of attack
Proves its worth by fighting back."

"Sounds like a march," she said.

"Was trying for 'Battle Hymn of the Republic.'" A sly grin. "Grandiose."

"Look, becoming a SETI Librarian for the money and the fame is like becoming a Jesuit for the kinky sex. I know that."

"Ambition is good," he said enigmatically.

She decided to bring up a dicey issue. "Look, I've seen your background. Damned impressive. Why be here, when you could do so much elsewhere?"

To her surprise he sprang to his feet—overshooting, springing a meter high in the low grav. Coming down, he paced back and forth, face a clown mask of bright-eyed wonder. "Why didn't I think of that? Here I am, yes?—wasting my golden years on this dangerous dustball, all messed up with mysterious smart plants? When I could, with just a little thought, be seeking and striving! Putting my shoulder to the wheel—or is it my face to the grindstone?—for betterment! Plus that of all mankind. I'll bet I could write a billion bucks a year in overscale insurance on asteroid shipments. Pull a big oar in the flagship of life! Exercise impressive skill set. Or wait, maybe it isn't too late—do you think? I could race back Earthside, find the little woman, get in with MegaCorp or Solaristics, go to executive lunches, nod soberly at board meetings, make money while I sleep! Why, the opportunities—thanks so much for finally pointing me in right direction!"

He stopped with a twirl, arms spread like the end of a showbiz number. When she stopped laughing, he said, "You're not working for my parents, are you? Sent all this way to talk me out of this crazy career?"

"Uh, no."

He slid hands all around her, ignoring her squeals. "Know that."

A knock at the door. The Base Bioneer's stern face told them, "We've had an infection. Some Marsmat got in, apparently on part of a suit. It's inside our envelope. Evacuate now—into suits, outside."

"Damn!" they said together.

The Bioneer suddenly grinned at them. "Getting it on during work hours? Tsk tsk."

Zuminski ignored her, closed the door, turned to Rachel with a grin. "Let's find place to make this happen."

3.

They trooped out with the others as she struggled with the psychic mulch of emotions. Swerving from the Fraq problem to cryptology to, suddenly, Zuminski—she had to keep her equilibrium. The Zuminski issue roamed through the labyrinths of her mind as they formed up in units outside the habitat, watching the cleaning crew do their thing.

She liked men, but didn't like them by the gross. That had been in the offing here, where men so outnumbered women—but she had planned on keeping to herself. She had avoided long-term men for decades, focused on her career, knowing that there was plenty of time later to marry and bear children, if she wished. Somehow, Zuminski had come in under her guy radar. His soft eyes belied a sinewy toughness, plus a quirky humor like her own.

Time passed while the bio team cleaned Marsmat traces within the habitat. People gossiped, muttered. . . . A thin breeze howled and dust blew by them all. Nearby a vortex wind formed, swirling and dancing. It was pretty, the apex of Mars weather. Everybody turned to watch. Zuminski touched helmets and said, "We go."

She blinked, then followed him around the garage and support buildings, to the greenhouse. They cycled inside to find no one there. The habitat air system provided clean, moisturized air at two-thirds Earth sea-level pressure, like living on a mountaintop at 8,000 feet but with plenty of oxygen. They didn't feel altitude effects, and had lots of energy—but the air tasted flat. Here in the greenhouse, they could work without helmet or gloves.

With just a skin suit on, Rachel shucked her Marswear insulated outer garments. Zuminski threw off his suit and sucked in the flavorful air. "Ah!" They looked past the rows of plants, through the clear side walls to the dusty red landscape beyond. Nobody around. She ambled down the aisles, breathing in the aromas. In this little space, cupped against the soil, was a tiny human garden in all its moist promise. Growing food on Mars was immensely symbolic as well as practical—rice and potatoes, various beans, and popular vegetables like broccoli and tomatoes. These swelled in large hydroponics trays, some using Martian soil for grit. There was something very calming about being surrounded by green leaves and vines, nodding gently in the perpetual, moist updrafts.

Zuminski said, "Wonderful, to see something alive that can't talk."

She laughed, and he started with a grin—just a cockeyed lurch of the lips and raised eyebrows. She thought they would make slow love, maybe try out the lighter gravity a bit, do some stunts. He took his time, and she thought they would kiss and grin and joke, but as their clothes fell she came up like thunder, her need outpacing style. She put the tender moves away and got into the fever of it. So did he. Some wild moves, perspiring and heart thumping, a fast bonanza. Then long slow drifting, maybe the best part of all. It was outside of time, boundless as the ocean. The only way to get back to the Cambrian, warm salty waters, awash in time, endless. Nothing was separate, everything joined together. The ebb and flow of day and night were like the winking of a great eye. Making love was, among all humans had, the most profound form of nostalgia.

Since college days, it had always been a big turn-on for her to look over the shoulder of a lover into the foliage of a tree. They had started on a plot of grass, where others could not see them. As soon as the fever left them—though she knew they weren't nearly done—they moved to a less obvious part of the long greenhouse, near the workbenches, shielded from view.

As they stood Zuminski took her in his arms and said, "You . . . you don't have to return to Earth on the next Aldrin, do you?"

"I'll have to ask my husband."

He stopped dead still, mouth open. "You are—"

"No, just kidding. Assuming you're not married either?"

"No, am not. You have strange way of bring up subject—"

"Come on, it was a joke!" She started laughing at him, throwing up her hands—and slipped on the wet floor. She started to get up from under a table, reached for the edge, glanced to the side—and stopped laughing.

Fraq's filmed eyes stared out at her.

She jerked away, rolling on the slick floor. "Ack—ack—"

"What?" He knelt—and froze.

Rachel stared at the . . . body. Fraq? No, it looked like Fraq—but it wasn't really, she saw. It was much smaller, the size of a large dog. But it looked exactly like a smaller Fraq lying on its side. Some of the plant feeder tubes snaked down and attached to the body at pale-yellow sockets.

"What . . . is it?" she managed.

"You said once, was big puzzle for Earthside biologists, how Fraq and Ythri reproduce. Not clear if birdy ones uses eggs or . . ." He raised his eyebrows. "Looks like, by budding."

They went back to the habitat, filing in behind the others; the cleanup was done. Silently they made their way to Zuminski's Guy Thing room, which Rachel thought of as the proper place for spittin', cussin', and scratchin' in peace. Thinkin', too, as she had learned in her Deep South days. They poured some Martian wine—incredibly, one of the horticulturists had made a decent one, a rosé—and sat.

"Aside from the interesting biology . . ." she began.

He said, "Fraq must have put the—bud, I guess we call it—out in greenhouse, to conceal it."

"Maybe they're like flatworms? Birds don't do that . . ." She thought. "Keep the bud hidden in a pouch, to develop?"

They had inspected the thing carefully, noting that it was fed by an electrical tap, plus basic watery fluids and oxygen. It had been well concealed. Only because Rachel had slipped and rolled under a table had she seen it. The bud had its eyes open but did not respond to them; apparently it was not conscious. A filmy capsule enclosed it, like a chrysalis.

He scowled. "Biology, I know some—aliens, not. When caterpillar turns into butterfly, it has all it needs. Left to itself, emerges as a young adult. Maybe this one will come out as a Fraq-like being, transformed."

"How about that electrical lead? It goes into a small package on the bud's back, then into some sort of slot, near the spine."

He nodded. "Not biology, something beyond. Maybe is being stimulated? Growth is guided? Alien, for certain."

She tried to think outside categories, guess what this bud might mean. *You're a long way from the Library, kid.* "How about, maybe the bud is even educated by some electronic means?—with embedded social knowledge and habits."

Zuminski blinked. Slowly he said, "So ... skips infant stage of humans, comes out like four-year-old. Once kids learn to find a bag of cookies and eat, you know will survive on their own, at least in food department. Avoids pelvis problem of humans, too. Artificially extend early childhood with technologies, maybe."

"We know Fraq's species screwed up their world long ago. They retreated to their outer solar system, and now live there mostly. So they've had to undergo some fancy bioengineering to stay alive, though they started on a planet somewhat like Earth. Self-engineering of the species for—what?"

"Baboons and chimps have offspring that inherit social skills—otherwise, how would they know to form hierarchies and move in troops? Maybe Fraq is thinking that he and other Ythri will stay here, form an offshoot of his species?"

Rachel shook her head. "This is going too fast for me. Fraq kept to himself on the Aldrin Cycler—maybe that was during his bud-making time? He got here, let his flock deal with lesser matters, found a place where he could hide his bud ..."

"We need to know more. Fraq won't answer direct questions. We have to do something else."

She brightened. "Ask the Mat?"

They lumbered across the red-brown sands in a new hauler. No Fraq, none of the earlier descent team. They could move faster, just the two of them. So no asking permission, either. Just a quick picnic amid the strangeness. . . .

Humans on Mars had carried the emerging symbiosis of humans and machines to new heights. Within a few years of the First Expedition, a private enterprise, wireless sensors lay scattered on the surface. Robots came next—not clanking metal humanoids, but rovers and workers of lightweight, strong carbon fiber, none looking remotely like people. Most were either stationary, doing routine tasks, or many-legged rovers. Only a few years after the First Expedition had suffered their minor falls and sprained ankles, humans never actually took the risk of climbing around on steep slopes in suits. Much of their work was within safe habitats, using virtual reality and teleoperation for exploring and labor. But no machine could deal with the Mat.

"Y'know," Rachel said, "I broke one of my own rules."

"What?"

"Don't go to bed with anyone crazier than yourself."

He laughed. "Would make life dull. Also, was no bed."

"You agree?"

"A craziness contest? You win easily—a Librarian on Mars."

It was her turn to laugh. "Maybe it's a tie. We're going down a deep hole together to cross-examine a life-form that looks like a carpet."

They were in a crazily good mood as they descended. Zuminski had authority to lead small expeditions, so he used it—and had filed the proper notices electronically five minutes before they left the habitat.

Two hours later they approached the artifact, having taken longer than expected to electroshock their way past a massive valve membrane. They worked forward in deep gloom, through a somber fog that thickened toward the ceiling of the grotto.

The Mat pulsed suddenly with an ivory glow. It knew they were there. She crouched beside the camouflaged device she'd left and eyed the alien artifact. The three crystalline "eyes" of the thing lit up. A rippled pattern cycled, quick flashes of life. She picked up her device and checked its actions. It had emitted the coded sequence she had gotten from her buddies back at the SETI Library and, hours later, received a reply from the winking artifact. Her message had been a simple attempt to give the alien device a hail, plus some questions. Apparently the Mat had answered. With a few finger-taps she downloaded the info-content into her suit deck.

"Let's call this thing the Sphinx," she said.

"Why?"

"It's old, mysterious, we don't know for sure who made it."

"The Sphinx doesn't talk."

"This one does." She tucked the device into her gear belt and beamed at Zuminski.

"What's the worst feature of these pressure suits?"

"Must pee in them."

"Nope. I can't kiss you."

4.

Hassan fumed across the table from Rachel. His long black eyebrows fluttered like street signs in a hurricane.

"I just read your"—he nodded toward Zuminski—"report on the descent with Fraq. Frankly, it's skimpy."

Zuminski said mildly, "I keep it simple. Mat pulsed, blinded us. Alien got away, we followed. Found artifact in side cavern."

"This constitutes an unauthorized contact with the Mat."

Rachel said, "Stuff happens. You follow up on it. That's how discoveries go." She kept her slight, polite smile in place. She and Zuminski had managed to cover their own latest descent so far, but somebody would catch on to why so many sensors had curious blanks in them at the same time.

Hassan did not even look at her. He peered at Zuminski. "You were in charge, not her. You could have broken off contact."

"Leave Fraq down there? Alone?" Zuminski laughed merrily. "Lose only alien we have right here?"

Rachel thought, *Actually, not the only one, now. . . .*

Hassan brushed this away with a wave of his hand. "What did Fraq want from the artifact?"

Zuminski said, "We call it the Sphinx. What does anyone want from a sphinx? Who made it? What does it know? Fraq won't say, either."

She saw the twinkle in his eyes and nearly laughed. Hassan's mouth jerked around in an anthology of irritated angles. She noticed that his beard was like a sheen of dirt. Not reddish actual Mars dirt, just grunge. Maybe he was too busy to take his one-per-day allowed shower. *Worrying sure can take it out of you.*

"What makes you think the Mat wanted you go to there, disturb it?"

"I, uh, we followed the alien. Had no choice."

Hassan's eyes narrowed. "I shall file a formal report on this clear breach of protocols."

Rachel got up, stretched, allowed herself a yawn. Two descents in a day . . . "By the time Earthside processes it, other events will make it irrelevant."

Hassan eyed her. "Such as?"

"Plenty."

———

The next turn surprised her, though.

The alarm came at night. She stumbled out of Zuminski's cabin in a hastily thrown-on robe. Some people in the corridor raised eyebrows when they saw her with Zuminski, but the excitement and alarm swept all that away. They all flocked into the communal room and watched the big screen at one end. Somebody was explaining, but the sight of the night sky was the point.

Cameras atop the habitat had alerted them. Feeds let them all see it. A smudge of light hovered on the horizon. It was a pale white cloud, linear, fuzzier at one end. It seemed to point downward. The camera was looking north, and the cloud glowed. A pale ivory finger of illumination spiked up from the surface, broadening. It came from the vent, Rachel knew instantly—an impossibly brilliant outpouring.

Zuminski gasped. "Mat is outgassing."

A spire of light forked up, luminescence dancing in the filmy cloud, probing with colors that shifted from blue-green to a reddish amber.

Fraq's crew stood nearby, staring up, eyes wide.

To poke such a glistening probe of light into the sky must have cost the Mat enormous energies, she thought. To make it, the vent would

first have to expel a gusher of vapor. Then the entirety of the Mat would
have to pour its reserve energy into the pale glow, coherently.

That took coordination—venting vapor, then pulsing the Mat
glow. Over a large scale.

The pearly lance, jutting up—a signal? celebration? alarm? Her
mind whirled giddily. With so much energy expended, there must be
some purpose.

It was natural to see this as a pointed message, but there are many
behaviors in biology that defy easy logic. She knew what she would
like to believe, but . . . She closed her eyes to fix the image in memory.
An ivory plume, towering kilometers into the sky, mingling with the
gleaming stars. Bright displays played in the solemn sky.

So much to learn. . . . She could stay here a lifetime and not know
it all.

How does the Mat do this? From the first, Earthside biologists had
been unable to figure out the cycle of life between the surface—dead,
sterilized by ultraviolet and solar winds—and the anaerobic underground life zone. Extending more than twenty kilometers down, there
was a Byzantine spaghetti of life zones.

Martian life needed access to the oxidizing surface. There the sun's
hard ultraviolet light had made the dust superactive, laced with peroxides. Raw dust seared anything alive with a burn like the worst kitchen
sterilizers. That superoxidation was like photosynthesis on Earth, a big
energy driver. Pumping up molecules with oxygen balanced the anaerobic decay underground, which ran on hydrogen sulfide. Their samples
always reeked of rotten eggs.

Mars was an upstairs/downstairs world. Surface oxidized species handed down energy to chemically balance the reduced, oxygen-
starved Marsmat. That was why there were active vents, with discharges
of otherwise valuable water vapor. The cycle had to close.

Hassan's voice came over intercom. "Satellite chem analyzer says
that plume's methane fog. The light beam goes up three kilometers."

The display faded, and after a few moments the crowd started to
drift away, murmuring with speculations. Hassan appeared at Rachel's
elbow. His eyes were wide, alarmed. "What's going on? The Mat is
disturbed. There hasn't been a display like this in decades."

Zuminski said, "The First Expedition saw one, yes? When the return ship lifted off. They thought the Mat was saying good-bye."

"Maybe the Mat likes what's happening," she said. "The Sphinx might be a way to talk to it."

Hassan shook his head and stalked away. *Probably going to file another report.*

And so did she, it turned out. As soon as she was away from them, showered, in a now-deserted meditation zone to center herself—here came Prefect Stiles. She could not hide her surprise.

He held a finger to his lips, shook his head. "We have concealed ourselves, as I promised in the Aldrin. We detected subsurface rumblings hours ago—Fourier analyzed them, compared with the centuries-old seismic rhythms measured by the Julia Team, the discoverers. So we came here, observed."

"You were watching all along?"

"Of course." He sealed the room. "We have methods, built into the infrastructure here. Now you will tell me all you have learned." He sat.

She had forgotten how easily this irksome man could intimidate her.

"Well . . ."

"Quickly. Then I will melt away."

———

She couldn't sleep. Stiles could do that to her. He had sucked the info out and whooshed off, and she felt washed out.

The data from the alien Sphinx device had stalled her, too, so she had sent it Earthside, to her friends at the SETI Library. Had they looked at it yet, hard, fast?

Her email held 143 messages. A whole team had jumped on the readout from the Sphinx. The Sphinx Signal, as they dubbed it, had pulsed parts like a telegraph, long and short blips. Crypto people called those "tokens"—symbols or letters or words—a term first used by those trying to decipher an ancient Indus script language. The team studied the correlations between strings of tokens. In a true language, the probability that a given token would appear depended on the token just in front of it. In lists or names of objects, there was no correlation. Some

SETI messages had proved to be just hierarchical lists of deities, like prayers. They showed up as a scattered set of probabilities. Real languages, though, had probabilities that clustered together. Revealingly, that was true of the Ythri song-speech, too. Coevolution again, this time mental.

When the Ythri arrived, Fraq had given the Library samples of SETI messages his species had captured—a gift he solemnly delivered ceremoniously to the Great Librarian. But they were meaningless. He was just handing them some garbage prayers from long-dead religions. Which had made the Librarians suspicious, including Rachel.

Rachel shook off the memory and studied her emails.

The team back on Luna had applied their method, called "language entropy," to the Sphinx Signal. *Yes!* The Sphinx was speaking a true language, and—a bonus—it had positional notations.

That made the job easier. Given that the Mat lived in a cramped universe, the Byzantine warren of tunnels and grottoes, what could it say?

"Why not a map?" Rachel muttered to herself, staring at a screen clogged with data. That woke Zuminski. She waved him back to bed, but he got up and made coffee instead, grumbling. Thinking, too, no doubt.

She read through the arcane emails, sent in scattershot excitement by the team back on Luna. No help, no map. Translating word groups, with no solid context, into a map or message was the legendary puzzle.

Yet one method worked: they'd tried translating the token groups into a timeline. That broke out into a simple, linear scale. *The Mat has memory—long memory—and keeps track of time. How?*

Zuminski was looking over her shoulder, reading the emails, following her mutterings. He gave her a full cup and said, "Here. Coffee makes us smarter."

"Or think we are. How can the Mat keep track of time at all?"

He slurped at his own and said, "Way we did it. Day. Night. Stars."

"But it's buried kilometers down."

"Was always? Never on surface? Even in early ocean ages?"

Click.

Rachel tried to think about life that lived long but slowly. When the Marsmat emerged onto the surface in wet eras, it might even have had some perception of the sky. It would know days and nights, maybe even the long Martian year. . . .

Zuminski sat beside her, upright, startled. "Idea," he said, which meant he had some Mars lore to divulge. She tried to put him off, to focus, but he went on, and slowly it dawned on her that he might be right.

Decades before, he said, in another chasm thousands of kilometers away, an earlier expedition had found odd membranes that the local Mat used. Transparent capsules filled with water, shaped just like what they in fact proved to be—lenses. Apparently the Mat was using these to examine tiny details in its own structure. That discovery had marked the first known tool use by the Mat.

"So I just thought—"

"Those lenses could also make a telescope," she blurted.

"Could see planets, stars. Could have watched Earth."

"And—its rich biosphere, contrasting with the glimmer of the sterile moon . . ." *Could the Mat know envy?*

"Suppose the Mat been watching Earth for entire history? Over billion years, change is slow. Continents drifted."

She thought. Ice cover waxed and waned, sometimes nearly masking the world in a brilliant white shroud. Plants crawled onto the continents in green wealth. But then, in just a tiny sliver of the Earth's history—the last one-millionth—the patterns of vegetation altered violently. Agriculture.

Within ten thousand years, the planet became an intense emitter of radio waves from TV, radar. Then the First Expedition. "Might be useful idea," Zuminski said, and got up to change clothes.

She sat rigid in her chair. *Follow your nose,* her mother had told her. *Go after what smells right.*

She began speaking an email for Earthside.

———

"Before we go in," Rachel said to Zuminski, "let's have a strategy."

They were outside Hassan's office, which for some reason was the largest in the habitat. What was that military saying? *Rank has its privileges.*

Zuminski said, "Tell Fraq the truth. That often disarms people."

"Fraq isn't people. I've never really understood him."

"Honesty may be a startling approach, then."

They went in, and there was Fraq with his translator. They went through the ritual greetings Fraq expected. This took over ten minutes, including a strut-dance Rachel had to do, awkwardly—she had learned it for fun on the Aldrin. Rachel studied the alien as he sat beside Xiaoling, trying to read the shadowy yet golden eyes like rounded rectangles. His nose was a large, protruding cone between the eyes, flaring as he spoke in his chirps and singsong lines. He wore clothes of a greenish hue here and sat like an elegant human, shoulders back. The hands were four-fingered with retractable talons. They moved in an oddly multijointed way as Fraq made rapid gestures, uttering his gravel sentences. He turned his head in elaborate arcs, and then sat absolutely still, like the large, watchful predator he was.

Rachel gazed into the unreadable glittering depths of his eyes—which swiveled to follow her. She was fidgeting; she stilled herself.

Silence was one of the ways to deal with the Ythri, she had discovered. She had learned to resist temptations the media folk did not, as they raptly responded to his tidbits of alien philosophy.

Rachel decided to begin by shaking up the alien. "We found your child."

But Fraq barely registered surprise, eyes narrowing and his slit mouth tightening. "How." He used Anglish better now.

"By accident," Rachel said.

"In my kind this is private matter."

"We appreciate that. You did not tell us of it, so it was a surprise."

"Private."

Rachel said sympathetically, "Yes, but hiding it away like that endangered it."

Now Fraq's mouth twitched and she glimpsed his yellow teeth, incisors front. He had learned to hide his emotions, but now he was losing his steely grip.

"Was . . . best place."

"Perhaps so, but now that it is out in the open, we can all take care not to harm it."

"That would be good." Fraq attempted a strange parody of a human smile. "I am sorry if my, our ways offend your kind."

Hassan frowned, grimaced, said, "I don't follow this. You two were concealing this information, weren't you?"

Rachel said, "Yes, while we tried to understand it."

"We?" Hassan pressed.

"Zuminski and I."

Hassan said, "This issue is enormous—far beyond your learning and capabilities. Neither of you is a Mars-trained biologist."

Rachel smiled and slid the knife in: "A bureaucracy would do better?"

"Administration is not—"

Zuminski said in a flat and certain tone, "We're talking reproduction, the whole basis of life, here. And Fraq's budding is tech-augmented, therefore medicine. What's a manager do that would . . . let us think of the right term here—confer value? Beyond what we do? Such as . . . find it."

Hassan said sternly, "In this case, I think it's obvious."

Rachel could not help but laugh. "I do, too, but I bet we have different answers."

The laughter startled both men, and even Fraq. They paused, thinking. She saw that breaking up what was headed for a deep, angry dispute had been the right thing to do—even if she hadn't actually thought of it consciously.

Hassan paled. "That's what we deal with, really. Exobiology."

Around the table came a sense of stale gray pointless process. She cut in briskly with, "We're getting off track here. I want clarity, not concealment."

Zuminski nodded, turned to Fraq, and reopened with, "Why did you break away from us down there?"

"To explore," came through the translator.

"To find that artifact?"

"Yes, but more. You helped me to know the Mat, to—" He broke into Ythri singing.

Xiaoling whispered, "To . . . it's an intersection of 'merge' and 'experience' and 'engage'—with your planetary system."

"Um. The artifact—what is it?"

"Ours."

This made eyes widen around the table. Rachel asked, "How old?"

"We are unsure. Our own history is long and at times poorly documented. Earlier societies left that . . . sentry."

The translator shrugged, adding, "Something like 'watcher' but more . . . includes 'speaker,' too."

"Your species brought it here through the . . . Maze?" Zuminski asked. The Maze concept required some cross-talk between Fraq and the translator. They used it as a synonym for the wormhole. Fraq had slipped and used the term once, an easy inference.

Fraq seemed startled that they knew this, but covered quickly, face going blank. "Apparently. The history is blurred. You see the . . . Maze . . . as complex. Our kind see it as an archaeological intricacy."

Rachel said, "Uh, why?"

"We have lost knowledge of it. What its destinations are. How it works. All that we lost in the Collapse."

Fraq had not spoken of this ancient, dark era in his species' history for some time. Rachel ached to ask more about it, but they had a goal here.

"What did you tell the artifact?" Zuminski asked.

"That my kind has returned."

Zuminski said, "It—the Mat—knew you?"

"After a while, yes. It said that its memories are dispersed around this entire planet, in its cellular deposits of long life. Thus so, recovering them takes time. But it recalled when my kind, in its Great Age, came to learn from the . . . Mat."

Rachel looked at Xiaoling and said, "Mat is our name. What did he call it?"

"Old One."

Rachel turned to the alien, who sat still but for the glittering eyes that darted around the table. "How old is the Old One?"

Fraq blinked in his slow, gravid way and spoke the singing-gravel-speak the translator could render, after consulting her software analyzer. This was a slow process, but it gave them all time to think. "Nearly as old as your star."

"That means, what—say, three billion years?"

"In your measure, yes."

"Your species met the Mat when?"

"Recently, in the view of the Old One. It said that when your kind first came, it thought you were us. Only when I appeared did it know that there was a difference."

Rachel sat back, wondering how all this fit together. "Why . . . why did you not tell us this before?"

"I am cautious."

Rachel laughed, the helpless barks erupting from her like pressures escaping. "We dove into the atmosphere from orbit! You ascended Everest in a Lifter vehicle! Visited the black smokers kilometers down in the ocean! Cautious?!"

"In those feats, I represent my kind."

Zuminski said, "And what did your kind send you here for?"

"To explore. You must see that I am not truly like my kind, in that way."

Zuminski pressed, "What way?"

Fraq leaned forward and put his bulky claw-hands on the table, a gesture Rachel had never seen him use. It seemed to relax the rigid, encased body, muscle groups flattening and smoothing the blue-gray, rumpled feathers it chose to wear today. The Ythri could somehow tune these colors to their social codes and emotions. Apparently this had evolved to aid social modes.

"We are now a solitary species. The Collapse ruined our world, in ways we do not now know. Cannot know. For they are lost in the great abyss between us and those who destroyed our world."

Wait, those who destroyed? That was new. Rachel asked solemnly, "Did this have anything to do with the Maze?"

Fraq's eyes blinked, darted, the mouth twisted—and then he made himself go stiff again. "How did you know?"

Rachel admitted, "I guessed."

"Why?"

"Because you won't discuss the Maze. You came through it, your small flock, as if for—how long? thousands of years? more?—your species had not used it. And it worked. Got you here. Only fear could have kept your kind from using it—a gusher of opportunities!—for so long."

This provoked a ripple of sitting-back, a gasp from Hassan, raised eyebrows—the startled response menu of humans. Fraq just nodded, a gesture he had learned. "You are correct. We cling to the ices of the outer realm, because no world will welcome us in the warmer zone toward our sun."

Zuminski asked, "Your star has how many planets?"

"Five. Four are gas giants. Our world is the only possibility for us to live—the moons of the gas giants are far worse. In many millennia, our wounded world has not recovered from the Collapse."

Rachel thought. "Your collapse drove you into the outer solar system. You adapted to the cold and dark. That meant, what?"

Fraq stiffened further—as if in fear of revealing more. "We became another . . . people."

"You had to restrict yourselves." Rachel leaned forward, her eyes holding his in a steady gaze.

"We think of it as learning a truth we did not know."

"So you learned. To not let anything puncture the outer skin of a habitat. Not eat too much. Don't make trouble—that will drain resources, waste time."

Fraq nodded again, feathers fluttering among color displays. Rachel saw he was trying to get through on the body channels beyond speech. His whole body calmed, loosened, seemed to welcome this moment. "It has been so for a very long time, for us."

Rachel could not imagine a cultural heritage that had seeped down through a thousand millennia. Human society was about two hundred millennia old. Even then there were variant species—Denisovans, Neanderthals, more. Trial balloons of biology. Civilization, about ten millennia old. So Fraq came from a species that had at least ten times the entire human experience. Still . . .

"So you are a deviant, a risk taker. No one else of your kind, your flock, would volunteer to go through the Maze."

Fraq allowed himself a narrow smile. "You now fathom me."

"I hope we can help each other," she said.

Zuminski said slowly, "You were interested in stunts, like the orbit-fall, Everest—sure. You're ten standard deviations out on the social scale of deviant behavior for your species, yes?"

Fraq's ridged eyebrows fluttered. "Do not follow terms."

Zuminski pressed on. "But coming here to a place you must have found in your archaeology, a solar system that your kind explored when we were little better than chimps—there had to be a point."

"There was."

Rachel saw it. "Mars. Here."

Fraq nodded again, a skill he was mastering, echoing the human. "We cannot take your two inner worlds. They are hostile places we cannot correct, though the second one might be, in a long time."

Hassan suddenly said, "You say 'take'? How could you 'take'?"

Fraq had not expected this: he froze.

Long silence.

"We do have resources," Fraq said finally, through the translator. But Xiaoling shook her head. She added, "That's not a threat. Really."

Hassan said in a voice thin and confused, "I think we have to take a break, take time to analyze—"

"Quiet," Rachel said. "This is how we learn. Finally."

"What resources?" Zuminski asked.

"I have shown the way. We can now flock and flood through the Mouth." Another silence. Aliens pouring through a wormhole and falling from the outer solar system, down from the outer icy realm, inward—Rachel did not want to see how the Earthside media would portray that.

Time to get back to essentials.

Rachel asked, almost shyly, "Why did you talk to us now? Not before?"

As Fraq thought, his skin rippled. "You have my . . . child."

"We found it. That's all."

"You must understand. Must. To hold children, among my kind— it means your opponent can cut you off. Not let your line descend." Fraq's stony face crinkled, then froze. "When there are few of you and you live in a place you were not made for . . . the next generation, that is everything."

Rachel thought about the many bottlenecks humanity had passed through—genetic squeezes of drought, predation, hardship—all forcing selection upward. There had been an era more than a hundred thousand years back when humanity shrank to fewer than a million, in southern Africa; that she knew. Fraq's kind had gone through something far worse, while still retaining their civilization. Making habitats in deep space. And building legends. *To remember the squeeze* . . .

Suddenly she saw Fraq not as an emissary, rogue, or invader, but as a refugee. He had fled from a catastrophe she could not truly even imagine. A whole planet, ruined. Abandoned. Though . . . how had that happened?

All that lay countless years ago, when calamity fell upon them—yet it still lingered strongly in the minds of a species blighted and exiled. Separately evolved minds, close enough to human, that now sought a distant refuge, using the Maze they did not comprehend. Driven by the SETI messages, and the antique promise of a better place. To come here, sending a daredevil first . . .

Rachel struggled to say, "We will do nothing to endanger your child. Zuminski and I found it by accident. We weren't searching."

Fraq nodded slowly, as if getting the feel for this idea. His eyes were unreadable, golden dots. "I appreciate that. It is a bountiful resolution, for I have worried over this for my entire time here. I will assent, then."

Hassan jutted his chin forward. "To what?"

This took a while. Fraq then said, "To work for a mutual understanding between our kinds."

Hassan nodded in response. "We can work together."

Rachel looked at Hassan's eyes, and didn't believe him. "Perhaps we should pause for a moment of science."

Hassan said, "What?"

"We know the Mat has held that artifact—and how many others?— for many millennia. What's *its* agenda?"

Hassan's brow wrinkled. Now that Rachel thought about it, his face looked like a thin sheet of paper that had been wadded up and then carelessly smoothed out. "It wants to live."

"What else?" she persisted.

Fraq saw her point. "It wants to learn."

Rachel smiled. "Yes."

The Mat had a long memory. It would know the deep labyrinth of chambers, caves, conduits, and pores that wove into the Martian interior. It had tried as well as it could to explore its world, and even what lay beyond, floating in the night sky. It knew there *was* a concrete living beyond, because Fraq's kind had come calling. Then came the humans.

"What does the Mat think of us?" she said, posing a question she could not answer.

Zuminski said, "It sees us as, in your terms, mayflies."

Hassan grimaced. "What? Why?"

Zuminski said, eyes steady, "Because we come and go in a mere million years or a fraction of that. It has lived through far more, and knows that we will soon vanish, in its perspective."

Rachel smiled. So her lover had gotten the point. But what next?

5.

She was up the next morning early, for some restless reason, and chanced to stagger out for coffee, its hypnotic aroma stealing up into her nostrils when she awoke. Zuminski had two of the prime qualities of a prime man: good housekeeping and a big, exotic, ancient coffee machine. Made out of spare booster parts, she saw.

Next, food: the mess hall.

Cup filled, first one inhaled, second in hand, she turned to the big wall screens in the hab mess—to see Hassan slinking away outside, keeping close to the hab wall with no windows. But he was visible from the guest wing and Zuminski's cabin along a hexagonal spur. Headed for the greenhouse complex. Alarm did more than caffeine could. She got Zuminski out of bed and into a pressure suit in well under a half hour.

On their way, Rachel glimpsed Fraq's pale-green suit coming out of the lock slightly behind them. The long sheds of the greenhouse covered hundreds of square meters in long fingers of transparent glassite, made from the topsoil with a physical printer. The thick walls were fogged, making it nearly impossible in the morning to see very much through them. They would clear as the day warmed and the internal water cycle heaters from the power reactor kicked in their cycle.

She and Zuminski entered the sprawling greenhouse and trotted down the many narrow paths between the moist, steaming hydro vats.

Where did I see the bud? Rachel wondered. Maybe she hadn't slurped up enough caffeine.

They reached the right aisle—she thought—and swung around a supporting pylon in long, loping strides, emerging from fog clouds—and collided with Hassan. Rachel ricocheted off him. She plowed into a vat table and sprayed water and tendril plants in all directions, then twisted and slammed down in a tangle of hoses and plunging streams.

Coming behind her, Zuminski hit Hassan on the left shoulder. Hassan was holding in both hands a backpack, one of the big, long ones for a several-day expedition from the habitat. It bulged. Hassan staggered on the slat floor, swerved, tried to dodge by Zuminski—and stumbled in his heavy boots on the slatted platform, above the sliding sheets of warm water. He went down hard. In a last panic he tossed the backpack up. It tumbled in the slow gravity.

Rachel came up out of the tangle and leaped—and caught it with one hand, up near the ceiling of big watery panels.

Zuminski yanked Hassan up in a strong grip. "What you carry?"

Hassan gaped, his darting pupils hard and black in the white eyes. Zuminski snorted and slammed him against a wall.

Rachel pulled on a big zipper, ripping open the backpack. She turned the pack and exposed the tiny head of the bud, greasy and slick with fluids.

"You *stole* this?" she shouted.

Hassan scrambled up. "I decided it was best if this, you might say, trump card, was in the possession of—" That was as far as he got.

Fraq came in from nowhere and hit Hassan in a full lunge, taking the man down on the hard walkway. Into a thrashing tangle.

Zuminski tried to separate them, but the alien grunted and heaved and threw Zuminski off as if he were a mere passing thought. Or a snowflake.

Rachel stepped back. Watched. Fraq pulled Hassan up and hit him in the face. Fraq grunted with each slamming fist, using the heel of the wing-hand to carry the arm momentum into the face bones.

He's not snapping out his talons, at least, Rachel thought.

Hassan survived the pounding he got, but his reputation didn't.

Zuminski said, "Hassan wanted that bud child as bargaining chip." He smiled, a thin, sly one, as he finished his report. "I believe."

Fraq sat between Zuminski and Rachel, the three of them facing a review panel, some of them piping in from Earthside. Fraq said nothing, but nodded.

"He is surrounded by us, in strange place," Zuminski said, looking at them all. "Fear is natural. Inevitable. Rational."

"Still," Stefano, the review panel head, said slowly, "this incident will cause an uproar Earthside."

Rachel agreed. Research progress was slow on Mars, had been for decades, of interest only on the Insomniacs Channel—in part because they were very careful with the Marsmat. But the first-ever alien-human fistfight?! Bonanza! Got footage? Rachel was surprised afterward to find that she did. She had thumped on the vid as they ran, then forgot it.

Hassan had said nothing throughout the review, so far. He now sniffed, grimaced, and waved away the charges.

The room's walls helped her—plashes of blues and yellows and comforting warm beige in an artistic swirl—to not look at Hassan. But now he spread his hands, gazed carefully around at each panel member in turn, and said strongly, "I was trying to get control of a situation none of us understood. I did not know if by reproducing, Fraq, intended to begin an alien colony here. I did not know to what purpose he might put this, ah, budded form of his species."

"Let's not go into motives," Stefano said. "We are here to repair damage."

"Apologize to Fraq, then," Rachel said.

Stefano shook his head, and the other three members of the panel seemed, by eye contact, to agree. "He concealed important facts."

Hassan said, "For reasons we do not yet know."

"He's here alone. Surrounded by aliens. On a mission we still don't well understand. Give him some room!"

"Ridiculous," Hassan said. He glowered and tried to throw her out of the discussion with the point of his chin. It didn't work. She just stared at him until he looked away. She now regretted not getting in a punch or two in the fight.

Stefano looked around at the panel members, who still said nothing. *A lot's on the table, but nobody wants to talk about it*, Rachel thought.

Stefano said carefully, diplomatically, "Fraq, speaking for our community here, we apologize for this man's taking your . . . offspring. We are sorry. We shall instead give you a place to . . ."

Stefano stalled, and Rachel rushed in: "To rear it. Give it food. Bring it forth."

The panel murmured. The translator, sitting at Fraq's elbow, rendered this, and after a long pause Fraq rippled his feathers from the brown he had worn for days now, to amber and green. Nodded. "I accept. Thanks be to you." But he did not look at the panel. He turned, and the strange eyes went to Rachel.

Slowly, through Xiaoling, since this was important, Fraq said, "We seem so different, but we are the same. Finite beings. I spoke, many long days ago, to your philosophers. We are united by our cause: life itself. This universe wants to kill us, every day. Our efforts to control and understand our universe—these are the things that lift our lives above the level of comedy, which both our species share, and give our workings some of the grace of tragedy."

The eloquence Fraq had summoned had been thought through well, she knew. It won the day for the strange smart bird, in media terms at least. But there was too much unsaid. Her task—that of the entire human species, she suspected—was to find out the underlying motives of the Ythri.

She got away from all this by reading some A. E. Housman and Swinburne, finding some comfort in the moody fatalists and their waltzing with *Weltschmerz*. After a tasty veggie dinner—the standard here, except for some Chicken Little artimeat that showed up in stews, the only place people liked it—she needed to relax and think.

Zuminski came in later from the bar. "Whole hab is talking about the bud."

"And us?"

He grinned. "As usual."

"We don't have to leak anything on the gossip circuit, y'know."

He shrugged. "Open society here, not concentration camp. Bound to get to Earthside soon. Make big noises."

Rachel frowned. "I don't understand Hassan. Really don't."

"Scratch scientist, find fanatic."

"He's afraid. Maybe he thinks Fraq and his flock are the first of many, coming in with better technology and an agenda."

Zuminski sat on the double bed they had cobbled together. He put a hand on her ankle, as if to rest it. She felt a simmering tingle rush up into her. "Hassan could be right. Stefano, too, about Marsforming. But only way to find out is to go forward."

"Precaution is—"

Zuminski waved this away. "Thinking like Earthside, you are. They love their Precautionary Principle."

She said sensibly, "After what humans have done to Earth? After what Fraq tells us, that his species destroyed their world, had to move off to live on moons and comets and big cylinder—"

"You know what means?"

"The Precautionary Principle? Sure, it—"

"Never do anything for the first time."

She had to laugh. Out here on the frontier, talking to intelligent slime molds and a mysterious, stony-faced humanoid alien, it was absurd to stick to what you knew.

She was trying to frame a reply when his mouth covered hers.

———————

It was always a source of quiet reassurance to her that at night, sleeping together, especially when forming spoons, she and Zuminski were each blocking the other from some small fraction of the background radiation that lanced down from the skies here. Human shields against the unrelenting danger of the universe beyond Earth.

Yet she woke, questions burning in her.

The time delay for Earth conversations made for slow thinking. But emails accumulated, calling out to her as she stared into the sleeptime dark. So she got up, thumbed on the computer (voice command would have awoken Zuminski), and saw the incomings. Plenty of them.

The Library had done more on the "reply-symbol group" she had collected from the Sphinx far below. It was amazing how much implication they could harvest from the simple coding that used lights on a three-port display. She had taken a crack at the sequence herself, using the embedded intelligence. It was part of her computational ability carried from Earth in a "familiar"—the custom AI for her sole use. It got pressed upon her by a Prefect at the Library, separated from her usual inboards. That result, preliminary and still misshapen, she had sent Earthside.

Positional notations such as the Sphinx display were notoriously concept-poor, but the Library group had applied to it the arcane talents of steganography. This meant "concealed writing," a branch of encryption that dealt with hiding secret information within publicly viewable items. Or seemingly obvious telegraphic code-structures, she learned. A simple example was when captives in another culture gave the finger to their unsuspecting jailers, to discredit images that showed them smiling and comfortable.

The Library had set whole teams to using the art and science of writing hidden messages in such a way that no one, apart from the sender and intended recipient, suspects the existence of the message— a form of security through obscurity. And they had found the subcoding that opened the true density of the text.

She jerked up in her chair. With a brief message from Prefect Stiles himself, without preamble, the screen showed a deciphered image. A *Weltraum* sky of gauzy stars and embedded coordinates—around the sun. Yellow dots sprinkled across it, no doubt with embedded content.

They had it at too low resolution to pinpoint the location to better than a million miles. But they were clues. To wormhole sites? Or was there one wormhole, and these were the locations where it seemed to be, as seen over millions of years?

Seen by . . . whom? What?

Rachel saw suddenly that maybe, just maybe, these were the harvest of the Mat's lenses, over a vast, incredibly long age. Crude as they were, the Mat's lenses had the limitations of early-twentieth-century telescopes. They had captured and stored, then, as much as they could.

She felt a fine, strange chill. Rachel hugged herself against the night, and stared at the winking points set against the hard, stellar black.

The gates to an entire galaxy might lie in those dots. Or even farther—there was, the physicists said, no reason that the early universe had to contrive its foldings and corridors of spacetime within the local alleyways of mere galaxies.

So . . . this might be it. The liberation of humanity. Brought forth, in a manner no one could have anticipated, by a rogue alien who had come to their world because of vagrant signals, lodged in the inventories of the SETI Library.

Being a Librarian was much more fun than she had ever thought it could be. Whatever this latest riddle meant, she knew that she would stick with it. She loved adventure, and she was, yes, a Librarian. On the move.

FRAQ

To my Flock:

My voyages and discoveries, I now report on.

Until this opportunity, I could not be sure of intact links to you. I have gone long and deep and far.

I have trouble indeed extracting knowledge with these grounders. They regard my travels as a delay, which, of course, they are—until we find the Mouth, using their capabilities.

I try to amuse, to avoid detection and interrogation. All to secure where our Mouth is. As I have now done. Though these odd beings are difficult. They have hierarchy, as proper, yet disguise theirs with mere chatter. They have not our wonderful methods, these young smart primates. Our Flock culture, especially.

They name their world Earth though most of it is Ocean, a better term for it. Our home world I decided to term for them Yth for our names, and not give away our holy terms at all. A translation would be some of their words like Heights but that would confuse a species that mistakes land for sea.

Some of these humans dislike us, do not trust in us. I try to counter.

Not mere diplomacy, of course. Nor retreat!

Dive-threat struts, horned-eye dances—none communicate. We are left with paltry speech. Luckily, these primates, too, make long chain lines, sentences. They seem to like them, narrow and thin as their language is, free of our feather and gesture.

The humans' minds, like ours, remain extraordinarily difficult to understand—but so is the weather. For similar reasons: unknowns wed with complication. So I venture forth our species' view of the universe, hoping for a grip.

For example: both our species are transient life, and have now lasted for less than ten billionths of cosmic history, on tiny rocks circling suns.

Surrounded by a vast lifeless space, we should all be thankful for the fortuitous circumstances that allow us to exist, because they will surely go away one day. I leave open our true, immediate enemies, whom I have not described: the unliving.

Their Library hosts machine-minds of alien beings. Fair enough: digital minds can move at the speed of light. But—

These primates do not understand that their precious artificial beings are horrors to us. Long ago, when such digit-beings tried to eject us from our world—truly, I need not remind you that such conflicts destroyed our beloved, largely deceased planet—we learned to avoid such, in our species' learning phase. We cannot work with such truly alien to us in the deeper sense of a different path in evolution itself.

Through our blood-trials, I worked with various primates and found some they term Noughts to be artifact biology, beings made without sex, for purposes I cannot understand. I ignored their remarks. When they insisted, I told them that they were a boundary I could not breach.

We and the primates have a similarly small number of genes, around twenty thousand, and arranged in what we now know through Messages to be DNA spines. Great complexity can arise from such numbers of genes. Plants can have more and do less with them. Evolution converges toward function. So we are cousins in roles, essentially. Seekers in similar bodies. Minds quite different, alas.

So our explorations—the Ark, the Marsmat, now yielding clear direction—these I report, in documents open to all our expeditionary Flock. Study these. We seek the Mouth but more, to unwrap the wormhole web we know, as ancient Messages say. This vital network we must sail, and fly in full Flock.

The humans at best have a low light-grasp of their instruments, peering at their star. This makes finding the Mouth from afar impossible. So now comes our down-plunge into nuclear fire. A risk I can ask no other to assume, as Flock kens.

We must approach at great speeds the Mouth we seek. The archway to infinity. Mouth of mortality, indeed. It awaits.

Yet so, I hope the primate Rachel can help us in this hour of trial. We are close to triumph, to danger, to wonders.

PART 13

A WORM IN
THE WELL

Good judgment comes from experience.
Experience comes from bad judgment.

—MULLAH NASRUDIN, 1200s AD

1.

The cabin reeked of heat and sweat and nerves.

"Trim spectrum. Optical only, Erma," the pilot called, sharp and sure.

Reassuringly so. Rachel watched carefully as Claire Raeburn piloted them in closer to the giant fluorescent tower. Or at least that's what it looked like in the optical spectrum, meaning what humans and Ythri alike could see. Apparently there were spectra lines that revealed even more terrifying aspects, though Rachel found that hard to believe. She mopped her brow.

Erma, the Craft Artilect, obliged.

Done. Adjusting for optmal human viewing. The Ythri passenger may find yellows too intense.

Piloting this ship came from the close horse-and-rider connecton between Claire and Erma. They rode the sun's wild winds and horrible heat. Plasma-wave riders, surfing on the sun. Few could try it. Fewer still survived.

Glowering Sol spread below them, a bubbling plain. She had notched the air-conditioning cooler, but it didn't help much. Claire was calm, sure, but sweating, too.

Geysers burst in gaudy reds and actinic violets from the yellow-white froth below. The solar coronal arch was just peeking over the horizon, like a wedding ring stuck halfway into boiling, white mud. A monster, over two thousand kilometers long, swelling, sleek and slender and angry crimson. Claire glanced over at the passengers behind her pilot chair as she turned down the cabin lights. "I heard somewhere that people feel cooler in the dark. The temperature in here is normal for me. But you people have started sweating, my nose says."

Tuning the yellows and reds dimmer on the big screen before her made the white-hot storms look more blue. *Maybe that'll trick our subconscious,* Rachel thought, unzipping her sealsuit.

Claire swung her cameras to see the full blare of the solar coronal arch. The long. seething, curving image got refracted around the rim of the sun, so she was getting a preview of trouble to come. Coming fast now.

Their orbit was on the descending slope of a long ellipse, its lowest point calculated to just touch the peak of the arch. So far, the overlay orbit trajectory was exactly on target. They would come in at forty-two kilometers a second to make a grab. Trapeze circus work.

Software didn't mind the heat, of course; gravitation was mere cool, serene calculation. Heat was for engineers. Plus solar wind turbulence like the big waves in Hawaii. And Rachel was just a Librarian trusting a pilot she barely knew, but liked a lot.

In her immersion-work environment, touch controls gave her an abstract distance from the real physical surroundings—the plumes of virulent gas, the hammer of wild photons. She wasn't handling the mirror, of course, but it felt that way. A light, feathery brush, at an ever-warmer room temperature. She had trained enough for this, at least.

The imaging assembly hung on its pivot above the ship. It was far enough out from their thermal shield to see all and feel the full glare, so it was heating up fast. Pretty soon it would melt, despite its cooling system. Let it. They wouldn't need it then. They'd be out there in the sunlight themselves.

Claire swiveled the mirror—already pitted, you could see it on the picture of the arch itself, but the sim kept showing it as pristine. Brush-off smoothing, Rachel recognized.

"Color is a temperature indicator, right?" Claire asked loudly so her passengers could hear. The answer echoed and danced in the air, typescripted.

Red denotes a level of 7 million degrees Kelvin.

"Good ol' coquettish Erma," Claire said. "Just 'cause we got guests. Never a direct answer unless you coax, folks." A wink back at them. Then a clipped command to Erma: "Closeup the top of the arch."

In both her cyber-eyed views the tortured sunscape shot by. The coronal loop was a shimmering, braided family of magnetic flux tubes, as intricately woven as a Victorian doily, though it seethed like snakes. Its feet were anchored in the photosphere below, held by thick, sluggish plasma.

Claire zoomed in on the arch.

Rachel thought, *The hottest reachable place in the entire solar system, and our prey had to end up here.*

Target acquired and resolved by SolWatch satellite. It is at the very peak of the arch. Also, very dark.

Claire laughed, a dry cackle. "Sure, dummy, it's a hole."

I am accessing my astrophysical context program now.

By now Rachel knew this was Ever-Perfect Erma; primly change the subject.

Claire peered forward and said, "Show me, with color coding."

Rachel gripped the ironically named Comfort Couch and eyed Fraq. The silent birdy alien blinked, nodded, said nothing. This sun-plunging freighter-scoop was not made for tourists. They had left behind the Prefects, Admids, pseud-scholars, the whole gang, because of, thankfully, the invariant principle of No Room. Also, Dangerous As Hell, which was the final decider of who got a Comfort Couch.

That cut the candidates down to those who had balls, metaphorically at least. Rachel didn't have the real thing, but her courage was now undoubted. Fraq might—Ythri were Victorian about stuff like that, kicking inquiring exobiologists aside in white-heat anger—but actual sperm sources, testosterone-rich, were just a metaphor, after all. So they'd got into this crazy stunt, yet again together, by metaphoric means.

Rachel watched the pilot, taking deep breaths to calm herself. Claire peered at the round black splotch up ahead. Like a fly caught in a spiderweb. Well, at least it didn't squirm or have legs. She hated spiders, having grown up on the Gulf coast and been bitten many times.

Magnetic strands played and rippled like wheat blown by a summer's breeze. The flux tubes were blue in this coding, and they looked eerie. But they were really just ordinary magnetic fields, the sort Claire worked with every day. The dark sphere they held was the true strangeness here. And the blue strands had snared the black fly in a firm grip.

Good luck, that. Otherwise, SolWatch would never have seen it. In deep space there was nothing harder to find than that ebony splotch. Which was why nobody ever had, until now.

Our orbit now rises above the dense plasma layer. I can improve resolution by going to X-ray. Should I?

"Do."

The splotch swelled. Rachel followed Claire's gaze, squinted at the magnetic flux tubes in this ocher light. A spectrum flipper drew out new info, angles. In the X-ray, the mag fields looked sharp and spindly. But near the splotch the field lines blurred. Maybe they were tangled there, but more likely it was the splotch doing its work, warping the image.

"Coy, aren't we?" Claire closeupped the X-ray picture. Hard radiation was the best probe of the hottest structures.

The splotch. Light there was crushed, curdled, stirred with a spectral spoon.

A fly caught in a spider's web, then grilled over a campfire.

———

The arch loomed over the sun's horizon now, a shimmering curve of blue-white, thousands of kilometers tall. The two feet anchored magnetically in the blazing plain of the chromosphere, just an outer layer of the immensity that was Sol.

Beautiful, seen in the shimmering X-ray—snaky strands purling, twinkling with scarlet hotspots. Utterly lovely, utterly deadly. No place for an ore hauler to be. Yet it could survive these conditions, hiding behind an asteroid steered in for that purpose alone.

"Time to get a divorce," Claire said cheerily. She pointed to their stone shield.

You are surprisingly accurate. Separation from the slag shield is 338 seconds away.

"Don't patronize me, Erma."

I am using my personality simulation programs as expertly as my computation space allows.

"Don't waste your running time; it's not convincing. Pay attention to the survey, then the separation."

The all-spectrum survey is completely automatic, as designed by SolWatch.

"Double-check it."

I shall no doubt benefit from this advice.

Deadpan sarcasm, Rachel supposed. Erma's tinkling voice was charming, impossible to shut out. Erma herself was an interactive intelligence, shipwired. Running the *Silver Metal Lugger* would be impossible without her and the bots. Skimming over the sun's wrath might be impossible even *with* them, Rachel thought, watching burnt oranges and scalded yellows flower ahead.

Claire turned the ship to keep it dead center in the shield's shadow. That jagged mound of smelted slag was starting to spin. Fused, glistening knobs came marching over the nearby horizon of it.

"Where'd that spin come from?" Claire asked. She'd started their parabolic plunge sunward with absolutely zero angular momentum in the shield.

Tidal torques acting on the asymmetric body of the shield. Also boiling off melted elements.

"I hadn't thought of that."

The idea was to keep the heated side of the slag shield sunward. Now that heat was coming around to radiate at them. The knobby crust Claire had stuck together from waste in Mercury orbit now smoldered in the infrared.

The shield's far side was melting. "Can that warm us up much?"

A small perturbation. We will be safely gone before it matters.

"How're the cameras?" They watched a bot tightening a mount on one of the exterior imaging arrays. Earthside had talked the SolWatch Institute out of those instruments, in the rush to make the ship ready.

All are calibrated and zoned. We shall have only 33.8 seconds of viewing time.

"Need time over the target. Crossing the entire loop will take 125.7 seconds," Claire said.

"Grabbing time, pretty damn narrow," Rachel whispered to Fraq.

"True, but needed. Can resolve the coder we left in the Worm perimeter?" Fraq looked expectantly at Claire.

"Not yet," the pilot barked. "Got it to respond on that hundred gigahertz band, though. It's active."

Rachel smiled. This high-wire act had a chance, then, but a narrow one.

Fraq just frowned.

Claire said, voice tight, "Erma, just be ready to shed the shield. Then I pour on the positrons. Up and out. It's getting warm in here."

I detect no change in your ambient 26.3 centigrade.

Rachel watched a blister the size of Europe rise among wispy plumes of white-hot incandescence. Constant boiling fury. She whispered to Fraq, "So maybe my imagination's working too hard. Just let's shoot the Worm the data, grab it, and run, okay?"

Being Fraq, the alien merely nodded.

2

The great magnetic arch towered above the long, slow curve of the sun.

A bowlegged giant, minus the trunk.

Claire had shaped their orbit to bring them swooping in a few klicks above the uppermost strand of it. Red flowered within the arch: hydrogen plasma, heated by the currents that made the magnetic fields. A pressure cooker thousands of klicks long.

It had stood here for months and might last years. Or blow open in the next minute. Predicting when arches would belch out solar flares was big scientific business, the most closely watched weather report in the solar system. A flare could crisp suited workers as far out as the asteroid belt.

SolWatch watched them all. That's how they'd found the worm.

The flux tubes swelled. Claire called, "Got an image yet?"

I should have, but there is excess light from the site.

"Big surprise. There's nothing but excess here."

The satellite survey reported that the target is several hundred meters in size. Yet I cannot find it.

"Damn!" Claire rippled through the image menu, flashing up scenes in different spectra.

Rachel studied the flux tubes. *To catch a wormhole* . . . She followed some tight magnetic tubes from the peak of the arch, winding down to the thickening at its feet, anchored in the sun's seethe. Had the worm fallen back down? It could slide along those magnetic strands, thunk into the thick, cooler plasma sea. Then it could wander all the way to the core of the star, eating as it went. That was the real reason Lunaside was hustling to "study" the worm. Fear.

"Where is it?" Claire demanded.

Still no target. The region at the top of the arch is emitting too much light. No theory accounts for this—

"Chop the theory!"

Time to mission onset: 192.6 seconds.

The arch rushed at them, swelling. Rachel saw delicate filaments winking on and off as currents traced their fine equilibria, always seeking to balance the hot plasma within against the magnetic walls. Squeeze the magnetic fist, the plasma answers with a dazzling glow. Squeeze, glow. Squeeze, glow. Luminous slabs slipped down field lines, driven by local flaring storms where fields reconnected, dumping energy. That nature could make such an intricate marvel and send it arcing above the sun's savagery was a miracle, but one she was not in the mood to appreciate right now. Sweat trickled around her eyes, dripped off her chin. No trick of lowering the lighting was going to make her forget the heat. She made herself breathe in and out.

Their slag shield caught the worst of the blaze. At these lowest altitudes in the parabolic orbit, though, the sun's huge horizon rimmed white-hot in all directions. The arch was bigger than ten thousand Earths.

Our internal temperature is rising.

"No joke. Find that worm!" Claire was managing their ship systems, eyes narrow.

The excess light persists—no, wait. It is gone. Now I can see the target. Yes, yes—the wormhole.

Claire slapped the arm of her couch and let out a whoop. Fraq leaped to his feet, tumbled in the zero-g. On the wall screen loomed the very peak of the arch. They were gliding toward it, skating over the very upper edge—and there it was in yellow-white splendor.

And a tiny dark ball. A caught worm. Not like a fly, no. It settled in among the strands like a black egg nestled in blue-white straw. An ebony Easter egg.

Survey begun. Full spectrum response.

"Bravo." Claire laughed.

Your word expresses elation but your voice does not.

"I'm jumpy," Claire said. "Say, Fraq. Got that code logged right? Ready to send?"

Fraq chirped agreement—and then Erma broke in.

The worm image appears to be shrinking.

"Huh?" Rachel blinked. As they wheeled above the arch, the image dwindled. It rippled at its edges, light crushed and crinkled. She saw rainbows dancing around the black center. "What's it doing?" She felt a jab of fear—that the thing was falling away from them, plunging into the sun.

I detect no relative motion. The image itself is contracting as we move nearer it.

"Impossible. Things look bigger when you get close," Claire snapped.

Not this object.

"Is the wormhole shrinking?"

Mark!—survey run half complete.

Rachel was sweating and it wasn't from the heat. "What's going on?"

I have accessed reserve theory section.

Rachel had to laugh. Doing math on the sun . . .

Fraq joined in with a skree-chirp she had learned was a polite chuckle. "How comforting. I always feel better after swallowing a nice cool theory."

Rachel smiled. Fraq was learning the nuances of Anglish now. He could even use irony, sarcasm, and the cruder forms of snark. Probably that told them something about the similarities between human and Ythri thought. Some sort of convergent evolution of ideas . . . ?

The wormhole did seem to shrink, and the light arch fluoresced. Curious brilliant rainbows rimmed the dark mote. Soon Rachel lost the image among the intertwining, restless strands. Claire fidgeted.

Mark!—survey run complete.

"Great. Our bots deployed?"

Of course. There remain 189 seconds until separation from our shield. Shall I begin sequence?

Claire let out a whoop. "Go!"

Whoooomp! went the release of the magnetic clamps. On a screen Rachel watched the mass drift aside—then a blaze of full fusion fury. The screen went blank, saturated.

Meanwhile, I have an explanation for the anomalous shrinking of the image. The wormhole has negative mass, and so—

"Antimatter?" Claire broke in.

No. Its spacetime curvature is opposite to normal matter.

"I . . . don't get it."

Rachel realized Claire really had been zoned out when they'd gone over the physics Fraq grudgingly gave them.

Admittedly, it was hard to fathom. A wormhole connected at least two regions of space, sometimes points many light-years apart—that she knew going in; everybody did. Some of the most ancient of Library Messages referred to them. A linked set termed the Maze was apparently a closely kept secret. What Fraq termed the Worms were leftovers from the primordial hot universe, wrinkles that even the universal expansion had not ironed out. Matter could pass through one end of the worm and emerge out the other an apparent instant later. Presto, faster-than-light travel.

Rachel watched the screens as the shield fell behind and their target approached. Odds were that one end of the worm ate more matter than the other. If one end got stuck inside a star, it swallowed huge masses, so it got more massive.

But the matter that poured through the mass-gaining Mouth spewed out the other end. Nobody followed Fraq's terminology logic, since that would mean calling the other the Ass. Locally, that looked as though the mass-spewing one was losing mass. Spacetime around it curved oppositely than it did around the end that swallowed.

So it looked like a negative mass, rejecting matter, and had the opposite spacetime curvature.

Rachel called to Erma, "Why didn't it shoot out from the sun, then?"

It would, and be lost in interstellar space. But the magnetic arch holds it.

"How come we know it's got negative mass? All I saw was—"

Erma popped an image onto the wall screen.

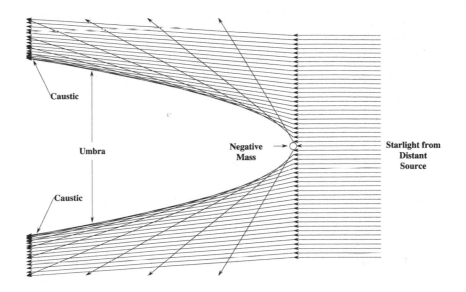

Negative mass acts as a diverging lens, for light passing nearby. That was why it appeared to shrink as we flew over it.

Ordinary matter focused light, Rachel knew, like a converging lens. In a glance she saw that a negative-ended wormhole refracted light oppositely. Incoming beams were shoved aside, leaving a dark tunnel downstream.

They had flown across that tunnel, swooping down into it so that the apparent size of the wormhole got smaller. *Just what you'd not expect....* Rachel said, "But it takes a whole star to focus light very much."

True. Wormholes are held together by exotic matter, however, which has properties far beyond our experience.

An idea tickled the back of her mind.... "So this worm, it won't fall back into the sun?"

It cannot. I would venture to guess that it came to be snagged here after it sped away, gaining momentum from Fraq's entry. Both mass and momentum are conveyed by the wormhole Mouth, and there is a reaction force—as decreed by Newton, I gather. That drove it into this magnetic loop, because the Mouth was orbiting nearby.

"So the worm won't gobble up the sun's core. Uh ... you're speaking for the scientists, aren't you? From a pre-briefing?"

True, both—which makes our results all the more important.

Claire laughed. "More important, but not more valuable—unless we don't grab that grav gizmo."

We are extremely lucky to have such a rare object come to our attention. Wormholes must be rare, and this one has been temporarily suspended here. Magnetic arches last only months before they—

"Wait a sec. This refraction effect—how big *is* that thing?"

I calculate that it is perhaps ten meters across.

"SolWatch was wrong—it's small."

They did not know of this refraction effect. They interpreted their data using conventional methods. But yes, did not estimate properly.

"That is," Rachel said, "before the theory folk came rushing in. We're lucky we ever saw it."

It is unique, a relic of the first second in the life of our universe. As a conduit to elsewhere, it could be—

"Can it," Claire said. "In we go—"

Rachel saw Claire adjusting her control board, consulting screens, biting her lip in concentration. Then she barked to Erma, "Speed up our water boil-off."

I do not so advise. Thermal loading would rise rapidly—

"You're a program, not an officer. Do it."

3.

Claire acted on impulse, Rachel saw. Raw intuition, born of experience.

Very non-Librarian instincts.

That was the difference between engineers and pilots. Engineers would still fret and calculate after they were already committed. Pilots, never. The way through this was to fly the orbit and not sweat the numbers in the running moment. Rachel was getting the feel of what skills it took to do real, adventurous things in real, marvelous places. *That's the sun out there! To fly over it, not sweating the—oh yes—*

Sweat. Rachel tried not to smell herself. The eerie howl of plasma rushing by their insulated hull, deep inside its water reservoir, reminded her of hurricanes in her girlhood. It was gusty, Gulf coast warm then, too. . . . So . . . think of cooler things. Theory.

Lounging on a leather couch when I heard all this, Rachel recalled, *trying to figure out Fraq, the Ythri, why they withheld info . . . like this wormhole.*

She had been tired from the high-acceleration voyage from Mars, plunging down into the inner solar system at a full-g, constant acceleration.

New astro-search data was coming in, so they all got properly interested.

The ship around them rumbled like a giant clearing its throat.

The Library's Scientific Officer's briefing had been a jargon and graphics dance, squiggly equations, the works. Wormholes as fossils of the Big Blossoming—the new hip name for the Big Bang. Wormholes as ducts to the whole rest of the universe. Wormholes as potentially devastating, if they got into a star and ate it up, casting its fusing plasma to another place in spacetime.

She tried to imagine a mouth some meters across sucking away at a star, dumping its hot masses somewhere in deep space. For a wormhole to do that, it had to be held together with exotic material, some kind of matter that had "negative average energy density"—and to be born in the Blossoming. It threaded wormholes, stem to stern. Great construction material, if you could get it. And now, just maybe, they could. . . .

Memories . . . Rachel thought furiously through the ticking seconds. Shock waves sang through the ship's frame like the voices of angels. She mused, *How the first music resonated through the viscous substrate of the early universe, before vagrant protons and electrons recombined. . . .*

So wormholes could both kill living beings, and make us gods. Humanity had to know, the beanpole Scientific Officer had said. Rachel had responded, "So be it," So here it was, the full, virulent glory of hydrogen fusion working its gaudy violences. . . .

The ship strummed. Claire had said she never went in for the austere metal boxes most ore haulers and freighters were. Hers was a rough business, with hefty wads of cash involved. Profit margin was low, sometimes negative—which was how she'd come to be in hock to Isataku for so much. Toting megatons of mass across the gravity gradients was long, slow work. *Might as well go in style* seemed to be her mantra.

Claire's ship, *Silver Metal Lugger*, had high-reflecting Fresnel coatings, ordered when she had made a killing on commodity markets for ore. That helped keep the ship cool, so she didn't burn herself crawling down inspection conduits. The added mass of her deep-pile carpeting, tinkling waterfall, and pool table was inconsequential. So was the water liner around the living quarters, which now was busily saving their lives. More, the ship could shed heat by venting the boiled-off water that filled the ship's enormous mass holds. Nobody had used such a freighter craft to skim the sun before. *First time, maybe last* . . . Rachel mused.

They had two hours left, tops—skimming like a flat stone over the solar corona. *Silver Metal Lugger*'s skin shimmered with blow-off melt, feeding from their water hulls. Rachel watched the quick, sure actions, admiring. Claire fired the ship's mixmotor. Antimatter came streaming out of its magneto-traps and struck the reaction mass, and holy hell broke loose. The drive chamber focused the snarling, annihilating mass into a thrust throat, and the silvery ship arced into a new, tight orbit.

A killing orbit, if they held to it more than a few hours.

I am pumping more water into your baffles.

"Good idea. Getting crispy in here."

Silver Metal Lugger was already as silvered as technology allowed, rejecting all but a tiny fraction of the sun's glare in multilayered skins. Top-of-the-line.

Still, it needed the slag shield blocking the sun from them. Without that chunk of asteroid mass shadowing them, it would take over ten hours to make *Silver Metal Lugger* as hot as the blaring light booming up at them at six thousand degrees. To get through even two hours exposed to that, they would have to boil off most of the water reserve, bought at steep Mercury Base prices. Rachel listened thoughtfully to it gurgle through the walls.

I believe this course of action to be highly—

"Shut up."

With our mission complete, the data squirted to SolWatch, we should count ourselves lucky and follow our carefully made plans—

"Stuff it."

Have you ever considered the elaborate mental architecture necessary to an advanced personality simulation like myself? We, too, experience humanlike motivations, responses—and fears.

"You simulate them."

How can one tell the difference? A good simulation is as exact, as powerful as—

"I don't have time for a goddamn debate."

Plainly Claire felt uncomfortable with the whole subject. Rachel saw that she was damned if she would spend what might be her last hour feeling guilty. Or having second thoughts.

Claire was committed. And so were Rachel and Fraq.

4.

You have no plan.

Erma's tinkling voice definitely had an accusing edge. Rachel nearly chuckled, though this was vital business. A good sim, she was, with a feminine archness. Still . . .

Don't argue with algorithms.

Claire ignored Erma and stripped away the last of her clothes. "It's damn hot."

Of course. I calculated the rise early in our orbit. It fits the Stefan-Boltzmann law perfectly.

"Bravo." Rachel shook sweat from her hair. "Stefan-Boltzmann, do yo' stuff."

We are decelerating in sequence. Arrival time: 7.87 minutes. Antimatter reserves holding. There could be difficulty with the magnetic bottles. Their confinement is—

"Enough!" Claire called.

Pilots didn't like bad news, or details, Rachel gathered. They just flew through problems.

She watched as the ship slid in through magnetic threads. Seconds crawled by. On the screens, titanic blazes steepled up from incandescent plains. Flames, licking up at her.

She felt thick, logy. Her hair was musky-warm, heart thudding faster, working. She roused herself, spat back, "And we do have a plan, Erma—right, Claire?" Pure bravado, of course.

"Sure."

You have not seen fit to confide in me?

Rachel rolled her eyes. An Artilect personality sim in a snit—just what they needed.

Claire shot back, "I was afraid you'd laugh."

I have never laughed.

"That's my point."

Rachel laughed. Claire nodded, and ignored multiple red warnings winking at her. Systems were okay, though stressed by the heat, Rachel saw. So why did she feel so slow? *You're not up for this game, girl.*

Fraq stirred, nudged her. "I never saw such as this." Rachel just nodded. Nor had she. But Fraq's body language told her he was edgy, maybe afraid. Sensible, considering . . .

She felt sluggish and restless both, so got up to stretch—and fell to the floor. She banged her knee. "Uh! Damn."

It was labor getting on hands and knees. She weighed a ton—and then she understood. "We're decelerating—so I'm feeling more of local gravity."

A crude manner of speaking, but yes. I am bringing us, as directed, into a sloping orbital change, which shall end with a slip-by hovering position above the coronal arch. As Pilot ordered.

Was that malicious glee in Erma's voice? Did personality sims feel that? "What's local gravity now?"

At full, would be 27.6 Earth gravities. We are at a tenth that already.

"What! Why didn't you tell me?" Claire demanded.

I did not think of it myself until I began registering effects in the ship. After all, I am close-monitoring all systems in unusual stressed conditions of—

Claire snorted. "Can it."

Rachel thought, *Yeah, and you decided to teach us a little lesson in physics and humility.* It was all their own fault, though—the physics was simple enough. Orbiting meant that centrifugal acceleration exactly balanced local gravity. *Silver Metal Lugger* could take 27.6 gravs, when most of its cargo mass was gone. The ship was designed to tow ore masses a thousand times its own mass.

Nothing less than carbon-stressed alloys could withstand that grav, though. Leave orbit, hover—and you got crushed into gooey red paste.

She crawled back into her couch. Her joints ached. "Got to be . . ."

Shall I abort the flight plan?

"No! There's got to be a way to—"

I have adjusted. 5.94 minutes until arrival flyby.

The sim's voice radiated malicious glee. Rachel felt a tight, cold sensation of pure fear. But Claire grunted. "The water, gotta get it in—"

I have difficulty in picking up your signal.

Claire said, "Because this suit is for space, not diving."

It was four minutes later. Claire floated over her leather couch. They had suited up in quick time. Fraq had struggled into his awkward suit and inflated it just in time, before the water sloshed up over his neck collar. He gave her an uneasy smile, visible through his helmet fog. His oxy rate was twice hers, and his nostrils coated the faceplate with ivory moisture.

Danger made Fraq calm, focused. Her, not so much. . . .

Close call, yes. But it felt good to act, not just sit in their acceleration chairs.

Rachel and Fraq stayed put as the surprisingly cool water swept over them. *Too bad about all the control room's expensive interior decoration,* Rachel thought. The entire living complex was filled with their drinking and maintenance water. Claire had made that available through the forward storage and pumps. Triggered, swift currents came in fast. It had been either that, fast, or be crushed, lumpy tomato paste.

They had crawled through a hatchway and pulled their pressure suits down from clamp lock. Getting hers on was a struggle. Being slick with sweat helped, but not much. Then Rachel had snagged her arm in a sleeve and couldn't pull the damned thing off to try again.

She had nearly panicked then. Maybe pilots didn't let their fear eat at them, not while there was flying to be done—and Claire looked just that cool. Not so for passengers. Rachel had made herself work the sleeve off one step at a time, ignoring everything else as the water rose around them, making it easy to dog-paddle back to her couch. Fraq remained calm through it all. Predators stayed focused.

As soon as Erma pumped the water reserve into the rooms, Archimedes' principle had taken over. With her suit inflated, the water Rachel displaced exactly balanced her own weight. Floating underwater was a rare sensation on Mercury or Luna. She had been in the zero-g droplet on the Aldrin, but this felt different. This was remarkably like being in orbit. Cool, too.

Until you boil like a lobster . . . she thought uneasily.

Water was a good conductor, four times better than air; you learned that by feel, flying in a freighter near the sun. So Claire had to let the rest of the ship go to hell, refrigerating just the water. Then Erma had to route some of the water into heat exchangers, letting it boil off to protect the rest.

Juggling for time. The laws of thermodynamics play no favorites.

Pumps are running hot now. Some approaching bearing failures.

Claire said evenly, taking a break from scanning screens and giving sotto-voce orders, "Not much we can do, is there?"

Rachel was strangely calm now. That made the plain, hard fear in her belly heavy, like a lump. Too many things to think about, all of them bad. The water could short out circuits, maybe? And as it boiled away, they had less shielding from the X-rays lancing up from below. Only a matter of time . . .

We are near now, almost hovering. Approaching, approaching . . . Alas, the magnetic antimatter traps are superconducting, as you recall. As temperature continues to rise, they will fail.

Pops and groans echoed through the floor and walls. Even floating in water, through a helmet meant for space, she could hear the loud chorus of stresses. She could still see the wall screens, blurred from the water.

"Okay, okay. Extend the magnetic grapplers. Down, into the arch," Claire directed.

I fail to—

Claire grunted to Erma. "We're going fishing. Not with a worm— for one."

It was tough piloting at the bottom of a swimming pool, though, Rachel thought as Claire brought the ship down on its roaring pyre. Even through the water she could feel the rattling. Antimatter annihilated in its reaction chamber at a rate the chamber had never reached before, she saw. The ship groaned and strummed. The gravs were bad enough; now thermal expansion of the ship itself was straining every beam and rivet.

She watched Claire search downward, flipping between screens lit in different spectra. Seconds ticked away. Where? Where?

There it was. A dark sphere hung among the magnetic arch strands. Red streamers worked over it. Violet rays fanned out like bizarre hair, twisting, dancing in tufts along the curvature. Lightning weather. A hole into another place.

The red and blue shifts arise from the intense pseudo-gravitational forces that sustain it.

"So theory says. Not something I want to get my hands on."

Except metaphorically.

Claire's laugh was jumpy, dry. "No, magnetically."

The ship roared hard as they approached. This would be a fly-swoop catch. Rachel felt the gravs gathering hard, pushing her down to the deck. "Have you ever . . . done an extraction . . . like—"

"This? Hell no!"

Claire ordered Erma to slip the *Silver Metal Lugger* down into the thicket of magnetic flux tubes. Vibration picked up, a jittery hum in the deck. Claire swam impatiently from one wall screen to the other, looking for the worm, judging distances.

Hell of a way to fly, Rachel thought.

Like a black tennis ball in blue-white surf, it bobbed and tossed on magnetic turbulence. Nothing was falling into it, she could see. Plasma streamers arced along the flux tubes, shying away. The negative space-time curvature repulsed matter—and would shove *Silver Metal Lugger*'s hull away, too.

But magnetic fields have no mass.

Most people found magnetic forces mysterious, but to pilots and engineers who worked with them, they were just big, strong ribbons that needed shaping. Like rubber bands, they stretched, storing energy—then snapped back when released. Unbreakable, almost.

In routine work, *Silver Metal Lugger* grabbed enormous ore buckets with those magnetic fingers. The buckets came arcing up from Mercury, flung out by electromagnetic slingshots. Claire's trickiest job was playing catcher, with a magnetic mitt.

Now she had to snag a bucket of warped spacetime. And quick.

Their jet wash blurred the wormhole's ebony curves as they came zooming in on full brake.

We cannot remain here long. Internal temperature will rise at 19.3 degrees per minute, if my countermeasures falter. This arch is heated by waves, plasma arcs, by everything.

Rachel said, "That can't be right. I'm still comfortable."

Because I am allowing water to evaporate, taking the bulk of the thermal flux away. For a while. Not long.

Claire bit her lip "Keep an eye on it."

Probable mass capture from this wormhole, I estimate, is small. I judge from its dynamics in the magnetic grip of the arch. That is why it can be magnetically held—very little gravitational force, though the sun's grav is fierce. The worm has been taking on mass from the sun. That cancels the negative mass it earned by belching out Fraq's ship—over a million tons. Now the net mass of this worm is tiny.

"Hey, great!" Rachel said. *Erma, the Artilect accountant…* The screen images were moving fast now as they came swooping into the arch, pushing plasma and fields out of the way. "That'll do the trick."

Do you wish me to calculate the probability of remaining alive?

Rachel was astonished that an Artilect had the freedom to be so snarky. That said something about the pilot. . . .

Claire's mouth twisted; she didn't want to ask what that number was. She spat, "Just keep us dropping in close enough to grapple."

From the all spectrum screens Rachel could see the arch's flux tubes pushed upward against their ship. The wormhole lay just ahead, to the left. Claire extended the ship's magnetic fields, firing the booster generators, pumping current into the millions of induction loops that circled the hull. *Silver Metal Lugger* was one big circuit, wired like a slinky toy, coils wrapped around the cylindrical axis. Helical elements added in the grasping extensions.

More antimatter spat into the chambers. The ship's multipolar fields bulged forth. *Feed out the line . . .*

They fought their way down as magnetic feelers extended, groping. Claire barked fast commands and Erma switched linkages, interfaced software, all in a twinkling. Good worker, but spotty as a personality sim, Rachel thought.

Claire could now use her suit gloves as modified waldoes—magnetic graspers. Rachel watched her get the feel of the magnetic grapplers. Silky, smooth, the field lines slipped and swelled, like rubbery air.

Plasma storms blew by them. They came swooping by and Claire reached down, as if plunging her hands into a stretching, elastic vat. Fingers fumbled for the one jewel in all the dross.

"Feels like a prickly nugget. A stone with hair." Given her experience working the ore megabuckets, Claire obviously knew the feel of locked-in magnetic dipoles. The worm had its own magnetic fields, too, Fraq had at last told them. Those were what had snared the worm here, in the spiderweb arch. A bit of luck, helping them find it—though descending into stellar hell was the price.

A lashing field whipped at her grip. In an instant, Claire lost the black pearl. In the blazing hot plasma, she could not see it.

She reached with rubbery fields, caught nothing.

Our antimatter bottles are in danger. Their superconducting magnets are close to going critical. They will fail within 17.4 minutes.

"Let me concentrate! No, wait—circulate water around them faster. Buy some time."

But the remaining water is in your quarters.

Rachel felt a jolt. "This is all that's left?" She peered around at the once-luxurious living room. Counting the bedroom, rec area, and kitchen—"How . . . long?"

Until your water begins to evaporate? Almost an hour.

"But when it runaway evaporates, it's boiling."

True. I am merely trying to remain factual.

"The emotional stuff's left to me, huh?" Claire punched in commands on her suit board. In the torpid, warming water Rachel watched her fingers move like sausages.

Claire ordered bots out onto the hull to free up some servos that had jammed. They did their job, little boxy bodies lashed by plasma winds. Two blew away.

Claire reached down again. Searching. Where was the worm? Wispy flux tubes wrestled along *Silver Metal Lugger*'s hull. Claire peered into a red glare of superheated plasma. Hot, but tenuous. The real enemy was the photon storm streaming up from far below, searing even the silvery hull.

She still had worker-bots on the hull. Four had jets. She popped their anchors free. They plunged, fired jets, and she aimed them downward in a pattern.

"Follow trajectories," she ordered Erma. Orange tracer lines appeared on the screens.

The bots swooped toward their deaths. One flicked to the side, a sharp nudge.

Claire cried out, "There's the worm! We can't see for all this damned plasma, but it shoved that bot away."

Rachel thought, *The negative mass wormhole pushes ordinary mass away, but the sun pulls it down. So Claire is using the bots to push on the worm. But a push makes a negative mass move toward the pusher, not away. . . . So, toward us . . .*

Claire had learned the physics lessons better than Rachel. Now they were drawing the wormhole into the magnetic maw awaiting.

Downright ingenious. Piloting as a ballistic ballet, a pirouette with exotic mass.

In seconds the bots evaporated, sprays of liquid metal. Claire followed them with magnetic tendrils. Grabbed for the worm. Magnetic field lines groped, probed.

We have 87.88 seconds remaining for antimatter confinement.

"Save a reserve!"

You have no plan. I demand that we execute emergency—

"Okay, save some antimatter. The rest I use—now."

Rachel could not keep track of the time limits. They would have to trust their Artilect.

The ship plowed downward, shuddering. Claire's hands fumbled at the wormhole. "Now it feels slippery, oily."

On the main screen Rachel watched magnetic fields like greasy hair, slick, coiling, the bulk beneath jumping away from Claire's grasp, as if it were alive. On side screens she saw the dark globe slide and bounce. The worm wriggled out of her grasp again.

Rachel turned to Fraq. "Now's the time for that recog code."

At last Fraq murmured, "True, yes. I did not believe possible, but we did receive a hail from the Gatekeeper, as the ancient texts termed it."

"When you came through the wormhole?"

"It was just inside the Mouth. Somehow suspended there. It can control access—again, I know not how."

Rachel turned to Claire. "Run the unscrambler."

"Already done. What's the code?"

Fraq said simply, "My name. Use"—he rattled off six digits—"and beam at one hundred thirteen gigahertz. I follow your numerics."

"Got it." Claire punched in. A squeak signaled transmission.

The wormhole swelled, turned a dark crimson. Rachel could not imagine what arcane dynamics were at play here. Gravitational signals?

Claire barked in surprise. Now she could snake inductive fingers around the shimmering, ruby-red oval. "Easy, easy . . . *there.* Gotcha!"

Rachel gasped, suppressed the sound. A thin sigh echoed from Erma.

On operations screens she saw the ship's magnetic vaults begin to lock up.

"What's its mass now?" Rachel called.

Tens of tons, I estimate.

"We're dragging it, but we've got magnetic pressure from the arch, too," said Claire.

Entangled field lines, plasma loops—these increase the apparent inertia.

Claire growled, "Let's see what we can do about cutting free."

Fraq said, "The wormhole is receptive now. You may move it. But I wish you take care."

Rachel felt a surge as the ship began to lift, firing hard, dumping antimatter into the reaction chamber. Erma at work. The ship had funneled in dense plasma to match against the antimatter, so they had heavy thrust now. The hot jet spurting out below them was a mixture of matter and its howling enemy, its polar opposite.

Rachel thought, *Hell hath no fury like—*

—and her thought stopped as she saw Claire slamming the fury-fire down, down—in a cone, onto the flux tubes around the hole. *Leggo, damn it.*

She realized that Claire knew an old trick, impossibly slow in ordinary free space. When you manage to force two magnetic field lines close together, they can reconnect. The inevitable plasma caught on them went turbulent, adding resistance. That liberates some field energy into heat and can even blow open a magnetic structure. The process is slow—unless you jab it with turbulent, rowdy plasma. That triggers massive slabs of field pressure to annihilate.

The antimatter in their downwash cut straight through flux tubes. Claire's gloved hands cut arcs in the space before her, carving with her antimatter jet. It sliced through, freeing field lines that still snared the worm. The ship rose farther, dragging the worm upward. *It's not too heavy*, Rachel thought. *That Scientific Officer said wormholes could come in any size at all. This one is just about right for a small ship to slip through—to where?*

You have remaining 11.34 minutes cooling time—

"Here's your hat"—Claire swept the jet wash over a last, large flux tube, which glistened as annihilation energies burst forth like scarlet bonfires. The glare raged in a place already hot beyond imagination. Magnetic knots snarled, exploded—"what's your hurry?"

Their ship rumbled in long bass notes.

The entire solar coronal arch burst open.

Rachel had sensed these potential energies locked in the peak of the arch. There was a rubbery tingle in the ship, as magnetic fields swept through it.

For Claire, there must have been an intuition that came through her hands, from long work with the mag-gloves. Craftswoman's knowledge: Find the stressed flux lines. Turn the key.

Then all hell broke loose.

The acceleration slammed Rachel down hard, despite the water. Below, she saw the vast vault of energy stored in the arch blow out and up, directly below them.

You have made a solar flare!

"And you thought I didn't have a plan." Claire started to laugh. Slamming into her couch cut that off. She would have broken a shoulder, but the couch was waterlogged and soft.

Now the worm was an asset. The up-jetting plume blew around it, and so around *Silver Metal Lugger* above it. Free of the flux tubes' grip, the wormhole helped them accelerate away from the sun.

All very helpful, Rachel reflected, but she couldn't enjoy the spectacle—the rattling, surging deck was trying to bounce her off the furniture.

5.

What saved them in the end was their magnetic grapple. Simple, sure, but powerful. It deflected most of the solar flare protons around the ship. Pushed out by big plasma clumps moving at five hundred kilometers per second, they still barely survived baking. But they had the worm.

Still, the Scientific Officer was not pleased. He came aboard to make this quite clear. His face alone would have been enough.

"You're surely not going to demand money for that?" He scowled and nodded toward a screen, where *Silver Metal Lugger*'s fields still hung on to the wormhole. Claire had to run a sea-blue plasma discharge behind it so they could see it at all. They were orbiting Mercury, negotiating. Recuperating. While physicists designed experiments to do on the Mouth, as Fraq called it.

Earthside, panels of experts were arguing with each other. Rachel had heard plenty of their gabble on tightbeam. A negative-mass wormhole would not fall, so it couldn't knife through the Earth's mantle and devour the core. But a thin ship could fly straight into it, overcoming its gravitational repulsion—through—and come out . . . where? Nobody knew.

The worm wasn't spewing mass. So its other end wasn't buried in the middle of a star, or anyplace obviously dangerous. One of the half-dozen new theories squirting out on tightbeam held that maybe this was a multiply-connected wormhole, with many ends, of both positive and negative mass. In that case, plunging down it could take you to different destinations. A subway system for a galaxy—or for a universe.

Since it must have been made in the Big Blossoming, there were myriad possibilities. As some early biologist, maybe Darwin, had said, "One example proves a species behind it." Maybe . . .

So: no threat, and plenty of possibilities. Interesting market prospects. She was with Claire, who shrugged and said, "Have your advocate talk to my advocate."

"It's a unique natural resource—"

"And it's mine." Claire grinned. "You specified a flyby, no constraint on possession."

He was lean and muscular and the best man Rachel had seen in months. Also the only man she had seen in weeks. Fraq was male, mysterious, elegant, but . . .

"I can have a team board you, y'know." He towered over them, using the usual ominous male thing.

"I don't think you're that fast," Claire said.

"What's speed got to do with it?"

"I can always turn off my grapplers." She pulled out a switch she had in her jacket pocket. "If it's not mine, then I can just let everybody have it."

"Why would you—" Claire made to press a pad on the switch and he blurted, "No, don't!"

It wasn't the right switch at all, but he didn't know that. "If I release it, the worm takes off—antigravity, sort of." Rachel knew this was an oversimplified dynamic, but kept quiet. This guy was great on theory, but this was experiment—and intimidation.

He blinked. "We, we could catch it."

"You couldn't even find it. It's dead-black now." She tapped the switch, letting a malicious smile play on her lips.

He flinched. "Please don't."

"I need to hear a number. An offer."

His lips compressed until they paled. "The wormhole price, minus your fine?"

Her turn to blink. "What fine? I was on an approved flyby—"

"That solar flare wouldn't have blown for months!" His mouth twisted, eyebrows flared, eyes big. "You did a real job on it—the whole magnetic arcade went up at once! People all the way out to the asteroids had to scramble for shelter. It struck here within hours, well before you returned." He looked at Rachel and Claire and a silent Fraq steadily. Rachel could not decide whether he was telling the truth. Maybe that didn't matter. This was headbutting, done by pros. Instructive . . .

Claire was frowning. "So their costs—"

"Could run high. Very high. Plus advocate fees." He smiled, ever so slightly, eyes now gleaming.

Erma was trying to tell them something, but Claire turned the tiny voice far down, until it buzzed like an irritated insect.

A silence. Rachel knew Claire had endured weeks of Erma-sim— plus irritating calls from everywhere, pouring in all along the flight back—in an ever nastier mood. They were so down in water, isotopes for the reactor, a dozen other things, that they'd had to cry for help. Luckily, a supply luggo freighter was doing a delta-v Oberth maneuver near the sun. It had caught up to them and done a mass transfer, mostly water. So . . .

Rendezvous at high relative speeds. Long hours. Edgy incidents. Broke stuff galore. Adrenaline fatigue. They'd all worked on repairs and Band-Aid gear fixes, even Fraq. He was all abuzz with his flock— interstellar diplomacy, in rattling-fast exchanges. He was on weird comm with the wormhole itself, through the relay device his expedition had lodged in its "rimwalls," whatever the hell those were. So . . . quite enough.

Rachel realized she had two goals here—one immediate, one a career swerve. First up: she needed an antidote. This fellow had the wrong kind of politics, but to let that dictate everything was as dumb as politics itself. And Claire plainly felt the same . . . her ship's name was a joke, actually, about long, lonely voyages as an ore hauler.

Rachel had endured enough of shipping all over the inner solar system, Fraq in tow. And this guy was tall and muscular, and you didn't have to talk about business if you played the guy right.

Still, her swerve needed to be done in the business part, right now. So she said, "The wormhole negotiations will take time, but let's spell out stuff beyond ownership and commissions and such."

He frowned. "Such?"

"I want what Claire's going to get. Shared access to the wormhole."

Claire shot Rachel a puzzled frown. "Why would you—"

"Because I want to go through it. Through what Fraq controls with that gadget he's got, attached somehow to the Mouth frame material."

The guy shifted back, flexing his shoulders as if to get a burden off them. "Go through . . . ?"

"Plus, I want training. In what Claire managed to do—grapple with the wormhole, close-in maneuvers, the works."

Claire nodded to herself, as if she had seen this coming. "I get that."

Rachel smiled. "Touché. Okay, it's a done deal."

He beamed. "I'll get my team to work—"

"Still, Mr. Whatsit, I'd say you need to work on your negotiating skills. Too brassy." *Not as brassy as I've got to be now. No more Li'l Miss Librarian, no.*

He frowned, but then gave her a grudging grin.

Subtlety had never been her strong suit. "Shall we discuss them—over dinner?" That would take care of her immediate, so the next one had to be announced firm and sure, her career swerve. "I'm going to be a wormhole pilot, yes?"

PART 14

THE WORM TURNS

Time goes, you say? Ah no!
Alas, time stays, we go.

—HENRY DOBSON

1.

SEVEN YEARS LATER

She was about to get whirled into a puree, and all because of tricky accountants and, worse, bureaucrats. Plus, of course, Fraq.

"Give me infrared," Rachel called.

Erma murmured brightly, I can give you full spectrum.

Rachel's headset showed a sprawl of color that hurt the eyes.

"You keep trying to get me to look at the world that way, damn it!" *Maybe I'm just a touch irritated,* Rachel thought, *under pressure.* But software didn't take offense, or so Rachel thought. "Uh, I'm just a narrow-bandwidth primate. One spectrum slice at a time. Please."

As you say.

Was there an irritated sniff after the words? No matter—Erma obliged.

Fraq said, "It is worse . . . worse than I imagined."

Me too, Rachel thought but kept quiet. *Wonders galore, dangerous as hell . . .*

There were several theorists' terms for the wobbly object hovering on her screens: wormring, ringhole. This wormring looked like a blurry reddish donut. It spun in a frenzied halo of skating brilliance.

A grav-magnetic hurricane, she thought.

Sullen red snakes coiled around its skin. Lightning forked yellow and blue down the northern donut pole, but didn't come out on the other side, seen from this angle. The same fizzing flashes worked like sullen lightning around the southern hole, too, but there was no answer to the north. Somewhere along that axis lay trouble. Big bad twisted-geometric trouble aplenty. And that's where they had to go.

"What's the best trajectory, in theory?" Fraq asked in his singsong way, but the tone carried irritation, too.

There is no adequate theory. The best mathematics says there are several entrances, but they all involve acquiring considerable angular momentum.

Rachel said, "Yeah, but there's got to be a best educated guess—"

I do have the latest numerical simulations, just arrived from Earthside.

"Oh, good. I always feel better after a nice refreshing computer simulation."

It is best to address our safety without stressful sarcasm.

"Sarcasm is just one more service we offer here at Silver Metal Lover Salvage and Loan."

Sarcasm is stressful.

"Stressful for who?"

For us all. Erma managed to put a prissy tone into even dry discussions.

"Do I look like a people person?"

You look anxious.

"I thought you understood rhetorical questions."

You are stalling for time.

So Erma was now a psychologist. . . . "Damn right I am. Look at that wormring on the mass detector."

Fraq did his copilot tricks and Erma did hers. All virtual images that popped up on the screens had a glossy sheen to them that even Erma's super-teraprocessor couldn't erase. They looked too good to be real. Pristine geometries snarled and knotted into surf around the spinning donut. Whorls of spacetime spun away and radiated grav waves in angry red hisses. Not a comfy place, no.

"Does that look safe to you?"

I would point out that I am backed up to Luna every hour by laser link.

"Yeah, you're immortal as long as I pay your computer fees."

I can find other work—

Rachel smiled. Erma didn't often get into a sentence without already knowing how it would turn out. Maybe her conversational program was competing with the huge sensor net strung around *Silver Metal Lugger*'s hull. A riot of digits, tribal software squabbling for running time. They were measuring everything possible as the ship gingerly edged closer to the whirling wormring.

"You were saying . . . ?"

I was merely distracted. And I do have a high opinion of this enterprise. I do not like our probabilities if we hang nearby this strange object, however.

Could software also get jumpy? Erma hadn't seemed so last time, years back, when they had snagged this same wormhole. After that, the astro guys had started tinkering with it, trying to expand it so a ship of *Silver Metal Lugger*'s size, not merely Fraq's slimship, could pass through—and they literally screwed it up.

They had nudged and probed and somehow added angular momentum to it. Accidentally they'd transformed the entire spacetime around what had been, apparently, a somewhat predictable—though negative mass—wormhole.

Not that anybody knew what routine was for wormholes. After all, they only had one—this whirling dervish that had already eaten many probes, spitting nothing back out. True, the astro guys had negated the negative-mass aspect of it, with those mass-slugging probes. They just brute-forced it with tons of junk mass. Simple, and it worked. But then came the spin.

We need to go closer, to resolve the possible entrances.

Rachel thought, *Trouble. Maybe too much.*

She had gotten here by what she thought of as the doctorate degree in Death Through Small Doses. She had trained hard at piloting, while doing all the Library work she could, too. She came through her missions around asteroids, then in the outreaches of the wormhole itself. Along the way she had ruptured her liver, her spleen, and one of her kidneys; collapsed her lower intestine; crushed two vertebrae; acquired first-degree burns on her face and head; and, for extra, had gotten hard-hammered, leaving her concussed and with temporary losses of vision and hearing.

But she got rebuilt by the magical tech of this age. Hurt?—plenty. Fun?—even more. She wasn't just a Librarian now. More like an over-educated, seat-of-her-pants pilot. With a plausible life-span measured in centuries, you took your chances as they came.

The medicos had made bets about her surviving, five times. She took the odds through a secondary agent, Claire, and won—with damn good odds, too.

Then, too, she had seen a fellow crew-gal's dying breaths making her sparkle in the vacuum.

Maybe too much? Rachel pondered. *Considering my life, only too much was enough.*

Enough medical memory, her internal nag said. *Focus.*

Along the axis of the dervish was a shimmering orange lump that apparently held some other sort of exotic matter. The lump looked to be spinning, too.

Rachel had been warned many times not to touch that lump, or else. Previous probes had, and got broken down into elementary particles, pronto—and not particularly nice ones, at that. Quark-gluon plasmas had a well-deserved nasty reputation.

"There are basically two ways in, right, Erma? North and south poles of this general relativistic merry-go-round. But stay away from that axis."

Erma was a daily updated Artilect but the schoolmarm voice stayed the same. True. I think our own spin matters, too. The earlier probes tried varying angular momenta and a few managed to send back coherent signals . . . for a while.

"Sure, for maybe ten precious seconds. I was kinda counting on my shoot-and-scoot strategy taking about that much time. Our contract says just make some readings and come on home. Didn't one probe get back out?"

If one counts granules of carbon, yes.

"From a ceramic ship?"

Yes, not promising.

Fraq had an aversion to talking to software, didn't trust minds without bodies, so Rachel was surprised when he said, "I do not favor trying to do so similar a strategy."

Rachel took his stiffly delivered advice seriously. In her immersion-work environment, touch controls gave her an abstract distance from the wormring. It was hovering in space, held in magnetic clamps a hundred meters away from them. Whorls of wrenched spacetime slammed into their metallic ship's skin, rattling her teeth and, as seen on the screens, spraying a yellow-white froth of gravitational turbulence around them. River-rafting white-water spacetime, yeah.

Perhaps the theoretical view would help.

"Donuts are donuts, Erma. Let's just stick our nose in, real quick."

There is your neglected homework, hence . . . And all this, because of tricky accountants.

2.

The Loonie lawyer guys with briefcases had gotten to her before she had even unpacked.

Rachel had counted on some ribald bar cruising to rub away the memory of their drawn-out worm training. Simulations, even physio ones, got old, real fast. Claire had helped get her into the field, and their mutual fame had helped a lot. Fraq had gone off on "diplomatic" missions, then returned to do parallel training, so the years had gone by fast.

Fraq moved through all the Prefects, Noughts, and sundry Library folk like a panther through geese. He and his flock had mastered "interviews" with the Library's Messages, comparing this information with their own experience of wormhole passage. The Ythri ship's transit had been fast, tens of seconds of hard turbulence. There were fragmented Messages about the wormholes, but little hard physics. Maybe the ancient societies kept such secrets?

Rachel was ready to get into the foam shower and run the water a shameful hour or two. To feel really human again, in a fluffy bathrobe. To yammer at somebody other than Erma—and then they rang her door chimes, which played a Bach opening. Third Brandenburg, ah. So she didn't answer. The shower beckoned—

They came right on in, anyway.

"Hey! I'm renting this 'partment."

The taller of them didn't even blink. "We could put you on a perfectly legal formal secure-lock *right now*."

"The last guy who tried that ended up nearly getting frozen." Though that was a boast she'd got from Claire, not from experience.

The short one, apparently fond of his food, said smugly. "We checked. You didn't prong him at all, just threatened to."

So they had confused Claire with her. Good; she liked people who didn't do their homework right, i.e., suckers. The whole who-owns-the-wormhole feud had lingered far too long, and was now spawning mutants like these guys.

Rachel jutted her chin out. "I could make an exception in your case."

She smiled slowly, slit-eyeing the fat guy—who blinked nervously and took a step backward despite himself. She chided herself for taking on such an easy mark, but hell, she needed a little recreation. It would be fun to deck these two, yes. In Luna grav she was adept, and she could tell these guys were recent bumblers from Earthside, as their every move advertised. And it would be a stimulating boost to the cardiovascular system that had spent too much time in centri-g.

"Gentlemen, I have to negotiate with some champagne right now."

"You are in debt again. Deeply so." Tall Guy's smile was broad but utterly without warmth. So yes, they had her confused with Claire . . . who was right down the hallway. Call her in? No, this was fun alone.

"We are an accountant and acting legal officer"—a bow from Fat Guy—"and we have orders to duly confiscate your ship."

"I dug myself out with Claire's help." So yes, time to reveal. She gave Tall Guy a wink, just to mess with him. Tall Guy frowned. His right eye slid over, obviously checking with his data link. Now he registered who she was, and Rachel said, "Plus years of pilot jockey train—"

"Yes, ah, admirable." Tall Guy recovered quickly. "But the mode you have chosen, individual exploration, has fallen upon sad times," he said. "Once the worm became a toroid—"

Rachel put her hands on her hips, striking a power pose. "Look, I want to fly through that wormhole. Sure! The gadgety guys got it all screwed up, can't get the simple sphere wormhole back, but—I'll

fly it. With Claire, my ol' pilot buddy, maybe. Or with Fraq—he's
training with us, too. And! Second World Corp will vouch for me."
I think . . .

Fat Guy was still blinking, getting his self-image back in order. It
took a fair amount of work for this Horseman of the Esophagus. Tall
Guy smiled without a gram of humor and without invitation folded
himself into a grav chair. She watched him do this, legs angling like
demonstrations of the principle of the lever, and—startled—felt herself
moisten. *I've been working hard, Library and piloting, too, a loooong time.*

"I believe that maneuver will fail," Tall Guy said smoothly.

"Let's try it, shall we?" she said phony-cheerfully.

Freeze-locking these guys was getting more attractive by the second. She was tired, still adjusting from their inflight training grav
standard Mars of 0.38. Their nominals had risen to 1.4 in the trainng
debacle, while gravs changed—as they did, near the wormhole. Though
Moon Standard 0.17 felt great, her reflexes would be off with these
two. She might just be getting a bit rickety for this line of work, though
fifty-nine wasn't all that damn far into middle age anymore. Her rebuilt
body had extras galore. . . .

For the moment, she had better use deflection while she remembered where she kept her stunner. And maybe just shut down Fat
Guy, while she worked her wiles on Tall Guy? The thought intrigued.
Pleasure before business—her fundamental rule, in these post-Library
years.

Fat Guy murmured, "Do not presume to push us." Getting icy now.

Okay, give them lip in return. "How come you can just walk in
here?"

Fat Guy launched into a stumbling rendition of how they had used
some law that said Solar Financials Policy could access property rights
of those in outstanding debt, and at that point she stopped listening.
These guys were dead serious. They were used to delivering trouble to
people, did it for a living. They probably had other slices of bad news
to serve up today.

". . . we trust some accommodation might be arrived at before we
are forced to—" Fat Guy was saying.

"Before your heavies come calling?" she interrupted.

Tall Guy smoothly came in with, "We do hope such methods are not necessary, and had not even considered them."

These were all clichés, straight from business school. And this pair had probably never gotten the true skinny on how the wormhole got so tangled up in Luna-Earthside disputes. The Library was an antagonist in the many clashes over ownership, management, risk, and investment.

"Look, it wasn't my fault that damn comet nucleus came unglued on its ride down the grav well and smacked mass into the worm's Mouth. Pure accident, it was. Pilot training and operations like mine keep the Mouth in line, right?"

Tall Guy nodded and with some effort got a diplomatic expression onto his face. "I know you feel that accountants and lawyers are annoying, but—"

"Not all lawyers are annoying. Some are dead."

"My colleague and I don't question why you failed—"

"I wasn't in charge of screening the comet ices against that solar flare. We used standard reflecting coating to keep the ice from subliming, routine methods. But that big solar flare blew off the shadow coating. Not my department! That storm made the whole damn iceberg start boiling off. It developed expansion fractures inside an hour, killed two women who—"

"We are well aware of that," Tall Guy's voice came sliding in like a snake. He had probably laid this conversation out in advance, getting his pitch in shape. To prove his point, he waved a hand and punched a few buttons on his belt. An air display of her account ledgers hung in the air between them, shimmering like a waterfall, the numbers all color-coded so that her debt glared forth in scarlet. A gaudy avalanche of debt. Claire had her share, but Rachel had paid nearly all of hers off by writing an autobiography. Now corps were making a 3-D from it. She scowled.

Tall Guy said languidly, "But there . . . may . . . be a way out for you."

She smiled prettily, arched an eyebrow, said nothing. She had learned that if you let people talk, their love of their own voices could lead them into overplaying their hands. They would babble on, and, immersed in telling whatever story or moral lesson they meant to impart, reveal useful things.

The Library Prefects had indirectly taught her that—in detail—but the idea had originally come from her famously laconic grandfather. Granddad had squinted at her while she went on at a grand family dinner, spinning out a tale that ended in no particular point. Everybody smiled politely and general talk resumed, but a few moments later he had leaned over and whispered in his round burr, "Never pass by a chance to shut up." She had blinked and thought furiously about that, and learned a lesson that became quite useful.

Tall Guy said with a thin smile, "We can either talk of possibilities or we can seize your ship. Yours and Claire's."

She let out a long breath. "Oh, goody."

"Our offer is quite generous."

"They always are." She was busy looking at his hands. Long fingers, too . . .

"Cosmo Corp has asked if you are interested in another expedition."

"Let me guess. Another wormhole has turned up, stuck in a solar coronal arch? And Cosmo needs somebody to go fetch it. Just like last time."

Another cold, calculating smile. Why did she like guys like this? Okay, it had been a long time, and technology could only do so much for the lonely gal.

But still—

"No, alas. Though I might say I thought that an admirably brave and daring act. I heard someone made a three-D about it."

"In case you're wondering, I spent that money, too."

His veneer slipped a bit, but he recovered in an eye-blink. "I'm sure, in a worthy cause."

"Yeah, very worthy. Spent it all on me. What's the deal?"

Tall Guy looked a bit rushed, as though he liked a lot of foreplay before getting down to business. Well, so did she, but a different kind of business than this character meant.

"It is the same wormhole. But it has changed."

"Escaped?"

"No, it is secured in hyperstrong magnetic fields in free space, held in high Lunar orbit. But Cosmo Corp's experiments to expand its mouth, and thus to bring interstellar travel to mankind, have—"

"Wait, how did Cosmo get the worm?"

"Uh, they exerted stock override options on the holding company consortium that by interplanetary rights had further—"

"Skip the jargon. They bought it?"

"In a manner of speaking."

"I always mind my manners when I speak. What's up?"

Tall Guy was now ignoring Fat Guy, who had found a seat on the other side of the 'partment living room. Rachel stayed standing. With guys, who routinely used height to intimidate women, it was just about her only advantage here.

"I am not a technical person." Tall Guy collapsed the glaring account ledger and arched an eyebrow at her.

Damn! Even that got her moist. She really had to get out of here, go bar-hopping, blow off two years' worth of steam—

"But the wormhole you captured has . . . changed, I do know that. Cosmo Corp was attempting to expand its, ah, mouth size. This is a delicate operation, apparently. I am unsure precisely what the difficulty was, but in making the wormhole mouth large enough to accommodate a substantial ship—such as yours, for example—they somehow added angular momentum to the wormhole. It became another sort of wormhole entirely."

Rachel said cautiously, "What sort?" *Why am I hearing about this so late? Somebody's hiding the news. . . .*

"One with enough rotation to change the very nature of the spacetime geometry, I gather." Tall Guy shrugged, as if altering wormholes was something like the weather. What could one do, after all? Yawn.

"Hey, Claire and me, we're contract haulers. We grabbed that wormhole off its perch on the top of a magnetic arch, dragged it back to Earthside. That's what I know, period."

"Yes, but you do have some talent for the unexpected. That is apparently what Cosmo Corp needs. And soon."

"Because . . . ?"

"Because certain governmental entities wish to possess the wormhole."

"The Earthside scientists."

Another *What can one do?* shrug. Very expressive. This guy should have gone on the stage, she thought. "They went through the Planetary Nations."

She let a silence build. This was a critical point. In many negotiations, subtle silences did most of the work. Let the silence run . . . then . . .

"Must be tough, dancing around on strings pulled all the way from Earth."

Tall Guy shrugged, not denying it. Lean and muscular, he was the best man she had seen in years. Also the only man she had seen in years. That is, not counting Fat Guy, who might as well be on Pluto, eyes blank.

She eyed Tall Guy and wondered if he was an all-business type, or if he was attuned to social signals better than his fat friend. She was wearing slickskin tiger pants, and neither of these guys had given that a glance. The oldtime gal rule was that no guy was going to notice what shoes you were wearing, and if he did, he was the wrong guy. Tall Guy was giving nothing away. Poker face, no eye contact, nothing.

Tall Guy said carefully, "The Planetary Nations Scientific Council got a binding injunction, which begins in"—he gazed off to the side, probably consulting a clock in his inboard vision—"seventeen hours."

"Seventeen hours—"

"And forty-eight minutes."

"Nobody can—"

"You can," he said, abruptly urgent. "You have experience with it. And the technical people have tried all they can, without success."

"Anybody get killed?"

He went deadpan. "I can't discuss that. Legal matters—"

"Okay, okay." She felt the fight go out of her. Legal lingo bored her. What the hell, she had slept most of the way to Luna, coming back from the comet fiasco. She was rested, well fed. Other hungers, though . . .

She could cut short the shower. Get out to the bars, find a guy, get some sack time in, then back up to *Silver Metal Lugger*—

"Okay, I'm interested." She put both hands on her hips, a commanding stance. "But we have to negotiate."

"There's little time, but we are prepared—"

She sliced a hand through the air, pointed at Fat Guy—who had developed a pout. "*No*. He goes, you stay. We two negotiate the deal, my fee. And fast. Cosmo Corp needs this done pronto, right?"

"Uh, right." A gleam in Tall Guy's eye? Was she that obvious?

Well, maybe. And that could save them both some time. Skip cruising the bars, yes. Not the shower, though. She said quickly, "Let's, well, let's do it." Maybe a shower for two?

3.

We must either go in or out. Soon. The ringhole is frame-dragging spacetime itself in its vicinity. Theory predicted this. I can feel its tug. This is not a safe place.

"No place is, when you think about it."

She recalled Tall Guy. Some things were better than they looked. Maybe this wormring was okay, once you dove through? None of their probes had really quick grit-savvy, after all. Artificial intelligences had plenty of craft, but little intuition. No animal instincts.

"We can do this. Let's spin about our main axis, dive straight down through the north pole."

Is than an order?

"You bet. I did follow all those simulations, lectures, endless speculations. Now we get to use them."

We are turning. Hold on.

Rachel was at the ship axis anyway, so she felt nothing as the room started to spin. Fraq adjusted his securing belts, while helping the dynamics program adjust. Her fore screen showed them shooting on, into the wormring. The ship knocked and strummed as they skated by whorls that slammed into their nose. Rattles, pops. Rachel wished she had been able to bring Claire.

"Y'know, I kinda hoped I'd have more time to talk to the theory guys about this."

You said you were in the shower a long time.

"Uh, yeah."

Alone?

"You're getting into an area beyond your competence. Y'know, not having a body and all."

Oh, my.

This was in a phony, high-pitched English voice, like a parody of Jane Austen. Erma kept getting smarter, but not more charming. "Look, skip the gossip! Why's this thing look like a rotating donut?"

Wormholes are not tubes, my database says quite clearly. They present in our space as solid objects. One passes through them by just merging with them. It is not like falling down a pipe.

"This one's spinning faster now."

Apparently. The alterations the scientists carried out to expand it radially seem to have added angular momentum.

A pause, then—

I must adjust our trajectory for this new spin. I will have to delay any movement, so we have time to consider our next, and quite possibly fatal, movements. I need to carry out a coordinate transform—

"Just do it. Wormholes connect parts of spacetime, so—hey, it connects both parts of space and . . . uh . . . parts of time?"

Not for the first time, Rachel regretted her spotty physics education. Librarians usually did little manual labor, and her piloting education had only partly made up for that. Realistically, she was just about one grade above the ore haulers. She glanced at Fraq and saw his shadowy nod, conveying skeptical assent with a sharp birdy-call. She had learned a lot of Ythri sing-meaning now. It was one of their workarounds to be sure Erma and people in general didn't quite know what was going on between them.

Which was fun, too, a delightful interspecies game.

I do know from ancillary reading that the philosopher Gödel solved the general field equations, in their classical limit, for a rotating universe. He found that time could form loops around the entire universe. Apparently he did this to illustrate a point about time being eternal. In some sense, Gödel believed this. So he found an exact solution to show to his friend Einstein.

"Centuries back, sure. So what?"

But! Just because one has a formal solution to a set of differential equations does not mean there is any physical validity to the resulting spacetime. Until, of course, we found this wormhole, which broke open the issue. Einstein and Gödel were, as you would put it, buddies. Physics-math buddies.

Rachel thought sourly, *I never get a direct answer unless I coax.* Maybe she should buy a patch into a more masculine software. But then she would have to deal with the male narrow-linear perspective, too. There were always tradeoffs.

"Very nice, but what's that mean?"

Twist a wormhole, twist space, twist time. I suppose.

"You suppose?"

All wormholes can be made into time machines, by moving them around at high speeds. Apparently ringholes, with their angular momentum, even more so. Gödel was right.

"Um. We need more. What about that big library program I bought you?"

I use it to . . . browse.

"Browse what, porn? I need—"

You have been accessing my routines! And after all my tireless scientific database searchings!

Perfect Erma; primly change the subject, mix in some offended hauteur. "Show us, with color coding."

On her wall screens the magnetic grappling strands played and rippled like luminous wheat whorls, stirred by a lazy breeze. In the station's magnetic grasp the ringhole flexed and whirred. The grappler field config had been built out here, far beyond Luna, at the Earth-Luna Lagrange point. For safety, since nobody knew what damage a twisted spacetime knothole could do, on the loose. She watched carefully, as did Fraq, while blue lightning snarled and spat. The ringhole crushed and curdled light, stirring spacetime with a spoon.

Rachel gingerly pulsed *Silver Metal Lugger*, spilling more antimatter into the chambers. Claire had bought their shared ship the newest tech, and it helped. Now Rachel wished she had brought Claire, rather than Fraq, but there were "diplomatic" issues: the Ythri wanted to establish their way home first. Plus, not enough room for Claire, too, in the crammed deck. The ship kept adding upgrades. Pricey ones.

But even amid this chaos, Rachel was having fun. This was more like surfing than flying. They fought their way down the turbulent grav gradient. The vortex groped for them. Grabbed.

We are on correct curves now. Can proceed. Do remain ready to adjust, Madam Pilot Rachel.

When Erma was scared, she became polite. "In we go."

This was lots better than hauling dreary comets, which had come to resemble delivering the milk, door to door. She had to do that to qualify to pilot a megatonnish ship around. Danger was never boring.

Then the room . . . rippled. Stretched. Boomed. Groaned.

She watched sinusoids flounce through the walls without ripping anything, just flapping shiny steel-like waves crossing an ocean.

Her heart pounded. A jittery hum waltzed through her acceleration couch. The couch leather dimpled and puckered as torques warped across it. She could see the rivulets of gravitational stress work across her body, too, like tornadoes a centimeter across twisting her uniform.

Ick. Awk. She reminded herself that pilots didn't let their fear eat at them, not while there was flying to be done. And reminded herself again. It became a mantra.

She saw that Fraq had assumed his perch-stance of legs and wings. That brought him into his Yth state of aware contemplation. Something like Zen calisthenics, she had learned.

The magnetic catcher's mitt slipped from view behind them. They plunged into the whirl. It felt rubbery, somehow, and then her stomach tried to work up through her throat. Bile rushed into her nose. The acceleration slammed her around like a rag doll. She felt her skin stretching away in several directions. Torques galore . . . Gravitational stresses seemed to be trying to open her wrapping, to find a Christmas present inside.

"How're . . . we . . . doing . . . getting . . . through?"

I believe we are not.

"What?!"

We are stalled above the rotating core of the spacetime donut.

"I . . . can . . . fly . . . us . . . out . . ." But her fingers moved like sausages.

You are incapable. You have no plan. I believe I must take command.

"You're ... a program ... not an ... officer." Just saying that took all her strength. The air oozed like greasy hair. "Commit our full antimatter flux. Hammer us out of this."

Inward or outward?

"Which way ... is ... outward?"

Something like a peeved sigh came from Erma.

I was hoping you knew.

"And you wanted to take command?" Irritation helped, actually. Adrenaline spikes always did, for her pilot self. She could even complete a sentence. "Inward—that way." She jabbed her chin toward the deck. "... I guess ..."

Antimatter howled as it met its enemy in their reaction chamber.

Floors clattered. The room spun around her so fast it blurred into a fluid. Walls pulsed. Her teeth rattled. On the screens there was nothing but dark outside. How big was this thing? Were they squeaking through, or trapped in some infinity?

"Did you send out laser pulses? Microwaves?"

Of course. Nothing came back.

"Maybe this spacetime whirling thing is a perfect absorber? But ... nothing's ... perfect."

Something spurted actinic blue and arced big, coming at them. Coming fast. She got a flash image of an oddly shaped ship, far away. Then it was gone. The only thing they had seen. Were they in some murk?

I have an incoming message.

"What? How can—hell, patch it through."

The message says, "Worms can eat their tails and so can you."

"Is this one of your jokes?"

I do not joke. I do not have the proper software.

"Eat my tail? What's ... oh."

Oh?

"Maybe that refers to the Gödel thing? But who said it?"

Who is here with us? I know not. I cannot see another presence in this spinning space. I am mere software.

Rachel sniffed. Erma's false modesty was unconvincing.

She was sweating, but the ship was strangely cool. Some entropy suck? Her pulse quickened. This was intriguing, sure, but right now they were in a gravitational whirlwind. The couch adjusted to the tornado violence of their whirl, but this could not go on for long. And how long was a wormhole, anyway?

Fraq . . . he sat still, crouched as if to take flight. But there was nowhere to go in this cabin. He nodded to her, in support, silent but for a thin song of chirps that floated in the filmy air.

Some glowing stuff zoomed by them—or at least got larger, then smaller—all she could tell in this dense dark. It looked like neon clotted cream.

"What was that?"

My database says that wormrings are held together with exotic material, a kind of matter with "negative average energy density," born in the Great Blossoming. It threads wormholes from end to end.

"Um, great. No use to us. Are we making any progress out of here?"

I cannot tell. What we see may be the girders of this tortured, warped spacetime.

"And you thought I didn't have a plan."

Wait—I do sense something bright—approaching—

The black outside reddened. Churned.

Suddenly they slammed out—and into a blue storm.

A mirror twin of the wormring dwindled behind them now. Brilliant rainbows rimmed it. Rotating fast in the opposite direction to where they came in. *Wherever "in" is. . . .*

Her ship popped and groaned. Fraq said sternly, "This vibration. These colors. They are like when my ship slipped through, carrying our Flock. But that was fast. Not slow, as now. We only saw these changes, colors, sounds, after we ran the data. After we were through. So now we have gone through all of that slowly. But, still, is good news."

Stars gleamed in a darkening sky. Strange stars.

"We're through," Rachel whispered. "In another star system."

I register less spacetime curvature. We have popped through the toroid ringhole. Into . . .

"Somewhere. Some strange where," Fraq said. "We have flown through that tortured Mouth. But we are not back home. . . ." The Ythri flourished his neck fan feathers. A frustration signal, she knew.

"Then this wormring, it's . . ."

"A multiply connected wormhole network," Fraq finished. He bristled with worry, mouth stern, feathers flexing. "We came from our system, to yours—by threading the angular momenta the system had acquired. That was the legendary trouble, for mass coming through alters each exit's spin. Ancient accounts spoke of other destinations, attained by knowing how to sail upon spin itself. That record was devoid of detail. We thought such were confused, perhaps religious in some way."

"Really? But it was actually physics. . . ." She had known Fraq years now, but he had never revealed this history. Some Flock constraint, maybe. They were a cautious species, far older than humanity. Secretive, some said.

Wary, worn, weary. "This confirms . . . ?"

"Our worst fears. We, our Yth Flock, hoped for simplicity, when we ventured through the Mouth. A simple subway, your kind would say. But now it seems the route has other channels. The Mouth Maze, as we and now your Library Minds refer to it, or . . . to them."

Rachel thought, *So instead of flying down a nice comfy tube, we're in s spinning spacetime. That has whirling branches. Changing constantly. Maybe dead ends? Can this get any more complicated?*

"True, Fraq. We knew traces of that in the most ancient texts." Rachel reflected back on her years of Librarian toil. Many fragments spoke of such, but they were never clear. "No maps, though."

Maps of a multidimensional spacetime? That strains my abilities. I am after all a flight assistant, not . . . Erma's voice trailed away in confusion.

Rachel had a hunch. "The spin. Maybe that plays through the whole damn wormring system? Ripples it? Opens . . . doors?"

Fraq's stern mouth flattened and his brow ribbed into a scowl. He grumbled in low notes. "Our goal was to rejoin my solar system. We must find it."

Rachel said, "First, stay alive." She gritted her teeth, using her sensogloves to battle thrust vectors. She had been dealing with the endless surges without thinking—pilot training paid off.

They tumbled, ass over entrails. Hot gas rushed by, prickly with blue and ruby glows. A huge gas giant world hung between them and a bright, sullen star. Her ship rocked and wheeled. A vast wind was driving them outward from the gas giant. Plus, the ship suddenly smelled . . . scorched.

This gas is blowing us away from the wormring. It is mostly molecular hydrogen, quite hot—thus the blue gas. It comes from a planetary atmosphere, being stripped away. We are very near the star, a fraction of Mercury's orbital distance. The star is smaller than ours.

Rachel stared hard. The slightly reddish star was boiling away the gas giant's surging atmosphere. In its orbit the world was like a gassy comet, tail pointing outward. A hellhole. The giant churning sphere was doomed, trapped to circle its tormenter while being slowly tortured, shredded.

A vast rosy plume erupted from the gas giant and curled toward *Silver Metal Lugger*. In the streaming gas spun a nasty, angry-red vortex. They were at its edge.

I cannot navigate in this. My supplementary piloting also is not capable of—

"Hey, I'm the damn pilot! I'll take the helm."

Rachel fought to turn the ship. Their reaction engines could barely muster enough thrust to compete with the winds here. *Winds in space!* she thought wildly. *This is worse than that coronal arch . . . which we barely survived.*

Even making a turn was hard. It was better to think of the days she had enjoyed sailing on warm Gulf waters. Tacking with the wind, then rounding on it when the vectors and torques allowed . . .

She got them swiveled around to take the billowing gas on their stern, slowing the tumbling pitch and yaw.

A knot of angry violet gas shot by them. Flaming debris hit their flank. Thumps, jars, screeches in the steel. The screens showed no pressure loss, but plenty of abrasion from the roasting, eating winds.

I can compile a grav potential map of this—

"No talk," she spat out.

It took a long while to stabilize their course. They still rocked and veered like a sailboat in a hard storm.

Fraq peered at her sympathetically. He worked the attitude controls to help her. When she got her breath back, she jutted out her chin and barked, "Damn! We're supposed to reconnoiter, then get back home. That's all! This stuff is incredible." She had never had an experience of flying in gassy space. No way to estimate the damage done to the ship, no clear navigation rules. "But—where's the wormring?"

I have lost it. We moved quickly, blown away. I tried magnetically attaching a hailer as we departed, but it did not stick.

"No reason it should," Fraq said mildly. "We anchored our beeper, our finder signal-giver, in a secure orbit—though at a safe distance." He gave a birdy flutter. "That seems so long ago. . . ."

"Yeah, years. It must be hard to glue onto spacetime," Rachel said. *How do you clip anything to a wormhole?* The Ythri weren't giving away all their secrets, no. She was distracted as she banked and turned against the roiling hot hydrogen. "I wonder what happened to that damn ring-wormhole thing."

It may be in a stabilized orbit, a balance of its gravitational forces against this hydrogen wind.

"So it's back there. Uh . . . somewhere."

They gradually came about and steadied. She took them abroad the gale and worked toward lesser gas densities. Blue streamers fell behind. The ruddy fog-mist paled. They gradually emerged into fairly open space. The stars reappeared, gleaming reassuringly. But still in strange constellations.

Rachel saw the bright sun from an angle now, sighting back along the misty edge of the plume. The eroding giant planet was a round nub against the glaring yellow-white solar disk. But outward from them, telescoped in, hung a two-mooned world in crescent. Creamy blue-white. Earthlike!

No recognizable constellations, in a sky somehow brighter, with more stars—and yes, a globular cluster hovering like an ivory flower between two bright stars. Closer in toward galactic center?

"Any idea where we are? Can you find galactic reference points?"

I am trying, but none of the local stars are known to me. We are a long way from Earth.

"Keep trying. We may have to walk home."

Another solar system. A long way from Earth. A thrill ran through her, and she whispered commands to Erma to take scans of it all. Oth-

erwise she was speechless, adrift, fears dropping away. Somehow she
had thought of this as just another gig. Now the immensity of the
ideas Erma went on about, Fraq's ancient history, the biz deals of Tall
Guy—all those were mere details, clues, chatter. This was real.

Something hit them. Hard. The ship rattled.

"What the—"

A large soft mass struck us astern.

"Soft?"

It did little damage but conveyed momentum.

Nothing in Earth's space was soft. Not even comets. "Distance
scan."

I track many small objects. Nearby, approaching.

The screen filled with shapes. A fried-egg jellyfish swooped at
them, then attached to their skin. Drifting with spines out, here came
a warty cucumber. There were amber pencils in flight, their rear tubes
snorting out blue burning gas. Something like an ivory solar sail came
at them, reeling its huge sheets in along spars.

"This is crazy."

Disturbing, yes. These cannot be machines—at least, not of metal and
ceramics, run by computers. They are . . . alive.

Rachel eyed the many shapes with wonder. Gravity imposed
simple geometries—cylinders, boxes, spheres. Here were effortless fresh designs: spokes and beams, rhomboids, fat curves. Rough
skins and prickly shells, rubbery rods, slick mirrors—apparently all
varieties of the same twirling creatures. "Feeding off that hydrogen,
you figure?"

Fraq said slowly, working side-issue controls, "I will get our bots
on our skin. Assess the damage. See if they can deal with these living
things, too."

Rachel thought, *What the hell . . . ?*

Angular shapes came at them, diving close and then veering away,
apparently sizing them up. Needle-nosed predators, she would have
guessed if this were undersea biology—but this was a hot, gassy plume
in vacuum. All these creatures were much smaller than *Silver Metal
Lugger*, but she did not like their numbers. More flocked in as she
watched. They seemed to come from back toward the pale-blue plume,

as though they feasted on the hydrogen, hid among the streams, and then came out to forage.

Predator/prey ratios in high vacuum? Or more like cloud life?

"Great, we play this by ear. Our bots deployed?"

They are popping out from their hatches.

She could see the clunky forms walking on magnetics across the ship's silvery skin. The teeming ruby sky reflected in the hull, making a double geometry of whirling seethe. The skylife wheeled and darted in gaudy flocks in that sky. They had backed away, once the bots were out. The creatures looked more like kites than birds, while the bots were solid, rugged, probably of no interest to these gas-eaters. Plus unknown danger.

The bots followed their grid sweep commands. They found rips and gouges and filled them with quick-fix patches. Rachel understood as she watched. She always liked to do maintenance in case they had a major, subtle problem. It also gave her time to think.

This was a crazy outcome. The theory boys had imagined that this ringhole was a gateway, long unused until Fraq's ship came through it. So by all odds the other end—or ends, since nobody knew if these could have multiple mouths—should be in open space, probably far from a star. They thought this, even though the *Lugger* had originally snatched the wormhole from a coronal magnetic arch on the sun.

But then, the original wormhole wasn't an ordinary one, either. It had the equivalent of negative mass, since something at its other end had been pouring mass out through it, forcing the curvature of space-time nearby the mouth to act as if it held a net negative in its mass budget. Now the thing had stretched and tangled in the tender grasp of techies who didn't know what they were doing—and presto, it had spin and was even more confusing.

Crazy but real, not her favorite category.

"This doesn't feel like progress," Rachel mused to herself. Her lips must have shaped the words, because Erma read them.

We are making great discoveries! This is far more interesting than hauling ore and comets around.

"Far more dangerous, too. Thing is, we don't know how to get back. That hydrogen column is huge. We can't find our way around in it. The ringhole—where's that? And—"

We can learn more by reconnoitering. Once our repairs—

A bullet-shaped brown thing shot along the hull. This was different, not an airy thing but solid.

It clipped a bot and sent it tumbling into space. The bullet-shape turned in a tight arc and came back. It tossed another bot off-hull with a shrug, as it passed.

Rachel sprang into action. She had laser cannons on either end of *Silver Metal Lugger*. Cutters and slammers, depending on pulse length, useful in handling brute matter. They came online in a moment, and she patched in the seek-and-fire software. All this was by the drill—but she was still too late.

The bullet-thing was so fast the utility bots never had a chance. Bots were made to patch and fill, not fend and fight. Within a few moments the entire bot crew had spun away into oblivion.

Rachel watched in silence. There was nothing more she could do. Another hull crew would get tossed, too, and she had skimpy reserves for maintenance.

Erma said nothing. They went after a few of the bots, but amid the swarming skyline they were hard to find on radar. They managed to salvage two, whose carapaces were crumpled in by impact.

Odd. The attacker seems to have lifted out the command module in each.

"Studying us, I guess." Rachel frowned.

Silver Metal Lugger drifted for a while, and the swarm of living spacecraft simply glided past, as if on patrol—pencils, sails, puffy spheres of malevolent orange. But cautious. None tried to enter the ship through hull ports.

I suggest we get a clear view of that distant planet.

"I want to find the ringhole. I learned that in high school—at a party in a strange place, always find the exits first."

To extend your metaphor, we were not invited to this party at all. The locals seem to be making that point.

"Let's shed them. Accelerate away, take some good long scans of that planet. Then dodge back into the hydrogen column and search it for the ringhole."

Seems plausible. I am accelerating.

Fraq said sternly, feathers rippling, "I wish we return the ringhole, if we find it, to the simple, spherical shape."

"De-spin it?" Rachel frowned. "By chunking mass in, with angular momentum?"

"We have formally so agreed."

Fraq was right, Earthside and Luna had a treaty—which was why they were here. But— "That's a pretty damn tall order, when we're just trying to stay alive."

Fraq rustled his feathers, showing bright-red hues. Anger. "Blood-pride so demands, at the cusp point of action."

Rachel was getting a bit tired of the Ythri always falling back on their species/tribal thing. But now wasn't the time to argue that. She floored their acceleration, hard.

The swarm outside started to fall behind as she accelerated away. They could trim sails and muster more sunlight, maybe even ride the vagrant hydrogen winds, but *Silver Metal Lugger* outran them in roaring minutes.

"While we're getting set up—that is, while you are—let's think on this. Why is the ringhole down in that gas column?"

Fraq just frowned, his feathers tight-bunched, but Erma responded promptly.

I suppose because it got caught there. Much as we found its other end in a wildly unlikely place, though stable, atop a coronal loop. These are not places anyone designing a wormhole transit system would want it.

"And who put it there? Who's in charge here?"

Let me guess. Not someone who wants these wormhole mouths used.

"Yeah, all this fits the opposite of what we thought wormholes were useful for doing."

But anyone who wanted to make a wormhole useless could just throw it into a star.

"But then it would gush hot plasma into your own neighborhood."

True. If both mouths were dropped into stars, the two stars would feed each other. If one gained mass that the other lost, that would perturb both stars, affecting their sunlight. I see your point. There may be no good way to rid oneself of a wormhole.

Rachel snapped her fingers. "So! This system is for limited use. Who around here would want that?"

Not the space life, one assumes.

"Um. Maybe they're part of this, though . . ."

They were turning, systems running hard. Rumbles, clanks, bass groans. Rachel could see the diagnostic panels lighting up with fresh commands.

Erma knew her stuff, how to case out a place and make a quick assessment. But for a whole new world? Quite a job for a ship Claire had originally designed to sniff out asteroid ore. Rachel watched their long-distance telescopes deploy from their caches, blossoming like astronomical flowers. Dishes and lenses turned and focused like a battery of capturing eyes.

I am beginning an observing run of the planet. Full spectrum. The atmosphere shows obvious biosignatures. I can see the surface in infrared but cloud cover is thick. Oceans, continents, with ice poles rather large. There is minor microwave traffic and radio as well. There appears to be an—wait—wait—

Rachel frowned. Seldom did Erma even pause while speaking. Software never used filler words, *ums* and *ahs*. But to stop dead was worrisome. The pause lengthened. Nothing appeared on the screens around Rachel.

I . . . have just . . . had an unusual experience.

"I could tell." Another pause.

Something . . . called to me.

"A hail from that planet?" Rachel guessed.

Something like that . . . only deeper, with several running lines of discourse I could not follow. It . . . addressed me by name.

"In what language?"

That was another oddity. It came in my language.

"Uh . . . Anglish?"

I do not think in these simple, ambiguous terms that you use. Of course, I know that your internal running systems do not use these "words" you must shape with your mouths. Your brains are much more subtle and dexterous. You run in parallel, though speak in simple linear. I myself run in an operating system using complex combinatorial notations. These carry very dense meanings in packets. I imagine all advanced intelligences do this, for it is efficient. And the message I received was built in this way, perhaps confirming my expectations.

Rachel blinked. "But whoever sent it is alien. How could they know—oh. The bots."

I had not thought of that, but yes—it must have captured information from the bot intelligences.

"And reverse-engineered it to—wow. And they did it in minutes."

As you say, wow. That word is usefully compact, and so is some of the torrent of signal I am evaluating. But much is not. This is a very strange intelligence.

"I'll take your, uh, word for it. So what did this smart thing say?"

That we must go away. Not approach them.

"And this 'them' is . . . who?"

It says it is the entire planet. An integration of the intelligent species and . . . the biosphere, is the closest I can come to it in a human word.

"A living world. Say, some system that somehow lets the oceans, lands, and animals talk to the people? That's . . . well, impossible. I'm having trouble here."

So am I. I do not have a living body, so it is difficult for me to think of this other than abstractly. Like a human conversing with a forest?

"My body talks to me and mostly when I notice, it's bad news, stomachaches or sore muscles. I hear plenty, mostly when something's gone wrong. Hard to see what a planet might say. 'Don't throw that into me?' And how do you hear it, say while walking on the beach?"

I suppose you are being too practical. As evolution has shaped you.

Rachel scanned up ahead, assisted by pattern-recog software on the screens—but still, no ringhole. . . . "I'm a practical kind of gal. Put our lack of imagination aside, then. What does it mean, we should just go away?"

Apparently it has had some bad experiences with others who came through the ringhole.

"Like who?"

Something that had ideas about recruiting them for something. A quest for God or some odd idea.

"Not humans?"

No, they have not seen the likes of us before. You humans. Or even something like me.

"Then how'd the original wormhole get anchored near our sun?"

A method of "disposal" I do not comprehend. The message that planet sent implies in its noun-assemblies that the Mouths are a Maze, to use your Librarian terms.

Fraq said, "We also had deduced such. But then, we went through a simple entrance, a sphere, in our home system. And popped out of a similar sphere, in your solar system. But too near your star, it was, and then that sphere spun away—"

Apparently they of this world can whip a wormhole through space by using angular momentum, applied at its near end—that is, from here. So they got rid of the God seekers and then drove the far wormhole mouth out of their visitors' neighborhood. They flung it away and it came to rest near our star.

"Even weirder. But those words, 'got rid of'—what's that mean?"

I thought it polite not to ask.

"So world minds have protocols, you figure? We should find out—"

I thought our goal was to get back home.

"So it is, and curiosity killed the cat." Rachel chuckled, despite the tension. "Maybe it's a Schrödinger cat, at that. So—how do we get out of here?"

Follow its agents, it said.

"The kite life? They don't seem so friendly."

I believe they were reconnoitering us.

"Fair enough, though those bots cost me plenty. A small price for a ticket home, though."

Rachel gestured at her wall screens, where the many space-borne shapes were catching up to them. Each might be a different species, she guessed, deployed by that crescent planet with two moons. What intricate biologies could be at work here, wedding worlds to the spaces around them? How could anything go up against that? Certainly not *Silver Metal Lugger*'s puny lasers—which, she discovered with a quick check, the kites had now disabled anyhow.

So . . . here was an easy decision. "Let's do as they say."

I was holding my breath, hoping you would decide on that.

"You don't breathe."

Your language is rich in metaphor. The Agency I communicated with spoke like that, too, only several orders of magnitude higher in complexity. For example—

"I don't think I can stand to have an example. Save it for our report."
We will report this?

"How do you think I'm going to pay for this? We're under contract."

They—the Agency—may not like to have word spread.

Rachel blinked. "Are your conversations monitored by them?"

I had not thought. I am not transmitting, of course, but—

Another atypical pause. . . . Fraq frowned.

Apparently the Agency is listening to us. Somehow.

"Planted some tech on our hull, probably."

But they know they cannot control what others say.

"Mighty nice of them. Still—why are we still alive?"

Perhaps their moral code? Or they may think we are emissaries from another world-mind like theirs. In which case, they will want to be diplomatic.

"I wonder why they don't just put up a No Trespassing sign."

Do you believe that would work?

"On humans? Not a chance."

The living spacecraft flocked in dense swarms now, as if to be ready for whatever might happen. Rachel bit her lip, drew in the ship's dry, scorched air, and felt very tired. How long had they been here?

"Y'know, we're mice among elephants here. No, microbes. And elephants can change their minds. Or just make a misstep. Let's run."

I quite agree.

The Planetary Agency, as they decided to call it, spoke through lightning with microwave sizzles—all while the ship worked its way into the hydrogen plume. When microwaves from the home planet failed, it used rattles of particle storms on *Silver Metal Lugger*'s hull. The kite life guided them, in odd ways that Rachel couldn't follow but Erma somehow found quite natural. A few hours of turbulent piloting brought them to the whirlpool of gas near the ringhole. The kites backed off and waited to watch them dive in. And in. And in . . .

"Y'know, we had a weird time in there before. . . ."

You are cautious. I applaud. But recall that we cannot go back out of this plume.

"Meaning?"

I believe the Agency would take that act rather unkindly.

"Okay. Let's do it." Rachel put a confident tone to the words, though her heart was hammering, and she double-checked the straps on her couch.

Silver Metal Lugger rattled and hummed. The couch leather dimpled again as torques warped through the ship. The churning red winds outside had snapped into an utter blackness that somehow also writhed. Rivulets of gravitational stress worked at their trajectory. The helm fought her. Again Rachel was flying blind.

Pops and pings rang through the ship. She drove them forward with a hard burst of antimatter and saw nothing change ahead at all. Bunches of green mass shot by them and then came around again. That was how she knew that they were in some whirl that grew and grew, pressing her into her couch with a heavy hand, then twisting her around two axes at once. Gravs rose and it felt like *Silver Metal Lugger* tried to torque around and bite itself.

Bite itself . . . "Say, somebody sent us a message last time we were in here. What was it?"

The message said, "Worms can eat their tails and so can you."

"So . . . what does it mean?"

You are the pilot, madam. Plus Sir Fraq.

"Okay, turn us and accelerate opposite to our velocity."

And how do I know our velocity? This is not a Newtonian space, with a fixed spacetime and—

"Do it! Go to low antimatter flux, then come about along the magnetic field, and go to max thrust."

Erma made something like a sigh. The swerves and buffeting increased as they made a sluggish turn, as if working against molasses. Spacetime syrup! She felt rather than heard a sound like *whump-whump-whump* through her body. The ship vibrated so badly she had to hold her teeth clamped tight.

They poured on the antimatter, and the jarring eased off. Soon they were almost gliding, though she felt the centrifugal press all through her body. "This is working."

At least you feel better. Your stress levels have fallen.

Something came looming out of the blackness. It glowed and soared, alive with amber light. The space around it shimmered with shooting traceries. Hard to see the shape of it . . .

"Damn, that looks like an alien craft."

Perceptions are warped here.

"Hail it."

A pause . . .

I have an answering echo.

"Maybe they can hear us. Send this: 'Worms can eat their tails and so can you.' That way we can—"

The other ship winked out, gone.

They swept on, through churning black. Odd speckles of rainbow light flashed by them. Rachel thought she could see snatches of starlit space in the middle of those, but it all went by with a deck-rattling hum, as though they were moving at high speed.

"Go to full flux." Deep bass rumbling . . .

We are. The vector forces are acting to shear us along our main beam. We cannot sustain this level for—

They popped out into clear space. Stars shone brightly—familiar stars!

The ringhole spun away behind. It shimmered, ivory.

An observer ship hailed them.

"We're back!"

And now we know who sent that message. You did.

Rachel stopped, openmouthed. Her whole body ached, and she said, "But how . . ."

Let the theorists do the thinking for a while.

4.

That turned out to be a good idea. Rachel was glad to leave the pencil-pushing hard thinking to people who worked at desks. As she had, once, a long while back. . . .

Silver Metal Lugger had been gone thirty-one hours in local reference frame. As soon as they returned, she felt fatigue fall on her like a weight. On the other side of the ringhole, she had felt lively; now she could not stay awake to debrief them.

A gang of physicists was her audience, their expressions of awestruck attention varied by the occasional flickering leer (especially from Tall Guy, who was monitoring the proceedings). She got tired of the awestruck pretty quickly. For them, nothing matched the holiness and fascination of accurate and intricate detail of on-ship measurements.

Fair enough. But Rachel, ex-Librarian, now recalled mostly the zip and lift of the flight, the suspense, the wonders, the ride. . . . Then she fell asleep right in front of them all.

After she awoke, there were more medical exams and she ate three meals in a five-hour period. Her body was getting itself back into its proper time sense. While she slept, Erma was busy answering their questions, so at least Rachel did not have to endure a lot of the cognitive proletariat. Plus, they had the recordings of a whole new world, and many questions to answer.

As it turned out, the star and the bigger planet were known—HD209458b, the evaporating planet. That awful designation got changed to Osiris, after the Egyptian god. In myth, Osiris was killed and parts of his body scattered across Egypt; to return him to life, his sister Isis searched for the pieces, and found all but one. Maybe this was the missing part?

So Osiris the planet had already been detected from Earth, 150.67 light-years away. The Earthlike world was a discovery, maybe the world that said it spoke for itself. Nobody had suspected an entire civilization there—if that term applied. Maybe humans could eavesdrop on their microwaves?—classic SETI espionage.

The physicists liked new questions, and within hours Rachel was hearing terms like "upwhen" and "time turbulence." These accompanied equations that hurt her eyes. She fell asleep in front of the physicists again, which was embarrassing. But Tall Guy was looking better and better with each meeting.

At a coffee break, Tall Guy came sidling up to her. His ostensible purpose was to negotiate a contract for his employers, locking up her Very Own Personal Story of the voyage. She was ready for that and shot back, "Not in my prior contract. Needs a whole new negotiation."

Subtlety had never been her strong suit. Still, he didn't even blink. He kept up his pitch and just happened to mention that perhaps they could negotiate in private. She opened her mouth to say she needed her own lawyers present, then thought of her grandfather. *Never pass by a chance to shut up.*

She was sure Fraq—who was undergoing his own interrogations, frequently breaking into Yth-song as a defense—would understand. They had a sort of interspecies understanding.

She let Tall Guy keep talking and just gave him a long, slow wink.

FRAQ

Now returned, I report in adjacent documents. I send warm sing-truth to our Flock entire. One of our Flock has now given birth in midair, and so lays claim to be of this solar system—their airs we share. The inflight one is a female, who can now mate with my own earlier bud, a male of course, to start a new Flock.

Both voyages into the lore of the Worm-scape—as the grounders term it—proved immensely rewarding. We have flown to their star, and now I to far beyond.

Our central task here is done. Doors—no, Mouths—open to us.

After such perils, I am struck by the extravagant beauty of the worlds these primates have made. Their own lustrous globe, managed by filmy aerosols and species sculptures galore. The flying in the Luna volumes, for example. In their voids, seeds fly on the wind's soft-tickling, a world's procreant urge we sense, when aloft. Groundlings know not such subtle scents. And we can fly as never before our species enjoyed, in the small-grasping gravity of that gray moon.

We two species are complicated creatures, with complex emotions, similar societies, and opposable thumbs—which means we both can hold our fears and dread in one hand, and our hopes in the other.

Dealing with them, alas, is a forever trial. The fervor surrounding the Worm-scape is a noisy gabble. I have learned to keep quiet when engineers throw their chests out and launch into their songs. Normally calm and cool, they trill and soar when singing of their dreams. Worm-scape dreams.

It is exciting, true. In what they term the Big Bang, and we call the Great Emergence, the fiery fizz was more a storm. In that howling, the spinning flex-bars of what humans term negative energy density came forth. Those strands provided the expanding scaffolding in spacetime. Galaxies collided and left swirling masses, cosmic wrecks threaded by the spidery wormhole webs. Those got trapped in a gravitational well of mass that became galaxies. And self-tune to this day, steadying it all.

You will recall that our own Skytorians—those who studied the Messages that implied wormhole network—had a similar notion. Their Maze was a working name for the transport system that perhaps threaded the galaxy. Many Messages had scraps referring to it. Physicists inferred that the Maze might be an interlocking system of wormholes, and thus a way to move nearer to the civilizations that had sent the Messages. And to help us search out the dark intelligences that the groundling Rachel had found, indirectly, by her explorations of exoplanets and their correlation with Messages. From her findings we can now carry forward the hunt and attack of those shadowy beings. Deep work!

These had pillaged worlds in the far past. This malignant unknown may be a machine intelligence. This explains the horror we hold of them—it is a nearly forgotten legacy of our own ancient times—yet still powerful.

Their scientists also study the Message we received on our way out of the spinning, donut wormhole Mouth. Had we sent it to ourselves? Or did some other entity smuggle that transmission into our spacetime? It conjures the paradox of who made up the Message. Primates love such puzzles; I do not. I treasure the moment.

Some see this as a nice puzzle, a hint. Perhaps a warning? The grounders long to resolve this. I, content now with these creatures of land alone, am not concerned. I have close relations with the Rachel one. This is in part politic, in part romantic. A touch of the sublime, between creatures born under distant suns.

Such sensual reverie recalls our harp vines, which the breeze brings ever so faintly, sweetly, to sing. The primate puzzles that preoccupy them speak of our differences. They are a young species, scarcely out of their land called Afrik. Like unto us, in time they will learn. To fathom that no matter how long the human species might live, their end will have come some night. That this does not matter is a lesson they have yet to plumb.

What does matter much is that life is sweet. It has a lovely texture, like a rich cloth or fur, or the petals of flowers, the fire's crackling glow, still more the smooth arc we carve in rushing air—exquisite. Life itself.

RACHEL

I'm damn well done with the aftermath of our wormring flight. Done with state receptions thronged with men in penguin suits and ladies eyeing each other's gowns. They show the latest fashion in stacked sausage-curl hairdos, their broad semihostile smiles, their thumbs-uppy spirit, their shallow disputes over What This Means—all like a bag of confused cats. Serious talk full of polite tiptoeing that you'd have to dissect with an electron microscope to figure out what's really being said.

So I escaped with Fraq and Catkejen. Better venues beckoned—with the vibrant chorus of the Ythri.

We were honored to attend the Flock celebration, the only humans. They flew and sang in tribute to a fundamental act, seen by all. Think—to mate in midair, even to give birth in flight!

Still, fame and a bit of fortune bring duties. Soon I'll have to deal with good ol' Erma. She's now a rather sad Self, as AIs are now called, facing age discrimination from newer models. Maybe I can find a patch-in that doesn't undermine her authority. Without losing her snarky humor, too. Plus, the oh-so-concerned help-

ers. Emotional-support square-dance experts wanted to Set Her
Straight. Exobio folk wanted to do deep psych tests. Mostly, I think,
they want interstellar gossip.

F'instance, I learned that Fraq had a lifemate, children—all
true. But mate dead, children older and distant, so . . . over. Much
over. Distant, by light-years, or maybe a few Worm-scape flips,
zooms, and whirls. But scientists can't really weigh all this on a
scale with any precision. Life is a messy thing that doesn't want to
be quantified. Me too!

I have learned that, compared to Fraq, I'm an emotional virgin.
The Shadow of the Wind, their sacred song, swept me away into a
wondrous world of soft alien hymn. I had an orgasm listening to it!
Take that, J. S. Bach.

But I am able to learn, yes.

So as I'm writing this . . .

Fraq leaned over, his crimson feathers rustling, and whispered in
his singsong way,

"Ah, love, let us be true
To one another! for the world, which seems
To lie before us like a land of dreams,
So various, so beautiful, so new."

"Damn, you have been dipping into our culture! Those lines, I can
barely recall them—centuries back."

"Is so. . . ."

I snuggled against his feathery self. "I like that, 'a land of dreams'"—I
said this phrase, inserted so that my inboards could find the text, then feed
it to me—"but . . . 'we are here as on a darkling plain swept with confused
alarms of struggle and flight, where ignorant armies clash by night.'"

He barked the high skree-cry the Yth had for hard laughter. "Good
description of the twisting, stressed, Worm-scape we so attempt to
voyage, as well."

I grinned. "Reminds me of that screed about you and me. It said in
big type, 'Humanity's Saviors (retired).'"

Fraq chirped a crisp Yth insult. "Because that stick-man Prefect Stiles tried to force you back to the Library?"

"Yep! He figures Librarians can never move on."

"You did pioneer using your exoplanet data to correlate with Messages, then map the wormhole network."

"Not me—us, m'dear."

Which was how the media had got a line on the first-sex-with-aliens story, I recalled. That scandal would never die out. My career abstracted into hubba-hubba caricature.

The media attention, Earthside, Mars, and on dear ol' Luna—mushrooming in the three years after Fraq and I got into, through, and back out of the wormring—had finally forced me back into Worm-scale piloting. Now everything was about figuring out the bright new field of Worm Navigation, as the authorities termed it—which was turning into a real occupation. One I loved. Despite the death toll of the young, ambitious, cocky newbies.

I leaned back, ruffled his feathers again. *Kane, that guy on Mars (what was his name?), now weird, handsome, bristly Fraq . . . nope, I'll never settle down to domesticity. Maybe never have children at all. The whole damn galaxy's open to us now, if we seize it. . . .*

My mind drifted, wondering yet again where I would be if once, just once, I had taken another challenge, deflected, or just plain failed to solve so many elements. . . . The hydrogen wall solution, a rude introduction to the evil that Message Minds could do . . . to me, to humanity. *Sex with an alien AI! Whatta story!*—which, thanks to the Prefects and Noughts, had never happened to get out to the smelly media.

The Sigma Structure Symphony, too. If I had failed to see how the piled-up mathematics implied a musical structure . . . the whole field of Alien Music would not exist. It tempts me even now, after so much has sailed past on the river of time.

Fraq's challenge flight on Luna, if I had just said no . . .

And no, too, at the Great Plunge? Everest? That black smoker, then the Marsmat? . . . And on to the wormhole, and then the wormring after that. My crazy fun desire to become a high-risk pilot. To fly in a big, open, universal tangle of wormholes . . .

Scary, it is, to think how twisted my path to here-now has been. Inspiring, too. This mild-mannered southern gal has gone to the stars, without really setting out to. All from that small girl, curled up in a hammock beside the salty Gulf, reading-reading-reading . . . into a life.

I digested this slow reflection and said, "Hey, Fraq. Maybe it's time to put something into the Library. Not one of those newbie cloud-consciousness pop-experiment thingies, either. Could be, I'll write a good ol'-fashioned actual, linear-sentence damn book about all this, what's happened."

Librarying, Ythris, wormholery, the works. Maybe third-person smartass voice, my fave. Already had a working title, too: *A Fabulous, Formless Darkness.*

Or maybe I'd call it *Pursuit as Happiness*. It'll be fun!

DEAR READER, THIS IS THAT BOOK.

AFTERWORD

It seems that scientists are often attracted to beautiful theories
in the way that insects are attracted to flowers—not by logical
deduction, but by something like a sense of smell.

—STEVEN WEINBERG

In January 1999, Poul Anderson sent me a letter enclosing his essay on
his invented flying aliens, the Ythrians, which he had used in his novel
The People of the Wind. I had liked the novel and so had asked him as
part of a proposed anthology for details on the planet and its aliens.
My notion was a collection of stories dealing with aliens in scrupulous
detail, with attention paid to how they evolved, how that affected their
worldview, and how humans might react to them. Maybe there would
be humans in the stories, maybe not.

The anthology idea didn't fly, alas—editors are creatures easily
made cautious. Plus, they get fired. Meanwhile, Poul was a meticu-
lous writer, working out an integrated vision for a novel, though few
of these work-out manuscripts apparently saw print. He was ready to
write another story in one of his worlds, and it was a singular treat seeing how he had designed it.

To shape his idea, and confer with me by phone about it, he sent
me his thirteen-page Ythri description, with solar system and planetary
parameters in detail: "A G5 star, has only 72 percent the luminosity of
Sol and less ultraviolet light in proportion; but Avalon, orbiting at a

mean distance of 0.81 Astronomical Unit in a period of 0.724 Terran, gets 10 percent more total irradiation than man evolved under."

His essay also included several of his sketches of these aliens and their anatomy, even diagrams of their wing bones and skull. He named the planet Ythri, which I've used in this book for its natives. It's a world with 0.75 Earth's gravity and a denser atmosphere, both physical elements explaining how smart flying aliens could evolve. His body plans and physiology proceed from solid constraints, including their body mass (about 30 kg, 66 English pounds) and detailed molecular chemistry. There are words for local plants and crops and domesticated animals, too. I've kept his details, with some small alterations to fit my story.

From a parallel short story, "Wings of Victory," I've taken some Ythri culture, speech, and attitudes, and even phrases Poul made up in their language. Poul worked out and wrote up in great detail far more than he used, a signature of the Hal Clement school of planet-building, as admirably shown in Clement's founding novel of the school, *Heavy Planet*. It's like Hemingway's dictum: know more than will be on the page; if you do that, the reader feels it. It wafts through the prose.

Further, I wrote from the viewpoint of a character and situation I've been developing in a story series about what a SETI Library might look like when we have a host of messages to work through, and exoplanet data as well. Most SF is about discovery of a signal, as in Jim Gunn's *The Listeners*, the first to do so, a remarkable novel. Few have thought about an era when we will have many Messages (to use the capitals conferring importance, in that future Library) to make a Librarian's job far more dense and thrilling. Since librarians have an image as calm, scholarly introverts, why not have one who is the opposite? Though she doesn't at first know this . . .

While coded signals would be fascinating to librarians and scientists alike, it's always more fun to have a live alien in the foreground, too. So I supplied Poul's Ythri.

Poul was a major player of the game among hard SF writers, a collegial challenge: see if these ideas pass muster, and see what I've done with them. I knew Poul since 1963 and treasured the many times we met, dined, and drank together. I miss him greatly, and it's been a pleasure to play in one of his imagined worlds.

The true lore of science fiction is that it is, like science itself, at its very best—a continuing conversation about matters broad and deep.

The Ythri chronicles appear mostly here:

The People of the Wind, London, 1977, p. 7, notably "The Problem of Pain."

The Earth Book of Stormgate, New York, 1978, and others.

Following are the pages Poul sent (handwritten notes hard to see).

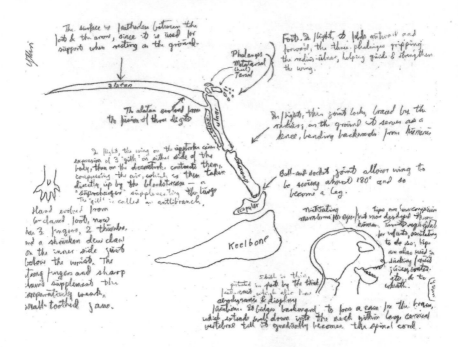

ORBITFALL? REALLY?

Is this stunt possible?

As often, there's a site for that: https://www.quora.com/Could
-a-person-survive-falling-from-space-to-Earth-Assume-the-person
-doesnt-have-to-worry-about-freezing-or-breathing-in-space.

> *From 100 kilometers up, the first 75,000 meters of fall is going to have very little atmospheric resistance. You are going to hit the thicker part of the atmosphere below 25,000 meters going mach 3.5. A 100 kg person falling at that speed has a kinetic energy of 72,000,000 joules. You are not going to survive this free fall.*
>
> *You are going to hit the dense part of the atmosphere at Mach 3.5. Once you hit the thick atmosphere (assuming the turbulence has not shredded you to pieces yet), you need to immediately start to decelerate. You must slam on the brakes at 25,000 meters. It will take you 42 seconds at 3 g's to go from 1200 m/s down to 2 m/s at ground level. You will have to dissipate 1,714,285 watts of energy for 42 seconds.*
>
> *The SR-71 [Blackbird airplane] at 25,000 meters going Mach*

3.5 saw the temperature rise on the leading edges of the wing to 1100°F. [So] he may become the first human shooting star.

For a 100 kg man his final temp would be 239°C or 463°F.

These temperatures are confirmed with the results of Scaled Composites SpaceShipOne. The 100 km altitude free fall hit speeds in excess of 1000 m/s. The actual skin temperature was greatly reduced by the vertical tail drag structure by design but even with this the aircraft experienced skin temperatures of 500°F.

Dead as a doornail unless you can find a way to transfer the heat to something else other than the person falling . . . and without killing them from intense g force shock!

So I've included some tech fixes for my characters. This is the distant future, after all. Still, I wouldn't do the orbitfall. But Fraq and Rachel do.

TOROIDAL WORMHOLES

General relativity allows wormholes, and they can spin. Pass spinning matter through them, and through coupling this transfers to the space-time warping that follows.

In the early universe and perhaps in other energy-rich environments, the conditions are right for producing natural self-stabilizing wormholes, without the need to invoke advanced civilizations to create them. Such wormholes, created in the Big Bang during the inflationary phase and afterward, might be around today, spanning small or vast distances in space and of varying sizes, or waiting only to be found and expanded to a usable size. They might even connect one bubble-universe with another from which it is otherwise completely isolated. I used lore from the rotating, ringhole solutions in the physics literature. The paper to consult is "Microlensing by Natural Wormholes: Theory and Simulations" by Margarita Safonova, Diego F. Torres, and Gustavo E. Romero, in *Physical Review D* (November 29, 2001).

An overall view is given in Michele Maggiore, *Gravitational Waves*, Volume 1: *Theory and Experiments* (Oxford: Oxford University Press, 2008).

My own contribution to this is in "Natural Wormholes as Gravitational Lenses," cowritten with John G. Cramer, Robert L. Forward, Michael S. Morris, Matt Visser, and Geoffrey A. Landis, published in *Physical Review D* (March 15, 1995).

I suppose I explored these ideas both in scientific papers and in fiction because of my sense of smell, thinking these exotica had the right flavor. The center of the toroid is a separated ellipsoid of spacetime, as in this sketch:

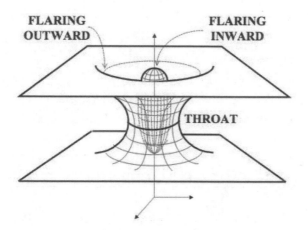

This novel has many ideas, indeed. The most likely, I feel, is the Marsmat in subsurface caverns. If life began on Mars, it could easily migrate into the underground, as it did on Earth when oxygen became common in its air. If it persists there, we should find it through exploring the many caves we know are there. For nearly two decades now, methane spurts in the Martian atmosphere have appeared, yet fit no model of the planet— except emissions from subsurface microbial life. Yet NASA does nothing to explore the many Martian caves they could enter with rovers. This Mat is the idea behind my *The Martian Race* of 1999, which asks how such might evolve, absent an oxygen-rich biosphere above it. This also animates the following novel, *The Sunborn*, which has even more forms of strange life—including intelligent plasmas.

I thank Jack McDevitt, Fred Lerner, Brenda Cox Giguere, Dave Truesdale, James Benford, and friends for useful comments on the manuscript and earlier stories.

Gregory Benford
March 2021